TREECAT WARS

IN THIS SERIES BY DAVID WEBER

For a complete listing of Baen titles by David Weber, please go to www.baen.com.

TREECAT WARS

A Star Kingdom Novel

DAVID WEBER & JANE LINDSKOLD

TREECAT WARS

A Baen Books Original

Baen Publishing Enterprises
P.O. Box 1403
Riverdale, NY 10471
www.baen.com

ISBN: 978-1-4767-3663-1

Cover art by Daniel Dos Santos

First Baen paperback printing, August 2014

Distributed by Simon & Schuster
1230 Avenue of the Americas
New York, NY 10020

Library of Congress Control Number: 2013023283

10 9 8 7 6 5 4 3 2 1

Pages by Joy Freeman (www.pagesbyjoy.com)
Printed in the United States of America

TREECAT WARS

"YOU WANT TO SEND US TO MANTICORE?"

Despite her best effort at adult composure, Stephanie Harrington's voice rose in pleased astonishment. Beside her, she heard her good friend Karl Zivonik swallow a chuckle. Even Lionheart, the treecat, perched on the edge of Chief Ranger Shelton's desk emitted a small "bleek" of amusement.

Only the chief ranger himself did not seem to notice the enthusiasm with which Stephanie had met his proposal. He continued his explanation without pause.

"That's right. Two slots have opened up unexpectedly in a special accelerated training program for Forestry Service personnel on Manticore. The Sphinx Forestry Service has regularly sent its full-time members to the course. This year, given that we're facing the aftermath of such an exceptionally bad fire season, I can't spare any of my rangers. However, I can—just barely—spare my two provisional rangers."

"Me and Stephanie," Karl said, only the fact that he needed to make this unnecessary clarification showing how excited he was.

"You and Stephanie." Chief Ranger Shelton motioned toward two chairs. "Sit down. Before you accept, I need to explain to you just what you're getting into."

The young people sat, although Stephanie had to fight back an impulse to perch on the edge of her chair. Lionheart made sitting back easier for her by flowing gracefully from the desk onto her lap. At around 140 centimeters, Stephanie was relatively small for her fifteen and a half years, petite, rather than just short. Holding Lionheart's sixty-five centimeters took all of her lap and then some. Somehow, though the treecat's face was gray tabby-striped and his eyes green, while the girl's short hair and eyes were both brown there was something similar about the pair.

Karl, Stephanie's senior by two and a half years, seemed to have no trouble keeping his composure, but then in many ways Karl was old beyond his years. Stephanie knew tragedy had shadowed his first real romance, a loss he had apparently gotten beyond but never over. Dark-haired, dark-eyed, already 185 centimeters tall, with a strong boned frame, Karl at eighteen was very much a young man.

Chief Ranger Shelton studied them thoughtfully for a moment before continuing. "I'm going to admit right off that there was some protest when I suggested we send you two to Manticore. The provisional ranger rank is new enough that some people still don't accept it as real. Moreover, Stephanie in particular is quite young for the program."

Stephanie swallowed an automatic protest. Chief Ranger Shelton knew better than most how much Stephanie was capable of doing. Indeed, he'd created the rank of provisional ranger as a way to acknowledge those achievements. She just had to trust that he was on her side.

A gentle mental "nudge" from Lionheart brought Stephanie out of her thoughts. She still wasn't quite sure how Lionheart influenced her moods, but if there was one thing she was sure about regarding treecats it was that they were both telempathic and telepathic. Of course, the fact the treecats were telepathic was a closely guarded secret and would remain so until they'd been acknowledged as a fully sentient species with the rights and protections granted to such by law. For now, it was enough for Stephanie to know that what most people saw as a sort of long-bodied, long-tailed, furry, six-legged weasel-cat was as much a person as she was—and the sort of person who wasn't above reminding her to pay attention, even if he used rather unconventional methods.

"You, Karl," Chief Ranger Shelton was saying, "are a legal adult. Based on your achievements as a provisional ranger, if I'd wanted to push the matter, I could have promoted you to assistant ranger and avoided the entire question of eligibility. You, Stephanie, have shown by your actions that you're not only competent but completely devoted to the well-being of our forests and their inhabitants. Let's leave it that, after considerable debate, I've garnered permission for you to attend the course if you choose."

Stephanie wanted to say "I choose! I choose!" but she restrained herself to murmuring a polite, "Thank you, sir."

In any case, something uncomfortable was niggling at the back of her thoughts, something that was making her wonder if she really *did* want to take up Chief Ranger Shelton's offer. She shoved the doubt away and concentrated on listening.

"The course is geared to teach you about more than just forestry. At least as applied to Sphinx, you could learn plenty about forestry right here—and in some instances, probably teach. Sadly, though, being a member of the SFS on Sphinx includes a lot more than simply caring for plants and animals. Because Sphinx has so much undeveloped land and so few people, we also have fewer police forces compared to Manticore. That means the law enforcement aspects of a ranger's duty are at least as important as firefighting, search and rescue, and protecting the environment. That's why part of what you'll be learning will be law enforcement technology, forensic techniques, basic legal theory and content, and how to handle civilian relations.

"All of this is on top of taking tests to show your competency in basic, practical forestry knowledge. Since you, Karl, have spent your entire life in a single biosphere— here on Sphinx—you can expect some individual studies designed to plug the gaps in your knowledge base. Stephanie, I know you spent your first ten or so years on Meyerdahl, but don't be surprised if your instructors come up with individual studies for you, too. If there's one thing I've learned during my years in forestry service, it's that you can't know too much."

The coursework did sound intense, but Stephanie had been at the top of her class for as long as she could remember. Some of her grades had slipped a little when she joined the SFS, but her parents weren't the sort to complain about a few percentage points—especially when it was evident to the meanest intelligence what career path Stephanie planned to follow. Thinking of her parents reminded her. . . .

"Chief Shelton, you mentioned I'm still a minor. Have you spoken with my parents yet?"

Chief Shelton's lips shaped what, on anyone other than his dignified self, Stephanie would have thought a mischievous grin. "I have not. Consider convincing them you should take part in the program the first proof that you're old enough to do so. They may, of course, contact me for details."

Karl cleared his throat nervously.

"Chief Shelton, there's the question of tuition. I have a bunch of brothers and sisters. Our family has a lot of land, but I'm not sure my parents could come up with interplanetary tickets and living expenses, especially on short notice. Even with my job with the SFS, I've been helping out at home, too, but I think they can work around that."

"Tuition's one thing you don't need to worry about," Chief Ranger Shelton assured him. "If you go, you'll be going as a member of the SFS. Other than money for personal indulgences, we'll be covering all the bills."

"Thank you, sir!"

Stephanie thought of another complication.

"Chief Shelton, what about Lionheart? I can't leave him. It's not that I won't; I *can't*."

She hoped the chief ranger understood. She suspected he did. Not everyone knew about the Stray and the lengths that 'cat had gone to avenge his murdered human partner, but, even with only the evidence of the few bonded human/treecat pairs that existed, it was apparent that being separated overly long caused a great deal of distress for both human and 'cat. They could be apart for days at a time but, as Stephanie had explained it to her parents, after a while she felt anxious, like one of her senses had been dampened or even cut off.

She'd talked about this negative aspect of being part of a partnership with a treecat with her friend Jessica Pheriss, the most recent adoptee. Despite the fact that she and her Valiant had only been together for about six months, Jessica felt the same way. Now just thinking about leaving Lionheart behind on Sphinx while she went to another planet made Stephanie feel prickly. Her palms grew damp, and she surreptitiously wiped them on the legs of her trousers.

"I've already considered the problem of Lionheart," Chief Ranger Shelton assured her. "Dr. Hobbard was a great deal of help in convincing the appropriate authorities that it would be beneficial if Lionheart went with you. So if you choose to go to Manticore, Lionheart may travel with you."

"Thank you!" Stephanie let out a breath she hadn't known she was holding.

"You're certain to find that there will be many places on Manticore where Lionheart won't be permitted to go, however," the chief ranger cautioned her. "Here on Sphinx, particularly near Twin Forks where both you and Jessica live, the tendency has been to let the treecats into whatever facilities their humans use. I already know the instructors for most of the courses you'll be taking won't wish Lionheart to be present. He'd be a distraction, you realize."

Stephanie did realize. Even in Twin Forks, Lionheart continued to attract attention. Not only were treecats a relatively new discovery—Stephanie had "discovered" them when she had been only eleven—but with their thick, silky fur, enormous green eyes, and prick-eared heads, they were undeniably cute as well.

Cute, that is, Stephanie thought, *until you learn how sharp their claws are and how good they are at using them. Then, I think, except for the dimmest of the dim, respect just has to temper the "cute."*

Even with modern technology, treecats were almost impossible to locate in the wild and, despite some pressure in that direction, none were on display in the zoos where people could see other Sphinxian creatures like hexapumas and peak bears.

Chief Ranger Shelton was continuing. "You may think that the more high-profile achievements each of you has racked up over these last few years are the reason I was finally able to convince my associates to permit you two to represent the SFS in this year's training course. Certainly, it didn't hurt that you both showed initiative and bravery during the recent wildfires. Moreover, it can't be overlooked that Stephanie—and you, Karl—are among the most knowledgeable when it comes to the treecats. However, in the end, none of those things tipped the balance. Can you guess what did?"

Stephanie shook her head, but Karl said slowly, "If it isn't the high-profile stuff, then it must be the rest, right? The time we put in as provisional rangers?"

Chief Shelton nodded emphatically. "That's it. Your demonstrated willingness to do the nonglamorous and routine patrols that are part of a ranger's daily job is what convinced the worst of the doubters. Stephanie, in particular, has a bit of a reputation for impulsive behavior."

He paused, but Stephanie didn't protest. She supposed some might see her as impulsive, but she preferred to think of what she did as taking necessary initiative. Chief Shelton gave her a sideways smile and continued.

"However, our computer logs don't lie, and they show how faithfully you've done your shifts—even when those shifts have consisted of nothing more romantic and exciting than covering headquarters so someone with more experience or a wider range of skills could go out into the field. Remember that when you—if you—get to Manticore.

"I'm forwarding all the necessary information to your uni-links so you'll be able to show it to your parents. I'm afraid I'm going to need to ask for a decision fairly quickly. Time was wasted while we went through our rosters looking to see who we could spare. Then more time was wasted while we convinced various people at various levels that our provisional rangers would fit the bill. Can you give me an answer within a week? We can stretch to ten days, but a week would be better. The class starts in two weeks."

"A week?" Karl seemed momentarily astonished, then nodded and got to his feet as if he was prepared to start the trip back to Thunder River that very moment. "I can do it."

"Me, too," Stephanie said, "but my folks will want a few days to make sure they've considered everything. Neither of them are impulsive."

"Unlike you," Karl said, grinning at her.

All too aware of Chief Ranger Shelton, Stephanie refrained from sticking her tongue out at Karl, but the rumble of Lionheart's purr against her chest as she picked him up and got to her feet let her know that more than one of her friends was laughing at the joke. Immediately, the treecat flowed into approved "carry" position—his remaining front foot (his true-hand) on her shoulder, his rearmost set of feet (or true-feet) on a specially built brace she wore with all her clothing. This was a compromise her dad had recently agreed to, although Richard Harrington still preferred Stephanie let the treecat do most of his own walking.

"Good luck," the chief ranger said, waving them toward the door. "I look forward to hearing from you both."

Karl stopped in mid stride. "I suppose the information's in our uni-links, but I forgot to ask. How long is this course, exactly?"

"Three T-months," came the prompt reply. "As I said, there's a lot that needs to be covered."

Stephanie's feet kept moving, but inside her something froze as the shapeless dread that had been haunting her for the last few minutes suddenly came into focus.

Three months! Anders! I want to go to Manticore, but can I bear to leave him for three whole months?

Despite her sudden emotional turmoil, Stephanie managed to talk naturally to Karl during the trip back to Twin Forks from Yawata Crossing. Thankfully, they had a lot to talk about. If Karl thought Stephanie was acting at all oddly, he probably put it down to her thinking about ways to convince her parents to let her go off-planet for three months.

"I'll com you later," he said, as she got out of his air car, "and let you know how it goes with my folks."

"Me, too," she replied. "Remember—don't let your folks call mine until I get a chance to talk with them first. I need to figure out how best to let them know."

"I promise," Karl agreed. Then he shifted the car up to where he could pour on speed as soon as he was out of the city limits. The Zivoniks lived near Thunder River, a good many hours travel away even at top speeds, but Stephanie didn't doubt Karl would have the car on autopilot and be on the com to his mother as soon as he was in clear airspace.

Her own mind swirled as she walked to her dad's office. Of course, the fact that Richard Harrington had an office in Twin Forks didn't mean he'd be in it. Stephanie's father was a veterinarian, a job that, on Sphinx, embraced not only the care of the animals belonging to the colonists, but often of creatures native to Sphinx, as well. Add to that the numerous genetically altered creatures that were being tried out as the colonists looked for the best way to work with their environment and still have some of the meat and dairy products they were accustomed to, and one could argue that Richard Harrington was one of the most irreplaceable professionals on Sphinx. Certainly Richard's interest in exotic creatures, combined with the fact that his wife was a plant biologist and geneticist, had assured the Harringtons of a warm welcome when they had immigrated to Sphinx back when Stephanie had been ten.

Six years later, Stephanie could hardly understand the girl she'd been then—a girl who'd been so overwhelmed by her changed environment and the loss of all her previous dreams and goals that she'd spent a lot of time sulking. Now Stephanie loved Sphinx with all her heart. She'd be happy to go visit Meyerdahl, but she knew she'd always come home to Sphinx.

Given how scattered Sphinx's human settlers were, Stephanie wasn't surprised when she got to her dad's office and found both him and the Vet Van missing. Besides, his recently hired assistant, Saleem Smythe, would be in shortly to cover the evening shift. Under the circumstances, she wasn't unhappy to have the office to herself until Dr. Smythe's arrival, though. There was celery in the fridge, and she gave Lionheart a big stalk as a thank you for his support during the meeting. Uncharacteristically, she didn't feel very hungry, but she got herself a fruit and nut bar, which she nibbled more from duty than desire. Next, she commed her parents to let them know where she was. She didn't mention the meeting with Chief Ranger Shelton. She hadn't been lying to Karl when she said she needed to figure out the best way to present the proposed trip to Manticore to them, but there was something else she needed to figure out first.

Anders.

Anders Whitaker had come to Sphinx last year, not long before Stephanie's fifteenth birthday, as part of an anthropological expedition from Urako University, headed by his father and formed for the express purpose of studying the treecats. From the first time Stephanie had seen Anders, she'd been overwhelmed. It wasn't just that he was good-looking, although with his wheat-blond hair and dark blue eyes he was undeniably handsome. Anders was also smart, smart enough that he didn't feel a need to hide his enthusiasms—and one of his enthusiasms turned out to be treecats.

At nearly seventeen, Anders was quite a bit younger than the next older member of the Whitaker expedition, which meant he was happy to spend time with Stephanie. She'd found ways for the two of them to be together, although often enough Karl (who frequently boarded with the Harringtons, since Thunder River was so far from where he and Stephanie did their ranger work) made a third. In fact, for the first time since Stephanie met him—back when Stephanie had started learning how to use firearms—Karl had definitely become less than welcome company.

Things might have gotten uncomfortable, but then the Whitaker expedition's air van had gone missing. In the intensity of search, rescue, and forest fire, somehow any uneasiness had vanished. Then after...

Stephanie felt her lips twist in an unwilling smile as she remembered the first time she'd kissed Anders. It hadn't been much of a kiss, but it had been her first time kissing a boy. Later, Anders had reciprocated a lot more enthusiastically than her careful lips against his cheek.

Although nothing had been formally declared, they'd become more or less a couple. It helped that part of Stephanie's and Karl's job as provisional rangers had been to act as advisors to the Whitaker expedition. Then, too, although he could assist, Anders wasn't a professional anthropologist. That meant he was free to ride along when Stephanie and Karl did their patrols. Before long, he was learning to hang-glide and becoming as much a part of Stephanie's circle of friends as any of those who lived in Twin Forks.

Things had appeared to be moving along very satisfactorily, but then, shortly after the fire, Dr. Whitaker had been sent back to their home world, Urako in the Kenichi System. His behavior on Sphinx had been...erratic, and the potential consequences could have ended his expedition to the Star Kingdom in academic disgrace. Stephanie knew Dr. Hobbard and Chief Ranger Shelton had both argued in favor of allowing the university's expedition to remain on Sphinx, with a Sphinx Forestry Service ranger or two permanently assigned to it to keep it out of trouble. Unfortunately, the Manticoran government had been unwilling to go along. Neither Governor Donaldson nor Interior Minister Vásquez had been satisfied with Dr. Whitaker's simple promise to behave himself. They wanted the same sort of guarantee from the university itself, and that meant sending him home to face a review of his actions by the chancellor of the university and the chairman of his department.

Dr. Whitaker hadn't been at all happy about that, but he'd clearly realized that he had no choice. However, getting there was easier to say than to do because the Star Kingdom of Manticore was so small and so far from the core systems...like Kenichi. There was very little interstellar traffic into or out of the Star Kingdom, especially now that the assisted immigration following the Plague Years had almost entirely wound down. There was little cargo to attract freighters, passenger ships had become less frequent, and even mail couriers arrived only at intervals which were erratic, to say the least. Worse, Kenichi was 400 light-years from Manticore, so even one of the fast courier boats would take literally months to make a one-way trip between them. By the best passenger ship connection Dr. Whitaker could arrange, the trip home would have taken at least six months, which meant it could easily be well over a T-year before he returned—*if* he'd returned—so he'd intended to take Anders with him.

The thought of having Anders snatched away for *at least* an entire T-year had been devastating to Stephanie, and she'd spent more than a night or two railing to Lionheart about stupid, small-minded, chip-pushing bureaucrats. There'd been more than a few tears involved, as well, despite Lionheart's comforting presence.

But then Dr. Whitaker's plans had changed.

Anders' mother was a cabinet minister in the Kenichi System government, and Kenichi turned out to have close trade ties—and treaty agreements—with the Beowulf System. Beowulf was one of the few core systems which maintained a full time consulate on Manticore, and Dr. Whitaker had appealed to the consul for assistance. As it turned out, a Beowulfan courier had been in orbit, there to collect the consul's regular quarterly report to his home government, and Kenichi lay almost directly on the route between Manticore and Beowulf. The courier boat was scarcely a luxury liner, but it did have the capacity to carry a *few* passengers, and the consul had offered the available space to Dr. Whitaker.

Unfortunately (from Dr. Whitaker's perspective; Stephanie had seen things a bit differently), there'd been room for only one additional passenger: him. There would be no place for Anders, if he took advantage of the courier boat, and he'd had only two days to make up his mind about accepting the consul's offer, given the courier's scheduled departure date.

In the end, he'd decided speed was of the essence, for several reasons, including the fear that some other anthropology team would be credentialed to study the treecats instead of his if the delay stretched out too long. So instead of taking Anders back to Urako, he'd left him in the Star Kingdom under the supervision of Dr. Emberly, the expedition's xenobiologist and botanist, and her mother, Dacey.

At first, Stephanie had been ecstatic over Dr. Whitaker's decision, but her joy had been short-lived. Until Urako University responded with the required assurances, Governor Donaldson had barred the Whitaker Expedition's team from further exploration. None of its members came from heavy-gravity worlds like Sphinx, and Sphinx, with a total population of less than two million, didn't offer a great many attractions to people who were prohibited from doing the one thing they'd come to the Star Kingdom to accomplish. Dr. Emberly had certainly felt that way, at any rate, and she'd decided to withdraw the expedition's personnel from Sphinx to Manticore, the Star Kingdom's capital planet, whose lower gravity was far more comfortable and whose larger population provided a lot more in the way of "civilization."

The decision had not met with unanimous approval. Unfortunately, the two people who'd most strongly objected—Anders and Stephanie—hadn't gotten a vote. And, in her more reasonable moments, Stephanie actually understood Dr. Emberly's thinking. Sphinx truly could be an uncomfortable planet for people who hadn't been genetically engineered for heavy-gravity environments, like the Harringtons, or grown up on its surface, like the Zivoniks, and Dacey Emberly, Calida's mother, wasn't a young woman. Not only that, but Dr. Whitaker had been adamant that Anders keep up his studies, and it was hard to deny that the planet Manticore's educational opportunities were better than Sphinx's.

But none of that changed the fact that Manticore and Sphinx were almost ten light-minutes apart even at their closest approach and, at the moment, they were over twenty-five light-minutes from one another. That meant any real-time conversation between someone on Sphinx and someone on Manticore was impossible, since it took nearly a half hour for any lightspeed transmission to make the trip between them. Somehow, asking a question and then waiting an hour for an answer put a damper on lively discussions.

Twenty-five light-minutes was a lot better than 400 light-years, but the communication delay had still limited Stephanie and Anders to letters and recorded vids. True, they could be sent back and forth a lot more quickly than they could have been transmitted between Kenichi and the Star Kingdom, but it just wasn't the *same* as face-to-face conversation... and Stephanie had discovered that even the warmest letter was a poor substitute for kisses and cuddling. There were things she just couldn't say, or explain, even in a personal vid. Not when she couldn't see his expression or hear his voice when she said them. It was a lot better than having him go all the way home with his father, but in some ways it was actually worse.

She'd been resigned to spending a whole half T-year pushing electronic mail back and forth, but she hadn't counted on Dacey Emberly, the expedition's painter and scientific illustrator. Dacey had decided that even if the entire team wasn't permitted to study *treecats*, there was no reason she couldn't be working on her portfolio of the rest of Sphinx. In addition, she'd discovered that Stephanie's mother was also a painter, as well as at least as good a botanist as her daughter, Calida. Marjorie Harrington had cheerfully offered her services as tour guide and fellow artist and invited Calida to join them. The botanist in Calida had jumped at the chance to explore Sphinx's plant life with a Sphinxian resident who was not simply a fellow botanist but probably the planet's best plant geneticist.

There were times when Stephanie thought it was just possible her mother had extended the invitation because she'd realized how miserable it was for Stephanie and Anders to be in the same star system but on different planets. There were other times when she wasn't so sure about that, but the result had been wonderful. For the last two months, both Doctors Emberly had been back in Twin Forks... which meant that *Anders* had been back on Sphinx, too.

The day they'd returned from Manticore, her parents

had invited them to a huge welcome back party, with all of Stephanie's—and Anders'—friends in attendance. Stephanie would have preferred to have Anders to herself, but her parents did so love a party and, anyhow, she'd suddenly felt a little shy. They'd never actually *declared* themselves "a couple"—not like Chet and Christine—but even so, there was a lot of teasing.

Later, they'd gotten some time by themselves. Soon they were over being shy and everything had been great.

"Great," Stephanie said to Lionheart, "except that now *I'm* going to be the one going away to Manticore! Three more entire months of nothing but *letters*...Can I do it? And even if Dr. Whitaker's university lets him come back, it won't let him stay here forever. I doubt Anders wants to give up his family. I mean, the only reason he's here now is that his mom's so busy with her position. What if it turns out Urako *won't* let Dr. Whitaker come back? What if Anders finds out he has to go home before I even get back from *Manticore?*"

The treecat evidently sensed her distress. He leapt lightly onto her lap and laid his true-hand—still damp and smelling of celery—on her cheek. His leaf-green eyes met hers, and he bleeked a gentle sound of comfort and inquiry.

"The problem is," Stephanie told him, "I don't know what I want. When Chief Ranger Shelton started telling us about the training program there was nothing in the world I wanted more than to go. Now...Now I find myself thinking that maybe it would be a good idea to let my parents talk me out of it for another year. I *am* only fifteen and a half—okay, fifteen and eight months. I could wait. A year won't matter too much. It's not likely the SFS will let me become an assistant ranger until I'm at least seventeen anyhow..."

The sound of her father's air van settling into its space alongside the clinic brought her back to herself.

Impulsively, she hugged Lionheart, feeling his fluffy tail curl around her in return. Then she took a deep breath and straightened up.

"Whatever I decide," she said softly, "I can't let Dad see I'm upset. That would sway him before I've even made up my own mind. Shall we go see if Dad needs help with his gear or a patient?"

"Bleek," Lionheart agreed, the sounds meaning far less than the enthusiastic flirt of his tail and the expectant prick of his ears as he led the way toward the door. "Bleek! Bleek! Bleek!"

Climbs Quickly didn't know exactly what had happened to generate such a stew of mixed emotions in his two-leg. When they had been in the meeting with Old Authority (as the treecats had dubbed the male two-leg to whom so many of their two legged friends deferred) Death Fang's Bane had begun by being excited and happy, her mind-glow overflowing with anticipation and delight. But then, somewhere in the midst of all the mouth noises, uneasiness had begun to tint the exuberance.

Climbs Quickly had not been concerned. For many season turnings, long before he had met Death Fang's Bane, he had served his clan as a scout. He was accustomed to the excitement that came with a new assignment, and how that excitement could be muted when one began to consider the challenges that would be involved.

However, at the very end of the meeting, Death Fang's Bane had experienced a surge of such intense emotional pain that it had been all Climbs Quickly could do not to wail aloud in response. One of the differences he'd discovered between two-legs and the People was that two-legs frequently attempted to conceal their feelings from one another. It had seemed bizarre, but then he had remembered the two-legs were mind-blind. They could not taste one another's mind-glows even if they tried, and it actually seemed to embarrass them sometimes if they revealed their emotions too clearly.

Sensing that the youngling was doing her best to hide what she felt at that moment, Climbs Quickly had muted his response and instead offered her a touch of comfort. He might not truly understand two-legs' odd attitude towards sharing their emotions, but he was proud to see that Death Fang's Bane was strong and had managed to hide her distress with very little help from him.

Once they had left Old Authority's place and Shadowed Sunlight had gotten into his flying thing and departed, Death Fang's Bane had let her feelings have freer play. At that point, Climbs Quickly isolated the source of her distress more clearly. He recognized the emotional notes that meant his two-leg was absorbed in thoughts about Bleached Fur, the young male in whom she had invested so much energy since his arrival back in the early days of the fire season.

Climbs Quickly liked Bleached Fur. The young male was full of lively curiosity. His mind-glow might not be as brilliant as that of Death Fang's Bane, but it had an enthusiasm that was very appealing, and Climbs Quickly had been happy to see his return from wherever he had vanished to. Despite this, there were times when Climbs Quickly was surprised by how intensely Death Fang's Bane cared for this young male.

At that thought, Climbs Quickly bleeked to himself in quiet amusement. Even among the People, understanding why one Person chose to be attracted to another could be a mystery—and at least the People could speak mind-to-mind. He supposed that, even as deeply as he and Death Fang's Bane were bonded, there would always be mysteries between them.

With her usual self-control, Death Fang's Bane had moderated at least the outer appearance of distress when her sire, Healer, had returned. She had helped Healer to settle in his latest patients—a pair of medium-sized plant-eaters with what smelled like some sort of respiratory distress—and had waited while he made mouth noises at the male who was his chief assistant. However, as soon as they were alone in the big flying thing, Death Fang's Bane started making mouth noises.

Soon the pair of two-legs were in animated discussion. Since Death Fang's Bane did not seem unduly agitated, Climbs Quickly contented himself with sniffing the interesting odors carried to him from the forests below. He heard the mouth noises that he knew indicated himself a few times, as well as the single hard sound that indicated Shadowed Sunlight, but most of the time the sounds meant far less than the flow of his two-legs' mind-glow.

He kept track of it, but Death Fang's Bane seemed to be doing fine. Climbs Quickly relaxed into the moment, the better to be prepared if a crisis did arise.

"SO YOU SEE, MOM," STEPHANIE ENDED HER SUMMARY of the meeting with Chief Ranger Shelton, "it's a terrific honor. What do you think?"

Marjorie Harrington tucked a lock of curly brown hair behind one ear before answering, a gesture that meant she was deep in thought. Her hazel-brown eyes had held only interested curiosity as Stephanie told her about Chief Ranger Shelton's offer. Now the keen mind that spliced and diced genes of just about anything that grew was at work on the pros and cons of her daughter's newest opportunity.

Needless to say, Stephanie had told her father about the offer on their flight out to the Harrington freehold. Not to do so would have been uncharacteristic, and the last thing Stephanie wanted either of her parents to guess was how undecided she herself was. From her father's response, Stephanie had a pretty good idea what her mother would say. She wasn't disappointed.

"Download the information to my computer, would

you? I'll want to review it myself, then talk with your father. How do you feel about it, Steph?"

"I'm excited," Stephanie said. "It's a huge opportunity. Still . . . Three months on Manticore is a long time. Manticore's not at all like Sphinx."

Marjorie nodded. "And, strangely enough, that might be the best reason for you to go. I know you're madly in love with Sphinx, but it might be a good idea for you to see something of other planets before you get pot-bound here. You didn't like Sphinx much at first, remember?"

"Mom! That was in winter! Now I've had a spring and a summer and we're moving into autumn."

"And winter will come again."

"Yes, but now I know so much more about Sphinx that I'm almost looking forward to winter. I can't wait to see how the animals and plants deal with all that snow. Before, I wasn't allowed to go anywhere unless you or Dad were along, remember?"

"You were only ten," came her mother's mild reply.

"Exactly!"

"Still, Stephanie, the more I think about it, the better it seems that you spend some time on another planet. I'm not saying I'm giving permission, mind you, just that I can see some good points. You're just a wee bit obsessive—I can't think where you might have gotten that trait; certainly your father and I are never the least bit obsessive—and it would be good to give you some balance."

Since Stephanie knew both her parents were perfectly capable of being quite focused—her mother had been known to spend entire nights without sleep waiting for some rare blossom to open so she could collect pollen— she knew she was being teased. Still, she couldn't quell a certain uneasiness. She'd counted on at least one of her parents being somewhat resistant to the idea, just in case she decided to back out, but so far both had been surprisingly receptive. She wondered if—despite what he'd said—Chief Ranger Shelton might have dropped a hint or two.

"I'll com that information from my uni-link to your computer," Stephanie said. "Can I help with dinner or anything?"

"That would be great...."

For the rest of the evening, talk was pointedly centered on domestic matters. Eventually, Stephanie excused herself.

"I'm supposed to show Dacey that waterfall of Jessica's she wants to paint tomorrow," she reminded them. "She and Anders are picking me up pretty early, so I need to get some sleep."

"You're coming back early enough to talk this over, though, right?" Richard said. "Since we need to give SFS our answer, a family conference would be in order."

"Absolutely," Stephanie said. "I don't see that there'll be any problem with my getting back in time."

Up in the privacy of her room, Stephanie considered screening Jessica. In the end, she decided that while her own feelings were so unsettled, even talking to her best friend wouldn't help a lot. Instead, she sat at her desk for a long time, thinking over her options while a slideshow of her favorite holo images from the time she'd spent with Anders marched across her desk. When she eventually tumbled into bed, the same images—animated and making cryptic statements—marched through her dreams. Stephanie thought that somewhere in what they said was the answer she needed, but when she awoke at dawn the dream images fell mute and only the uncertainty remained.

"Hi, Dr. Richard," Anders said when Stephanie's dad opened the door to the big, rambling stone house. "Is Stephanie ready?"

"Good morning to you, Anders," Dr. Harrington replied. "Steph ran upstairs to get something. Can I offer you some coffee?"

"Dacey and I already had some," Anderson said, "but I could use a bit more. Were you up all night again?"

The veterinarian nodded as he led the way to the kitchen. "Saleem called from the clinic. We have two nipper-hoppers with some sort of respiratory infection and one went into crisis. Probably reaction to the antibiotic. I didn't have to fly in—Saleem's a good vet himself—but we were in consultation until we pulled the patient through."

"You did, then?" Anders accepted the large mug of steaming hot coffee and sipped it gratefully. Stephanie preferred sweets, but he liked a bit of bitter. "Congratulations!"

"Thanks. I think they'll both make it, but sometimes I long for the days when my practice consisted of dogs and cats, and remedies tested by centuries of care."

Anders grinned. He knew Dr. Harrington was being melodramatic. The truth was that he was a trained xenoveterinarian who'd treated a lot of non-Terrestrial creatures even back on Meyerdahl.

He heard the sound of Stephanie spilling down the stairs at her usual breakneck pace. A moment later she burst into the kitchen, Lionheart loping with sinuous grace beside her, her travel pack swinging from one hand.

"Sorry, Anders. I realized I'd forgotten to bring those extra nets I have for your dad."

As always, Anders found his heart giving a joyful leap when he saw Stephanie Harrington. He knew she didn't think much of her looks. She thought she was too short, that her hair was too curly and too boringly brown. He knew—more from watching Stephanie's reactions than because she'd actually admitted it—that she envied girls with more curvaceous figures like Jessica or Trudy. He'd tried and tried to tell Stephanie that curvy figures were all right, but how to explain to a girl that she reminded you of an eagle lofting on a breeze or a deer leaping with lithe grace? It just didn't come out like you meant it to, especially when the girl's dad was a vet and she tended to think of animals from a very practical perspective.

"Dad will be really pleased to have those nets," Anders assured her without adding "if he's allowed to come back to Sphinx." That was something he and Stephanie had decided by unspoken agreement not to discuss. "He never gets tired of comparing one physical artifact to another," Anders went on, "even if they all look pretty much the same to most of us."

"Great!" Stephanie said, turning to give her dad a quick hug. "I'll be back for dinner. Remind Mom not to tell Jessica, okay? I want to do it myself."

"Right," Dr. Harrington said. "I will."

Anders thought this last exchange was very odd. Over the last six months, Stephanie and Jessica had gotten so close that sometimes he was just a little bit jealous. He guessed their closeness had to do with the fact that both had been adopted by treecats, but maybe it was just that they were girls. Either way—even though they didn't spend all that much time giggling over clothes or hairstyles—there were times he felt distinctly left out. What wouldn't Stephanie tell the other girl?

Maybe it's near Jess' birthday or something, he thought, *and Stephanie is present shopping.* He resolved to ask later. Jessica Pheriss had become his friend, too, and he wouldn't want to miss her birthday.

"Can I help with any of that junk?" he asked Stephanie as they headed towards where he'd parked the rented air car.

"I've got it," she assured him. "It's less awkward than it looks, really."

Anders didn't protest. He'd gotten used to the fact that, tiny as she was, Stephanie was a lot stronger than he was. She moved easily in Sphinx's 1.35 gravity without needing the counter-grav unit that Anders wore day and night, sleeping and waking. He supposed it didn't bother him because Stephanie would be the first to remind him that she hadn't done anything to earn that extra strength. The Harringtons were all genies—genetically modified humans. Their home planet of Meyerdahl had cultivated several variations, all meant to help humans deal with environments for which the unaugmented human form was not intended. Anders didn't know the full extent of those modifications, but he did know that Stephanie was strong and tough. She healed well, too. He didn't know if Stephanie's intelligence—she was scary smart—was a result of genetic modifications, too, or just good luck. After all, both her parents were obviously smart.

There were drawbacks to Stephanie's mutations, of course. The most obvious was that she had a huge appetite. Most of the time that meant she simply munched away without putting on an extra ounce, but there had been that time they'd been hiking and the extra food bars they'd brought along had been ruined when a pack fell into a stream. If Lionheart hadn't come up with some peculiar looking nuts, Stephanie would have suffered.

Anders knew from personal experience that it was a good thing humans could eat a lot of what grew on Sphinx. Of course, if humans only ate foods native to Sphinx, they would eventually suffer from dietary deficiencies. But the compatibility meant that the planet—despite its high gravity and relatively cool climate—was actually pretty friendly to humans. Friendly, that was, until something surged out of a bog and tried to eat you...

Anders grinned at the memory. Adventure was definitely more fun afterwards than when it was happening.

The air car was empty when they got to it, but Anders wasn't surprised.

"Dacey?" he called.

"Up here, just a sec. I saw something I wanted to sketch."

He and Stephanie looked up in time to see a tall, skinny, older woman drifting from the lower boughs of one of the many crown oaks that ornamented the area surrounding the Harringtons' house. She adjusted her counter-grav unit just shy of the ground and came to a light landing that spoke of a lot of experience using the device.

"Good morning, Stephanie," Dacey Emberly said cheerfully. "I hope your parents don't mind, but the light drifting down through the leaves—especially with the leaves turning that particular golden shade—was too much for me."

Stephanie grinned and stowed her pack in the air car. Lionheart leapt up and in, settling into one of the window seats and bleeking to have the window opened a crack so he could sniff out. Anders moved into the driver's seat and complied with the treecat's request.

"The autumn color's too much for Mom, too," Stephanie said. "This is only our second real autumn here on Sphinx, and we got here late last autumn, just as winter was coming on. Mom's making sketches or taking images every free moment. She wants to fill out her series of season paintings."

"I know," Dacey agreed. "And I understand, too. We've been here for nearly a full T-year, and as far as I'm concerned, Sphinx exists in a sort of eternal late summer, though the color shifts in the trees these last couple of T-months are making me believe in autumn."

"If you're still here," Stephanie laughed, "I can tell you, you'll seriously believe in *winter*. Take my word for that!"

The flight to the waterfall she'd described to Dacey was filled with conversation comparing Sphinx and Meyerdahl to Urako and to several planets Dacey had lived on during her long life. Eventually, Anders brought the air car down into the clearing Stephanie indicated and they piled out.

"It's still another couple of kilometers that way," Stephanie said, pointing to the northeast. "Sorry I couldn't find you a landing spot closer than this."

"We'll manage," Dacey assured her, watching as Stephanie checked the enormous pistol holstered at her right hip.

Anders had acquired the Sphinxian habit of always carrying a weapon in the bush, as well, although he preferred a rather more modest-sized gun, and he was busy checking his own pistol. Dacey, on the other hand, knew her limits. She had no expertise with firearms and no real desire to acquire it. If something with lots of teeth and claws came along, she'd do her bit by getting nimbly out of the way and letting Stephanie deal with it.

"Let's go," Stephanie said, shouldering her pack, and started off through the picketwood along the trail she'd marked on her and Lionheart's last visit.

Anders and Dacey followed her, and she heard them discussing Calida Emberly's most recent meeting with Patricia Helton, Governor Donaldson's chief of staff. It was clear from Helton's attitude that Donaldson's nose was still out of joint over Dr. Whitaker's actions, but he seemed to be settling down at least a little. The fact that Dr. Whitaker had been off Sphinx for almost five months might have something to do with that, she thought.

It felt a little strange to realize that Anders' father had been back in the Kenichi System for almost two months by now. She wondered how he'd made out defending his activities on Sphinx? He struck her as the sort who would be able to evade his fellow academics' condemnation, but what if he hadn't? Even if he managed to use his connections to nab another fast courier boat for his return to the Star Kingdom, he couldn't possibly be back here for another month, so there was a little time left with Anders, no matter what happened. But what if he did come back only to collect Anders and return to Urako University in disgrace? If he had to make the trip by regular passenger ship, she and Anders had at least another five or six months before he disappeared back to Kenichi. But if he *did* get passage back on a courier boat, Anders could be headed home to Urako before Stephanie even got back from Manticore!

Worrying about it won't change it, she told herself tartly, eyes and ears alert for any possible threat. Lionheart was pacing them, flowing through the picketwood a good fifteen meters above the ground, and she trusted him to spot potential dangers well before she did, but that didn't excuse her from the responsibility of looking out for herself and her companions, as well.

She thought about the Whitaker expedition as they hiked along. Assuming Dr. Whitaker was allowed to return, his staff would be rather different, and she thought that might help. She suspected that what had happened six months ago might actually have cured him of thinking he knew how to handle everything better than anyone else—nearly getting eaten by a swamp siren should provide a wake-up call for almost anyone. And the fact that he would no longer be as surrounded by people dependent on him for their careers would probably be good for him, too.

Virgil Iwamoto had resigned as Dr. Whitaker's chief assistant and managed to secure passage for himself and Peony Rose, his pregnant wife, aboard a starship headed for Beowulf about a month after Dr. Whitaker's departure by courier boat. Modern medical and technological improvements meant that pregnancies in high gravity weren't as risky as they had once been, but Anders had told her Virgil and Peony Rose were both concerned. Besides, they probably wanted to be near their families at this exciting time in their lives, and they'd barely get home in time for the birth, as it was.

Whether out of gratitude or because he was aware that Virgil could ruin his reputation if he chose to share certain stories, Dr. Whitaker had released him from his contract and given him the highest marks. He'd also granted Virgil permission to use expedition data to complete his dissertation, Anders had said, assuring that the document would get a lot of attention.

With Virgil's departure, Calida had become the senior member of the expedition in the Star Kingdom, although it seemed probable that Kesia Guyen would step into Virgil's place when—and if—Dr. Whitaker was allowed to return. Since Kesia's specialization was linguistics and the treecats were being remarkably stubborn about providing her anything to work with, she'd decided to expand her expertise. It turned out the the type of mind that easily organized tiny details of word order and grammatical rules also did very well in categorizing the minutia of an alien culture. Making matters better all around, Kesia's husband, John Qin, had made some profitable business contacts within the Star Kingdom. Unlike Virgil, who'd been all too aware of his dependence on his mentor, Kesia—eager to succeed in her field, but buffered by her husband's increased prominence—was unlikely to be the least intimidated by her boss. And from all Stephanie had seen, the other two Ph.D.s on the expedition—Calida and Dr. Nez—seemed to view it as part of their job to make sure the assessment of the treecats' possible sentience went beyond examining the flint tools, nets, pots, baskets, and shelters that made up their material culture, which should serve as another brake on Dr. Whitaker's occasional bouts of excessive enthusiasm.

If he comes back, and Governor Donaldson and Minister Vásquez let him stay, he'll behave himself better this time, she thought with a mental smile.

Anders hiked along behind Dacey, bringing up the rear and trying to emulate Stephanie's obvious alertness. He envied the way she seemed so completely at home here in the bush, striding along with the easy grace of her genetically engineered muscles and constantly aware of every sound, every flicker of light. This was exactly the world she'd been born to live on, he thought, and hoped his dad's past actions weren't going to get all of them permanently exiled from it after all.

He didn't much like thinking about that possibility, but it had occupied his mind more and more of late. It had been frustrating, to say the very least, to find himself stuck on Manticore until Dacey managed to convince Calida to return to Sphinx. Letters and vids just weren't the same thing as face-to-face conversations, although he *did* have to admit that he would always treasure the memory of the rib-popping hug Stephanie had bestowed when they finally did return. And whatever happened, they'd have at least another three or four months together, he reminded himself. And on the same planet, this time!

He smiled at the thought, and the smile broadened as he anticipated having her to himself for a change. Dacey would disappear into her sketch pad as soon as they reached the waterfall Stephanie had described, and that would give him a chance to sit and talk with Stephanie in the sort of privacy they seldom enjoyed.

Usually, when Stephanie guided him or other members of the expedition in the bush, Karl came along, as well. Anders liked Karl quite a lot, but the older boy was an intimidating presence. Like Stephanie, he often moved around without the need for a counter-grav unit. However, in Karl's case, the ability owed nothing to genetic modification and a great deal to sheer stubbornness. Karl had the determination of a nativeborn Sphinxian to be able to move about on his home planet without being constantly dependent on a counter-grav unit. Anders had been on Sphinx long enough to know that not every Sphinxian made that difficult choice, which added to his respect for Karl.

The fact was that Anders wasn't at all sure how Karl felt about him—Anders—and his increasingly important role in Stephanie's life. From various things he'd overheard—and from various things Stephanie herself had let drop—Anders had learned that after the Harringtons moved to Sphinx, Stephanie had resisted making friends among people her own age. She'd managed with her own company and—later on—that of Lionheart, supplemented by corresponding with people she met on the net through classes or clubs. If her parents hadn't pretty much forced her to join the hang-gliding club, Stephanie probably wouldn't have met anyone her own age at all. Then a couple of rangers had talked the Harringtons into having Stephanie take lessons in how to use a variety of firearms. Karl had been brought in to act as tutor, since the rangers couldn't always be available. It had turned out they shared interests in a lot more than target shooting, and Karl had become Stephanie's first real friend on Sphinx.

Anders knew Steph liked Karl but thought of him as a buddy rather than anything else. What he couldn't figure out was how *Karl* felt about Stephanie. There had been a few times early on when Anders thought he was being given "keep off" signals, but then Karl had seemed to accept that Stephanie would make her own mind up in matters romantic, the way she did about everything else.

Even so, when a couple of times Karl had come upon

them when they couldn't have been doing anything other than kissing, Anders had thought he saw jealousy—or maybe just protectiveness—flash in Karl's dark eyes.

Thinking about Karl reminded Anders of the other complication in his developing relationship with Stephanie. That was her link with Lionheart. The 'cat was far more than a pet. Anders thought that anyone who bothered to spend time with the 'cats would come to the conclusion that they were intelligent—although that intelligence had taken a somewhat different shape than it did in humans. Even someone who, like Dr. Whitaker, preferred to make assessments of a race based on its material culture had decided the 'cats were intelligent. Really, the only question that remained—at least as Anders saw it—was where on the sentience scale the treecats would end up being placed.

However, Stephanie had confided in Anders something that far fewer people had had the opportunity to learn. She was certain the 'cats were at least telempathic. She was less certain—but still pretty positive—that they were telepathic, as well. Anders had to agree that something was going on with the treecats that didn't lend itself to visual confirmation. He'd seen how Lionheart seemed aware of the flow of Stephanie's emotions. He'd also become pretty certain that Lionheart could read people other than Stephanie—although he wasn't sure if the 'cat got the same amount of detail from anyone else. Stephanie claimed that Lionheart was a really good judge of character. He liked Anders, didn't he? But he'd taken a strong dislike to another off-worlder, Tennessee Bolgeo, right off.

As to whether the 'cats were telepathic...Anders thought Stephanie was probably right. He'd had opportunities to observe Lionheart and Valiant acting in concert when the action in question implied a whole lot more information was being exchanged than could be held in some sort of emotional burst. One of the best examples was when

Valiant—who shared Jessica's interest in gardening—had reached for a specific tool, one Jessica had borrowed a few moments before. Lionheart had loped over, retrieved the tool from Jessica, and handed it to Valiant. There'd been no exchange of sounds. Valiant hadn't even turned around, so there couldn't have been any of the body language signals Kesia had thought might substitute for more complex vocalizations.

All of this made Anders less than comfortable when he was alone with Stephanie and things were getting... romantic. Were the two of them really alone? How much did the treecat share in Stephanie's reactions? How much did he feel of Anders' own reactions? Anders was determined to keep his and Stephanie's mutual explorations within Stephanie's comfort range, but that didn't mean he hadn't had thoughts, some of them pretty detailed and pretty graphic.

It was bad enough to think that Lionheart might sense some of what he was thinking, but what if the treecat shared those feelings with Stephanie? What would she think of Anders? Would she be enticed or horrified? Could the treecat somehow contaminate or influence their feelings for each other?

Such conjectures were enough to make Anders stop short every time he got a bit carried away, even when he was pretty sure Stephanie wouldn't mind trying a little bit more. Now, just thinking about what Lionheart might or might not know was enough to make Anders hot under the collar.

He shook his head, smiling at himself, and concentrated on paying attention to his surroundings.

"It's gorgeous, Stephanie!" Dacey Emberly exclaimed as they came to the foot of the waterfall.

It plunged over a precipice ninety meters above them, plummeting down in a single long spill, flanked by two secondary falls that descended in a series of roaring cataracts. The seething pool at the base of the cliff was at least fifty meters across, its surface perpetually dimpled by fine drops condensing back out of the falls' spray. The river was twenty meters across where it flowed away from them, brawling through a forest of rapids and sliding down deep, glassy smooth chutes between mossgrown boulders. The backdrop of trees and undergrowth—most of it the distinctive deep blue-green of summer red spruce but touched here and there with paintbrush kisses of autumn—framed it in a rich, luxuriant tangle of color.

It was just a bit difficult to hear Dacey over the steady, unremitting thunder of the falls, but her expression was all Stephanie had hoped for.

"Jessica was the one who spotted it, really," she told the older woman. "She and I were mapping the freehold's plant diversity from the air for Mom. You wouldn't think something that tall would be hard to see, but those crown oaks"—she pointed back over her shoulder—"do a really good job of hiding it from the air unless you hit the angle just right."

"It's spectacular," Dacey said, head swiveling as she absorbed the falls' entire impact. "And speaking of crown oaks, I think that might be my best vantage point. If that's all right with you, of course, Probationary Ranger Harrington!"

She smiled broadly, and Stephanie chuckled.

"I think it's probably perfectly safe," she replied. "Look—Lionheart's already checking it out!" She pointed, and Dacey followed her finger to see the cream-and-gray blur of the treecat swarming up the tallest of the crown oaks. "We'll just make sure nothing's hanging around up there to eat any of us, and then Anders and I will find a good lookout post about halfway up. You can climb as high as you like to get the exact angle you want."

Climbs Quickly flowed up the towering golden-leaf, exploring his surroundings with eyes, ears, nose, and mind. He had realized early on that they must be bringing Eye of Memory out here to see the waterfall Windswept had discovered, and he was happy that they had, because he loved to watch Eye of Memory at her craft.

It would never have occurred to one of the People to make a permanent image of something one of them had seen, since they could always pass the actuality of it from mind to mind. Because of that, it had taken him longer than perhaps it ought to have to associate even the moving images on the bright, flat memory thing Death Fang's Bane spent so much time sitting in front of with things he had actually seen. Then he had realized that of course the poor, mind-blind two-legs could not possibly exchange the memory of things seen with one another. He had been pleased by the clever way they compensated for their inability, yet the images that Eye of Memory made were even more pleasing. They were not as *accurate*, perhaps, and they did not move, but gazing at them was like savoring the tiny differences between two of the People's remembered images of the same thing. It was as if Eye of Memory was able to share her own perceptions of the things whose images she captured despite the fact that she was mind-blind, and watching those images come to life under her clever, skilled fingers was almost as pleasing as the taste of her happy, focused mind-glow as she worked.

He and Death Fang's Bane had accompanied Eye of Memory on several expeditions, and so he had already guessed where she would be most likely to perch while capturing this image. When Death Fang's Bane turned and looked at the tallest of the golden-leafs, he had known he had guessed correctly, and it felt good to climb swiftly up the enormous tree. Well, of course it did! Had not his clan named him Climbs Quickly because climbing was one of the things he most enjoyed in all the world?

He reached a wide fork in one of the branches and paused, looking back down the way he had come. This would do well for Eye of Memory, he decided. The branch was broad enough to give her a comfortable place to sit or stand and shaded from too much direct sunlight, and the entire waterfall was clearly visible. He had detected no sign of any danger, and so he scurried out to the end of the branch, sat up high on his true-feet, and waved his true-hand at Death Fang's Bane.

He could not make her hear his mind-voice, but he knew she would be watching him through the far-seeing thing she carried at her belt, and he felt her understanding as he beckoned to her and the other two-legs. She waved back, and he settled down on his bright, breezy perch, waiting.

"How long do you think she'll paint *this* time?" Anders asked, grinning at Stephanie as they sat on their own branch, twenty meters below Dacey's, and leaned back against the crown oak's enormous trunk, sharing the thermos of lemonade Marjorie Harrington had sent along.

"Until she runs out of light, probably," Stephanie replied with an answering grin. She'd become very fond of Dacey Emberly, but having a mother who was also a painter had taught her a thing or two about the breed.

"Yeah, you're probably right," Anders agreed.

He looked around, thoroughly enjoying the sunlight and the cool breeze singing through the crown oak's leaves.

He might not have felt quite so happy about perching so many meters above the ground if he hadn't had his own counter-grav, but he'd gotten accustomed to climbing trees here on Sphinx. Stephanie and Lionheart seemed to spend at least a third of their time in the treetops, after all!

The thought of the treecat drew his attention to where Lionheart clung to a branch just above Dacey, gazing intently over her shoulder as she worked. He knew Lionheart seemed to love watching Dacey paint, and he wondered how focused he was at the moment on *Dacey's* emotions instead of Stephanie's. Could he be distracted from his person's emotions, or was the link between them—whatever it was and however it worked—always in the forefront of his attention? It was a question which had occupied Anders more than once, but in a lot of ways, he was grateful, since no one objected when he and Stephanie went off on a hike together, even without Karl. Apparently they assumed that Lionheart made an adequate chaperone.

And I guess he does, Anders thought ruefully. *Even if Stephanie flat-out invited me to . . . well . . . to do more than we've been doing, I don't think I'd try. I saw the records of what Lionheart and his family did to the hexapuma. I don't really want him to decide I was offering his human some sort of threat.*

Today, however, Stephanie seemed to have something on her mind other than their usual explorations of the local wildlife and each other. He hadn't been able to put his finger on what that something else might be, but several times he'd thought her usual smile seemed a little more forced. Now she looked at him for several moments, smile fading. Then she reached to hold his hand, and Anders didn't need to be a telepath—not even a telempath—to know she was looking for comfort, not inviting a snuggle.

His eyebrows furrowed as he searched for a way to ask what was wrong without implying that she was acting particularly weird, but he didn't have to.

"Anders," she asked, "how did you feel when you realized you had a chance to go to Sphinx?"

Anders was surprised. They'd talked about this before when comparing notes on their various trips to other planets and it hadn't seemed to worry her any then. Why should it be worrying her now? Unless...

Guessing this was a lead to some other topic, he answered honestly.

"Pretty happy, really. I'd already gotten interested in treecats, you know. Here was my chance to see them—not in recordings, not some captive being brought around as a display—but where they lived. I was really excited."

"You weren't nervous about going to a strange place?"

"Not really. I mean, it wasn't like I was going alone. Yeah, Dad can be really obsessive, but if I got in trouble he'd be around. Anyway, despite my mom's impression that a colony world was going to be pretty backward, I knew Sphinx was cutting edge in a lot of ways."

"Manticore is even more cutting edge," Stephanie said. "I haven't been there since we stopped over on the way to Sphinx. I was only ten and fresh from Meyerdahl, so it didn't seem too much to me then. Now I know lots of people on Manticore think people from Sphinx are complete rubes."

"Some of them probably do," Anders replied. "I don't remember anyone actually saying anything like that to *me*, but most of the people I talked to knew I was a visitor. They probably wouldn't have talked down about their neighbors to a stranger." He smiled slightly. "I don't think most of them think that way, though."

"No?" Stephanie looked away for a moment. "*I* sort of felt that way when we first got here, you know. Until

Lionheart and I met, anyway. So I guess it wouldn't be too surprising if somebody on Manticore felt that way. Or if... if they might, I don't know, look down on somebody from Sphinx if they were to run into them wandering around Landing or something."

The meaning behind her somewhat jumbled words registered on Anders suddenly.

"You've got a chance to go to Manticore? That's really cool, Steph. I enjoyed my visit a lot—except for the fact that *you* were on a different planet, that is. I think you'll really enjoy it! What is it? Some sort of educational field trip? A competition, maybe?"

"You might say so," Stephanie agreed. She took a deep breath, and then, the words spilling out of her in a torrent, she told Anders about her and Karl's meeting with Chief Ranger Shelton.

Anders listened first in delight, then—as he realized just how long Stephanie would be gone—with increasing dismay. He fought to hide his reaction. He was sure Stephanie didn't guess how he felt, but he was pretty sure that if Lionheart was paying attention to them instead of Dacey, *he* wasn't fooled at all.

Stephanie ended her account on a sort of choking note, like she was swallowing back a little sob. She'd told the last part to some point on the tree limb near her right foot. Now Anders reached and tilted back her head so he could see her face. To his amazement—Stephanie was a queen of self-control—her brown eyes were swimming with unshed tears.

He thought she might pull away, but instead she flung her arms around him and squeezed him with a bone crushing intensity that demonstrated that, for once, she'd forgotten her own strength. Anders tried not to show he was gasping for breath, but hugged her back as hard as he could.

"Oh, Anders! Anders! What am I going to do? I thought that maybe Mom or Dad would be against it, but as far as I can tell, if I want to go they're going to let me. But *you* only just got back from there! And...and we don't know yet how long you're even going to be here in the Star Kingdom at all! How can I tell them I don't want to go because I don't want to leave you?!"

She relaxed her hug so she could look at him. To give himself a moment to catch his breath, Anders kissed her lightly. Then, trying hard not to show how mixed up he himself felt, he settled her back next to him with his arm around her.

"I don't want you to go, either, Steph. But I'm guessing that you don't know what you really want."

Stephanie gulped something between a sob and a laugh. "I do know, actually. Absolutely. I want to go and take that class *and* I want to stay right here on Sphinx with you. Since that's impossible, I'm going to have to make a choice."

Anders cuddled her against him. He'd grown a bit in the last six T-months, but Stephanie hadn't much. Against his side, she felt deceptively fragile and delicate, like a baby bird.

Stephanie is fragile and delicate, he thought. *Maybe not in her body, but inside, where it counts. I've got to help her make the right decision or something might break—and along with it, whatever it is we have between us.*

"We've never really talked about being from two different planets—what that means to 'us,'" he began.

Stephanie sniffled a little bit. When she pulled away just enough that she could look up into his face, Anders saw that she'd stopped crying.

"No," she agreed. "I think we were just about to when your dad decided you could stay here in the Star Kingdom while he went back to Urako. I guess I didn't want to jinx the good news. Maybe I just hoped the reprieves would keep coming."

Anders flashed a grin that quickly faded into seriousness.

"Yeah. Me, too. And the truth is that Dad's good enough at working the system back at the university that I really do think the odds are that he will be able to get the guarantees Governor Donaldson and Minister Vásquez want. If he does, they may even extend his contract, leave us here longer than any of us thought. But one way or another—you going to Manticore, me going back to Urako—we're going to be separated. Even if Dad's contract gets extended until I reach my majority, there's no way I'm never going to leave to see my Mom or something. And it's not like we weren't already separated while I was on Manticore and you were here on Sphinx, either. Right?"

Stephanie nodded. "Right. But do we need to speed up getting separated? What if I come back from Manticore and you need to leave for Urako a month later? What if you get a message from your dad telling you to come home next month while I'm stuck on another planet? We would have wasted whatever time we might have had together!"

Anders wrapped a lock of her hair around his finger. "I doubt even Mom would hire a private courier just to send word to me to come home. So we're probably looking at at least another four months before I'd have to go—and we'd probably have to wait another month longer than that, at least, before we found a passenger ship headed in the right direction. So, at worst, we'd have another couple of months after you got home. And if Dad does manage to convince everyone to let him come back and stay, we'll be here at least until the snow makes excavation impossible. That gives us eight, nine—even ten months. Then, yeah. I'm going to have to go."

"And if you're wrong? If you have to go sooner?"

"Leave off my going for a minute," Anders said. "Before we go any further, there something I've got to say. I'll be honest. I don't want you to go to Manticore. I really, really don't. But I don't want you staying because of me, either. I think in the end it would ruin whatever we've got. Karl would come back with his certificate or badge, and you'd be thinking 'That could've been me.' Worse, you'd be thinking, 'That could've been me and I missed the chance to be one of the youngest ever to get that badge. Anders held me back and there's Anders, getting on a ship for home anyway.'"

Stephanie sighed. "You know me too well.... I thought about all that. I think I might have felt that way if I hadn't considered it ahead of time, but now I'd be making the decision knowing up front what the trade would be. I don't think I'd be so small-souled that I'd resent a trade I made, well, knowing I was making it."

"I'll give you that, Steph. You might sometimes be impulsive, but you're never small-souled. But you have to consider that you would've wasted a unique opportunity." Anders hated the words that were taking shape in his own mouth, but he knew he had to say them or he'd be a hypocrite. "Earlier you tried to give the impression that this training class wasn't a one-time offer, but do you know that?"

Stephanie frowned. "I want to be a member of the SFS. This is part of SFS training. Of course there'll be another chance."

"You're being difficult," Anders said. "You know exactly what I mean. You're fifteen and, what, eight months? Chief Ranger Shelton made clear that he had to argue to get you included. Now, what if word gets around that you turned down the offer because you were obsessed with some boy? How seriously will people take you? I'm guessing not very. They'll decide you're one of those intense prodigies who burn out young, or, worse, one of those girls who excel in some hobby until they discover boys."

Stephanie winced. That last had hit home. Recently, her rival in the hang-gliding club, Trudy Franchitti, had quit, saying she had more interesting things to do than play at butterflies with a bunch of kids. The fact that her on-again off-again beau, Stan Chang, had dropped out a few weeks before made it pretty clear what those "more interesting things" were.

"So you're saying I might not get another chance next year. I might not get a chance until I was actually in the SFS."

"Right," Anders agreed. "Worse, you might find yourself waiting until you're in your early twenties for that other chance. You're still a probationary ranger. The SFS has just opened up its ranks and started active recruiting, so there are going to be new assistant rangers ahead of you next year. This opening only came up because the fire season this year was so bad Chief Ranger Shelton can't spare any of his full-timers. I'd say this is a one-shot offer until you're at least an assistant ranger, maybe until you're promoted to full ranger. Wouldn't you?"

Stephanie bit her lower lip. "I can see what you're saying, but, Anders, you're a one-time offer, too! I've heard your dad. He's really proud of what you've done with your independent study here, but he wants you to finish up school back on Urako so you're on hand to apply for university, go on interviews, do internships, all that kind of thing."

Anders felt his mind go all cool, the way it did sometimes when he was helping Dr. Emberly or Dr. Nez sort through samples. His heart was still pounding fit to burst at the idea that Stephanie might actually go off to another planet. In some ways, the fact that they'd already endured that kind of separation only made it even worse. He thought that if he wasn't careful he was going to embarrass himself by crying, but, thankfully, the coolness held.

"So you accept that I have to get a proper education? Apply for college. All that?"

"Of course! You're smart! You have promise!"

Anders bent to kiss her again, this time softly, gently, on the lips.

"Then, Stephanie, my darling, how can I wish for anything less for you? You've got to go to Manticore. It's really our only choice."

ALL THE WORLD HE HAD KNOWN WAS BURNT AND broken, reeking of ash. Keen Eyes, scout of what had been the Swaying Fronds Clan, looked over the ruins of his former home. A few of the tall gray-bark trees still remained, but their bark was blackened and ruined. The fat, wide limbs that had protected the People when they foraged for the tangy seeds among the springy boughs were gone, except for an occasional skeleton that both evoked and mocked the trees' former beauty.

As for the wide-leafed ground plants that had given the clan their name, they were not even skeletons, not even ash, only memory.

The People had known such destruction before and moved on. The songs of many clans contained details of migrations when fire or flood made a range no longer suited for habitation. Those songs were heart-swelling and inspirational, filled with challenges met and overcome before, at last, the clan settled into its new home.

But this time is different, Keen Eyes thought. *The fires were vast. Even with the two-legs intervening to put the blaze out, the destruction spread farther than any in the recent memory of our clan and even—so Wide Ears reported before she died—in the memories of neighboring clans. Many have praised the two-legs for their intervention, but I cannot believe they did so for the good of any but themselves. No doubt it was to protect the range they have made their own, and they seem to take more of it with every turning! I have scouted to the sun-setting of what was once our range and the two-legs have settled themselves throughout that area. True, there are none of the larger settlements, but the presence of the two-legs contaminates what was once open range, and with so much burned and destroyed . . .*

He had recently returned from scouting deeper into the mountains. The fire had burned fiercely there, making the lower elevations uninhabitable. The higher elevations were not inviting, especially since the year had already moved into the changing of leaves. Were this the time of new growth, his clan might manage in higher elevations while searching for a new range, but not now. Not with the coldest times marching closer.

Swaying Fronds Clan could not move in the direction of moss-drying. Bright Water Clan held the range there. They were known as a generous clan, but they already faced the strain of supporting their own clan with the more limited foraging offered in higher elevations. Bright Water's range was large, so they had plenty of good hunting, but their hunters worked hard and they did not have a great deal to spare.

Moreover, Bright Water had long been considered uncomfortable neighbors by many of the older members of the Swaying Fronds Clan. Bright Water consorted too freely with the two-legs. One of their scouts had even bonded with a youngling of that strange, naked-skinned, mind-blind people. Some whispered that this Climbs Quickly had become nothing more than a lazy hanger-on, trumpeting through his memory singer sister tales of his own importance.

Keen Eyes didn't believe this last. He had never met Climbs Quickly, but he had listened to the song of that Person's courage and valor, not only when he had rescued the two-leg youngling who was now his partner, but during the last fire season, when he had intervened to help save members of the Damp Ground Clan who otherwise might have been trapped on their island home and burned to death.

No. Climbs Quickly was not anyone's lazy hanger-on. Nonetheless, moving in the direction of Bright Water's range was not an option.

So, farther to sun-setting into the mountains was ruled out. The mountains to moss-drying were out. So were the mountains to moss-growing, for the fires had been worse there. That meant the only direction in which Swaying Fronds could move was the lowlands. Here the problem was that many areas were already the territory of established clans. They might let the remnants of Swaying Fronds Clan pass through their lands, but they would not wish them to settle.

The two-legs were more common in the lowlands, as well. Even where they had not claimed land for themselves, they seemed to prefer the lowlands for their own hunting and foraging. From what had been learned of the two-legs from People who lived near them, the strange creatures had a marked preference for warmer areas. Although their various made things let them do remarkable things, without them they were astonishingly defenseless. Seemingly, some of them even had trouble walking about without the aid of their made things.

Therefore, Keen Eyes did not find it at all surprising that

the two-legs preferred the softer lowlands, but their activities in those regions made the already complicated problem of finding a new place for his clan almost impossible.

He breathed deeply and the bitter odor of ash and burned wood flooded his lungs. Even though the fires had been quenched since the warmer days of turning leaves, Keen Eyes still found himself inclined to cough. The smoke had done damage to his lungs, damage that might not ever heal, even with the passage of many turnings.

Others of his clan had been weakened by the smoke as well. Struggling to subsist on the tattered edges of their old range had made others thin and weak. Only the ripening of nuts that came at this time of year and the plentiful fish in the streams had let them survive thus far, but soon the nuts would be gone and the fish sealed up beneath the unrelenting ice.

Swaying Fronds must find a new home range, and soon, but where? Where could they go?

Never had the world in all its vast green reaches seemed so small.

Four days had passed since Stephanie had broken the news to Anders about her possible departure from Manticore. That night she'd talked to her parents. They'd agreed that, if she wanted, she could enroll in the Forestry Service training program. Apparently, they'd taken advantage of her being out to com Chief Ranger Shelton and were content with how the program would be managed. They'd even excused Stephanie from her regular studies here on Sphinx until after her return from Manticore.

"Even you deserve a vacation now and then," Mom had said, "and you'll need to be fresh to soak up everything expected of you in the training program. It's not only a lot of information, but a very diverse curriculum."

Now Stephanie and her best friend, Jessica Pheriss, sat on the bed in Stephanie's room. They weren't much alike. Jessica was curvy to Stephanie's still-boyish figure. Jessica had vibrant hazel-green eyes and wild masses of curly light auburn hair. She was taller than Stephanie—but then, just about everyone was—and knew a lot more about "girl stuff" than Stephanie had ever bothered to learn. But they were alike in one very important thing: both of them tended to speak out about what they thought was important, no matter the cost. That had drawn them together even before Jessica had been adopted by the treecat, Valiant. After that, their friendship was sealed.

Despite cooler autumn evenings, the casement window of Stephanie's room was cranked open, and Lionheart and Valiant sat up in the limbs of the closest crown oak, taking advantage of the convenient sunbeam. The two 'cats, superficially alike with their gray-striped tabby fur trimmed in cream, were apparently dozing, but for all Stephanie knew they might be as deep in conversation as two businessmen lounging in chairs before the fire in their favorite club.

Alike, Stephanie thought. *Well, they would be if it weren't for Lionheart's injuries. No one could miss all the ripples of his scars under his coat, or that he's missing his right true-hand.*

Jessica often came out to spend a few days with Stephanie, so that each of the treecats could have the companionship of another of his own kind. By nature, the 'cats were social. Stephanie had often worried that Lionheart had condemned himself to loneliness by choosing to stay with her. Valiant's availability had eased her guilt on that matter, but now she felt it rising all over again.

"Jess...How do I tell Lionheart I'm taking him not just on any old trip but off the entire planet?"

To her credit, Jessica didn't even suggest that Stephanie

not try, that Lionheart would go with her anyhow, so why get stressed? Nor did she say that maybe he wouldn't even realize what had happened. Why worry about it?

Stephanie knew Jessica understood the relationship she and Lionheart shared in a manner that even Stephanie's parents or Karl or Anders couldn't. Jessica's relationship with Valiant was a little different, forged in fire rather than in blood and battle, but no less intense for that. What made the difference were the personalities involved.

Like Stephanie, Lionheart was impulsive. After all, he'd been breaking into one of Marjorie Harrington's greenhouses when Stephanie first met him. Valiant, by contrast, was a steady soul. He was no less inquisitive in his own way, but his interests ran to what was for treecats—at least by every indication the humans had gathered to this point—the cutting-edge science of agriculture. If Climbs Quickly was the explorer and adventurer, Valiant was the innovator, eager to watch and learn from the humans, showing every sign of not merely copying but adapting what he had learned.

And Jessica is steady like Valiant. Maybe it's because her family's moved so much, or because she's had to pitch in with caring for all the littler kids, but she values stability and comfort in a way I don't. She's far from dull, or I couldn't like her so much. She's just different from me.

Typically, Jessica's answer to Stephanie's question hadn't come quickly.

"I think that, since you can't tell Lionheart, you're going to need to show him," she said finally. "Does he understand what he sees on a computer screen? I'm never sure how much Valiant gets or if what he sees just bores him so he doesn't pay any attention."

"I think Lionheart gets at least some," Stephanie said. "I've shown him images and he seems to grasp what he's seeing. It's hard to tell how much. I've wondered how much a purely visual or even visual/audio presentation would mean to a treecat. They rely on their sense of smell a lot more than we do, and on their sense of touch—not just in their fingers and whiskers, but in a whole-body way."

"I know." Jessica nodded. "And then there's the added element of their empathy and telepathy. Yeah. I can see what you mean. It may not be that Lionheart and Valiant don't 'get' the images. It's just that to them even a really good HD clip with full sound gives them about as much dimension as we'd get out of a flatscreen when the audio went dead."

"You mean show Lionheart images of shuttles taking off and like that... Wait!" Stephanie threw one hand into the air to hold back whatever Jessica might say in reply. "I've got it! We can make a movie of our own. It won't be great, but we can use the animation program on my computer. We'll feed in images of Lionheart and me from my files, then..."

Jessica got into Stephanie's idea at once. They settled side-by-side at Stephanie's desk and started pulling up files. Stephanie was the better programmer, but Jessica had more of an artistic flair. Her suggestions were invaluable for transforming what would otherwise have been a rather stiff presentation into something fluid and alive. The girls had to take a break for dinner, but afterwards they galloped up the stairs. Before they went to bed, they'd put together a short but detailed film showing Stephanie and Lionheart—each distinctly recognizable—entering a shuttle and what would happen afterwards.

"Of course," Stephanie said with satisfaction after they'd reviewed their work, "Lionheart's probably going to have to be in a carrier of some sort, not walking like we've shown him here. I'd want him in a carrier for his own safety, even if no one else did. I don't want him poked by the other passengers. For that matter, we know he doesn't get airsick, but he might find liftoff and all unsettling. Better that he have a secure place of his own."

"I agree," Jessica said, "but for the video, I think we're better off showing him moving around. Adding him getting put in a carrier and hauled around would distract from the real purpose—showing him going up in the shuttle and where that goes. Are we going to show him our vid now?"

"Let's wait," Stephanie said. "I'm beat and I bet you are, too. When we show it to him, I want to try something to go with the images. I was hoping you and Valiant could help, too."

"Sure. What?"

"Remember how I told you that when Bolgeo had that 'cat trapped, Morgana—Lionheart's sister—kept staring at me like she was trying to put ideas into my head?"

"Sure. You didn't understand, did you?"

"Not really, but I did understand that whatever it was she wanted was important, and I've often wondered how it might work the other way around. After all, I'm not a telepath, but clearly Lionheart can read me more than I can him. I'm going to try get across to him that this isn't just an image or something fun we made, but that it's *real*—a representation of what's going to happen."

Jessica nodded. "We know they could at least get a mental picture through to Scott MacDallan. From the way he described what happened, it took a bunch of treecats working together for them to communicate even with someone who has 'the sight.' Well, we're not telepaths, but maybe if both of us concentrate really hard on our specific 'cat then we can boost the signal strength enough that they'll be able to understand this isn't just pretty art."

"Right. After all, if they can talk to each other..."

"And we're both sure they can..."

"Then they can discuss what we're showing them. It might help them work through what we're telling them."

"I like it," Jessica agreed. "Anyway, it can't hurt to try, can it?"

"Guess who's coming to Manticore?" Oswald Morrow couldn't hide a certain sly, self-satisfied smile as he spoke. He was a big man with dark skin against which his teeth flashed in brilliant contrast.

"Who?" Gwendolyn Adair asked, not even looking up from examining her manicure.

"Stephanie Harrington. I have it on good authority that not only is she coming without any adult supervision, she's bringing the treecat with her."

That got Gwendolyn's full attention. She sat up straight, showing off a trim, youthful body.

"You're joking! That's too perfect."

Oswald Morrow gave her another flash of the dealmaker smile that was so very well known in certain exclusive Manticoran business circles. "I'm not joking. I'm perfectly sincere. Stephanie Harrington is coming here with the famous 'Lionheart.' I'm not one to brag—"

"Hah!" Gwendolyn's comment was little more than a breath.

"—but I might even say I had something to do with arranging their trip."

"How could you have done that?"

"You know I keep alert for any information at all having to do with the SFS."

"Through your brother-in-law, Harvey. Yes, I know."

"Well, I asked a few leading questions when Joan and I had dinner with Harvey and his family a while back. Harvey started ranting about how Shelton of the SFS had actually had the audacity to suggest two kids be enrolled in the Forestry Service training class. Harvey was pretty indignant. He had a hand in getting that program into its current shape, and he sickeningly proud of it for turning out tough, well-trained men and women who can deal with flood, fire, or panicked tourists with equal ease. He felt Shelton was degrading the program by assuming two kids could pass."

"And you asked who the kids were..."

"I did. And when he'd confirmed that they were indeed Stephanie Harrington and her sidekick, Karl Zivonik, I hinted that it might be a good idea to admit them. It would show he has an open mind towards those back-woods bumpkins. If—I might even have said 'when'—the kids failed his demanding program, well, the one who'd look bad would be Shelton, not Harvey."

"Brilliant!"

Morrow shrugged in mock humility. "I'm not saying I was the only one speaking out in favor of including them. In fact, the number of people who wanted the Harrington kid included was part of what had Harvey so riled. My comments might have tipped the balance, that's all."

"But Stephanie and Lionheart will be here!" Gwendolyn looked as pleased as a cat that had gotten the cream. She was an attractive enough woman, but her real gift was not beauty. It wasn't even her family connections, valuable as those had been on occasion. It was in acting. She was a chameleon, filtering effortlessly through other people's lives and being whoever she had to be for each of them. She'd worked profitably with Morrow before, shifting appearance and attitude with such skill she sometimes frightened him. "It's been so hard to influence the treecat question from off planet. The Bolgeo plan was a disaster because he had a few too many irons in the fire. If he'd stuck to doing what we paid him for instead of resorting to poaching—"

"That's water under the bridge," Morrow said dismissively. "Bolgeo didn't do us any favors, but now Shelton's ambition has handed us just what we need. With Ms.

Harrington and her 'cat here, we can engineer situations that show them in a less than ideal light. And with them off Sphinx, we can send in new agents without worrying about her interference."

"You're not afraid of a fifteen-year-old girl, are you?" Gwendolyn's laugh held an acid bite.

"I'm not *afraid* of anything," Morrow countered. "We simply can't ignore that Stephanie Harrington seems to view anything to do with the 'cats as her personal domain, or that the SFS plays up to her because it's good for their public image. No one else is the 'treecat discoverer,' though, so no one else can butt in quite so objectionably. We'll do very well out of both her presence here and her absence there."

Gwendolyn looked at her manicure again as if she were considering it in a new light. "Yes, we will indeed. I have some very interesting thoughts on how we might befriend the young lady."

"I'm sure you do, my dear," Morrow chuckled. "I'm sure you do."

Climbs Quickly watched as the images moved before him. If he had not lived with Death Fang's Bane for so long, observing her as she spent long hours in front of the thing—and if he had not watched Eye of Memory creating images of her own—he was not sure he would have grasped what his two-leg was trying to show him. Indeed, if she had not been so intense in her desire for him to look, to pay attention, to understand, he was not sure he would have grasped the importance of what he was seeing at all. As it was, he felt at least reasonably confident that he understood her meaning.

Mostly.

He thought, however, that some confirmation would

be a good idea, just in case he was jumping from limb to limb without testing his footing—something his elders were always telling him was one of his failings.

<Dirt Grubber,> he said, <I wonder. What to do you make of these images?>

The older Person—Dirt Grubber's long tail had two more full rings than did Climbs Quickly's own—rubbed at his nose with his true-hand, much as he did when he had finished digging and wanted to clean his whiskers.

<In those images, empty of thought as they are, I see a song—a song of future travel. I think we now know why Death Fang's Bane has been so unsettled since she met with Old Authority. She has decided to go in the big flying thing, up higher even than the tallest mountains, then to land on this other thing. I think perhaps it is an even bigger flying thing, but what these colored balls are I cannot quite guess. Are they islands?>

Climbs Quickly shook his head, a mannerism he had picked up from the two-legs.

<I do not think so. I admit, something like that was my first conclusion. Then I considered. We know that two-legs are from elsewhere. We have both listened to those old memory songs that tell of the egg-shaped things that roared down from above and returned to the skies. I know some People persist in believing that the two-legs come from somewhere else in the lands we know. I have heard the theories that the two-legs live on some isolated island where net-wood does not grow, and so the People have not ventured there. However, I think that unlikely.>

<I agree,> Dirt Grubber said. <The two-legs did not suddenly create the flying things we see them using now. There must have been steps in between, perhaps along the lines of the folding flying things that Death Fang's Bane and Windswept use as toys. But if they had such flying things and were anywhere near the lands that we know,

certainly, a bold two-leg or two would have come into the net-wood forests before Death Fang's Bane, and that meeting would be recorded by the memory singers. Therefore, they must have come from elsewhere.>

Climbs Quickly was pleased that his friend agreed. He had not looked forward to arguing with him. Dirt Grubber could be as stubborn as the deep-rooted weeds he was always pulling from his garden patches.

<I think,> Climbs Quickly continued, *<that Death Fang's Bane is going to journey back to where the two-legs came from before coming to the world. The first ball in her images is here. The second ball is where we are going. She is trying to make sure I understand because she does not want to make the journey without me.>*

<So she anticipates a long journey,> Dirt Grubber commented.

Climbs Quickly agreed. Bonded pairs could separate, sometimes for days on end, else how would a male feed his mate and kittens? However, a long separation was wearing on both. Many mated males tried not to be away from their nesting places overly long. Some, especially the older ones, chose to give up hunting entirely, focusing on contributing to the clan in other ways. Making stone tools took time and patience, and so did scraping straight shafts and tying nets. Or a mated pair might go foraging together, for although the People mostly ate meat or fish, they supplemented their diets with nuts and roots.

Since the coming of the two-legs, the People had begun to imitate them in the cultivation of plants. At first this had merely been the tending of plants that were already in place, bringing them water when the season was dry, clearing away competing plants that might choke them. In this way, the yield had increased. Now there were those such as Dirt Grubber who wanted the People to actually put useful plants where they would thrive, or bury seeds and protect the young shoots from opportunistic bark-chewers. Plant growing took a lot of attention. It was proving a very good way for bonded pairs to help provide food for the clan without taking the same degree of risk as when the male went hunting.

And avoiding that risk was important. Only rarely did one half of a bonded pair survive the death of the other. Minds that had been so intertwined that they intensified each other's glow did not often survive the loss of their match. Sometimes a female with kits would survive because they needed her, but often the clan would need to care for doubly orphaned younglings.

Climbs Quickly shook himself as if he could shake away the unhappy memories as easily as he could a bug climbing through his fur.

<I am glad that Death Fang's Bane wants me to go with her. I am not certain she understands the dangers when a bonded pair is separated. I think she knows she would be unhappy, but I do not know if she realizes that our separation could mean my death, especially if our mindglows were so far separated. Even if I must go beyond the tops of the mountains and to this other ball—this other world—I will go. It is our pact. It is our bond.>

Anders tried not to let Calida—or even Dacey—know how mixed up he felt about Stephanie's going off to Manticore. For the moment, he was glad Bradford Whitaker wasn't on Sphinx. Dr. Whitaker wasn't the most sensitive of humans, and Anders doubted he would really have understood his son's feelings—or even noticed them. Of course, there was something to be said for that. If Anders' *mother* had been there, he would have been forced to have a heart-to-heart or two whether he wanted to or not. There was a reason she was a politician—and a good one of the old type, the type who'd gone into politics not because she saw it as a route to fame and fortune, but because she saw it as a way to help people.

He'd had to message Mom, of course, but the nice thing about interstellar communication—well, nice in this case, although he doubted his father saw it the same way at the moment—was that there would be a considerable time lag. By the time he had to answer Mom's well-meaning and thoughtful questions, he thought he'd have his head together.

For now, though...

His heart twisted painfully whenever he saw Stephanie. He thought she didn't guess, but he was pretty sure Lionheart did. Oddly enough though, Anders also felt sure the treecat was keeping his secret. It made him realize the 'cat was his friend in a way he'd never felt before, so he guessed at least one good thing had come out of this impending heartbreak.

Geez, though, I'm an insensitive jerk, aren't I? All the time Stephanie and I have been 'canoodling,' as Dacey puts it, I hadn't given a lot of thought to how Steph would feel when I went back home. I knew how bad I felt when I got dragged off to Manticore and she got left behind, but at least we could still message each other and get a reply back the same day! I figured that felt pretty darn bad anyway, but now that the shoe's on the other foot, I know she felt even worse watching me go than I felt going, and I was so busy feeling sorry for myself I never realized it. Now that I'm the one being left, well, I can say it doesn't feel good. In fact, it feels worse than being the one doing the leaving. The leaver has something to do; the left just gets to build life around the hole where the other person should be. And what are we going to do when I have to leave and we both know I won't be coming back? There won't be any same-day messages then!

Stephanie was being really sweet, Anders had to admit that. Even though she must be up to her ear in plans—he knew there'd been a shopping expedition all the way to Yawata Crossing for stuff that couldn't be found in little Twin Forks—still she never chattered about how excited she was. Even better, the holiday Stephanie's parents had let her have from her studies meant they still had time to meet every day, even with preparations for departure.

Today they were linking up in Twin Forks where they planned to join the hang-gliding club meeting, then go out—just the two of them—afterwards. Anders had his own glider now—a cutting-edge model that had been an "I'm sorry I screwed up" gift from his dad before Dr. Whitaker's departure. It was really nice looking, in vibrant green and turquoise that the girls had all assured him went well with his own coloring. A few months hadn't been enough to get Anders up to speed with the rest of Stephanie's gang, but at least he no longer embarrassed himself.

Maybe because Stephanie's pending departure was making him think back to when everything was fresh and new, Anders found himself thinking how much people had changed in the last six months as he hurried over to join the others.

The changes were most obvious in Toby Mednick. Toby was just a few months younger than Stephanie, and when Anders had first met him, he'd been Stephanie's size or a little shorter. Certainly, the way the boy had carried himself—shy and meek—meant he might have been three meters tall and still have seemed small. Now nature had stepped in to give Toby more height. His shoulders were showing powerful muscle, although overall his build remained gazelle-graceful. The biggest change, though, was in his attitude.

Toby came from a very conservative family. The hang-gliding club was the only such organization he was allowed to join, and that was because it was run by Mayor Sapristos. But hang-gliding had proven to be just what Toby needed. He was well on the way to making good his vow at Stephanie's fifteenth birthday party to become the best flyer in the club. No longer did dark brown eyes peek up shyly through a curtain of silky black hair. They met other people's eyes directly, and the dark hair was tied back in a fashion that Anders thought—without undue modesty—was copied from how Anders wore his own.

The "Double Cs," Chet Pointier and Christine Schroeder, had changed differently. Chet had finally slowed the growth spurt that had—he admitted cheerfully—been the bane of his parents' clothes-buying budget. At seventeen, he was settling in at something over 188 centimeters in height, and these days his body seemed determined to fill in the frame it had stretched out. Chet's natural hair color was just slightly lighter than Anders' own wheaten gold, but he and his girlfriend Christine had recently indulged in matching dye jobs. Both now sported indigo blue hair, highlighted with violet. When they got set to go out, they also sported matching cat's-eye contact lenses in silver.

On Chet, the alterations looked a little affected—or so Anders thought—but from their very first meeting Anders had always thought that Christine had something of the exotic bird about her. She'd kept her cockatoo crest, and it looked as good in indigo and violet as it ever had in white-blond. If Christine's graceful, willowy figure had changed at all, it had been to smooth her curves into something more delightfully feminine. Silver contact lenses were hardly an improvement over her naturally ice-blue eyes, especially when contrasted with the warm sandalwood hue of her skin, but if she wanted to experiment, Anders wasn't going to complain.

Stephanie and Jessica arrived in Jessica's junker just as Anders was unfolding his glider. He turned to meet them, his heart lifting as always when he saw Stephanie smile at him.

How am I ever going to let her get on the shuttle without me? I've got to do it. I know I've got to do it, but I can't let her know just how very much letting her go is going to hurt.

4

WHEN KEEN EYES VENTURED INTO THE FOOTHILLS, HE found himself fighting the sensation that he had moved in time, rather than space. In the mountains, snow was falling at night. The icy whiteness was neither deep nor dense, and it melted within a short time after the sun's rising. But the coming of snow meant that many of the small ground grubbers and bark-chewers upon which the Swaying Fronds Clan had been relying to augment their food were harder to find.

Some of those creatures slept all through the winter. Others were simply spending more time in burrows beneath the earth. When true snowfall came, many of them would make tunnels in the snowpack itself, their foraging concealed from all but the sharpest-eared hunters. Knowing this time of relative safety was coming, they waited patiently for the same snow that Keen Eyes dreaded.

Here in the relative lowlands, even though the trees showed signs of damage from the fires that had raged so much more powerfully in the higher elevations, opportunities for hunting and foraging were more plentiful. Leaves were shading into yellow and red, but still bore traces of green. In some sheltered areas, trees were sending up shoots through the thick soil. More quick living plants were taking advantage of the damper weather and rich ash, and some of the grasses and shrubs were adorned with fat seeds. Although the People could not subsist wholly on a diet of leaves, seeds, and shoots, these would help to bulk up their bellies—and they attracted prey animals.

The difficulty did not come from the lowlands themselves. Rather it came from those People who had already claimed these lands as their own. Keen Eyes met up with the first of those one afternoon as he sat on a net-wood branch enjoying a small but plump bark-chewer he had caught.

<*We thought we smelled something sour.*> The mind-voice came without warning. <*How do you name yourself, poacher?*>

Keen Eyes sniffed the air, but these People must be approaching from upwind, because he could not catch their scent. True, a mind-voice could call over a far greater distance than anyone could detect with certainty the mind-glow of another Person, but these People had obviously sensed his mind-glow and realized that it did not belong to someone they knew.

Relaxing over his meal, Keen Eyes had taken the obvious precautions, but he had not been actively searching for other People. Now he attempted to do so. Distantly, he sensed at least two People. The fuzzy quality of the contact indicated that they were attempting to mute their mind-glows, but one of the pair was upset enough that his anger came through strongly. Even as Keen Eyes sought to get a clearer reading, this one moved deliberately to take his mind-glow out of range.

Keen Eyes shaped his reply carefully. <*I am not so much a poacher as a traveler. I was not aware I had crossed into another clan's range. May I ask to whom I am speaking?*>

<*I am Nimble Fingers of the Trees Enfolding Clan.*> The voice of the person with the less angry mind-glow shaped the answer. <*My uncle, Swimmer's Scourge, hunts with me. What are you called?*>

<*I am Keen Eyes of the Swaying Fronds Clan.*> Keen Eyes did not open his mind to them, but he did allow his sense of loss and sorrow to color his reply. <*Although you might say that those of us who survived the great fires of last season are now the Landless Clan, for our burned and tormented forests will not support us through the coming winter.*>

Nimble Fingers' mind-voice shaped the reply. <*So your clan is homeless? Are you scouting for new lands?*>

<*If so, scout elsewhere, Keen Eyes of the Landless Clan,*> Swimmer's Scourge's mind-voice cut in. <*Our own range was burned by the fires. Our hunting has been badly reduced. We need all of what our range produces to survive the coming snows.*>

Keen Eyes shared a mind picture of the lands surrounding his clan's ravaged range. He showed them the barren land, how even where trees still stood so many were nothing more than blackened spires, the remaining limbs charred skeletons that would not hold even a small bark-chewer, much less to a robust Person.

<*We would not intrude into your range if that could be avoided in any way,*> he said then. <*Would it be possible for us to pass through? Perhaps your scouts know of a range that is unoccupied, or that a smaller clan might be willing to share.*>

Swimmer's Scourge's response came so quickly that Keen Eyes had the impression he had deliberately stopped his nephew from answering. At the same time, his faint awareness of Nimble Fingers' mind-glow vanished, so that he suspected that the other had moved—or been moved—out of range.

<We know nothing of any place where you might go. Perhaps your memory singers could reach out to others of their kind and learn where there may be an open range.>

Keen Eyes could not have hidden his grief, not even if he had tried. <Wide Ears and our other memory singers fell victim to the flames. A tongue wrapped around and cut them off. We tried to save them, but they would not let us risk ourselves on such a thin chance. They had an apprentice, but Tiny Choir is still very young. She shows promise, but her voice is hardly stronger than that of an ordinary adult. She needs time.>

<And time,> Nimble Fingers replied, <is what you are seeking. Time as much as land.>

<Yes. Precisely that,> Keen Eyes replied, glad to be understood, but Swimmer's Scourge was unable—or unwilling—to join in his nephew's opinion.

<Stay out of our range,> came his stiff rejoinder. <Your clan may lack memory singers, but surely some of the elders have heard tales of what happens when range rights are challenged. Your clan is already reduced. Do not press a course that may lead it to become even smaller.>

With that, Keen Eyes could no longer sense the pair, even faintly. He sat perched in the net-wood tree for a long time, searching, but met only with silence.

The two weeks before Stephanie and Karl's departure rapidly dwindled to days. Time and again, Stephanie considered backing out, considered making some excuse for not going. At one point, she was even so desperate that she thought about injuring herself so she couldn't go. The problem with modern medicine, though, was that even "accidentally" forgetting to turn on her counter-grav unit so that she fell out of a tree wouldn't have helped much. Even badly broken bones could be patched up pretty quickly.

So began the days of saying goodbye. Stephanie thought that she and Jessica had managed to get across to Lionheart what was going to happen. Certainly, the 'cat cooperated admirably with drills designed to get him used to the standard interstellar pet carrier they'd bought for him. She'd even demonstrated the emergency life support, so the noise wouldn't bother him in the unlikely event she had to use it.

The first of the goodbye parties came when she and Lionheart visited Lionheart's extended family where they were settling into winter quarters in the mountains northeast of the Harrington freehold. They went out as they often did, using her hang-glider rather than an air car. As a present, Stephanie had brought with her several bunches of celery. Lionheart loved the stuff, and his family did, too.

However, Stephanie was certain that it wasn't just the celery that gave this visit the feeling of "event." For one thing, most of the clan was there. Even the hunters who were often away or asleep were present and active. For another, Morgana took the post of honor and gave a speech.

Stephanie knew she'd have trouble explaining why she was sure that was what Morgana was doing. Certainly she didn't hear anything. To someone who wasn't inclined to think of treecats as smart, it probably looked like a lot of 'cats drowsing in the sun. Still, she felt certain. Maybe it was the way the kittens, usually as ebullient and active as their feline equivalents, sat attentively prick-eared, green eyes focused on Morgana. If they were holding still, something important must be going on.

However, party or not, long before dark Lionheart marched over to where Stephanie had stowed her hang-glider, pointedly reminding his human that they had a long flight home. She took the hint. Now was not the time to start taking dumb risks.

The next party came the following day and was held at the Harrington freehold.

"Don't think we're just making a fuss over you and Karl," Marjorie Harrington teased. "Actually, this party is to celebrate Frank and Ainsley's promotion to Senior Ranger. You can't imagine how difficult it is to get both of them scheduled for the same day off. It's just a coincidence that we managed for a few days before you were due to leave."

Stephanie wasn't fooled, but she was glad to have some of the focus away from her and Karl going off to Manticore. Frank Lethbridge and Ainsley Jedrusinski had been among the first rangers she'd gotten to know well. Frank had been her handgun and rifle instructor and had introduced Karl to her, and Ainsley was his frequent partner. Celebrating their promotion to the newly created rank of Senior Ranger seemed a very good excuse for a party indeed.

Since both Frank and Ainsley were longtime friends of Karl's family, that provided a natural excuse for all the Zivoniks to be invited, again, without too much emphasis on the departure of the probationary rangers. With them came Scott MacDallan and his wife, Irina Kisaevna, also as longtime friends of the guests of honor. Scott was the only other living human—other than Jessica and Stephanie—who had been adopted by a treecat.

Given that all of Stephanie's friends had volunteered during the worst days of the forest fire, it made sense to include them, as well, and Anders came along with Dacey Emberly. So pretty much everyone who would have been at a going away party also ended up at this "promotion party."

As was natural at a gathering of such size, people eventually broke into smaller groups. Irina, Marjorie, and Dacey sat in a cozy huddle around the high-ceilinged great room's huge fireplace, discussing art while the antique ceiling fans' blades turned lazily overhead and Richard stood with an elbow propped on the mantle and listened, interjecting an occasional comment of his own. Karl and Toby were out on the wide snow porch, its sliding sides open to the pleasant autumn breeze, organizing foot races for the younger Zivoniks. Jessica and Scott were in deep conversation, probably about living with treecats, as they tidied up the stone-flagged kitchen where hectares of the buffet dinner's bowls and serving platters had been stacked to one side. The guests of honor had gathered around the pool table in the family room, just off the great room, cues in hand while they chatted with Christine and Chet about a new guide program the SFS was introducing to deal with the growing influx of tourists.

Coincidentally or not, Anders and Stephanie found themselves alone near the great room's wide front windows, looking out at the mountainous trunks of the crown oaks. Even Lionheart had absented himself to visit with Valiant and Fisher.

"Want to go for a walk?" Stephanie asked.

"Sure."

When they were out of direct sight of the party, Anders wrapped his hand tightly around Stephanie's.

"It's weird to think that in a few days we're not going to be able to do this again," he said after a long pause. He leaned and kissed her. "Or this. Or even talk to each other in real time." He grimaced. "Messages and vids just aren't the same, whatever anyone says."

"I know." Stephanie's response came out a bit more emphatically than she'd intended as she recalled the months *Anders* had spent on Manticore. "Still," she went on after a moment, "I think maybe it's better for the transmission lag to be as great as it is. I mean, there's no way anyone could possibly hold a conversation with a fifty-minute hole between every question and answer, and we both know it. But it was only, say, *ten* minutes each way, we might just try it, and think how miserable *that* would be!"

"Yeah, recorded messages are a lot smoother than that," Anders agreed.

"And the delays would just make the separation more real."

"So you'll message?"

"I promise. I won't let homework and all the rest get in the way."

"Me either."

More silence, though there was quite a bit of nonverbal communication to fill the space.

Eventually, Anders sighed and pulled back, though not before he'd carefully nested Stephanie's head against his shoulder.

"Who was it who said that bit about parting being sweet sorrow?"

"Shakespeare."

"I think he was cracked. I thought it the first time we went through this, and I'm sure of it now. Parting isn't sweet at all. It's just sad."

Stephanie offered an explanation. "It's sweet sorrow because you have someone to feel sad about. If you didn't have anyone, then, well, it wouldn't be sad, but it wouldn't be sweet either. It would just be going different ways."

"So this is sweet sorrow?" Anders asked, although the expression in his blue eyes when Stephanie moved to look up into his face left no doubt.

"It is," she said. "Very sweet and very, very sad."

✧   ✧   ✧

Two days later, she was at the shuttleport. Her baggage had gone ahead, and she was hugging everyone who'd come to see them off—her folks, Jessica, Anders, Karl's family—some of them more than once. Karl was doing the same. He even hugged Anders, who laughed and hugged him back.

"Take care of our girl, Karl," Anders said. "Don't let her intimidate all those Manticorans."

"Promise," Karl said. "And you be careful here. Remember, we won't be around to rescue you."

"I'll remember."

A recorded voice announced final boarding, and Anders gave Stephanie one more huge, bone-cracking hug.

"I guess we've got to go," she said. "I'll message. I'll message everyone!"

"C'mon, Steph." Karl's tone was gruff. "We'll be back before they get used to having us gone."

"Right." She grabbed Lionheart's carrier, then darted back one more time to hug each of her parents. "See you when you come to Manticore for your holiday!"

Then she turned and almost ran to the shuttle.

Anders was glad he'd brought his own air car to the shuttleport. He didn't really feel like being with anyone right now. He saw Jessica and Valiant go off with the Harringtons. Jessica looked as if she was crying. The treecat was reaching up over her shoulder to gently pat her cheek.

It's going to feel weird for all of them, being without Stephanie. And it's going to be weird for me to be here with all of her friends while she's off on another planet. It's all backwards and upside down from the way it was last time. And Steph and I have been so focused on what this means to us, I haven't really thought about how it's going to change things for everyone else.

He was still replaying the image of the shuttle's port sealing behind Stephanie, of the final pale flash that might have been the wave of her hand, when he got back to the apartment building where Calida had rented their quarters.

Kesia Guyen tried to wave him down as he passed through the lobby, but he pretended not to see her. Normally, Kesia would be just the person to talk to about his bruised feelings, but right now he still wanted to be alone.

To his surprise—Kesia was normally good at picking up on nonverbal cues—she came trotting after him and caught up just before he reached the lifts.

"Hang on a minute!" she called, and Anders was forced to stop and turn around to face her. She took one look at his expression, then smiled gently and reached up to pat him on the shoulder. That smile was so sympathetic Anders felt his own expression waver uncertainly for a moment. Funny. He'd thought he was doing a better job of hiding his feelings than that.

"I know you probably have other things on your mind right now," Kesia said, "but I thought you'd like to know about this. We got a com message from Manticore about four minutes ago, probably about the time you were parking the air car."

"What kind of com message?" Anders asked, trying to figure out exactly how to describe her tone. She sounded both excited—almost jubilant—and irritated in equal measure.

"Your dad's back," she told him. "The university sent him back out in a fast charter."

"*Dad's* back?" He stared at her in shock, and she nodded.

"Just hit Manticore orbit a bit over two hours ago," she confirmed.

Anders shook his head as if to clear it while he tried to process the completely unexpected news. Then it hit him. If Dr. Whitaker had been sent out here to collect the rest of the expedition's personnel—if the university had chartered the courier boat in order to hustle everyone else home in disgrace as quickly as possible—then he might have just seen Stephanie for the very last time! He felt as if someone had punched a big icy hole through the spot where his stomach used to be.

"Hey!" Kesia reached up, grabbed him by both shoulders, and gave him a shake. "Lighten, Anders! Lighten! It's good...mostly."

"What do you mean 'mostly'?" Anders demanded.

"Well, the good news is that the university's excited enough about what we've already turned up that, despite any...minor irregularities, they've authorized your dad to seek a contract extension from the Star Kingdom. It's open-ended as far as the university's concerned!" Her eyes twinkled at the sudden leap of hope in Anders'. "And, the chancellor and the head of department—and your mom, on behalf of of the government—have all promised everything Governor Donaldson and Minister Vásquez asked for. So I think we've got a pretty good chance of getting the extension. Maybe in a single time block, maybe with a break over the winter while we return to Urako with our data."

Anders nodded. All of that *was* good news...except, maybe, for that bit about going home "over the winter," since Sphinx's winter was over sixteen T-months long. But Kesia had said...

"So what's the news that *isn't* good?" he asked. *And for that matter,* he thought, *if Dad's been back more than two hours, why didn't he com us quicker than this? It's only a twenty-five-minute transmission delay, after all!*

"It may be good, and it may be bad." Kesia shrugged. "He says that when he logged into the system data net and commed Dr. Hobbard to tell her he was back, she told him there's been a change of plans. She says some bigwig on

Manticore—Morgo, Morrow, something like that; your dad wasn't sure of the name—is sponsoring what he called 'some tourists with an interest in xenoanthropology.'"

"Uh-oh."

"Exactly." Kesia actually chuckled. "Actually, once he calmed down a bit, he admitted they seem to be a little better than that. In fact, some of them have pretty good credentials. But your dad's really ticked. He thinks it's a violation of our contract's exclusivity."

"Well, it is," Anders pointed out. "On the other hand, we're probably luckier than we deserve to still *have* a contract. If we do, that is."

"I think that was pretty much your dad's conclusion, too," Kesia said with a grin. "Apparently this Morrow or whoever he is is associated with something called the Adair Foundation. It's some kind of nonprofit involved in preserving biodiversity that's interested in treecats, and apparently it's thinking about endowing a real xeno-anthropology chair at Landing University. So the dean of Dr. Hobbard's college asked her—told her, really—to make the foundation's team welcome."

"Of course." Anders sighed and shook his head, feeling sympathy for both his father and Dr. Hobbard.

Sonura Hobbard was the current chair of the Anthropology Department at Landing University. She was also the head of the Crown Commission on Treecats and so, in a sense, his dad's boss here in the Star Kingdom. However, the Whitaker expedition had been allowed to work on Sphinx in direct reaction to the Bolgeo disaster. The Crown wanted to be certain the people studying the 'cats were real—and reputable—scientists, and they'd been granted a considerable amount of latitude in their operations in light of their academic credentials. *And* their contract had specifically protected the all important academic rights of first publication.

But that had been before Dr. Whitaker had taken his entire team off and marooned it in the bush without mentioning his plans to anyone. It was inevitable that there'd be tighter oversight in the wake of that near disaster—his dad had to know that even better than Anders did—and if there was one thing his father understood—outside of xenoanthropology, of course—it was academic politics and funding. And that meant that he knew he had no more choice about accepting these newcomers than Dr. Hobbard had about taking her dean's "request" to heart.

"Is Dad sure these people are legit?" he asked.

"He says they look that way so far." Kesia shrugged. "Apparently, this has been brewing for a while and Dr. Hobbard says the background checks have been in motion for a couple of T-months now."

"When will they get here?"

"Probably not for at least another T-month. From your dad's message, they're already on their way, but they're coming from several different out-System universities."

"So this Adair Foundation gets an inside look at the treecats and Landing University gets the money for a chair." Anders snorted. "Sounds as if everyone except Dad and you guys get something out of this!"

"Your father's feelings exactly."

"Hey!" Anders perked up, interest briefly pushing back his depression over Stephanie's departure. "If Dad plays this right, you could get some prepublicity for your work out of this when these visiting scientists head home again. The sort of thing that will have people panting to read your 'full and complete' *definitive* reports when they come out!"

"You really are your parents' son, aren't you?" Kesia said with a laugh. "I foresee a bright future in politics for you if you can only stay out of the swamps of academia! I think that's a suggestion you should make to him as soon as he gets off the shuttle. Maybe even sooner if you want to message him!"

"Oh, I can wait till I see him in person," Anders replied, the reference to messaging reminding him that he wouldn't be seeing Stephanie again in person for another whole three months. The gloom came rushing back, but it was a lot less deep this time.

No, I won't see her for another three months. But if Kesia's right, we'll have at least six months together after she gets back. And if Dad really is able to extend his contract into an open-ended study . . .

It was amazing how much brighter the universe had just become.

The taxi slowed, banking to the left across Jason Bay and circling toward the landing pad, and Stephanie rested one elbow on Lionheart's carrier as she peered out the window beside her.

Her regret at leaving Anders behind on Sphinx was never far from the surface, but she had to admit that the trip had had its amusing moments. She'd completely forgotten that Karl had never been off the surface of Sphinx in his life—never been aboard even a little puddle-jumper ship like HMS *Zephyr*, their transport to the planet Manticore, far less on a visit to the "big city" of Landing. Big, tough, strong, competent Karl had been completely out of his depth aboard ship, and Stephanie had found herself in the role of senior partner for the voyage.

Nor had Karl been able to conceal his near awe at the sheer size of Landing and its gleaming pastel-tinted ceramacrete towers. After so long on Sphinx, Stephanie had been a little taken aback herself, but that hadn't lasted long. For all its impressive ground plan, there was still plenty of room for Landing to grow, and none of the towers were much over a hundred meters tall yet. In fact, the total population of the Star Kingdom's capital city was less than a quarter of the population of Hollister, back on Meyerdahl where she'd grown up.

Was kind of interesting to see where "Mount Royal Palace" is going to go, though, she reflected. The taxi pilot had deliberately detoured over the construction site to give the off-world kids a look. *It'll have a really nice view of the Bay, anyway. Going to be big, too, but I'd think they'd want a tower all their own, and from the architect's drawings posted all over the city landing pad's smart screens, they won't be over four or five stories anywhere.*

Now, as the taxi settled the last few dozen meters, she looked around Landing University of Manticore's campus and decided she liked what she saw. They could have put the entire university into a single tower easily, since the total student body was no more than thirty thousand, but they'd chosen to scatter it around the ample four hundred-hectare site.

They'd fitted it elegantly into the landscape, doing as little damage as possible to the local ecostructure, too, and her eyes brightened as she saw species of Manticoran trees for the first time. Somehow, even though she'd known better (especially after boning up for this trip), she'd half expected Manticore's flora to be similar to Sphinx's, yet they looked nothing at all alike. Most of the trees she could see had a distinctively blue cast to their foliage, and everywhere she looked she saw brilliant blossoms nodding under the late morning sun. Landing was almost on Manticore's equator, and the Star Kingdom's capital world was almost ten light-minutes closer to the Sun than Sphinx, which gave it a substantially higher average temperature to begin with.

"It's going to be a lot hotter out there than we're used to," she said, turning her head to look at Karl, and then glancing down at Lionheart's carrier. "A *lot*."

"I did read the handout, too, Steph." Karl sounded just a little snappish, she thought. Maybe he was feeling more nervous about visiting the "big city" than he wanted to appear? "I slathered on plenty of sunscreen, too," he added a bit pointedly.

"And a good thing you did," she agreed equably, then leaned closer to the carrier, looking into the open side at Lionheart. "Too bad we can't use sunscreen on *you*," she told him.

Climbs Quickly's ears pricked and his nose twitched as Death Fang's Bane made her mouth noises at him. He didn't much care for the scents inside this flying thing—there were too many of them, as if hands of hands of two-legs had come and gone—but new, different ones were coming to him now. He could smell them only faintly so far, since the flying things were stingy about letting smells in and out, but they were much more interesting. Indeed, they were *very* interesting, for they were obviously the smell of plants, yet he'd never smelled anything quite like them before, and he felt a burning need to be out and about to explore them.

But that is going to have to wait, he reminded himself. *You are in a new place, Climbs Quickly! Best you not rush off like a new-weaned kitten so sure of all you* think *you know that you come nose-to-nose with a death fang!*

He laughed silently at the thought, though he knew there was truth as well as humor to it. And even as he laughed, he wondered how much of his eagerness to explore was a way to distract himself from anxiety. He had no idea how far he and his two-leg had come from their home, but he was beginning to suspect it was even farther than he had believed it could be before they departed. The trip aboard the big flying thing from the two-legs' nesting place hadn't seemed to take that long, but when his person had lifted the carrying thing and let him look out the window, he had quickly realized they were traveling far faster than they had ever traveled before. They had been far *higher*, as well, and they'd gone on getting higher until the very sky had turned from blue to black! Yet even that had been only the beginning of their trip, for they had transferred to the biggest flying thing he had ever seen through a vast, hollow tube, and it seemed reasonable to conclude that it was probably even faster than the one which had delivered them to it. After all, it had even farther to go and there was clearly no limit to the sorts of speeds at which two-legs could travel when the mood took them! And the hollow tube had had windows, too—windows that let him look down upon the world . . . and know he had been right about the reason Death Fang's Bane and Windswept had used round blue shapes of their images for this journey. They had not been islands, whatever others of the People might have believed.

Yet Climbs Quickly had found himself almost more daunted than pleased at being proved right. The blue shapes *were* entirely separate worlds . . . and that meant he was far, *far* away from Bright Water's nesting place. That was a sobering thought for even the hardiest scout, for it meant he was the only Person in an entire world, and he was surprised how small that made him feel.

Still, he could not feel *lonely*, even if there were no other People to whom he might speak, for he was with Death Fang's Bane, and he looked back up at her, holding tight to the flare of her mind-glow and treasuring its welcome.

✧   ✧   ✧

"Bleek!"

There was something especially warm, especially loving, about Lionheart's sound, and Stephanie blinked quickly. Somehow, she knew he was trying to reassure her that he was fine . . . and probably to take reassurance *from* her, as well.

"It'll be fine," she told him just a bit gruffly, reaching into the carrier's side to stroke his ears with her forefinger while Karl popped the hatch. "It'll be fine."

"I THINK YOU'VE GROWN," BRADFORD WHITAKER SAID, standing just inside the apartment door.

He was a big man, and he'd put back on at least a little of the weight he'd lost on Sphinx. He'd always struck Anders as being tall, and Anders supposed he was, yet he didn't seem quite as tall as he had, and Anders realized with something of a shock that he truly had grown in the six and a half T-months his father had been away. Not all that much, perhaps, but enough. Only it wasn't just physical height, he thought. It was that he was older ... and not just by six and a half months.

Anders had already recognized that their near-disastrous excursion into the Sphinxian bush had changed his relationship with his father, but he hadn't really thought about just *how* it might have changed. Dr. Whitaker had not showed to advantage dealing with the consequences of their destroyed air van, Dr. Nez's near death, the forest fire, and the swamp siren which would have killed them all without

83

the treecats' intervention. He'd retreated into a sort of obsessive behavior in which his decisions had been . . . suspect, to say the very least, and it was his subordinates—and his son—who'd managed somehow to keep all of them alive until rescue came.

There hadn't been much time to talk about what had happened before Dr. Whitaker had been jammed aboard the courier boat and sent home to Urako. Frankly, Anders doubted his father had been in any great hurry to talk about it, anyway. He'd probably seen the tiny starship's cramped isolation as an escape from the way he'd humiliated himself. But Anders knew now that he'd never be able to forget that he'd been right and his father had been wrong. That he, Anders, truly had stepped up and contributed to the expedition's survival while Dr. Whitaker occupied himself excavating treecat waste dumps and cataloging potsherds.

And yet, as he looked at his father—at the receding brown hair, the complexion which had regained its library pallor since his departure from Sphinx—he realized something else, as well.

He wasn't angry anymore. He'd been so *mad* at his father—and, he finally admitted, ashamed of him. Embarrassed *by* him. His father had failed him, and he'd failed in his academic responsibilities . . . and in his responsibility for the lives of his team. Kesia had told him even while it was happening that Dr. Whitaker had been suffering from "displacement." That he'd been so overwhelmed by his own awareness of his ruinous decisions and their consequences that he'd withdrawn into that obsessive concentration on something he understood, something he could convince himself he was actually capable of dealing with. But Anders was his son, and Anders had been failed not simply by the leader of their expedition, but by his *father*. And that had been the true source of his anger—that sense of *betrayal*.

But somehow, during Dr. Whitaker's absence, he'd gotten past it. Not completely, of course. Their relationship would never be the same again, but perhaps it didn't have to be ruined after all.

"Maybe I have grown...a little," he conceded after a moment.

"I think you have. But, you know, I think most parents really have a memory of their kids as children, no matter how old they get," Dr. Whitaker said. "Silly, I know, but here you are, almost seventeen standard, and somehow the mental picture of you I carry around is maybe twelve." He smiled. It was an odd, almost tentative smile, and he shook his head.

"I brought you a *stack* of messages from your mom," he went on in a lighter tone. "I won't say she's delighted by the prospect of having you here in the Star Kingdom for at least another eight to ten months, but I told her it was being good for you. In fact, I told her something that she told me it was time I told you, too."

His voice had turned serious once more and Anders cocked his head, wondering why.

"Told me what, Dad?" he asked.

"How proud of you I am," Dr. Whitaker said softly.

Anders blinked. He couldn't help it, and he felt himself staring at his father. He couldn't help that, either, and to his astonishment, his father met his eyes levelly, his expression as serious as Anders had ever seen it.

"I screwed up, son," he said. "I made mistakes, I almost got people—including you—killed, and it was all my own stupid fault. And after I'd made the mistakes, I didn't know how to fix them, so I didn't even try. I let you and Kesia and Calida and Virgil and Dacey deal with them, because...because I didn't know how to."

Anders couldn't have been more surprised if a hexapuma had walked in the door and begun singing "Auld

Lang Syne." He couldn't remember the last time he'd heard that steady, serious tone from his father. It was obvious Dr. Whitaker didn't like saying that—admitting that—but he went on unflinchingly.

"I had a lot of time to think about it on the courier boat, and before I went to talk to the chancellor and the department chair and the faculty senate. And before I had to face your mom, too." His voice changed slightly on the last sentence and he rolled his eyes. "If I'd been tempted to lie to anyone else about it, I knew I'd never be able to fool *her*. So I didn't try, and she was just as mad at me as I expected her to be. Especially when she looked at the vids Calida made. She was ready to take my head off for putting you in a position like that, but— somewhat to my surprise, actually—she was mad at me for putting *myself* into it, too.

"But that was when I told her how you'd stepped in to take up the slack. I had to go over my notes, and Calida and Virgil's, to prepare my report for the chancellor. That didn't leave me a lot of room to fool myself, Anders. It's all there in the record and the vids, even if I wasn't paying enough attention at the time. So I guess what I'm trying to say is that I'm sorry. I'm sorry for the mistakes I made, sorry for the responsibilities I dumped on your shoulders, and sorry for not being the person—the father—you needed me to be. But one thing I'm not at all sorry for." Dr. Whitaker's eyes met his son's unflinchingly. "I'm not sorry that you showed me that whatever other mistakes I've made along the way, and however much your mom deserves the lion's share of the credit, between us, we raised a boy who's turned into a fine young man. One I'm prouder of than I'll probably ever be able to tell you."

Anders swallowed hard, feeling his eyes burn. For some reason, his father's words—the kind of words he'd wanted to hear from him for so long—made him want to break down and bawl.

He wanted to tell his dad that it was all right. That it didn't matter, since everyone was safe in the end after all. That it was okay. But it wasn't all right. His father's apology couldn't change the past. What had happened, had happened. It couldn't be undone anymore than a chicken could return to the egg. And even now, he knew his father was still his father. That he was going to be himself again— focused, driven, ambitious—once he got back to work. But maybe if they couldn't change the past, they could at least change the future. Maybe his dad really had learned something, been humbled by his experiences. He certainly *sounded* as if he had, and he must have been able to convince the university—and Anders' mom!—that he had, or he wouldn't be back here to stay. But there were limits to just how much someone could change, weren't there?

And would I even want *him to really turn into someone else completely? I mean, he is my dad, and despite everything, I really do love him.* Anders shook his head mentally. *Sure, he's going to backslide. But not as far—not when he knows how much is on the line if he screws up again and that everyone in the Star Kingdom's going to be keeping an eye on him! And if he does start screwing up again, this time I'll have a little something to say to him about it, too.*

He looked at his father for another moment or two, then gave him a smile that was only a little lopsided.

"Hey, anybody can screw up," he said. "Even me, I guess. Maybe not quite *that* spectacularly, but I'll probably find a way to do something just about as dumb sooner or later. Heck, I'm *your* son, aren't I?"

Dr. Whitaker's serious, almost somber expression, transformed into a smile and he shook his head.

"Yeah, but you're your *mother's* son, too. Her genetic

contribution will probably come to the surface if you start to do something that 'dumb.' I sure hope it will, anyway!"

"Me, too," Anders told him, and then he was wrapping his arms around his father. "Me, too. But it's *good* to see you again, Dad. It really is."

Anders never knew exactly what his father had to say to the other members of the team. But he spoke to each of them individually, and whatever it was he had to say, it seemed to have worked. There was definitely a different atmosphere, and he thought it was going to be a much better one. Dr. Whitaker was still the senior member of the expedition, still in charge, still had the final decision, but none of the others—and especially not Calida Emberly and Kesia Guyen—were going to accept his orders without question if they disagreed. Not anymore. And that, Anders thought, was probably exactly what his father had needed for years. He'd become too accustomed to the unchallenged authority of his exalted academic position and reputation, but now he'd been brought face-to-face with an awareness of just how bad a mistake he could make . . . and so had the rest of his team.

The surprising thing was that their new relationships actually seemed to make everybody, including his dad, more comfortable, not less.

"—so Chancellor Warwick made the university's position very clear," Dr. Whitaker was saying now, looking at the people seated around the dining table in his and Anders' apartment for his first working meeting with the entire team. "Calida," he turned to Dr. Emberly, "you are now officially the team's executive officer. The chancellor didn't go quite as far as saying you have veto authority, but he didn't leave me with much doubt about whether or not I'm supposed to pay attention to your recommendations."

He smiled as he said it, and Anders wondered if the rest of the team was as surprised by his father's attitude as he'd been.

"The chancellor also made it very clear that if any of you choose to return to Kenichi instead of continuing with this expedition, you're free to do so and there will be no academic or professional consequences. I told him I was confident all of you would prefer to stay and continue our study of the treecats, but if you'd prefer not to, I'll understand your decision."

He paused, as if waiting for someone to jump up and leave immediately, but no one stirred.

"The chancellor also made it clear that any member of the university faculty will be liable for some pretty severe penalties, tenure or no tenure, if there's another incident anything like the last one," he continued, and grimaced. "I expect most of those penalties would probably come down on me, but from what he had to say, I'm confident there'd be enough of them to go around for anyone else responsible for it."

This time it was the others who smiled—Kesia actually chuckled—and Dr. Whitaker shook his head.

"I've delivered Chancellor Warwick's messages to Dr. Hobbard, and I spoke personally to Minister Vásquez before leaving Manticore for Sphinx. I have a meeting scheduled with Governor Donaldson this evening, as well. And then, of course, I'm going to have to sit down and discuss all of this with Chief Ranger Shelton." He shook his head again. "I'm not really looking forward to that conversation. Do you think you could get Ms. Harrington and Lionheart to come along and protect me, Anders?"

"I'm afraid not," Anders said. His father looked at him, and he shrugged. "Stephanie's on Manticore for the next three months. She's attending a forestry training program there for the SFS."

He'd thought his voice had come out perfectly naturally. From the flicker in Dr. Whitaker's eyes, he'd been wrong.

"I'm sorry to hear that," his father said after a moment, looking directly at him.

"It was a surprise for all of us," Calida said. "Frankly, I'm not sure it's a wonderful idea to take Lionheart into such a radically different environment, but none of the people involved in the decision asked my opinion. And even if they had, I don't know if Stephanie had any alternative but to take him with her."

"I don't think she did," Calida's mother put in. "At least, neither she nor Lionheart *thought* she did! And it's not as if we've been left without any ambassador to treecats. There's always young Jessica, you know."

"Jessica?" Dr. Whitaker repeated a bit blankly.

"Jessica Pheriss, Dad," Anders said. "Stephanie's best friend. She got hurt fighting the fire and wound up paired with a treecat of her own, remember?"

"Tall girl—red hair?" Dr. Whitaker said after a moment.

"More auburn than red, but that's her."

For some reason, Anders was a little nettled by the vagueness of his father's memory.

Well, of course I am, he thought as he recognized the reason. *Jessica was a big part of saving our butts, and Dad was so far gone I don't think he even noticed she was there!*

"I *do* remember her," Dr. Whitaker said. "She was with Ms. Harrington and young Zivonik and the others in the forest fire, wasn't she?"

"Yes, she was," Anders confirmed, pleased to discover that his father *had* noticed his rescuers.

"Well, if she's half as knowledgeable about treecats as Ms. Harrington was—and if she's willing to work with us—I'm sure she could be a very valuable asset," Dr. Whitaker went on. "And, in addition, Minister Vásquez made it abundantly clear that she wants at least one SFS ranger assigned as a full-time member of our team. I'd really like to object, but, unfortunately, I'm not in much of a position to do that. And there *is* a good side to it." Dr. Whitaker rubbed his hands together cheerfully. "If he's assigned as a full-time team member, we should be able to get a decent priority from the rangers when we need to go into the bush!"

Now *that*, Anders thought, sounded like the Dr. Whitaker *he* knew. He was a little surprised by how much the thought amused him.

"What about these other xenoanthropologists, Bradford?" Langston Nez asked. "How are they going to fit into the picture?"

"That's difficult to say at the moment." Dr. Whitaker scowled. "What Dr. Hobbard was able to show me about their credentials looked...reasonably good." He flipped one hand back and forth in a waving away gesture. "I wouldn't say any of them are absolutely top-drawer, but they all seem competent enough. And unlike that cretin Bolgeo, they're all from reputable institutions. *Really* from them, I mean. They were pre-vetted by the Adair Institute before they were ever proposed, and Dr. Hobbard and Minister Vásquez have double and triple-checked the documentation this time! Unfortunately, I'm still not very clear on exactly what it is they hope to accomplish."

"I did a little research on the data net after we got your message, Doctor," Calida Emberly said. "The Adair Institute has an excellent reputation. It was established in the first decade or so of the colony here and it's been dedicated to researching the biospheres of all three habitable planets ever since. According to its site, its primary emphasis up to this point has been on Manticore, rather than Sphinx or Gryphon, which makes a sort of sense. There are a lot more people on Manticore, and their footprint's already a lot bigger there. I think we can safely say that the institute's priorities shifted just a bit when the possibility that Sphinx has a native sentient species hit the boards, though."

"Yes, well whether or not the treecats are truly sentient— demonstrably and provably, I mean—remains to be seen," Dr. Whitaker said. "I hope these people are going to keep an open mind about that instead of slanting their findings to suit their sponsors! But from what you're saying, at least they're unlikely to want to rush in and contaminate our contacts with the treecats or start anthropomorphizing them with all sorts of untrained preconceptions. Unlike some other people."

Anders started to protest the obvious shot at the Forestry Service's handling of the human-treecat situation—and probably Stephanie, too—but stepped on the temptation. Whatever else might have changed, Dr. Whitaker was still a xenoanthropologist. He would have been far happier if the Star Kingdom's authorities had declared the entire planet a nature preserve and decreed that no one—no one at all . . . except, of course, for him and his team—could have any contact whatsoever with the treecats until he'd completed his study of them. Which probably wouldn't take longer than, oh, twenty or thirty T-years.

If he rushed himself, that was.

"Well, we'll just have to see how all of that works out," Dr. Whitaker continued. "Dr. Hobbard tells me that we probably have a T-month or so before they begin arriv-ing, and I'd really like to have our new relationship with the SFS worked out before we have to start integrating them into our team's schedule. So, bearing that in mind, Calida, what I'd like to do tonight is—"

ANDERS FOUND HIMSELF CHECKING HIS MAIL SEVERAL times a day, especially first thing in the morning while he ate his breakfast. He didn't go out of his way to bring that to the attention of any of the Whitaker expedition's other members, although he was certain they'd noticed anyway.

Stephanie's first few messages included copious quantities of video about the trip itself and the campus. The accompanying commentary was obviously genuinely enthusiastic... and equally obviously an effort to pretend she didn't miss Anders as much as she did. He found that rather sweet and touching, and he supposed he really had to admit that his messaged replies were intended to disguise exactly the same loneliness.

The vids got somewhat shorter as she started settling in, dealing with things like registration, dorm rooms, finding her way around campus, and all the other preliminaries for her course of study. Still, he was a little surprised when he received a message less than a week after her departure that was not only very short but text-only.

"I bet you thought I forgot your birthday," it read. "I didn't! Happy Seventeenth, Anders Whitaker! The attached file will show you where I hid your present. Hugs and kisses, Stephanie."

Anders blinked. Stephanie hadn't forgotten his birth-date...but *he* had. He supposed it was the fact that he was living on another planet, under a different calendar, which had mixed him up. At home on Urako, his birthday usually came sometime in summer; here on Sphinx it was autumn. He checked to make sure the date was right and noticed a flurry of messages in his queue from friends and family off-planet. They'd probably sent them—quite possibly with Dr. Whitaker on his return from Urako—to be delivered specifically on this date.

He read a bunch of them, saving Stephanie's attachment for last. It was very short, even shorter than the message to which it had been attached:

It starts your name.
It's cherry bright.
It gives a zing,
So you can stay up at night.

Anders stared at the four lines in confusion.

His name started with the letter "A," but the rest seemed like complete nonsense. How could this tell him where Stephanie had left his present?

"Anders?" Dad's voice came through the door. "Are you coming with us to the site today?"

"You bet!"

The entire team was upbeat and eager now that they'd been allowed back into the field. Anders was just as happy about that as any of the others, and he was ready to go except for his boots and jacket. He shoved his feet into the one and his arms into the other. Dad was never patient about being delayed but, to Anders' surprise, Dr. Whitaker hadn't even put on his jacket or picked up his pack. Instead, with a sheepish smile, he extended a large package to Anders.

"From your mother and me. We picked it out before the expedition ever left Urako. I've been hiding it for months!"

Anders ripped off the wrapping paper. Inside was a new uni-link, one of the fancy high processor models he'd coveted. Surrounding it were about six packages of socks in different colors—the need to have plenty of socks having become a running joke between Anders and his mom.

"Dad, this is super-hexy! Thanks so much. It's the exact model I wanted."

Dr. Whitaker looked very pleased. "And you can be certain that *this* model is calibrated to access the com net here on Sphinx."

Anders grinned. Screwed up communications equipment had been the cause of a lot of last year's trouble. He strapped on his new uni-link while his dad got into his jacket. Daytimes were still pretty nice, especially if the site was sunny, but the rest of the time a jacket was an absolute necessity.

Father and son hurried down the steps together. It rapidly became apparent that the rest of the crew also knew it was Anders' birthday. Once they were all in the air van and speeding toward the site, gifts came out. Langston Nez presented him with a text on how sentience and intelligence had been judged practically from the dawn of human history.

"Did you know that things like skin color were once considered indicators of human intelligence?" he said. "This book will help you understand why getting humans to admit anyone—even other humans—to the exclusive 'person' not 'animal' club can be so difficult."

Anders was a little overwhelmed. From what he could see, this was a pretty serious book, but then one of the reasons he'd always liked Dr. Nez was that he never treated Anders like a kid.

"Thanks!"

The rest of the gifts were less serious. Kesia Guyen and her husband had found Anders a selection of popular music from back on Urako—"So you won't be too behind when you get home." Dr. Emberly, true to her botanist background—and perhaps as a sly reference to all the foraging they'd done together—had given him an assortment of dried fruit from all the planets in the Manticore system. Dacey Emberly had painted Anders a portrait of several male treecats lolling on pads of leaves and branches, their gray and cream coloration blending in amazingly well with the long streaks of sunlight coming through the limbs overhead.

"I put in several of our friends and acquaintances," she said, pointing. "There's Lionheart. Valiant is over to the side. He looks like he's asleep, but you can see he has a root in his hand-feet and he's drowsed off while inspecting it. Right-Striped and Left-Striped are the two who're wrestling. Fisher is licking his true-hands clean. Next to him, you can see the bones and scales from his most recent catch."

Anders laughed. "Thanks so much. This is great."

"It's an original painting," Dacey said, "not a print. It's from the series I'm doing to illustrate the expedition reports."

"That makes it a real treasure, Anders," Dad cut in. "We'll wrap it very carefully when we pack up this winter."

Pack up, Anders thought. *This winter, when it will be my turn to leave. And not just to another planet in the same star system, this time. At least Dad sounds like he's given up on the idea of shipping me home early.*

All the gifts got Anders thinking about Stephanie's little rhyme. He played it over in his head, then used his new uni-link to check his guess. "Cherry" was one of those words that had mutated a lot since humans started cultivating the particular sub variety of genus *Prunus* back on Old Earth. When humans had taken off for the stars, they'd shown a strong tendency to name new things after what they'd left behind, whether they looked a lot like the original or not. Certainly the Sphinxian crown oak, with its arrowhead-shaped leaves and enormous size, bore only the faintest resemblance to the oaks of Old Earth. The same was even more true of the Sphinxian red spruce, which was not much like a spruce at all, given that it had blue-green leaves rather than needles. However, some colonist had seen a similarity between the timber produced by that particular tree and that of the terrestrial spruce. As was so often the case, the name had stuck.

So what remained "cherry" when everything else changed? Anders happily viewed a variety of fruits and fruit woods that used "cherry" in their names and spent much of the morning considering that question. In the end, he decided that—although even on Old Earth cherries had come in pink and yellow, as well in various shades of red, including a hue so dark it was almost black—to most people "cherry bright" would mean bright red.

Okay. He made a note to himself. *The letter A and bright red.*

For a moment, a potential answer tingled in the back of his mind, but it drifted off. Rather than chase after it, he decided to let it percolate on its own while he considered the next line. Unfortunately, he couldn't think of an answer for that one, either.

At mid-afternoon, the crew stopped for a break. Anders had been helping Dr. Nez sift through river gravels to see if the treecats might be able to forage for sufficient flint there rather than traveling—or trading—to get it closer to the source. He was glad to take a rest from the neck and back-stiffening work and play waiter to the rest of the group.

Kesia Guyen, who had managed to keep her plump— she referred to it as "full" figure—despite hours of hard labor, plopped down and leaned back against one of the picketwood trees that were always part of a treecat settlement.

"Anders, my boy, I know it's your birthday, but I'm too pooped to pop up again. Can you grab me something to drink from the cooler?"

"Sure, but would you like? There's a bunch of stuff here."

"Anything as long as it has caffeine." She chuckled one of her deep, throaty laughs. "This girl needs some caff if she's gonna stay on Dr. Whitaker's staff."

Anders grabbed a bulb of a cream-coffee drink he knew Kesia liked and tossed it over to her. He was reaching for a bulb of spike thorn tea with associated honey when an idea hit him.

Gives a zing. Caffeine. Caff. It's not the letter "A" only; it's a letter. A cherry letter. A red letter. Caff-A! The Red Letter Café in Twin Forks! That's got to be what Stephanie meant.

He knew the Red Letter Café well. The owner, Eric Flint, had been one of the first business owners to announce that—despite Lionheart's terrible table manners—his business was a treecat-friendly zone. In thanks, the Harringtons had frequented the café, although thanks alone probably wouldn't have kept them coming back if the Red Letter Café hadn't also served ample portions and made excellent milkshakes.

After Jessica had been adopted by Valiant, the café had become the preferred hangout for the hang-gliding club after practice. So when, on the way home, Dr. Whitaker asked, "So, son, where do you want to go for your birth-day dinner?" there was really only one answer.

"The Red Letter Café. All this shifting stone has given me a real taste for a milkshake."

Stephanie swung her feet out of bed as soon as her alarm beeped, but it was harder than usual for some reason this morning. Even having stayed up last night getting to know a few of the other students couldn't explain why she felt so dragged down.

Only after she'd gotten out of the shower and was strapping on her uni-link did she glance at the date and remember.

"Anders' birthday!" she said aloud.

Lionheart stopped scratching at his shedding fur. "Bleek?"

"It's Anders' birthday," Stephanie repeated. "I wonder if he's got my message yet?" She calculated the differ-ences in time quickly. "I bet he has...I wonder if he's figured it out yet?"

"Bleek!"

"Yeah. I think he will, too. He's pretty smart."

Her uni-link beeped and for a moment she had the crazy hope it might be a message from Anders. Instead, it was a text from Karl: "Heading down to eat. Meet you. Remember. Early target shooting before forensics."

Stephanie sighed and shoved her feet into her shoes. She thought about eating in her room—she'd laid in a stash—and seeing if she could record a quick message to Anders, a follow-up to the timed one. Then she shook her head and continued talking to Lionheart as she gathered up her stuff.

"No. I can't risk seeming standoffish, especially not so early in the session. Last night was fun. I especially liked that Carmen Telford. But there were a lot of people who were looking at me like I was a trained neomonk or something. And if the word somehow got out that I was brooding over a boy..."

She hugged Lionheart, sneezed at the cloud of shed fur that came up, and ran for the door.

Anders certainly hadn't been wrong about his solution to Stephanie's puzzle. What he hadn't expected was that it would have more than one part. After they'd had dinner, he'd gone up to Eric Flint and said, "I believe you have something Stephanie left for me."

Mr. Flint had grinned and immediately produced a slim envelope from one of the cubbies at the reception desk. When Anders got home and opened it, the contents read: "High, high, up in the sky, where purple moths go drifting by!"

He got this one immediately. Not long ago, when he and Stephanie had been hang-gliding on the Harrington freehold, they'd found themselves flying in the midst of a host of delicate little six-winged creatures that they'd dubbed "purple moths." They'd hovered on the counter-grav units built into the gliders, taking images and—when a few unfortunates chose to commit suicide against the glider wings—taking samples, as well.

They'd nursed hopes that they'd discovered another new species, but it turned out that their moths were already known under the name "lavender hexaflies." Nonetheless, the SFS was happy to have the samples and images, since it was suspected that various species of hexaflies played an essential role in the late-season pollination of some of the faster-growing Sphinxian plant species.

That had been a wonderful, magical day, and Anders was certain he could locate the place again. However, he also knew he was one of the less skillful flyers in Stephanie's gang, and air currents this time of year could be unpredictable. It would be a good idea to bring someone else along. He'd also better get the Harringtons' permission. Their freehold was huge—over six hundred square kilometers—and they would probably not even notice people poking around, but Anders' mother had always stressed that remembering one's manners applied even when no one was likely to notice.

Richard Harrington asked where Anders wanted to go and, after checking the coordinates, gave the okay.

"You're not going alone, are you?"

"I know the safety rules, Coach," Anders replied promptly. "I figured on asking the gang: Toby, Chet, Christine, and Jessica. Club games and races are nice but, well, there's something great about flying just for the fun of it."

"I agree. Have a good time, then."

Anders debated which of his friends to call first. He realized that despite the amount of time he'd spent with them, this would be the first time he was the one setting something up. Usually Stephanie handled that, following some shared unwritten assumption that they were "her" friends. Finally, Anders decided a blanket invitation had the best chance of succeeding.

He was delighted—and a little suspicious, when all four were available. Could Stephanie have set this up in advance? Maybe Mr. Flint had been asked to let them all know when Anders picked up the note, indicating that he'd solved the first puzzle. Or maybe Richard Harrington was in on it and had signaled when Anders called to get permission. Anders wouldn't have been surprised. If Stephanie hadn't wanted to be a ranger, she would have made a great fleet commander.

✧　　✧　　✧

"So that's Ms. Stephanie Harrington and the famous Lionheart," Gwendolyn Adair murmured, gazing at the imagery on her display. Harrington and the SFS had maintained a very low profile on her arrival and none of the newsies seemed to have realized she was coming, but Gwen had positioned her own camera team ahead of time.

"Yep," Oswald Morrow agreed, looking over her shoulder. "Doesn't look all that impressive, does she? She's just a kid!"

"Who went up against a hexapuma with just a vibro blade and a treecat," Gwen reminded him a bit frostily. "And you might want to remember what happened to our good friend Bolgeo when *he* crossed swords with her." She shook her head, never looking away from the imagery. "Don't sell this particular kid short, Ozzie."

"Umph." Morrow shrugged, but he didn't argue with her. Not out loud, anyway. Instead, he tapped the display with a fingertip. "That's Zivonik?"

"No, Ozzie; its Crown Prince Edward." She glared over her shoulder at him. "Of course it's Zivonik!"

Morrow glared back at her, but only from the corner of one eye, and she snorted.

"Sorry." There might have been just a *little* insincerity in her tone. "Yes, that's Zivonik. Bigger than I expected, really . . . though he could just *look* bigger because he's standing next to her."

"How did they do coming through the terminal?"

"Better than I'd hoped they would, actually." Gwen shook her head. "I'd sort of hoped all the people running around everywhere would spook the 'cat, but he seems to've taken it in stride."

"Too bad," Morrow murmured. "That probably means he'll behave himself in crowds on campus, too."

"We knew it wasn't going to be easy." Gwen shrugged, gazing at the imagery for another handful of seconds, then shut it off and tipped back in her chair. "Like I say, our young friend Stephanie's not someone to take lightly, and I'm beginning to think her six-legged friend isn't, either."

"Are you thinking about changing the plan?" Morrow sounded both surprised and perhaps a bit anxious, but then, despite his confident exterior and reputation for brokering big deals, he was much more of a creature of habit than Gwen. He liked to make a plan then stick with it, and her tendency to improvise made him nervous on occasion.

"No," she reassured him. "I *am* thinking about how best to apply it, though. And the more I look at the imagery, the less confident I am of our being able to convince people treecats aren't really sentient."

"Then why are we sending all those anthropologists to Sphinx?" Morrow demanded, and grimaced. "It's costing a pretty penny just to get them out here, Gwen. And even with your backing through the foundation, I burned more favors with the Interior Ministry than I like to think about getting Vásquez to sign off on making Hobbard give them access right along with Whitaker! If he hadn't messed up so badly during the forest fires, I don't think she would've overruled Hobbard, no matter how we'd approached her."

"Oh, stop hugging your wallet, Ozzie!" Gwen shook her head again. "Our people are going to argue against admitting sentience as long as they can, and even if Hobbard doesn't buy into it, it'll create plenty of confusion in the minds of people who aren't anthropologists. In the end, it doesn't really matter what the scientists decide, now does it? What matters is what *Parliament* decides, and that means we have to convince a bunch of voters who probably don't even know what 'sentient' means that the 'cats are only cute, cuddly woodland creatures."

"But you said—"

"I said it was going to be harder, not that I thought it

was going to be *impossible*. Besides, that was never more than our first line of defense. You just be sure your pet anthropologists' reports underline these things' inability to truly understand the implications of modern technology or the real impact human settlements are going to have on them. We deny their sentience as long as we can, and when we finally admit it, we argue that the reason it took us so long to realize the truth is because they're so *different* from human beings. And with the foundation sponsoring their research, it'll be easy to tell everyone how concerned we are about their well-being. How much we want to protect them from the corrupting influence of human contact. After all, think how other aboriginal cultures have been scarred and destroyed by contact with more advanced societies!"

He looked at her, eyes narrowing, and then began to nod slowly.

Stephanie finished the newly arrived message from Anders, freezing the final frame on her viewscreen so she could enjoy the warmth of his parting smile while she thought about the news. More xenoanthropologists! She was happy for Anders that his dad had returned, and she was *ecstatic* at the thought that the Whitaker expedition's time on Sphinx had actually been extended, rather than cut short. But she'd learned to *know* the members of Dr. Whitaker's team, and she *didn't* know any of these newcomers Anders was talking about. She wished she could be there to see them firsthand—and to have Lionheart check them out.

"We can't be there, though. But I wonder..." An impish grin lit her face, and she quickly set herself to record.

"Anders... I'm so glad you're enjoying the scavenger hunt. Thanks for telling me about this new group of xenoanthropologists. I never thought I'd say this, but I agree with your dad, and I wish Lionheart and I could be there to check them out. Since we can't, though, I've got an idea. How about Jessica and Valiant?

"Jessica's good with people—better than I am, really. She's been so many places. I think Valiant is a bit more shy about strangers than Lionheart, but he's a wise sort. I think he'd be able to spot a blackhole like Bolgeo right off. Then you and Jess and all would know who to keep an eye on.

"I'm going to message Jess right away and see what she thinks. If she's for it, then I'm sure something can be set up."

Her voice softened. "I really, really wish I could be there—and not just to check out these new arrivals. I can't believe I've only been here three days . . . Three *months* seem like an eternity." She blew him a kiss. "Miss you!"

The weather wasn't as cooperative as the human elements, so it wasn't until a few days after Anders' birthday that the group assembled on the top of a cliff that offered a good place to park Jessica's car and Chet's truck. Unlike traditional hang-gliders, the modern glider included a counter-grav unit that made the blind leaps into the air that belonged to the traditional sport unnecessary. A few of the stronger fliers—Karl and Toby among them—had experimented with jumping off cliffs anyway, but Anders was just as glad to let his counter-grav carry him up to where he could find a strong thermal.

As he shrugged into his glider, Anders noticed Valiant reaching up to accept a neat little shoulder bag from Jessica. The contents clinked slightly as the treecat slung the strap over one shoulder, then over his chest, positioning it so that it rested comfortably between his upper and middle sets of limbs. Then the 'cat wandered off toward a cluster of thick, shrubby trees that—despite showing evidence of having been bent by the winds—were evidently thriving.

"Dr. Richard helped adapt my glider so Valiant could ride with me like Lionheart does with Stephanie," Jessica explained, "but he's not as keen on flying as Lionheart. I get the impression that Lionheart's a bit of a daredevil."

"Like Stephanie." Christine chuckled, settling her helmet over her indigo crest. "Where's Valiant off to?"

"Collecting plants," Jessica said. "Dr. Marjorie set him up with little bags that will protect his samples. She figured that was a good compromise that let her encourage him while not steering him. Valiant has gardens at our place, in the Harrington greenhouses, and back with his clan."

Very much the anthropologist's son, Anders asked, "Does Valiant seem to be doing any sort of systematic gardening or is he just sticking things in at random?"

"Systematic," Jessica answered promptly, "although what his system is, I can't say. We can't talk, remember. The best I can do is observe, but it sure looks to me as if he's trying out the same plants in different locations. His clan lives where the soil is very moist compared to our garden."

"I remember." Anders grinned. "I don't think I'll ever forget. It's interesting that Valiant's clan moved back into that territory after the fires burned them out of their new home. My dad had the impression that they'd moved in the first place because the area near the bog was fished out or hunted out or something."

"Maybe," Jessica agreed. "But they're back—despite having to put up with a swamp siren for a neighbor."

"I wonder," Anders continued thinking aloud as he went through his preflight check, "if they didn't have a lot of choice. Maybe treecats are territorial."

"Maybe," Jessica agreed again. She might have said more, but at that moment, Chet cut in.

"Hey, are we going to fly and find Anders' prezzie, or are we going to yack?"

"Fly," Anders replied. "Let's go prezzie hunting."

The small flock of gliders rose on counter-grav, gleaming in the sun, and from his newly elevated perch, Anders checked his uni-link for the coordinates he and Stephanie had filed when they had first discovered the purple moths.

"There," he murmured to himself. "Over by those rocks, then over to the right...Uh-oh."

He spoke into his uni-link. "Guys, we've got a problem."

"Problem?" Chad asked. "Can't you find the spot?"

"Oh, I've found it," Anders replied. "But something's changed since Stephanie and I were out here." He read off the location, then pointed. "See? Looks as if a flock of some sort of avians has decided this series of cliffs would make a perfect autumn aerie."

"I've got a good visual on them," Toby commed in. "I think your avians are rock ravens. Karl told me about them when we went out to do some traditional gliding a couple of weeks ago."

Still listening, Anders called up the SFS ranger's guide on his uni-link. The information available was depressingly brief. Like most lifeforms native to Sphinx, rock ravens were structured on a hexapedal model. In this particular case, that worked out two sets of wings and a single pair of powerful talon-tipped legs.

The wingspan was about a meter wide, and their feathers seemed to change color between shades of blue and brown, depending on their surroundings. No one had yet had time to study whether the color variants indicated different species or whether some other factor was involved. That was it.

"The rock ravens weren't there when you were here before?" Christine asked.

"Nope. All that was here were a bunch of purple moths— like I told you when I showed you Stephanie's clue."

"They weren't here when Steph and I came out to—" Jessica cut in, then stopped. "I guess I've got to admit that I know where the prize is hidden," she continued after a moment. "Anders has pinpointed it exactly, so it's not like I'm helping him cheat."

"I've got a different angle on the cliff from Toby," Chet said. "Jess, is what we're looking for wrapped in purple?"

Anders shifted screens on his uni-link and saw that the star indicating Chet on his map was drifting higher than the rest of them.

"Yep."

"Then I've spotted it, and you're right, Anders has pinpointed the target. There's something wedged in a cleft down there, right where the rock ravens are thickest."

"What a lousy coincidence!" Toby said, his voice full of sympathy.

Anders cleared his throat. "Actually, it may not be a coincidence. It's possible the rock ravens were drawn here by the swarms of lavender hexaflies—or because they came to prey on the creatures that came to eat the hexaflies."

"The circle of lunch," Chet quipped. "I always thought that would be a better name than 'circle of life.' So, how do we scare them off?"

Anders shifted the sights on his flying goggles for long distance. He'd honed his skill at this when he went gliding. Stephanie's capacity for aerial acrobatics went far beyond what he could manage. Rather than slow her down, he sometimes preferred to switch to counter-grav mode and drift on the winds, observing the land below. Now he focused in on the area where the rock ravens were thickest.

Looking at the flock, Anders could understand why some long-ago colonist had given the birds ("bird analogs, not birds," he heard his father pedantically lecturing in his head) the name "rock raven." They definitely belonged to the group that possessed beaks and feathers—a group which included mountain eagles and finches—rather than the more batlike flyers like the condor owls. Where condor owls were covered with a fine down, these rock ravens had the Sphinxian equivalent of feathers—hollow quills with outlying veins that captured the air. The rock ravens were nicely streamlined, too, with wedge-shaped tails that gave them extra finesse as they dodged and dove, sometimes skimming right up against the rock face before looping around into open-air.

"They don't look too dangerous," he said. "I mean, they don't have nasty hooked beaks, so I'm guessing they're omnivores or scavengers rather than hunters. I can't really get a good look at their feet, though, so it's hard to say."

"Karl said something..." Toby's voice faltered. "I can't remember what."

"Did he say they were dangerous?" Christine asked. "I mean, do they have poison or spines or something that might make up for them not being super huge?"

"Naw, nothing like that," Toby assured her. "It was something about them being migratory and moving into lower areas when winter came on. Something like that. I'm pretty sure he didn't say anything about them being dangerous."

Anders wondered if he imagined the warble of doubt in the younger boy's voice, but when none of the others questioned Toby, he figured he must have. After all, they knew Toby a lot better.

"Here's my idea," he said. "Stephanie wouldn't like it very much if we hurt—or even really disrupted—the rock ravens, not just to get a present. So how about I go in alone? I'll grab whatever's there, then get out."

"I don't want to give away too much," Jessica said, "but I can say that what Stephanie left is small enough for one person to pull out. Still, wouldn't you like some of us to fly cover?"

"Or maybe go in for you?" Toby added. "Like you said, Stephanie wouldn't like it if any of the rock ravens got hurt and, well, you're not the best flyer here."

"I am," Anders replied, "the worst. I know that. You know that. More importantly, Stephanie knew that. I'm sure she wouldn't have set up something I couldn't handle. So I'm going in."

He didn't want to admit it, but he was actually nervous about taking his glider in among all those birds. However, he also didn't want to give anyone a chance to talk him out of it. Stephanie had set this up for *him*, not for the whole gang.

Shifting his goggles back to normal range, he readied himself for the maneuver. He knew that Christine or Jessica would have managed a fancy dive, but he figured prudence was best. He'd drop down to the level of Stephanie's purple whatever, then go in on a flat horizontal course until he came up alongside. He'd grab it and get out. Then they'd all scatter and the rock ravens could go back to doing whatever it was rock ravens did.

Perfect.

Except, as with most plans, it didn't work out quite that way.

The rock ravens didn't react until Anders was on their level and speeding toward them. Then, rather than scattering as he'd figured they would, they bunched up. Not wanting to hurt them, Anders started braking. That would have been a bad idea with a traditional glider, since he'd risk losing loft as well as speed, but he had the counter-grav unit to compensate.

He'd managed to slow up before he reached the flock. Then, to his horror, the flock came at *him*. The sounds they made were more like the shrill shrieks of a peacock than the hoarser caws and croaks of Old Earth ravens. They penetrated into his inner ear, creating a sensation of vertigo. His body felt as if he were wobbling, falling, even as his intellect assured him that the counter-grav unit had to be keeping him aloft.

The rock ravens were all around him, mobbing him, beating at him with their wings, pecking indiscriminately at the glider's fabric, his clothing, the exposed skin of his face, their hard beaks tapping against his goggles. He felt hot beads of blood coursing into streams. The edges of the feathers rasped against his skin, causing a small pocket of his brain to guess that whatever made the side veins was stronger and coarser than the material of terrestrial feathers.

For a long and terrible moment, overwhelmed on all sides and all senses, Anders found it nearly impossible to think. He was aware of the voices of his friends shouting at him on the open channel of his new uni-link, but he couldn't make out anything over the shrieking of the rock ravens. He had to get free of the flock before they drove his faltering glider into the edge of the cliff. The counter-grav unit couldn't stop that.

The cliff face swirled and danced in front of him. The shrieking in his ears reverberated louder and louder. Buffeted by angry aviforms, Anders struggled to find a way to avoid certain doom...

7

COUNTER-GRAV!

Anders fumbled for the control, then pushed the weight-control slide to make himself lighter. For a moment, he thought the sheer mass of the avians on top of him would hold him down, but although the mob of ravens was dense, it couldn't contain him. He peeled up and out, floating toward the sky with increasing speed once the obstructions had been pushed aside. Quickly, he leveled off, then brought himself lower once more.

The shrieks of the rock ravens had shifted to something that sounded suspiciously triumphant, and Anders craned around to see how much damage they done to his glider. Thankfully, Bradford Whitaker's usual tendency to skimp on anything other than anthropology hadn't won out when he'd been choosing his son's glider. The high-tech fabrics were dimpled but largely intact.

"Wow!" Toby's voice was the first to register on Anders' recovering ears. "That was amazing."

"Good thing you got out of there so fast," Chet said. "You think well on your feet—and off them, too, now that I think about it."

His warm chuckle startled Anders, until he realized that what had been to him a horrible ordeal had probably lasted no more than a few seconds. The peacock cries of the rock ravens had distorted more than his sense of balance.

"You okay, Anders?" Jessica's voice held deep concern. "They didn't get your eyes or anything?"

"I had my flying goggles on," Anders replied, "and I'm really glad. They definitely were going for my eyes. Clever little monsters."

"Land at base," Christine said firmly. "We better make sure you and your glider didn't take any real damage."

Anders thought about arguing. With the counter-grav unit on, it wasn't like he could fall or anything, even if his glider was damaged, but he knew that tone. If he argued, Christine would simply get Chet to help her grab him and tow him in. Chet would probably think it was really funny.

When they landed, the girls made a fuss over the peck marks on his face. When Anders got a look at himself in Christine's pocket mirror, he couldn't argue. He looked pretty bad, with blood and streaks of what he thought was probably bird shit all over his face. The shit wasn't restricted to his face, either. Neither were the feathers.... Bits of down and longer wing feathers stuck to him, giving evidence of how violent the rock ravens had been in protecting their territory.

Anders plucked off one of the larger feathers and tilted it back and forth, noting how the colors shifted in the light through blues into browns.

"Well, I guess something good came out of this," he said. "We can collect samples for the SFS biologists. Anyone got a small bag?"

Jessica said, "I'll borrow from Valiant's stash."

On Sphinx, even kids knew how to plan in advance for emergencies. There was a first aid kit in Chet's truck and another in Jessica's car. Fresh water wasn't a problem, either. Within a relatively short time, Anders was scrubbed off and had been deemed fit for action once more.

"Well," Toby said philosophically, "at least now we know rock ravens will fight back. I wonder if that's what Karl meant when he said we should keep clear of them?"

"Now you remember?" Anders retorted sarcastically.

"Hey," Toby said with an eloquent shrug of his supple shoulders. "I thought he was just worried about the birds. You know how he and Stephanie are. Nature first."

"You've got a point," Anders agreed. "Now, how do I get that thing? Obviously, it's not going to be as easy as just grabbing it. For some reason those idiot ravens have decided they want to keep it."

"I wonder," Jessica said, "if it's the color. Stephanie picked it because it was close to the shade of those hexaflies you two saw here. I wonder if the rock ravens think that that's the biggest stash of hexaflies they've ever seen and you want to swipe it."

Anders laughed. "I bet you're right. If they're sight hunters, the color would mean more to them than the fact that Stephanie's package is the wrong size and smell and all."

"Hey, don't be too hard on them," Christine said. "After all, there were a lot of hexaflies here not long ago. They've got a lot of reason to hope."

Chet nodded. "Color might be our answer. What if we waited until after dark? If the rock ravens are sight hunters, then it's likely they bed down or roost or whatever it is birds do it at night."

"That's a good idea," Anders said. "Do you think we need to tell the Harringtons? I mean, I'm not sure they'd like the idea of us cliff-diving after dark."

"I wouldn't bug them," Jessica said. "Stephanie always says it's better to not say anything if you think someone won't like the truth. We're pretty far from where they have their house. If we don't show a light, we should be fine. We'll wait until the rock ravens get quiet, then send someone—"

"Me!" Anders insisted when Toby looked all too ready to volunteer. "This is still my quest. Anyhow, I'll just use the counter-grav to lower myself. No problem."

"That's what you said last time," Toby grumbled, but he didn't protest further.

This time the plan worked. The rock ravens even cooperated by retreating into neat little holes in the rock as soon as the light began to lose its brilliance. They peeped a bit as Anders drifted by, but seemed to feel no inclination to go after him.

Maybe they think I'm a condor owl or something, Anders thought. *They know how to pick their battles. That's really not a bad lesson to take away from this. Not a bad one at all.*

"Wow, that's amazing what happened with the rock ravens," Stephanie told the pickup as she recorded her latest message to Anders. "I had no idea they'd react that way. Jess wrote me about what happened, and it sounds as if you were great—and not nearly as out-of-control as you made it sound when you messaged me last night.

"I'm really glad you and Jessica both like my idea about her serving as liaison. Jess said that she actually got the impression Chief Ranger Shelton was relieved when she—I mean Jess—volunteered to be interviewed and to let the xenoanthropologists meet Valiant. You know how protective Irina is of Scott's free time, but Chief Ranger

Shelton isn't the sort to assume that just because Jess is only fifteen she's automatically available. And she and her family can sure use the stipend. I think it was a good move on your dad's part to offer it."

Stephanie sighed, thinking about how much she wished she didn't have to delegate that particular job. She was glad Jessica would be able to supplement her family's income, of course, but still...

"The coursework is just as intensive as we were warned. We weren't even on planet two hours before a bunch of material for us to review was downloaded onto our uni-links."

She went on to describe some of the material, which ranged from social customs to elementary forensics, with a lot of botany and zoology in the middle.

"—so then we got the full tour." Stephanie giggled. "Poor Karl found out it's even hotter here in Landing than he thought it'd be. I thought he was gonna melt right down in front of me, but even the air-conditioning's set a lot higher here than it is back home! It's rough on Lionheart, too, but I think dad's right about how the 'cat shedding mechanism works. Lionheart's been shedding like crazy ever since we got here, and it has to've been kicked off by the rise in temperature. My dorm room looks like a permanent blizzard from all the hair he's lost! But the labs are nice, and the HD set up is a lot better than I thought it would be. I like my dorm room, too, even if I wish it was a little bigger. With all this space here on campus, you'd think they could give me more than one room! But I guess it's really all Lionheart and I need."

Lionheart jumped up onto the back of her chair as if summoned by the sound of his name and twitched his whiskers gravely into the pickup over her shoulder. She laughed and reached up to scratch him under the chin, then turned back to the message.

"I wish we could let him run around more on his own, but Dean Charterman—she's dean of students for the university—made me promise I won't let him out without me. She says it's for his own protection, but I think she's little worried about what sort of trouble he might get into . . . or cause." She grimaced, then shrugged. "On the other hand, it might be she's worried about contamination, too. I know some people're still nervous about how freely we let *humans* move back and forth between planets here in the Star Kingdom, and I think some of them are afraid Lionheart might be carrying disease or parasites or something."

Her expression made her opinion of that particular worry obvious, but then she shook her head with another grimace.

"I guess it shouldn't be too surprising after the Plague and all," she acknowledged, trying to be at least marginally fair about it. "But you'd think all of the screening and medical inspections they still have in force would help people get past it. It darned well ought to, anyway!"

She glowered, still scratching Lionheart's chin, while she contemplated such benighted attitudes for a moment.

"We've met our professors," she continued then. "Dr. Gleason's officially only a department head, but my impression is that he pretty much runs the School of Forestry, and I don't think he's too happy to see us." She snorted. "Seems downright determined to keep as far away from Lionheart as he can, too, which I think is just plain dumb. He's supposed to be teaching forestry and he doesn't even want to *meet* a treecat?" She snorted again, louder. "On the other hand, Dr. Flouret's chairman of the College of Criminology, and I'm pretty sure *he's* one of the good guys. Seems to be an old friend of Dr. Hobbard's, and he had some really nice things to say about Chief Shelton, too."

She paused, not quite sure what to say next, and felt a sudden burning sensation behind her eyes. She knew how interested Anders was going to be in everything she just told him, but she didn't want to *tell* him about it; she wanted to *show* him, because that would have meant he was right here on Manticore where she could!

She bit the inside of her lip for a moment, then drew a deep breath and made herself go on brightly.

"In the meantime, Karl and I have been checking out the dining hall. You *know* how much I love to eat, and, fortunately, there are quite a few Sphinxians here with the kind of metabolism I have. At least they're not going to starve me between official meals! And besides that..."

She trailed off. Much as she wished she could somehow *make* Anders be there with her, she knew wishing wouldn't make it happen. Instead, she went back to what was really bugging her.

"I was fascinated—okay, a bit horrified, too—to hear how much trouble you had retrieving the package from the rock ravens. I don't think anything could go that wrong with the rest of it, at least I sure hope not.... Message me every step, okay?"

She wanted to say more, to say how much more fun it would be if he was there with her, but she didn't trust herself not to break down. Instead, she blew a kiss toward the pickup. "Miss you...Lots..."

Keen Eyes was deeply worried. Over the last span of days he had searched for somewhere his clan—renamed in the depths of his mind the Landless Clan—might go. Given the hostility displayed by Swimmer's Scourge, Keen Eyes felt that the route into the lowlands was unsafe. If he had his way, he would have taken the remnants of the clan into Bright Water's territory and traded on that clan's known liberality. However, the older People of his clan—sadly the majority among the survivors—held firm against this.

<Better we die to the last,> said old Sour Belly, who was both the most senior hunter and the best flintknapper in the clan, <than become corrupted by the two-legs as Bright Water has.>

That Sour Belly was long past his best hunting days meant nothing to him—no more than did the fact that his current name came from the fact that he was old enough that his digestion was not what it once had been. He viewed this infirmity as an indication of his extreme age, and extreme age as reason enough for his opinion to be better than anyone else's.

Keen Eyes couldn't agree, but, short of reducing the clan even further—and robbing it of its source of stone tools—he had no choice. If Wide Ears or one of the other memory singers had survived, she might have overruled the elders, but Tiny Choir was less than a turning old, far too young to be recognized as an adult, much less take over as the clan's memory singer.

Keen Eyes was also crippled in his ability to press his opinion because, before the fires, he had been among the younger scouts. The fact that many of his elders, including his beloved teacher, had died seeking the routes that had enabled the clan to get at least the elderly and the kittens to safety, did Keen Eyes no favors now. He was now the most senior scout... but not—at least in the minds of those such as Sour Belly—because he had earned the rank, but because he had been too careful of his life to die.

The decision—if any decision could be said to have been made, rather than simply made necessary by the creeping advance of colder weather—was to shift down into the lowest parts of their range and hope for the best. Keen Eyes suspected that by the reasoning of the Trees

Enfolding Clan they had already violated the boundaries of their territory, but, thus far, the intrusion had been tolerated. How much longer—or further—that intrusion would be tolerated, Keen Eyes could not guess.

He could only hope that this fragile period of grace would extend until he could find them a new home.

Although the gang offered to help Anders with the rest of his scavenger hunt, none of the other clues offered the same level of threat. Probably the most "dangerous" challenge was one that took Anders to the burned out island where Stephanie and the others had fought to save Valiant's clan. However, the danger offered by the island was due more to people than to the environment. It shared a border with lands held by the Franchitti family—a family that believed animals were for hunting, shooting, and imprisoning rather than preserving. They'd already received several reprimands for abuse of flora and fauna alike. As a result, they'd become very guarded about who crossed their airspace.

But Anders carefully kept his air car within the boundaries of public lands and, although there might have been an annoyed Franchitti or two just waiting to warn him off, he gave them no justification to intervene.

His prize in the end was worth every minute of his effort, though—as he wrote to Stephanie—the hunt in itself was a present.

"It kept you near me," he dictated, taking care with every word. "I could feel you there before me. Sometimes you seemed so close that I felt if I hurried just a little faster I'd glimpse you, be able to reach out and hold your hand."

He wanted to say more, but it was harder to talk about how much you wanted to kiss your girl than it was to do it. Weird.

Stephanie's present managed to be both romantic and practical—rather like the girl herself—a custom band for his new uni-link. She'd crafted it herself in her family's workshop and had inscribed the band so that the words would nuzzle up against his wrist, "To Anders, from his Steph. The void between worlds cannot divide hearts."

Dad grinned when Anders showed him the custom band.

"I can't say I'm completely surprised," he said, admiring the careful workmanship. "She did ask me what we were getting you. She's quite a talented young lady. I certainly wish she were still on planet."

Despite any other changes in attitude, Anders doubted that his father felt that way because he commiserated so deeply with his son's emotional life, so he said, "Still upset about those touring anthropologists? Have you learned anything about them that will help you deal with them?"

"Not much," Dr. Whitaker replied glumly. "It's been twelve days now, but given the lags in inter-system communication, all we have to go on is what we brought with us and what the Manticorans had on file. Langston and I cross-referenced the information Sonura Hobbard sent us against our own research libraries, of course."

"And?"

"And if these are the people who wrote the articles we've turned up, then we don't have any excuse not to offer them at least professional courtesy."

Anders understood why his dad had included that wistful "if these are the people." Tennessee Bolgeo hadn't been any of the things included in his academic credentials. However, it was too much to hope for the same thing to happen twice and save the Whitaker expedition from the interlopers.

"In fact," Dad sighed, "we'd be idiots not to offer them

a reasonable amount of access. Dr. Radzinsky is quite respected for her work on nonhuman intelligence. In my opinion, she's a bit conservative, but it was too much to imagine she wouldn't be interested in developments here."

"She's not the only one coming, though, is she?"

Dad shook his head. "Under other circumstances, I could actually enjoy meeting Gary Hidalgo. He shares my interest in archeoanthropology. Mind you, I don't agree with a lot of his conclusions, but he definitely knows his stuff. He feels very strongly about the preservation of indigenous cultures in an uncontaminated state, so I'm sure he'll have fits over how the SFS has given some treecats knives and axes. He's certainly going to be in favor of having them protected from interference."

Anders didn't think this sounded too bad. "Anyone else?"

"They've got a linguistics specialist coming, too." Dad scowled. "I had Kesia Guyen check him out, and she immediately got the shakes. Apparently, this Russell Darrolyn is on the cutting edge of nonverbal communication studies."

Anders felt a flash of worry. He knew Stephanie and Scott had been torn from the first as to whether or not it would be a good thing to have the treecats recognized as as intelligent as they were. Better for humans to get used to them, come to like them, before they had to face the undoubted threat another sentient species could offer to human interests.

"Still, a linguist is good, right?" he said. "I mean, Kesia hasn't been able to find any evidence that the treecats use complex verbal communication. Maybe this Dr. Darrolyn will have some new insights."

Dr. Whitaker made a "tcching" noise with his tongue. "I'm not so sure providing that sort of proof will be his aim. Kesia says this Darrolyn is positively 'cranky' on the subject of communication forms that don't involve words lined up into neat sentences."

"Huh? I thought you said he was a specialist in non-verbal communications?"

"He is. But, basically, Darrolyn is very limited as to what he'll agree is a viable communications form. Kesia said she thinks he'd doubt that even he is communicating, except for the undeniable fact that he gets replies."

Anders blinked. The very idea made his head ache. He'd heard of specialists who were extremely careful, but this seemed like going to extremes. Still, on the good side, it didn't look as if Dr. Darrolyn was going to immediately jump to the conclusion that because treecats were telempaths, they were also telepaths. In fact, it sounded as if Darrolyn would need to prove to himself that the 'cats were even telempathic, despite ample existing evidence.

"Anyone else?"

"No one as important," Dr. Whitaker said, sounding just a little happier. "Of course, each of them has a hanger-on or two, but none of them have the same level of prestige."

"Well, Dad, I'm sure you'll manage just fine."

"Still," Dr. Whitaker said, "I'm glad Ms. Pheriss volunteered to take over for Stephanie. Now she can waste *her* time talking to these people while I get on with my work."

"So, Ms. Harrington," Dr. Gleason said, regarding her with his head cocked to one side, "what can you tell me about picketwood?"

Gleason had brown hair and eyes, a slender build, and a fussy manner. He hadn't said so in so many words, but Stephanie was pretty sure he didn't think it had been a good idea to let a pair of "kids" jump the queue and use up two of the slots in the School of Forestry. Not that his classes were all that crowded, as far as she could see. There were only eighteen people in this lecture course, after all, including her and Karl. And she didn't much like the way he emphasized "Ms." whenever he spoke to her. She'd heard that patronizing tone from too many adults.

"Picketwood is the common name for any of at least six species of the genus *Neo-ulmus Sphinx*," she replied, "although '*ulmus*' is something of a misnomer applied by the original survey crew. It's really not very much like an Old Terran elm; it's more like a cross between an Old Earth willow and a Beowulfan ash tree, when you come down to it. The most common species are gray picketwood, yellow-leaf picketwood, mountain picketwood, magnolia picketwood, and narrow-leaf picketwood. They differ considerably in appearance, particularly in the fall, but all of them form a clear taxonomic genus. Picketwood is deciduous and unusual in that it produces vegetatively, not sexually, using a sort of proto-stolon well above ground level. The stolons are distinguishable from the picketwood's normal branches because they always form in groups of four, at right angles to one another, and grow horizontally, rather than spreading from the main trunk. They extend outward for from ten to fifteen meters, at which point they form adventitious buds that develop into nodes, extending rootlets vertically down to ground level. Each rootlet then establishes itself as a new 'main trunk,' extending the original plant and radiating stolons of its own. Sometimes, a stolon runs into one from another picketwood system, at which point they merge, sending down a rootlet from the new junction point. Because of that, it's difficult to say where one picketwood begins and another one ends—or if they ever *do* end, really. Studies indicate that the merging stolons share genetic material in putting down their rootlet, and the trunk which develops from that rootlet isn't a clone of either parent, but a new individual, although physically linked to both of the systems in which it arose. There's some speculation that—"

"Ah, that will do, Ms. Harrington," Gleason interrupted. His eyes had widened as she rattled off her description, and from the corner of one eye she could see Karl trying valiantly to suppress a grin. She hoped Gleason wasn't looking at him, and she smiled winningly at the professor.

He gazed back at her for several seconds, his expression thoughtful, and she found herself wishing (not for the first time) that she'd been allowed to bring Lionheart to class. Unfortunately, Gleason was clearly one of the faculty members who felt the treecat would be a "disruptive influence" in his classroom. She wasn't certain, but she suspected he was also one of the people who figured treecats had too little body mass to support a brain large enough for true sentience.

On the other hand, he obviously thought I *didn't support true sentience, either,* she thought. It was what her mother would've called "snippy" of her, but she didn't really care.

Obviously he hadn't paid any attention to who her parents were if he thought he could throw her with a question that simple.

"Yes, well." Gleason gave himself a shake, then regarded the class as a whole. Fortunately, Karl had his expression back under control.

"As Ms. Harrington has so . . . competently described, picketwood has a highly unusual mode of reproduction. It provides certain obvious survival advantages, but it also exposes the entire picketwood system to disease and parasite threats. There are additional drawbacks, such as susceptibility to fire, as recent events on Sphinx have demonstrated, but the speed at which picketwood grows and propagates is really quite remarkable. Since picketwood is so widespread and central to Sphinx's arboreal biosystem, and since over half of you will be returning to Sphinx after you complete your course work here, I thought it would be a good idea for this class if we began by considering those advantages and risk factors.

"Now, Ms. Telford, building on what Ms. Harrington's shared with us, how would you describe—"

"I thought old Gleason's jaw was going to hit the floor, Steph!" Carmen Telford chortled as she, Stephanie, and Karl headed for their next class.

"What's his problem, anyway?" Karl asked, and Carmen shrugged.

She was in her mid-twenties, at least five or six T-years older than Karl, and like him she was a nativeborn Sphinxian. Her father was Eduardo Telford, Baron Crown Oak, and he and her various uncles and aunts owned several thousand square kilometers of virgin woodland. They intended to develop the timber resources, but they also intended to be certain they didn't destroy the habitat, and Carmen was here on Manticore to learn the best silviculture techniques for reforestation and sustained timber production. Despite her age advantage and the fact that Stephanie was a mere yeoman's daughter, the two of them had hit it off well.

"I'm not really sure," Carmen said now, "but if I had to guess, I'd say it's probably that he figures the two of you only got here because of who you know. I don't think anyone here on Manticore was paying a lot of attention to the news when you guys were involved in those forest fires this summer. Gleason sure as heck wasn't, anyway!"

She made a face.

"He knows your dad's a baron, Karl, and I think he figures your father pulled strings to get you and your little buddy here—" she twitched her head at Stephanie with a grin that took the sting out of "little buddy"—"seats that should've gone to someone else. He doesn't take the whole 'probationary ranger' thing very seriously, I'm afraid. But Steph rang his chimes pretty good, didn't she?"

"I shouldn't have done it." Stephanie shook her head with a sigh. "Mom keeps telling me 'you catch more flies with honey than with vinegar.'"

"Hey, I *know* your mom!" Karl said, thumping her on the shoulder. "If she'd heard that look-down-my-nose-at-you tone of his, she'd've been standing in the back of the room cheering you on, and you know it!"

He probably had a point, Stephanie decided. And even if he didn't, it was nice of him to be on her side. Of course that, she'd discovered over the last T-year or two, was one of the things friends did for each other, and she smiled warmly up at him.

"Well, at least Mom wouldn't have *whacked* me for it," she conceded. Then she looked down at the time display on her uni-link, and her eyes widened. "Cripes! We're going to be late for class if we don't get a move on—come on!"

THE DAYS FOLLOWING STEPHANIE'S DEPARTURE TURNED slowly into weeks. Although he missed her, Anders kept himself busy helping out on his father's project and going on outings with his Sphinxian friends. Just about every day he messaged Stephanie, trying to provide her with a link to the people and events she'd left behind. She was incredibly busy but did her best to squeak off a message of her own most days.

Anders made sure he was on hand when the "tourist" xenoanthropologists arrived on Sphinx. Chet and Christine were there, too, as official wilderness guides in the new program established by the SFS and the Sphinx Department of Tourism. Until recently, the SFS had been able to handle what wilderness tourism there'd been, but the aftermath of the severe fire season put an extra strain on the Forestry Service's resources, even now, and the treecats had raised the profile of the Sphinxian bush.

Never mind that the known treecat areas were restricted.

That didn't keep some poorly informed visitors from thinking they could find a group of treecats and get themselves adopted—and have a nifty pet to take back home. There'd always been those tourists who wanted to "bag" a hexapuma, a peak bear, or some other sample of Sphinx's oversized wildlife, as well. Happily, the majority of the wilderness tourists were content with less dramatic goals: taking images of condor owls or of crown oaks in full autumn foliage, or viewing the magnificent vistas of Megana Canyon or Mikal Falls.

There were still plenty of ways people could come to grief in the bush, however, and the overworked and under-manned SFS rangers couldn't be everywhere at once. That was where the tourist escort program came in. The guides received a modest stipend for showing tourists the sights, answering questions, and forwarding special requests to the rangers. They could also help with things like hunting or fishing permits and do a preliminary review of "new species" tourists were certain they'd discovered. And, in the wake of the Bolgeo incident—and the *Whitaker* incident, for that matter—they kept an eye out for potential poachers and for those visitors stupid enough to try to "pet the hexapuma," as Frank Lethbridge put it.

And there would *always* be someone stupid enough to try to pet the hexapuma.

Or feed the swamp siren, Anders thought now with a mental chuckle. Although, he admitted, it hadn't seemed quite so funny at the time.

Actually, he was glad the guides program had been established. It kept Sphinx's visitors from coming to grief, and the pay provided a little extra pocket change for Chet and Christine. Jessica wasn't an official part of the program, but Dr. Whitaker had arranged for her to receive a retainer from the Urako University for assisting his expedition and making her own—and Valiant's—expertise

available to him on request. She'd argued against accepting it, initially, but Dr. Whitaker had convinced her to
agree, pointing out that the time she spent as his expedition's liaison with the treecats was time she couldn't
spend doing anything else. That was certainly true, and
Anders was glad his dad had thought of it, although he
did wonder sometimes if part of Dr. Whitaker's generosity
wasn't intended to give the Whitaker team rather than
the newcomers first call on her time. Either way, though,
it had created a welcome increase in the Pheriss family's
income stream. Jessica didn't talk about that much, but
Anders knew, and he was happy for her.

At the moment, the four young people stood toward
the back of the group which had come to greet the new
arrivals. Dr. Whitaker and Dr. Nez were up front to
represent the Whitaker expedition. Probably Dr. Emberly
should have been there, too, but Dr. Whitaker had insisted
that work go on at the site.

Chief Ranger Shelton was present to represent the SFS,
accompanied by Ainsley Jedrusinski, who'd been assigned
as direct liaison between the new arrivals and the SFS.
There were various other people Anders didn't know,
including the woman from the tourist office and a small
cluster of people who he guessed had something to do
with the Manticoran foundation which had arranged to
have VIP treatment extended.

The first person off the shuttle was Dr. Sonura Hobbard of Landing University. She was an old friend and
member of the unofficial "friends of treecats" group.
Following her came a pert woman with tanned skin and
obviously artificially red hair. She had a large button nose
that gave her face a rather clownish look, but her dark
eyes seemed to see everything.

"Dr. Cleonora Radzinsky," Christine murmured without glancing at her uni-link. "Specialist in nonhuman

intelligence, but obviously humanocentric in her analysis criteria."

Next came a very tall, very thin man. His pale gray hair was bristle cut, an unfortunate choice in Anders' opinion, given the way it emphasized just how much his ears stood out. He was carrying a bag in long, big-knuckled hands. Something in his manner dared anyone to touch it without his express permission.

"That has to be Dr. Hidalgo," Chet said. "I bet he and your dad are going to have some good arguments, Anders."

Anders nodded, but his gaze was fixed on the man who'd followed Dr. Hidalgo out of the shuttle. Dr. Russell Darrolyn was short and rounded, as if offering a direct contrast to the man in front of him. His hair was the defiant monotone brown of a bad dye-job, and his body language was lively and animated. Alone among the three senior members of the group, he was smiling widely as he debarked.

Each of these senior members had emerged from the shuttle in single file, as neatly spaced as if they were actors taking their places on stage. As soon as Dr. Darrolyn was clear, the remaining passengers came out in the more usual haphazard fashion. Occasionally, one or another would go over to join the group centered around Dr. Hobbard and Dr. Whitaker, but the shuttle held its usual quota of business travelers, families home for visits, and the like.

One of these days, I'll be waiting for Stephanie to come out, Anders thought. *But not for at least two more months...*

Eventually, the young people were motioned over to join the group. Needless to say, Jessica and Valiant attracted considerable attention right off.

Jessica handled the babble of questions with grace, becoming a trifle tart only when one of the assistants gushed, "Oh! He looks so soft! Can I pat him?"

"Only if he can pat you," Jessica snapped. "Seriously. Would you pat a chow-wolv when you first met it?"

Chow-wolvs were native to Trebuchet where, Anders knew, Jessica had spent several years. They were also about the same size as treecats and equally fluffy.

The assistant blinked. "No! They're known to be vicious."

"Well," Jessica said, "treecats aren't vicious. However, it's always a good idea to let any animal—even when it's an herbivore—get to know you before you assume it's pattable. There are quite a few animals here on Sphinx that would cheerfully take your arm off if they got the opportunity."

The assistant—one Gretta Grendelson—scowled. "I *did* ask."

Valiant patted Jessica gently on one cheek, then elongated himself from his position on her shoulder so he could sniff at Ms. Grendelson's fingers. He bleeked and gave the woman's hair a tug.

Ms. Grendelson squealed but didn't seem unduly upset—in fact, she seemed delighted.

Dr. Radzinsky chuckled. "Well, now you've been patted by a treecat, Greta. That's one for the records."

She turned to the woman from tourism. "It's very kind of all of you to come welcome us, but I think we'd like to go to our hotel. We're staying in Yawata Crossing for the first few days, but I believe we'll then relocate to Twin Forks to be closer to Dr. Whitaker's group."

"That sounds perfectly reasonable to me, Dr. Radzinsky. Please, come this way." The woman from tourism motioned to Chet and Christine. "Come with us, if you would."

The groups started breaking up. Anders looked at Jessica, then twitched his head after the departing new arrivals.

"Are you going with them?"

Jessica was frowning. "No. I don't think so. . . . I could, but I'm not needed for this stage. Later, when they do some of the longer landscape tours, I may go along. That's what I was planning on, anyway. But now I'm not sure that's such a good idea."

They'd turned and started walking to where the air cars were parked.

"Why not?" Anders asked, and Jessica blinked as if she'd only then really become aware of him.

"I'm sorry, Anders. You need a lift?"

Anders shrugged. "I can ride with Dad and Dr. Nez, but they'll probably want to talk about the new arrivals. I'd just as soon skip that."

"I can give you a ride back to Twin Forks."

"If I wouldn't be in the way..."

Jessica shook her head. "No. I'd be glad to have you."

Anders commed his dad, then they went along to Jessica's faithful junker. Once they were aloft, Anders noticed the frown hadn't left her face.

"What's wrong, Jess? I thought you were eager to be part of all of this." *And,* he added silently, *that you could really use the money.*

"I was," Jessica admitted. "But Valiant...I'm not as good as Stephanie at filtering my reaction to his reactions... or at figuring out just what he's reacting *to,* especially in a crowd like that."

Anders shrugged. "You haven't had as much chance to practice. So what about Valiant?"

"He didn't like someone there—maybe several some-ones. My feeling is that he'd prefer to avoid at least some of them."

"What didn't he like? Being patted?"

"No. Despite my getting cranky, I think he liked that idiot Greta. He's actually really good about patting. He even lets my little sisters comb him almost every night. Tiddles even put a bow around his neck yesterday, and he was nobly patient—although he took it off as soon as she fell asleep. No, it was more than that."

She piloted in silence for a while, then sighed. "I suppose what I should do is spend more time with them so Valiant can isolate whoever it is he doesn't like, but 'cats aren't like us. Because of the telempathy, I think it's sort of uncomfortable—almost painful—for them to be around someone they don't like."

"I remember Steph told me Lionheart would snarl and hiss when he sensed Bolgeo."

"Right. Not that there's any reason to think we have another Bolgeo here. I suspect there are many types of people Valiant wouldn't like—the hyper-ambitious or manipulative sorts, y'know?"

"I think I do. You realize that group's going to have a lot of that kind of personality? You've met my dad, so you know the type. Scientists working on the cutting edge of any field tend to be really competitive. Why not take it day by day?"

Jessica nodded. "That's what I'll do. Hey, thanks for listening."

"Any time." Anders grinned. "Any time at all."

"So always remember that the most important thing whenever you first approach a potential crime scene," Dr. Flouret said, standing in the middle of the holographic projection, "is to disturb *nothing*. The instant you begin interacting with evidence, you begin altering it."

The broad shouldered, blond-haired professor regarded his students sternly. He reminded Stephanie of a character she'd seen in an old HD which had been set in what its producers had fondly imagined Old Earth must have been like before the Diaspora. That character had been a professor, too, and he'd worn something called "glasses" to correct some sort of vision problem. He'd worn them low on his nose so that he could peer over their tops at his students, and she was pretty sure Dr. Flouret would have done exactly the same thing. But even if he was inclined to be a bit fussy, he was also one of the smartest people she'd ever met.

He was an old friend of Dr. Hobbard's, too, although Stephanie and Karl had been very careful to avoid even appearing to impose upon that friendship. Dr. Hobbard had told them they could turn to Dr. Flouret in case they had any serious problems, but neither of them was going to draw on what Karl had dubbed their "emergency hatch key" unless they really needed it. Not when it could have repercussions for Dr. Hobbard. Or for Dr. Flouret, for that matter.

They'd spent the last couple of weeks studying the theory of criminal forensics and the tools—from DNA sniffers to old-fashioned meter sticks—available to the criminal investigator. There were more of those than Stephanie had ever realized, but Dr. Flouret had emphasized over and over again that the most important tools of all were the human eye and the human brain behind it. All of the detection and measuring devices in the universe were useless, he pointed out, unless someone was able to combine their output into an *accurate* reconstruction of what had happened. This was the first time they'd examined an actual "crime scene" (or its holographic reproduction, at least), however, and Stephanie cautioned herself sternly against her normal tendency to rush in and take charge. She'd been working on developing what her mother called "more mature interpersonal skills," and she'd discovered that several of the students who were older than she was resented the way she tended to charge ahead when something caught her interest.

"Bleek!" someone said in her ear, and that same someone's whiskers tickled her cheek. One of the things Stephanie absolutely loved about Dr. Flouret was that, unlike any of their other professors here at the university, he actively encouraged her to bring Lionheart to class. She wasn't sure if that was as a favor to his friend Dr. Hobbard or because of his own fascination with treecats, but she deeply appreciated his attitude. And it was another reason she wasn't going to charge brashly forward and step on other people's toes—not when she was already receiving "special privileges" by being allowed to bring her "pet" to class with her!

"Evidence must be collected so that it can be properly assessed and analyzed," the professor continued. "And it must be collected and recorded in ways which can be reliably reproduced, not simply in the lab, but when the investigator's conclusions are presented in an evidentiary format in court, as well. If an investigator is to present evidence convincingly, he must not only be certain of his own conclusions but be able to reproduce that evidence, to demonstrate the *basis* for his conclusions reliably, accurately, and in a fashion which educates the layman. All of those things are critical portions of what a forensic criminologist is and does, but it's your responsibility to be as certain as humanly possible that the evidence you collect is accurate, honest, and unaltered. It's your job to form *conclusions*, not to pass judgment, and you have a moral responsibility as well as a legal obligation to do so as impartially as you possibly can. So before you pass your sniffer over the first piece of evidence, before you take your first step into the crime scene, record every aspect of it from as many perspectives as possible in as much detail as possible. Know where every single piece of evidence comes from. Be able to place it in a detailed computer model of the scene, and be certain before you disturb *any* of it that at a later date you'll be able to know and to demonstrate its physical relationship and proximity to every other piece of evidence you may examine."

His expression and his tone were very serious, and

heads nodded among the students seated in the lecture hall around the holographic stage. He gazed at them for several seconds, looking over the tops of those "glasses" he wasn't wearing, then nodded.

"Very well," he said, and glanced down at the "dead body" at his feet. "This is a re-creation of an actual crime scene. For obvious reasons, I'm not going to tell you what really happened here, or when, or even where. After all—" he raised his eyes, darting another look at the class, and Stephanie had the oddest sensation that he was looking directly at *her* "—we wouldn't want any of you looking the case up to find out what the *courts* decided had happened."

A chorus of student chuckles answered him, and he smiled.

"Now, Ms. Harrington," he invited. "Suppose you join me here and give us all the benefit of your insightful observations."

✧   ✧   ✧

"I feel like an idiot," Stephanie groused to Karl as they headed across the quadrangle towards their dormitory. "I should've realized that wasn't blood!"

"Oh, I don't know," Karl said judiciously, with something which looked suspiciously like a grin. "It looked like blood to *me*."

"Well, it wasn't," Stephanie replied in a withering tone. She really, really didn't like making public mistakes.

"Seriously, Steph," Karl said, his grin fading, "he was making a point. All of us have a tendency to jump to conclusions, especially when the evidence seems so clear. I don't think anyone else in the class questioned whether or not it was blood, either. That was the whole point."

"Well, I wish he'd chosen someone else to make it," she said feelingly.

"I guess I can understand that. But I kinda think he was killing two birds with one stone, Steph."

"Oh, yeah?" She knew she sounded sour.

"Yeah. I know you've been sort of hanging back in class to keep from getting up the noses of some of the other students, but you and Lionheart can't really *hide*, whatever you do, you know. I think it was his way of making the point that anyone can make a mistake . . . and of letting *you* be the one to make it this time. *Some* of 'em are going to take it as proof you're not as hot a hotshot as they think you think you are, but most of the others're going to sympathize with you. Might just help out in the long run, you know."

Stephanie regarded him skeptically, but once she thought about it for a few moments, she had to admit he might have a point. Not that it made her feel a lot better about jumping to conclusions like that. Still, it *was* something to think about.

A few days after the Radzinsky group arrived, a formal meet-and-greet was held so that the visitors could be introduced to various important residents of the planet. Anders went as part of his dad's expedition. Jessica and Valiant were there, as well, as were Chet and Christine. The "Double Cs" had tamed their flamboyant hairstyles in honor of their new job and looked very mature in their new guide uniforms.

The meet-and-greet was about as much fun as Anders had always found such events—that is, not much fun at all, unless you happened to be an enthusiast on the particular reason for the gathering. Anders was interested in treecats, but not so much in the fine points of anthropology which were under discussion. Still, between his parents' different jobs, he'd had a lot of experience with such events.

Jessica, on the other hand, was clearly overwhelmed. Valiant—hand-feet on her shoulder, true-feet on a support built into the back of her dress—stared at the humans clustered around, his green eyes wide with what might be the beginnings of panic.

Anders hurried over to Jessica's side, making his way through the little crowd of onlookers who'd gathered to get a better look at a real, live treecat. Dr. Darrolyn, the linguistics expert, was asking Jessica questions. For all that his smile was warm and affable, there was something hammering about how he fired them off.

"So, is Valiant communicating with you this moment?"

"I can feel a bit of what he's feeling," Jessica admitted.

"And that is?"

"Well, there are a lot of people here. I think he's a bit overwhelmed."

"But you have a large family, don't you? Two adults, six children? Certainly Valiant is used to crowds?"

"He *knows* my family—" Jessica began.

"But the treecat must know a fair number of the people here?" Dr. Darrolyn cut her off.

"He's met Dr. Whitaker's group, yes, but he doesn't really know them well. And most of the rest of you are complete strangers."

"Are you certain you're not projecting your own apprehensions on the animal?"

Jessica stared at the linguist in shock. "Are you saying I'm lying?"

Dr. Darrolyn smiled condescendingly, and his words took on a lecturing tone. "I'm saying that—in my field—we've learned that humans often project their own emotional landscape onto their animal companions. A man sees his dog wagging his tail and looking eager. He thinks, 'My dog is happy to see me.' This may be so, but only because the dog associates the man with food or outings. So what the man interprets as affection may only be a hope for some service the man supplies the dog."

Jessica's eyes narrowed. "I am not projecting my reactions onto Valiant. I really can feel what he feels. He doesn't—"

She cut herself off, but Anders could guess that what she'd been about to say was something like, "And he doesn't like you at all." From the flicker in Dr. Darrolyn's expression, he guessed the linguist had figured it out too.

Anders inserted himself into the conversation. "Jessica, I hate to interrupt, but Dr. Emberly was wondering if you could spare her a moment."

He'd checked, and Calida Emberly was just visible on the far side of the room, talking quietly with her mother, who appeared to be sketching.

"Sure," Jessica said. She bobbed her head politely to Dr. Darrolyn. "If you'll excuse me."

"I look forward to talking with you further," Dr. Darrolyn said.

Valiant's "bleek" could have meant anything.

"Thanks for rescuing me from those x-a's," Jessica said under cover of the room's general noise level as they walked away.

"X-a's?"

"Xenoanthropologists." Jessica laughed. "It's too much of a mouthful to say all the time."

"I like it," Anders said. "It sounds vaguely like a curse, which is about how I feel about the whole profession right now."

"Me, too. Valiant, three. I'll tell you more later."

As they approached Dr. Emberly, Anders said, "I brought Jessica and Valiant over like you asked."

Calida Emberly was not a pretty woman—in fact, she was actually pretty stern looking—but she had an enthusiasm for her profession and life in general that could make her almost beautiful. Now she extended a hand to Jessica and then to Valiant.

"I did, did I? Will that was very clever of me. Was Dr. Darrolyn getting intense?"

"That's an understatement," Jessica agreed. "You don't seem surprised."

"I'm not. They haven't been here even three full days, and Darrolyn's already had Kesia on the verge of tears. Radzinsky and your father are barely speaking, and Hidalgo has accused the SFS of corrupting a potentially sentient species."

"Kesia in tears?" Anders was appalled. He remembered how staunchly Kesia Guyen had stood up to his father when they'd been stranded. "I didn't think that was possible."

"Well, he all but promised to message the review board at our university saying she should be denied her doctorate on the grounds that she's fallen into superstitious thinking rather than good science."

"What a blackhole!" Jessica said. "I can see we're going to have a lot of fun while *they're* here."

"Don't worry," Anders said. "You volunteered to help them out, so you can un-volunteer." He smiled suddenly. "From what Dr. Emberly says, I'm sure it wouldn't break Dad's heart to find something else for you to do! The ones I feel sorry for are Chet and Christine. They're not going to be able to duck out."

"And to think I was disappointed that I didn't have time to take enough of classes to qualify as a guide," Jessica replied. "For today, though, I'm going to do my best. Time to march back into the fray. Thanks again, Anders, for getting me a breather."

"Let me come with you," he suggested.

Did Jessica blush? He couldn't be sure.

"No. I need to be at least as tough as Stephanie," she said. "She dealt with a lot of this sort of thing when she wasn't much more than twelve."

Dacey Emberly held up her sketch pad and showed them the quick drawing of Valiant she'd done. "There. That will justify your stop here. Jessica, you might consider taking Anders up on his offer if you need to do one-on-one interviews. He isn't an anthropologist, but he knows the jargon. They can't really send him off the way they could Chet or Christine without insulting his father, either."

"I'll think about it," Jessica promised. She gave them a lazy wave and moved off into the throng.

Anders watched her go.

"You know," he said to no one in particular, "in her own way, Jessica's just as brave as Stephanie. I wonder why she doesn't realize it?"

Dirt Grubber made certain Windswept was solidly asleep before he slipped outside to spend some time with his plants. If she awoke, she would know he was close, but he doubted she would. The day's events had been enough to overwhelm even a tough youngling like her.

Once outside, Dirt Grubber reveled in the night's coolness. The two-legs were now using some kind of heating thing to make the inside of their stone lair nearly as warm as summer. He supposed such devices were a good idea for two-legs, since they possessed no fur worth speaking of, but for a Person who was developing the beginnings of what would be a nice, thick winter coat, the interior heat could be a bit oppressive.

As he checked over his plants, patting the soil a bit higher to protect the stem of this one, nipping new growth off that one so the plant would not waste energy on leaves that would certainly be ruined by frost, Dirt Grubber sorted through his impressions of the large gathering to which Windswept had taken him that evening.

From the excitement and apprehension that had colored her mind-glow, he had known this was an important event. Therefore, although his immediate reaction to the crowded space had been to depart as soon as possible, he had given his two-leg his fullest support. It had not taken long for him to realize that he was the focus of a great deal of attention. When he considered who was present, this seemed reasonable.

Old Authority was there, along with several of his clan. Also present was Garbage Collector, as the People now called the father of Bleached Fur. This title was in memory of how Garbage Collector had gathered up the People's leavings and stood guard over them, even in the face of a hungry whistling sucker. Garbage Collector had brought his clan, as well, and Dirt Grubber had been particularly pleased to see Plant Woman and Eye of Memory, whose mind-glows he had found to be very compatible with his own.

Then there was the group he had seen arrive on a flying thing similar to that which had taken Climbs Quickly, Death Fang's Bane, and Shadowed Sunlight away. Many of these came and spoke with Windswept. He noticed she was careful to be very polite with them, but this was not the politeness of respect but that of being guarded.

Dirt Grubber could not read the mind-glows of all two-legs as easily as he could that of Windswept, but he would need to be far stupider than he was not to realize that one thing many of these two-legs had in common was an intense interest in the People. He had become accustomed to having two-legs stare at him when he went somewhere with Windswept. He had learned to be polite about the attention and, in turn, most of the two-legs were relatively good about keeping their distance. Tonight, however, was different. There was an intensity in the mind-glows of almost everyone who came near, as if—if they were given the opportunity—they would have counted his fingers and toes, checked the depth of his fur, fingered his ears.

That was uncomfortable. It was nothing, however, compared to the cold, hard assessment he had felt from a few. Reaching into his memory, Dirt Grubber compared what he was feeling to what Climbs Quickly had told him about his encounter with Speaks Falsely. There were some similarities, but the mind-glows were not the same. Speaks Falsely's mind-glow had been colored by a willingness to do harm. Dirt Grubber had not felt that sort of willingness from any he had encountered that evening. But what some of these did have in common with Speaks Falsely was a sense that they were holding back, calculating. Pretending to have one interest when what they really wanted was something else.

People did not speak falsely. They could withhold information, but they did not say or think things they knew were not true, nor could one Person deceive another about what he truly desired. Two-legs *could* deceive one another, but it was hard for Dirt Grubber to wrap his mind around such twisted thinking.

He was also aware that he had not spent time with all the two-legs present. Windswept had spoken mostly with those who had first initiated contact. He had sensed a few malicious breezes from the minds of some who had kept their distance, but that was not unusual. He already knew that not all two-legs liked the People. Sometimes what he tasted from them almost felt like tension over territory or a particularly succulent bit of food. He thought they saw the People as competition.

Reluctantly, Dirt Grubber decided he must do his best to learn more about these new arrivals. From Windswept's mind-glow, he could tell she expected to meet them again. For the good of the People, Dirt Grubber must try to make the most of those encounters.

9

THE MORNING AFTER THE MEET-AND-GREET, ANDERS felt tense. He might not be a treecat, but he was enough his politician mother's son to feel uneasy about the hidden agendas he'd sensed the night before.

Sure, he'd expected some tension. However chastened his dad might be, he was still as protective of his permit as the mother of a newborn baby. What Anders hadn't expected was how, well, political Dr. Radzinsky had been. He'd overheard her talking with Chief Ranger Shelton. From her questions, it was apparent that she had far more knowledge than he would have expected from an off-worlder about the implications treecat sentience could have for Sphinxian land ownership.

He didn't want to make Stephanie edgy. Her messages were full of how demanding she was finding her classes. He didn't doubt that she was doing great—Stephanie really was as smart as everyone thought she was—but she was working harder for those perfect grades than she ever had before. And she was *so* hard on herself when she did mess up. Weeks later, she was still beating herself up over some minor gaffe in forensics class.

Still, he had to let her know something was rotten on the planet Sphinx, so he gave her a quick summary. Then he went on:

"I let Christine and Chet know I thought Radzinsky, at least, has an agenda, and they're planning to keep a special eye on her—including making notes of those times when she wants them out of the way. Meanwhile, Jess will see how many of the x-a's we can meet in small groups. She thinks Valiant will be able to get a better read on them that way. I think it will be interesting to see just who *doesn't* want to spend time in a small group with a treecat, too.

"Listen, Steph. I'd really like to keep an eye on Jess and Valiant. I've got this idea, though, that she thinks she'd be imposing. Could you message her, tell her it would be good to have me along? I know what my dad is capable of and—hard as it may be for you to believe—he's actually really ethical. He'd never cook his data or anything. I'm not so sure about some of the others.

"I'll cover things here for you. You study hard. That's why I let you out of my reach, right? Say, hi to Karl and tell Lionheart I'm saving part of my allowance to buy him a bouquet of celery when he gets back."

He mimed giving her a big hug. "Miss you!"

Climbs Quickly stretched out along the smooth, rocky shelf outside the nesting place they had given Death Fang's Bane and panted quietly. The sun was unnaturally hot, burning down out of a sky which wasn't quite the right shade of blue, and he found himself wishing he had had some warning about just how warm this new place, this new world, was going to be. At least Death Fang's Bane's nesting place's window faced toward sun-rising, so the bulk of the structure threw a welcome patch of shade over this shelf each afternoon. For that matter, things in general had improved since he'd started shedding, and he could always retreat to the coolness of Death Fang's Bane's sleeping place. But it was still hotter here—even in the shade—than any of the people could ever have anticipated.

He disliked being separated from his two-leg so much of the time. She did not like it either; he could tell that from her mind-glow, even when she was far away. She had made it clear enough that she had no choice, however, and Climbs Quickly had learned more than enough about how the two-legs' clans worked to understand that neither Death Fang's Bane nor her parents could always arrange things the way they might wish to. The two-legs' elders clearly had a great deal to say about how all two-legs lived their lives, and he had discovered that Sings Truly's warning that it was important for the People to understand how these strange creatures thought had been even better taken than he had thought at the time.

Still, it would help me to understand them better if I could accompany Death Fang's Bane more places, he reflected, flattening even closer to the cool, shaded shelf. *It helps that she is so happy to be learning so many things—it is like watching a kitten scamper down a ground runner's burrow! Yet I know she misses Bleached Fur, and she feels guilty about leaving me so much to my own devices.*

He treated himself to a quiet mental laugh at that thought, for he was confident few of the older two-legs realized what sorts of opportunities this nesting place offered to one of the People. Death Fang's Bane did, although she had done her very best to warn him about being careless. It had amused him, for even though their inability to communicate clearly with one another remained frustrating, she had reminded him irresistibly of old Broken Foot, the half-crippled scout who had been entrusted with teaching Climbs Quickly and his fellow kittens about the perils of the world. Of course, that had been more hands of turnings ago than Climbs Quickly really cared to think about, but the message had been clear enough. And so had the fact that Death Fang's Bane had been fairly sure she was not supposed to be encouraging him to roam.

It was a long way from this ledge to the nearest of the strange trees growing in this place, but not so far that a healthy scout could not make the leap between them, especially when he seemed to weigh so much less than he was accustomed to. And even though he knew Death Fang's Bane worried about him whenever he was out on his own, she also understood that he was a scout of the People. She might not like it, and he had sensed her concern about the sorts of trouble he might find to get into in this world which was so different from his own, but she had not attempted to lock him up here in her nesting place. Instead, she had trusted him *not* to get into trouble and he had not. For all his sister's and Broken Tooth's lectures about impetuosity, he was not *really* heedless enough to take foolish chances. So his explorations had been cautious, largely under cover of night, and more for his own amusement and to defeat boredom than anything else, when he came down to it.

Now he rolled back over, ears twitching as he sensed Death Fang's Bane's mind-glow coming back towards her nesting place. Her mind was already reaching out to him, despite the fact that she had no idea what she was doing or how, and the inner warmth of that touch flowed through him like a welcome sigh of wind creeping delicately through the leaves of Bright Water's central nesting place.

✦   ✦   ✦

Anders didn't know exactly what Stephanie said to convince Jessica, but about a week after the meet-and-greet, after she'd brought Valiant along to solemnly consider the Whitaker expedition's latest collection of treecat artifacts, she asked him if he'd go with her the next day when she had a private interview with Dr. Hidalgo.

"I'd really appreciate your coming," Jessica said as he walked back to her air car with her. "He's the one whose area of specialization is like your dad's right? Would he mind? And should I get his permission first—because of the retainer, and everything?"

"You mean, would Dad think I was consorting with the enemy or something?" Anders laughed. "Not really. He'd probably be grateful, actually—give him an idea of how the other side is thinking. And that retainer's really just to reimburse you for the time you're spending helping him out. It doesn't mean you can't help anyone *else*, you know."

Although, he reflected, knowing his dad as he did, Dr. Whitaker wouldn't object if Jessica *thought* it did.

"Great! Thanks. I'm a little nervous. This is going to be my first interview with one of the big guns."

"You're kidding! I thought you'd had a bunch of meetings already."

"I've had a couple," Jessica admitted, "but they've been with some of the assistants. That Gretta Grendelson—the one who wanted to pet Valiant at the shuttleport—we've had a couple of meetings, but she's more a biologist than an anthropologist. She's really interested in things like the treecats' tails—how they are prehensile and how the gripping surface is designed."

"Did Valiant like being poked?"

"Actually, he was pretty good about it. I got the feeling he's neutral about Gretta."

Anders frowned. "That sounds sort of like you've met with someone you don't think he's neutral about."

"You sound," Jessica giggled, "like an anthropologist. You're right, though.... One time Gretta brought along one of Dr. Radzinsky's other assistants—a man named Duff DeWitt."

Anders searched his memory. "I think I've talked with him. Good-looking guy, blond hair, looks like he lifts weights?"

Did Jessica blush?

"That's him. He had lots of questions about treecat behavior."

"You said you thought Valiant didn't like him."

Yes, she *was* blushing.

"Well, yeah...Mr. DeWitt is...I mean, he likes... He's sort of a flirt. Gretta thought it was great, but how he talked made me uncomfortable."

Anders snorted. "You're really pretty, Jessica. It doesn't seem strange to me that he'd flirt with you."

Jessica rolled her eyes. "It was more than that. He was the sort that made me feel like he flirted by reflex. He knows he's good looking, so he sees where that might get him."

"And you think Valiant didn't like that."

"I think it's as good an explanation as any as to why Valiant was obviously uneasy with him. I messaged Stephanie, and she agreed the treecats don't seem to like insincerity."

"Neither does Stephanie." Anders laughed. "Anyhow, I'd be glad to go with you when you meet with Dr. Hidalgo. When is your appointment?"

"Is tomorrow too soon?"

Anders shook his head. "What time?"

"Mid-morning," Jessica replied as they reached her parked air car. "We're supposed to meet in one of the conference rooms at their hotel. Do you need a lift?"

"I wouldn't mind," Anders said. "The expedition's air

car's been a lot more in demand since the x-a's got here and not everyone is going out to the site every day."

"Great! See you then!"

Anders was right in his prediction that Dr. Whitaker would approve of his son going along for the meeting with Dr. Hidalgo.

"He's very good," was the reluctant admission. "He really appreciated my artifact collection. In fact, I think he's the closest of the three senior members of the group to coming around to accepting that the treecats should be placed somewhere on the sentience scale."

"Somewhere? Human somewhere?"

"Oh, probably not." Dr. Whitaker waved a dismissive hand. "I'd like to see what conclusions you reach about him."

"So you're not going to contaminate the sample further." Anders laughed. "Okay, Dad. I'll let you know what I think."

The next morning when Jessica picked him up, he asked, "Does Dr. Hidalgo know I'm coming along?"

"Yep. I told him I might need a translator who spoke anthropologist."

"And he didn't have any problems?"

"Not that I could see. Actually, he said some good things about your dad's collections."

Dr. Hidalgo had folded his long, thin length down into a chair at one end of the conference room, but he unfolded himself as soon as they entered. "Good morning and thank you both for coming, it's—" He stopped, shook his head, and corrected himself. "Thank you *all* for coming."

Anders wondered who'd been omitted in that first greeting—himself or Valiant—but he didn't think asking would be polite.

Dr. Hidalgo continued, this time addressing Jessica in particular. "I believe Valiant is a gardener. Would he be more comfortable if we went outside for our meeting? This complex has some very nice gardens, and they're just about empty this time of day."

Jessica beamed at him. "He'd like that. Besides, I think he finds indoor heating a little uncomfortable this time of year. His coat's been thickening since the nights started getting cooler."

"And how do you cope with that?" Dr. Hidalgo asked as he waved toward a door that led out into the promised gardens.

"Well, he always has the freedom to go outside, and I keep my own room cooler. I don't mind wearing a sweater. My family got here in summer, so I haven't actually lived through the winter, but I've heard a lot from my friends. I think Valiant's going to need as dense a coat as possible when the snows fly."

"Very thoughtful." Dr. Hidalgo nodded approval.

Anders thought though that the x-a had arrived at a slightly different conclusion than his words might lead one to imagine. He glanced at Valiant, trying to see with the treecat was thinking, but Valiant was busy stretching up from his perch on Jessica's shoulder so that he could inspect a vine that had been trained along a nearby trellis.

Dr. Hidalgo's questions followed a predictable pattern. He asked about Valiant's carry net and whether he had made it himself. He asked about the other tools Valiant used, and how easily he adapted to human technology— both those things he could employ himself, like the sample bags, and those things he used indirectly, such as riding in an air car.

Eventually, they arrived at a neat little gazebo, furnished with tables and benches. When they settled there, Dr. Hidalgo asked Jessica if Valiant would mind showing off some of his basic skills, like tying knots or handling various tools. The swiftness with which Valiant agreed told Anders even without the "thumbs up" Jessica gave him that the treecat found nothing threatening about this particular member of the x-a group.

Jessica obviously liked Dr. Hidalgo, too. Anders had to admit that there was something charming about the way he'd tug at one of his jug-handle ears and murmur, "Amazing!" or "It's different to see it in person rather than recorded." He always asked for permission before recording a particular action, too, never simply assuming that permission previously given flowed over to the next.

When they'd been in the gazebo a while, Dr. Hidalgo announced, "I think we all deserve a break. Shall I call and order some refreshments? Perhaps lunch?"

They agreed and not long after, as they sat munching on sandwiches piled high on thick-cut bread, Jessica asked, "So, off the record, what do you think of treecats?"

Dr. Hidalgo stopped disassembling his sandwich and considered. "Off the record?"

Jessica held up her uni-link as if to show she wasn't recording.

"Very well." Dr. Hidalgo slowly rolled a slice of roast capri-cow and considered. "I think that there's no doubt that the treecats will place somewhere on the sentience scale. They're tool-users and tool-makers. They also show a desire for more tools to fill their basic needs. Some of the potsherds and fragments of gourds Dr. Whitaker's collected show definite ornamentation. It's not elaborate, true, but it serves no other function than a desire for, if not beauty, then at least differentiation."

"And that raises them up the sentience scale?" Jessica asked.

"Especially at this primitive level," Dr. Hidalgo agreed. "Watching Valiant has been very interesting. I chose these gardens because they contain plants that are purely orna-mental as well as some that are both ornamental and edible. While Valiant shows a preference for those that are edible, he doesn't seem to be immune to beauty.

"Of course," he added, sounding embarrassed, "some of my colleagues would say I'm being subjective."

"How do the others in your group feel about the tree-cats?" Anders asked.

"They're proving more difficult to convince," Dr. Hidalgo said sadly. "I indicate the artifacts, and Dr. Radzinsky counters with examples of other creatures that make tools or elaborate dens. I mention the ornamentation, and Dr. Darrolyn asks if I see any evidence of written language—or even spoken language."

He sighed, tore a small square of bread from his sand-wich, squashed it into a pill, and swallowed it. "Then there's the problem that we're dealing with contaminated samples."

"Contaminated?" Jessica asked.

For reply, Dr. Hidalgo pointed to where Valiant was carefully sliding some seeds into one of the sample bags.

"Where once there was a potentially pristine culture," he said, "we now have one irrevocably contaminated by its contact with humans. I'm not blaming you, young lady. The SFS gave tools to treecats before you ever set foot on this planet. However, once the damage is done, it becomes more difficult to judge just how intelligent a species is. Take Valiant's interest in gardening. There's some evidence the treecats observed humans practicing agriculture and decided to imitate. That's quite different from evolving the skill on their own."

Jessica looked uncomfortable as Dr. Hidalgo went on.

"I, personally, would like to see two things. First, I'd like to see the treecats recognized as sentient. Then I would like to see some effort made to protect them in their uncontaminated state. Populations that haven't had human contact should be kept *from* human contact. Populations that have had human contact—for example, the clans from which Valiant and Lionheart originated—should be relocated to areas where they can practice their indigenous lifestyles in a manner uncontaminated by human influence. Only in this way can they evolve into the people they were meant to be. Otherwise, they'll become poor imitations of humanity."

"You must be joking!" Jessica exclaimed. "Treecats are treecats. They could never become humans."

"Precisely," Dr. Hidalgo said. He pulled at one ear lobe and smiled sadly. "Earlier you mentioned the care you'd taken to make sure Valiant developed his thick winter coat. However, if something happened to interfere, would you let him freeze?"

"Never!"

"So you'd either keep him indoors—an unnatural state for a treecat—or you'd provide him with clothing of some sort. Even in Dr. Whitaker's most careful excavations, we've seen no evidence the treecats need clothing other than their natural fur. Therefore, your desire to protect him would introduce an alien element into his life. If treecats do have some form of communication—something I believe is so, although Dr. Darrolyn differs with me—that idea would be spread further."

Jessica looked stunned. It seemed to Anders that she was wilting where she sat. He knew how much care both Jessica and Stephanie took to make sure that their treecat partners visited not only with each other, but with their clans. What would happen if treecats were isolated on reservations for their own good? Would those treecats who had adopted humans become exiles?

Valiant set aside his sample bag and bleeked softly. Then he loped over to Jessica and snuggled his furry head into the wild mass of her hair. However, he neither snarled nor growled at Dr. Hidalgo, so Anders guessed that the treecat could tell the man meant him no harm.

No harm. Only imprisonment. Only isolation from his own people and those people sealed away in tidy little reservations where they can practice their folkways in peace. Anders swallowed hard. *And you can bet that the lands "given" to treecats wouldn't be the best. They'd be destroyed by the "kindness" of people like Dr. Hidalgo.*

He remembered a section from the book Dr. Nez had given him for his birthday. There'd been an entire chapter on how less advanced cultures had been destroyed by forced assimilation into more advanced ones. But that same chapter had also offered up examples of how often well-intended efforts to *protect* those less advanced cultures had ended up confining, strangling, and ultimately destroying them just as thoroughly as assimilation possibly could have.

"I'm sorry, Anders," Dr. Hidalgo said. "Did you say something?"

"No, sir." Anders tried hard to sound normal. "Just thinking about some of the long-term implications."

"Ah. A natural anthropologist, following in your father's footsteps."

Anders forced himself to grin, but inside he winced. He thought about Stephanie's reports about how Lionheart was shedding. When Stephanie and Lionheart came home, would she put the 'cat in a sweater? He imagined the x-a's reaction, how Hidalgo would be sorrowful about the contamination of culture, how some of the others would certainly sneer.

For the first time since Stephanie had left, he found himself wishing her return could somehow be delayed.

In addition to his usual scouting duties, Keen Eyes went out of his way to patrol along the sun-setting edge of the clan's range where he had sensed Swimmer's Scourge and Nimble Fingers of the Trees Enfolding Clan. Aware that this was a dangerous area, Keen Eyes requested that the other members of the Landless Clan keep back from it. He did not meet with any complaint, for he had shared Swimmer's Scourge's warning with the rest of the clan. Moreover, the loss of their home meant there were tasks enough to keep every set of true-hands and hand-feet busy every waking moment of the day.

Keen Eyes himself hunted when he could, setting traps and snares for small game. He was removing a tree-hopper from one of his snares when a mind-voice spoke.

<Those snares may catch you more than tree-hoppers and bark-chewers, Keen Eyes of the Landless Clan. You might want to move a little farther towards sun-rising.>

Keen Eyes recognized Nimble Fingers of the Trees Enfolding Clan, but when he searched for the other's mind-glow, he did not touch it. He wondered if Nimble Fingers had a mate, for one benefit of such a partnership was that both the mind-voice and ability to detect the mind-glows of others intensified. That would explain why Nimble Fingers could find him while he could find no trace of the other. He suspected Nimble Fingers was at extreme range, but, nonetheless, he took care to dampen his own mind-glow, uncomfortable that someone who was not a clan member or a friend would have such an advantage over him.

He replied politely. *<May I keep my prey, or do you claim it?>*

<Keep it, but when you reset the snare, move it farther to sun-rising. There are those in my clan who fear that your People will seep into our territory as water overflows the banks of a river.>

<And you would dam the spread of that river?>

<Such is the command of the elders of my clan.>

Keen Eyes thought that perhaps Nimble Fingers did

not completely agree. However, the way of the People, as contained in the oldest songs of the memory singers, was that the wisdom of the elders was to be listened to by the younger members. In this way, the entire clan could avoid errors made in the past.

Usually, Keen Eyes had no problem agreeing with this approach. A traditional way of teaching hunting was to let the youngling attempt a hunt or two without coaching. Only after the youngling had gone hungry from a pounce too soon or from not knowing a particular trick of the intended prey did the serious teaching begin, for only then did the youngling realize that there was something to value in past experience.

Lately, however, he had begun to wonder why the elders should have the final say when the problem was one in which they had no genuine experience to guide them. Of course there had been forest fires in the past, but these fires were among the first where the ability of the People to move into new ranges was complicated by the presence of the two-legs.

He heaved a gusty sigh but, as it was his own policy not to challenge the rights of the Trees Enfolding Clan lest they decide the time of toleration was ended, he could not protest.

<*I thank you, Nimble Fingers, for letting me keep my prey. Would you perhaps like to come share it with me?*>

<*That is kind of you, Keen Eyes, but I had better keep my post. Our clan has not suffered as severely as you report your own has, but the mind healers have asked us to do as little as possible to upset our clan's internal harmony—and that means not upsetting the elders.*>

Keen Eyes was very interested. Even the ability to share thoughts did not mean the People were immune to disagreement. When consensus could not be reached, that disagreement could sometimes become intense enough the mind healers stepped in. Healing always involved a certain amount of work on the mind of the victim as well as the body even for purely physical injury—moderating of pain, offering comfort and reassurance. Mind healers, however, specialized in touching actual minds, feeling where they had become twisted from the true and helping them return to understanding that the needs of others were as important as the needs of the individual.

<Your elders are stretched thin?>

Nimble Fingers' reply overflowed with exhaustion. <We lost much of what had been stored up against the winter to a fire on our moss-growing border. We also lost several members of the clan.>

<And suffered injuries no doubt.> Keen Eyes was glad they were communicating only by mind-voice. If Nimble Fingers had been close enough to immerse himself in Keen Eyes' mind-glow there would have been no hiding the bitterness Keen Eyes felt.

<Many injuries. Not so much from the fire itself as from the smoke. It blanketed the forests for a great distance beyond where the fires burned.> The innocent agreement in Nimble Fingers' reply confirmed Keen Eyes' guess that Nimble Fingers could not read his mind-glow. <Several of our wisest elders were killed or disabled. The clan is still trying to sort out who has the most balanced view of how we should deal with our changed situation.>

<There are different opinions, then?>

<Many, from whether we should change our central nesting site to what to do about...>

Nimble Fingers' mind-voice trailed off. On the whole, People were not very good at hiding things. They were simply too accustomed to shared mind-glows. Scouts and memory singers probably had the most teaching in that area, for they were the most likely to deal with People who did not share the same priorities.

Keen Eyes wondered what Nimble Fingers had been about to say. "What to do about the invaders?" Or something more mild, "What to do about those poor refugees?" He considered asking, but decided against it. On the whole, Nimble Fingers had been kind to him and, by extension, to the Landless Clan. Nothing would be gained by challenging him.

Instead, he said, <*Our clan has been relying heavily on our mind healers. We are lucky that although we lost all our memory singers, we did not lose our mind healers.*>

<*You are fortunate. We lost our most senior mind healer, a true wellspring of wisdom about the twisting paths down which the pain of a few strong minds can lead a clan accustomed to following them.*>

That told Keen Eyes quite a lot. If the People of Trees Enfolding were dealing with conflict within their own clan, it explained why the Landless Clan had been kept in their particular limbo, neither welcomed and helped, nor driven away.

<*I am sorry. I hope the healing comes quickly.*>

<*I do as well. This is a bad situation for all of us.*>

His phrasing included the Landless Clan as well, and Keen Eyes was warmed. But Nimble Fingers' next thought reminded him that the danger was far from ended—that, indeed, it intensified with every sun's passing that brought them closer to the need to make a final decision.

<*Swimmer's Scourge comes. He would not like to find me chatting at my post. Remember. Move your snares farther to sun-rising. Remember...*>

Keen Eyes sent back a quick promise that he would, but as he shouldered the carry net with his catch and prepared to lope in the direction of home, he wondered just how long they could obey such warnings. In time, his clan must press to sun-setting...or die.

10

"STEPHANIE! KARL!"

They halted and turned in the direction of the shout. A young man, perhaps five years older than Karl, waved and came towards them, accompanied by a somewhat older, blond-haired, green-eyed woman. Stephanie recognized Allen Harper, one of Dean Charterman's assistants. He was a grad student—in geology, she thought—and he was also from Sphinx, which was why Charterman had assigned him to show her and Karl around campus for their initial orientation. She had no idea who his companion might be, though.

"Are we catching you between classes?" Harper asked as the newcomers reached them, and Karl shook his head.

"We're done till supper," he said. "Just heading back to the dorm to get Lionheart back into the air-conditioning."

"Just Lionheart, eh?" Harper laughed.

"Well, maybe me, too." Karl wiped sweat from his forehead and smiled. "Blame me?"

"I'm from Sphinx, too, remember?" Harper shook his head. "But I am glad I caught you. Dean Charterman asked me to introduce Ms. Adair to you." He indicated the woman beside him. "Stephanie, Karl, this is Gwendolyn Adair. Ms. Adair, Stephanie Harrington and Karl Zivonik."

"I'm so glad to finally meet both of you!" Ms. Adair smiled, holding out her hand first to Karl and then to Stephanie. "I've heard a great deal about you—and about Lionheart, of course." She smiled at the treecat on Stephanie's shoulder. "He's even more impressive looking in person than he is on HD."

Stephanie smiled back, but it was difficult. She'd felt a sharp spasm of something very like wariness the instant Ms. Adair had come within fifty meters, and she knew where it had come from. Now she reached up to touch Lionheart's ears.

"I don't know about impressive looking," she said, "but he's always been pretty impressive to me."

"I imagine so, given the circumstances under which you met." Adair shook her head. "I've been to Sphinx for visits, but I've never met a hexapuma in the wild, and I never *want* to, either."

"It isn't the sort of thing we encourage," Karl acknowledged. "Bad for tourism if too many tourists get eaten, after all."

Adair laughed, and it was Harper's turn to shake his head.

"Karl has what he thinks is a sense of humor, Ms. Adair. Despite that, he's really a very nice guy, once you get to know him."

Karl only smiled unrepentantly.

"At any rate," Harper went on, "the dean wanted me to make sure you three got introduced to one another. Ms. Adair's cousin is the Earl of Adair Hollow, one of the university's more generous donors, and she's been very active in supporting the university herself. She's also one of the directors of the Adair Foundation."

He looked at them expectantly, and Stephanie glanced at Karl to see if he'd recognized the name. She'd done her own research on the Adair Foundation after viewing Anders' and Jessica's accounts of their meetings with the "x-a's," and from everything she'd been able to discover, the foundation was about as respectable and reputable as nonprofit organizations came. Its list of donors and patrons read like a Who's Who of the Manticoran aristocracy— including the King—and it had a distinguished record of aggressively protecting the biodiversity of the Star Kingdom's habitable planets.

She'd felt reassured as she read over its charter and viewed the catalog of its accomplishments. Yet despite that reassurance, she'd still felt...uneasy. She knew she tended to be protective, maybe even overly protective, where the treecats were concerned, but it wasn't like Anders and Jessica to imagine things, especially with Valiant along to keep them straight. If they had their doubts about some of the x-a's, they probably had a reason, and there'd been no information on the foundation's site—or anywhere else in the public record—about how exactly it had decided which visiting xenoanthropologists to sponsor to Sphinx.

The corner of Karl's right eyelid dropped in what might have been the smallest of winks, and Stephanie suppressed a sudden smile. Yes, Karl had recognized the name. In fact, Stephanie was willing to bet he'd guessed who Ms. Adair was associated with the instant Harper had introduced her. That was probably what had prompted his remark about hexapumas and tourists.

"I've heard about the foundation, Ms. Adair," she said. "I've been messaging with a couple of our friends back on Sphinx about the expedition it sponsored."

"Oh, I wish we could take the credit for that," Adair said. She had a melodious contralto voice, and the gleam in those green eyes invited them to laugh with her. "Unfortunately, honesty compels me to admit that we only expedited it. I wish we'd been the ones who thought of it—and a lot sooner than this—but, well—"

She shrugged, her expression wry.

"Sooner than this?" Karl repeated, and Adair nodded.

"We're dedicated to recognizing and protecting biodiversity. It's what we do. Most people aren't that worried about things like that just this moment, given three entire planets that are basically still empty of humans, but the foundation figures it's only a matter of time before humanity starts really extending its footprint here in the Manticore System. We're already doing that on Manticore itself, you know, and it won't be so many more years before the same thing begins happening on Sphinx. You would've thought that an organization worried about things like that would have been on its toes enough to immediately recognize what Stephanie's discovery of the treecats meant—or might mean—for our declared mission, but frankly we were asleep at the switch. *We* should have sponsored a *reputable* xenoanthropologist instead of letting that horrible Bolgeo person slip past us. For that matter, we should have insisted on vetting his credentials better, in which case that whole mess might not have happened.

"But we were too focused on what we were doing here on Manticore, I suppose. And by the time we realized just how bad a choice 'Doctor' Bolgeo had been, the Interior Ministry and Governor Donaldson had written a contract with a reputable, properly credentialed team from Urako. We decided the situation was properly in hand, but then there was that whole incident this past year's fire season. To be honest, we began to feel... concerned over the future of the Whitaker expedition, and until the status of Dr. Whitaker's contract was fully resolved the entire treecat situation was in limbo.

"Frankly, we've let some other people steal a march on us. By the time we started to worry, the Star Kingdom Chamber of Commerce, the Scientific Association of Manticore, the Royal Institute, and at least three or four other private and public organizations had already come to the conclusion that we needed to broaden and deepen the scope of our study of the treecats. In fact, they'd begun raising funds to bring in additional xenoanthropologists before we ever got involved. We're a stakeholder ourselves, of course, but our financial participation is relatively minor. Our biggest real contribution has been to facilitate the arrangements and to work with the university and the Ministry to assist in vetting Dr. Radzinsky's entire team's credentials and background, planning travel arrangements, and, to be honest, opening a few doors for them here in the Star Kingdom and integrating them into a noncompetitive relationship with Dr. Whitaker and *his* team."

"I can only assume you've never met Dr. Whitaker," Karl said dryly. Adair cocked an eyebrow at him, and he shrugged. "He's actually a really nice guy in a lot of ways," he said. "But where academic discovery's concerned, he's about as 'noncompetitive' as a pair of starving hexapumas with a single range bunny."

"Oh, he's not *that* bad, Karl!" Stephanie protested with a laugh, and Adair chuckled appreciatively.

"Trust me, even if he is, he won't be the first academic I've met who feels that way. No offense, Allen," she added with a glance at Dean Charterman's assistant.

"You do realize I spend virtually all of my time here on this campus, don't you?" Harper responded. "Trust me, I've had the range bunny's perspective on scholarly hexapumas just like Dr. Whitaker at quite a few faculty get-togethers."

"Exactly." Adair turned back to Stephanie. "The truth is,

one of the main reasons the foundation got involved—even at this late date—was to try to . . . smooth out some of the bumps where academic egos were involved. Obviously, we believe there's no such thing as too much knowledge about the treecats. That goes without saying. And the more people we have looking, the more perspectives we have, the more we're likely to learn. But at the same time, we have to limit our intrusiveness. Whatever else may be true of the treecats, they're the original owners of Sphinx, and we owe them a certain courtesy when we come visit. More to the point, we want to avoid contaminating the culture or overstressing their society. The last thing we need to do is to be crashing in with competing teams of scientists who might—with the best possible intentions—do a great deal of damage to the treecats out of pure ignorance simply because we haven't had enough time to learn some critical truth about them."

Her expression was far graver now, and Stephanie felt herself nodding in response.

"Bringing in those additional perspectives and viewpoints is important, but it was equally important to us to have everyone . . . under one roof, I suppose. *And* with enough direct Forestry Service involvement to preclude another Bolgeo slipping by us."

"I see what you mean," Stephanie said. "And I certainly agree that the last thing Lionheart or his family needs is to have hordes of strangers tromping all over their territories! I'd really prefer not to have brought in still more scientists, to be honest, but I do see your point, and I appreciate the way you're trying to look out for the 'cats."

"It's the least we can do," Adair told her. "And that brings me to why I asked Dean Charterman to provide an introduction to you. Allen here is more concerned with rocks than with trees and birds—or treecats—but given your status with the SFS, and especially your relationship with Lionheart, the foundation would be very interested in hearing your impressions of how well the human presence on Sphinx is interacting with the native ecology. And, of course," she looked at Lionheart across Stephanie's shoulder, "how humans on Sphinx are reacting to the discovery of the treecats. We're all aware that's going to become a major issue in the not too distant future, and we'd appreciate all the insight we can get into it is early as possible. We know you're only on Manticore for your coursework here at the university, but we'd really hate to miss the opportunity to pick your brain on something like this while we've got the chance."

Stephanie felt herself tighten a bit more internally, the way she always did when the issue of the 'cats' future was brought front and center, but there was a lot of sense in what Adair had just said. Not that recognizing that fact did much about the sense of wariness flowing into her from Lionheart.

"I hope it won't become a *major* issue," she heard herself say.

"So do we," Adair assured her, "but we can't pretend the human race has an unblemished record where aboriginal species are involved. Which is why we'd like to invite the two of you to attend the foundation's monthly dinner this coming Tuesday as our guests. Most of the directors will be present, and with your permission, we'd like to invite some of our more generous donors—and some members of the Star Kingdom's business community who it couldn't hurt to get on the treecats' side—and ask you to possibly give a brief presentation on the treecats and then take a few questions."

"The *two* of us?" Stephanie asked, and Adair grimaced.

"I know. I know! Here we want to talk about treecats, and we're not even asking you to bring Lionheart along, which is dumb. Unfortunately, we didn't realize you were on planet until last week, and we've run into a problem with the restaurant where we always meet. They aren't pre-pared to allow a treecat on their premises...yet." Her eyes glinted. "We're working on them, and I don't think they're going to be raising any objections by the time we're done with them, but we won't be able to get it resolved before this month's dinner. Hopefully, by *next* month, we'll have them sorted out and be able to invite Lionheart, as well, before both of you have to head home to Sphinx again."

"I see." Stephanie looked at Karl, who shrugged. Then she reached up to caress Lionheart's ears. "I imagine we could be there," she said after a moment. "Assuming our class load lets us, anyway."

"Oh, I think you could count on the dean to run inter-ference for you in this case," Harper assured her. "If it was necessary...which it won't be."

"In that case, we'd be happy to accept, Ms. Adair."

"Good!" Adair smiled brilliantly. "The entire board will be delighted to hear that, Stephanie, and I'm personally look-ing forward to a very interesting and informative evening."

When Anders saw Jessica's ID on his uni-link, he almost didn't take the call. By this point, he'd had enough of the x-a's and dreaded the thought of another interview. Still, if he was dreading it, how might Valiant feel?

"Hi, Jess. What's up?"

"Hey, Anders. Toby and I scored some free tickets to an open air concert in one of the parks outside Twin Forks. We were wondering if you wanted to come. We could swing by and pick you up."

Anders didn't even pause. "You mean an outing that has nothing to do with treecats and their technology—or lack of technology, or whether or not they can commu-nicate on a sophisticated level? I'm in!"

"Don't you even want to know what sort of music it is?"

"I don't care. Even monotone ding-jow would be a welcome break from anthropological sniping. When can you bust me outta here?"

Jessica giggled. "The concert starts just after lunch."

"Then let me buy you lunch first—and Toby, too. Can you get away that early?"

"Sure. Mom and I juggled schedules."

As it turned out, the music was really good—at least from a human perspective. Shortly after the concert started, though, Valiant pressed his true-hands to his ears.

"They must be using some sort of frequency he finds annoying," Toby guessed when Jessica grinned ruefully, then carried the treecat off.

She hurried back just a few minutes later.

"I took Valiant to the edge of the field. We're not so far from home that he can't make his own way back. I suspect he'll take his time and do some botanizing along the way. He brought a carry net and some sample bags."

The first band—the one that had so annoyed Valiant—was definitely of the high-brow, sit-and-listen sort, but most of the ones that followed encouraged the audience members to join in in some way. Anders found himself dancing with people he didn't know, laughing as they tried out unfamiliar steps. More than once, he danced with Jessica. That was really nice. Stephanie wasn't much of a dancer.

When Jess had said "she and Toby" had gotten tickets, Anders had wondered if there might be a bit of romance going on. *But if Toby's interested in anyone, it's that cute little redhead*, he thought. *I think I've seen her watching the hang-gliding club's demos. I wonder if he has an admirer?*

The crisp chill of the Sphinxian autumn evening brought the concert to an end. Jessica dropped Toby off first, then glanced at the HUD.

"Want to have dinner at my house? I helped Mom with prep this morning, so I know there's plenty. Dr. Marjorie asked Mom to help herself from the greenhouses. Otherwise, lots of stuff would go to waste. The freeze-unit's filled to bursting."

"You're sure it'll be all right?"

"I sort of hinted to Mom this morning, but I'll double-check, just so you can read her 'yes' yourself. So you'll come?"

"Absolutely! But swing by the Red Letter Café. I'll get a box of those iced pastries to sweeten my welcome."

"Oh . . . That's not necessary. You're sweet enough." Jessica blushed to the roots of her hair. "I mean you're welcome without the bribe."

Anders found himself coloring. "Seriously. Take it from the son of an x-a. Guests bearing dessert are always more welcome."

He commed his dad and left a message, saying he'd be back later. When he came back to Jessica's car after buying a large box of the promised pastries, he found her ending the call. She held out her uni-link so he could read the final text.

"You're very welcome for dinner," she said. "Mom and Dad haven't gotten home yet, but they'll be back soon. Right now, the twins, Melanie-Anne and Archie, are in charge. Mom has Tiddles and Nathan with her."

Anders and Stephanie were both only children. They'd shared their amazement at the disorganized but somehow still functional amoeba that was Jessica's large family. Actually, though, on Sphinx such large families were more usual than their mutual status as "onlies." Stephanie said her parents hoped to add a child or two, but so far the time hadn't seemed right. She'd been pretty philosophical about it.

"Actually, I'm almost out the door," she'd said when Anders asked her how she felt about it. "College in a couple of years. After that, well, I'd really like to take some posts on parts of Sphinx I don't know as well. There's a lot of this world I want to experience firsthand."

Anders was wondering if he'd feel as calm if his parents suddenly presented him with a younger brother or sister when he heard Jessica draw in her breath.

"Hang on," she said, reaching for the controls. "There's an air car down there I don't recognize. The twins know they aren't supposed to let strangers in, but Melanie-Anne in particular is just too trusting. Still, I'd rather not cause a fuss. I'll bring us down on the back lot and we can walk in without being noticed."

She pulled off the maneuver with such skill—and so quietly—that Anders entertained the thought that Jessica might have found it convenient to go in and out without being noticed from time to time.

Or am I just being suspicious? In a house with so many little kids, it's probably second nature to find ways to avoid waking the baby.

"Valiant's not back yet," Jessica said softly as she opened the air car door. "He's on his way."

Evening chill had driven everyone inside. Jessica led the way around the side of the rambling house. Anders had been here many times with Stephanie and knew enough of the basic layout to know they were heading for a side door that led into a corridor that bisected the front and back portions of the house. It was a good choice. They could enter without being seen and hear whatever was being said in most of the house.

Jessica slid the door open and motioned him inside quickly. Anders was immediately struck by the relative quiet. The Pheriss house was never quiet—too many people lived there for that to be the case—but this evening the usual lively ruckus was subdued. Music was playing somewhere, but no feet were thundering up and down the stairs, nor was cutlery clattering in the kitchen areas.

Instead, from the front of the house where there was as close to a formal living room as existed, an adult male voice was speaking. A moment later, it was answered by a piping childish voice that Anders thought belonged to Archie, the male half of the twins. They couldn't make out the words, but everything sounded calm enough, and Anders felt his shoulders relaxing from a tension he hadn't realized was there.

Jessica held a slim finger to her lips and motioned for Anders to follow her. Stepping over scattered toys, they went down the corridor toward the front of the house and paused outside the living room door.

The man's voice said, "So you've never felt threatened, even though you've heard that treecats are meat-eaters?"

"No," Melanie-Anne said thoughtfully. "Our dogs, Otis and Mookie, are meat-eaters, but we're not scared of them."

"Otis and Mookie," corrected a younger voice—Billiam?—pedantically, "eat kibbles. Valiant thinks kibbles are yucky. He ate a chipmunk. I saw him. He ate it all up."

"And did that upset you?" the man asked. "Some people keep chipmunks for pets because they're cute."

The voice was familiar. In a moment, Anders placed it: Duff DeWitt, assistant to Dr. Radzinsky. Just the other day, Dad had said something about him . . . what was it? Right! "I wonder what sort of connections that DeWitt fellow has. He's certainly not the best anthropologist I've met, not even close. Radzinsky must've picked him for some other reason."

DeWitt was a good-looking man with his fair hair, dark eyes, impressive musculature, and chiseled features. The leer in Dad's tone of voice had made it perfectly clear what reason *he* thought Cleonora Radzinsky had for bringing DeWitt along. At the time, Anders had dismissed his scorn for the other man as yet another example of Dad's professional cattiness, but now he wondered if Dad might have been right. Certainly, this wasn't a professional way to conduct an interview! All Jessica's siblings were younger than her—definitely too young to be interviewed without their parents present—and these were certainly leading questions.

Billiam, bless him, was prattling happily on about how Valiant's choice of a meal hadn't bothered him at all. In fact, he seemed to have taken a childish delight in the fact that Valiant had "even gulped down the guts!"

Anders expected Jessica—who'd shown herself at least as fearless as Stephanie in her own way—to go charging in to defend Valiant's character, but she hung back. Then she glanced at him, and when Anders saw the deep lines of worry etching her face, he realized what held her back.

Defending Valiant would imply that there's something to defend him against. Jessica—and me, too—would be just about the worst people to interrupt, because we're known to like treecats. DeWitt would find some way of twisting it to his advantage, I'm sure.

He reached for Jessica's hand and tapped the uni-link strapped to her wrist. "Go and make a call," he mouthed. "Interrupt that way."

Jessica nodded. She could have texted, but it was likely that the absorbed group would ignore that. However, with both parents out, it was unlikely the Pheriss kids would ignore the signal of an incoming call.

She was moving toward the back of the house when a very unlikely knight came to the rescue. There was the sound of the front door—which opened into a small foyer directly off the living room—opening. Buddy Pheriss' booted feet could be heard striding in.

"Who are you, young man? And what are you doing in my house?"

Jessica pointed to where a slight change of angle would permit them to watch the action in the living room in the reflection cast onto one of the many windows. DeWitt rose smoothly to his feet, apparently not in the least flustered, and held out his hand to Mr. Pheriss. Buddy Pheriss was a big, wiry man who made his living doing an assortment of jobs, many of them involving physical labor. Currently, he wore a beard that jutted out in a point and his dark auburn hair—as curly as his daughter's—was longer than the current fashion. He looked rather wild, but DeWitt didn't seem in the least intimidated.

"I'm Duff DeWitt, Dr. Radzinsky's assistant. I called earlier and was told I could come by and talk to your family about life with a treecat."

"And who gave permission?" The rumbling growl was addressed to the assorted children, and Melanie-Anne raised a tentative hand.

"I guess I did, Dad. I mean, he asked if anyone here knew anything about treecats and could talk to him. I didn't realize he was coming over, but when he did..."

She trailed off.

"Ah." The monosyllable promised repercussions later, but Mr. Pheriss wasn't distracted.

"Mr. DeWitt, you may not have realized it, but the front window has a cracked pane. Landlord keeps forgetting to fix it, and it's become an issue, so I won't."

Anders grinned. The Pheriss' landlords were the same Franchittis Stephanie so deeply despised.

"So I just happened to hear what you were asking my children. Quite a lot of what you were asking them actually. That bit where you showed them the diagram of a treecat's teeth was very interesting. So was the bit where you stressed how hard their claws are and how very many they have. Not exactly scientific, now, was that?"

DeWitt blinked. If he'd researched the Pheriss family at all, he'd obviously made the mistake of thinking that lack of formal education was the same as lack of brains. From the expression that flickered across his handsome features, he'd just realized that he'd made a major error.

The next few minutes were quite interesting from the observers' point of view—especially since those observers could now be assured that Duff DeWitt was not going to leave the Pheriss household with any juicy soundbites regarding vicious treecats. Not only did Mr. Pheriss make certain that DeWitt had been recording the conversation—Billiam was quite helpful there—but he thought to make certain that not only did the whole the record get wiped, but so did the backup being made by DeWitt's uni-link.

"I'll be talking to your boss, young man, about scientific methods and ethical treatment of minors as subjects," Mr. Pheriss concluded as he ushered his unwelcome guest out the door. "I will indeed. Can't have the sample ruined, now, can we? I might even mention what I think of the sort of bottom-feeding, slime-sucking scum dogs who would frighten small children. But if you leave quietly, I might keep that to myself."

When DeWitt, wrath lighting his dark eyes, had departed, Mr. Pheriss called out, "Well, you might as well get out here, Jessica. And that young man, too. Before your mama gets home for dinner, we're going to have a scavenger hunt to make sure our fine visitor didn't leave behind any other devices. Always pays to play it safe, at least that's how I see it..."

Jessica barreled out of her concealment and hugged her father. Anders followed more slowly, thinking hard.

Now I think I understand why—despite needing to move all the time—this family works. When it all comes down to it, they can count on each other. Here I'd been pitying Jessica, but now—Now I think I actually envy her.

The Charleston Arms was the fanciest restaurant Stephanie had ever seen. In fact, it was fancy enough to make even her a little nervous. Her mom had insisted that she pack at least one "good outfit," although Stephanie was always most comfortable in the sort of clothes better suited to knocking around the bush. At the moment, she was glad her mother had been so inflexible on that point, but she was pretty sure her notion of "good outfit" fell a light-year or so short of the Charleston Arms' standards.

She knew from her own experience on Sphinx that newly settled worlds tended towards lower buildings, without the hundreds of floors a proper tower might possess, but the Charleston Arms was ridiculous. Set in the midst of its own four-hectare expanse of meticulously landscaped grounds, it favored what its public site had called "neoclassic architecture," although Stephanie couldn't quite figure out *which* neoclassic style it had followed. It was no more than three floors tall, its roof was covered in red tile, its walls were made of native Manticoran granite, and its façade was fringed with tall, fluted columns whose bases were almost as thick as Stephanie was tall. It was the sort of place which simply reeked of wealth, power, and prestige, and despite the imposing sweep of its clear, clean lines, something about it set her teeth on edge the instant she saw it.

Probably just the fact that the people who run it won't let you bring Lionheart, she reminded herself. *So remember to be polite!*

The incredibly superior live human who insisted on opening the taxi's door as if Stephanie and Karl were incapable of such a complicated and demanding task managed—somehow—not to sniff audibly at their ragamuffin appearance, but it was obviously hard. She retaliated by smiling up at him sweetly as he escorted the two of them up the broad, shallow steps into the restaurant proper. She couldn't decide if he was more worried that they'd get lost or that they might decide to steal the antique doorknobs if he didn't keep an eye on them.

The interior had exactly the sort of wood-paneled walls,

polished marble floors, and ever so quiet and discreet background music she might have anticipated, and she found herself beginning to wonder just how much she could possibly have in common with the Adair Foundation if this was where it regularly held its meetings. She was just beginning to think about beating a strategic retreat to the taxi when someone called her name.

"Stephanie! I'm so glad you and Karl could join us tonight," Gwendolyn Adair said. She swept across the gleaming stone floor towards them, tall and beautiful in a "casual" little gown which had probably cost more than the Harrington air car, and smiled hugely. "I'm sorry you had to come by taxi. If you'd screened me the foundation would've been delighted to arrange to have you picked up."

"We managed just fine, thank you." Stephanie smiled again, politely, though she was tempted to point out that she and Karl were perfectly capable of finding their way around the Sphinx bush on their own. The terror of finding an air taxi was probably something they were prepared to face when they absolutely had to.

"Well, now that you're here, let me show you the way to our dining room." Gwendolyn wrinkled her nose with a charming little smile. "Personally, I think they were a little too concerned with making certain people would be properly impressed with the establishment's grandeur when they built this place. You need GPS just to find your way around inside it!"

There was so much rich amusement in her tone that Stephanie found herself smiling back at her again, much more naturally this time. She glanced up at Karl and saw him smiling, as well, as Gwendolyn somehow made their escort/keeper disappear without saying a word. Then she turned and led the two of them across that sea of polished marble, through an arch, down two flights of shallow steps, around a corner, down a hall, *up* a flight of steps, through an atrium with its own private grove of exotic ornamental trees and flowering shrubs, past a koi pond, and—*finally!*—through another door into a cozy little dining room which probably couldn't have seated more than three or four hundred of Stephanie's closest friends.

It was a journey which could make even Stephanie feel more than a little out of her depth.

Floor-to-ceiling windows looked out over a small, beautiful lake on the restaurant's grounds, and the setting sun hung directly above it, pouring down a rich, golden light. A lectern had been set up at one end of the dining room, forming a small, bare island among the ice floes of tables draped in white linen tablecloths and glittering with silverware and crystal glasses. A couple of dozen people were already present, waiting for them. The attendees seemed almost lost in that enormous room and (she noted glumly) just about every one of them was as elegantly dressed as Gwendolyn.

"Hey, don't sweat it," a voice said very quietly in her ear, and she glanced up from the corner of her eye as Karl smiled down at her. "*You're* the one they're all here to see and listen to, Steph," he added, and gave her shoulder a gentle smack.

She smiled back up at him, then turned and followed Gwendolyn calmly out into the banquet room's splendor.

"And now, ladies and gentlemen," Gwendolyn Adair announced the better part of two hours later, "it gives me considerable pleasure to present Stephanie Harrington!"

She smiled from her place at the lectern, inviting Stephanie to join her, and the seated diners applauded enthusiastically as Stephanie rose. The introduction wasn't strictly necessary, given the fact that she and Karl had already been introduced to a seemingly endless array of rich, aristocratic, and rich *and* aristocratic people. Still, the applause was heavier than Stephanie had expected it would be, and she felt an undeniable little stir of pleasure as it greeted her. At the same time, she felt a matching irritation that she was the only one being invited up to speak to them. Karl had been just as involved with the SFS—and with protecting the 'cats—as she had, but the Adair Foundation (just like everyone *else* in the Star Kingdom) seemed fixated on the drama of her original meeting with Lionheart.

Well, the "original meeting" they all know about, any-way, she corrected herself, remembering a thunderstorm and a small celery thief in the rain.

The applause continued until she joined Gwendolyn on the small stage, then died away, and Gwendolyn continued.

"I know all of you are familiar with the news reports about Stephanie and Lionheart, and I'm sure all of you are as irked as I am that he couldn't join us as well tonight. However, since you *do* know the public parts of their story, I think we can skip the usual flowery intro-ductions and get right down to the real reason all of us are here tonight." She looked at Stephanie. "I thought it might be a good idea to ask you to tell us a little about what treecats are really like and then, if you don't mind, take a few questions from the floor, Stephanie."

"Sure." Stephanie smiled back at her just a *bit* more confidently than she actually felt, then stepped up behind the lectern and adjusted the mic more comfortably to her height as Gwendolyn returned to her own chair.

"First," she began, "let me thank all of you for inviting Karl and me to join you this evening." She emphasized Karl's name ever so slightly and saw several people glance in his direction. "And, like Gwendolyn, I'm sorry Lion-heart can't be here as well. He's actually a much better spokesman for the 'cats than I could ever be... even if he can't talk."

A quiet rumble of amusement answered her last remark, and she drew a deep, unobtrusive breath. Now for the tricky part, she reminded herself. It was time to enlist these people in the 'cats' support, but she had to do it in a way that made them eager to protect Lionheart and the others without over-emphasizing their intelligence.

"When I first met Lionheart, I was doing something really stupid," she began, "and if he hadn't come along, I wouldn't be here today. I guess that means I'm probably a little prejudiced in his favor, and that makes me very happy to have the chance to talk to an organization like the Adair Foundation about him and the rest of the treecats. We're obviously only beginning to really learn about them, and it's going to be years and years before anyone's ready to provide any kind of definitive evaluation of them. But one thing that's already clear is that they were on Sphinx a long time before we were, and that's why the SFS has declared them a protected species. That's only a provisional status, though. It's subject to being changed or revoked, and Karl and I both think that would be a really bad idea. I hope that after this evening, you'll agree with us, because we can use all the help we can get making sure the 'cats are protected the same way they protected me against the hexapuma."

She heard the quiet sincerity in her own voice and, looking out at her audience, she thought she saw it reflected in attentive expressions and cocked, listening heads. She hoped so, anyway.

"That afternoon," she went on, "when my hang-glider crashed into the crown oak, I had no idea what was going to happen. I thought—"

"WELL, I HAVE TO ADMIT I'M GLAD *THAT'S* OVER WITH," Stephanie admitted several hours later as Gwendolyn Adair and Oswald Morrow, who she'd introduced as one of her cousin the earl's financial managers, accompanied her and Karl back towards the waiting taxi. "Talking to that many people made me a lot more nervous than I expected it to!"

"Really?" Gwendolyn tilted her head, looking down at her. "I don't think anyone would have suspected that looking at you. In fact, I thought you handled that extraordinarily well. Didn't you, Oswald?"

"I didn't see any signs of anxiety," Morrow agreed. "And I thought you handled the questions quite well, too."

"And...shrewdly," Gwendolyn said. Stephanie looked back at her quickly, and the older woman smiled faintly. "I hope you won't take this wrongly, Stephanie, but it was pretty apparent to me that you chose your words rather carefully a time or two. You're very protective of the tree-cats, aren't you?"

"Well, maybe I am." Stephanie tried not to bristle. "I think I've got pretty good reasons to be, though!"

She felt one of Karl's big hands settle on her shoulder and squeeze gently, and she made herself relax muscles that had tried to tighten up.

"Of course you do," Gwendolyn agreed calmly. "That was an observation, not a criticism. I happen to think you're entirely correct to be protective of them—that's what the Adair Foundation's all about, isn't it?—and I meant it as a compliment. I don't know where the final judgment on treecat sentience is going to fall in the end, but I thoroughly agree that this is a time to go slowly and carefully. The last thing any of us want to see on Sphinx is a repeat of what happened on Barstool."

An icicle touched Stephanie's heart at the reminder of the Amphors of the planet Barstool and how they'd been exterminated by the human settlers of their home world to prevent anyone from suggesting that it belonged to *them* and not the human interlopers. The hand on her shoulder tightened again, this time as much in comfort as in warning, and she made herself meet Gwendolyn's green eyes levelly.

"No, we don't," she heard herself agree calmly. "And you're right—thinking about things like Barstool does make me kind of careful about how enthusiastically I talk about the 'cats. Oh, I know it's early to be worrying about things like that in Sphinx's case, especially with the Forestry Service looking out for them and especially when there's no way we can demonstrate how intelligent they really are. I do worry about it, though. I owe Lionheart too much to just stand around and watch something bad happen to him or the rest of the treecats."

"Of course you do," Gwendolyn acknowledged as they reemerged from the Charleston Arms into the warm, breezy night of the city of Landing, where the taxi waited on the parking apron. "It couldn't be any other way, and I'm glad—I'm sure the entire foundation is glad—they have such a good friend in you. And in Karl and the rest of the SFS, of course."

Stephanie smiled brightly at her, then held out her hand.

"Thanks! And I'm glad the foundation's on their side, too!" she said, shaking Gwendolyn's hand firmly. "I wish we could stay to talk about them some more, but Karl and I have a nine o'clock exam in the morning, and I just *know* a certain 'cat is going to be waiting to demand an extra stalk of celery when we get back to the dorms!"

"We are so screwed," Oswald Morrow remarked quietly as he and Gwendolyn Adair watched the taxi lift away.

"She *is* rather more personable—and formidable—than I'd expected out of someone her age," Gwendolyn agreed. "I knew she had to be tough and determined just to have survived the hexapuma, and it was obvious she was smart as they come, too. But she's a lot calmer and more collected than I thought she'd be. She didn't even turn a hair talking to the foundation members, did she?"

"Not that anyone might notice." Morrow grimaced. "The newsies are going to just love her the instant she starts giving interviews, you know. Smart, cute, tough, mature—she's a PR campaign's worst nightmare, Gwen! If she starts handing out interviews like the little talk she gave tonight, but with the treecat sitting on her shoulder and looking just as cute—and tough, with all those scars and the missing leg!—we're going to have every gooey-hearted idiot in the Star Kingdom pulling for the little monsters. And if *that* happens, you can kiss all those land options on Sphinx goodbye. Parliament'll grandfather in those little beasties' claim to the planet, and their market value will drop straight into the basement."

"You do have a dazzling grasp of the obvious, don't you, Ozzie?" Gwendolyn observed acidly. "Of course the options' values will tank if that happens! Unless I'm mistaken, that's the very thing you and I are trying to prevent, now isn't it?"

"Yes, it is," Morrow replied tartly. "And at the moment, I'm thinking things don't look too good in that respect."

"Maybe not. But that was always a possibility, wasn't it? What do you hear from Dr. Radzinsky?"

"Nothing good," Morrow said glumly. "She says the evidence is pretty clear that they're not just tool-users but also toolmakers, and probably even more advanced toolmakers than we were afraid they were." He shook his head. "She's not going to be able to convince the academic community they aren't sentient, Gwen. Not for very long, anyway. And I think she's a lot less optimistic than she was about convincing people their sentience is minimal, too."

"I wish I could say I was surprised." Gwendolyn gazed thoughtfully after the vanished lights of the taxi and pursed her lips. "So unless we can come up with some sort of pesticide that'll kill only treecats without bothering the rest of the ecosystem, it looks like we're stuck with them."

Morrow glanced at her profile a bit uneasily. He *thought* she was only joking about exterminating the 'cats, but it was always a little hard to be certain about Gwendolyn. He'd realized some years ago that she was actually far more ruthless than he was once she'd fully committed to an operation ... and she had more of her own portfolio invested in those Sphinx land options than he'd thought she did.

"Well," she sighed after a moment, "if we are, we are. I know the others are going to insist on trying for the 'only animals' solution, but you're right; it's not going to fly in the end. That doesn't mean we can't get *most* of what we want, though. I think it's time you and I started concentrating on Plan B. At least that way we can limit the damage."

Morrow grunted unhappily. She was almost certainly right about that, but she had a point about "the others." The real moneymakers behind their efforts weren't going to be happy if *any* of the land on which they held options was snatched out from under them and handed back to the treecats. Nor were they going to be very happy with the people—like one Oswald Morrow—who'd allowed that to happen.

"Frampton and the others will scream," he warned.

"Then they'll just have to scream." Gwendolyn shrugged. "Once we convince public opinion that the poor, aboriginal, barely sentient little savages need to be put on reservations to protect them from the corrupting influence of humans, we're halfway home. We've got more than enough friends in Parliament to make sure the reservation boundaries get drawn in ways that don't include any of the *good* land on Sphinx, Ozzie. And if we don't—" she shrugged again "—Frampton and the others can always buy us some *additional* friends, now can't they? Of course, it wouldn't hurt a thing if we could also convince the big, bleeding-heart public that the little monsters are too dangerous to be allowed to run around loose where they might endanger children or other innocent bystanders, now would it?"

"No, it wouldn't," Morrow agreed around a fresh prickle of uneasiness. "Why? Have you got something in mind?"

"Oh, I think you might say that," Gwendolyn replied with a small smile. "It'll take a little time to set up, but I definitely have something in mind."

Because he knew how nervous Stephanie was about speaking at the Adair Foundation banquet, Anders waited until he heard back from her about that to tell her about

Duff DeWitt's less than professional behavior toward the Pheriss kids.

When he did, her next message showed she took the incident as seriously as he and Jessica—and Mr. Pheriss—had. They'd messaged back and forth so often over the last several weeks—a lot more frequently than they had when *he'd* been the one on Manticore—that any early stiffness had vanished. Stephanie sprawled on her stomach on her bed, wearing shorts and a sleeveless top. Her head rested on her hands and she was kicking her bare feet up behind her. Lionheart rested nearby. The fact that the 'cat wasn't sitting on Stephanie—as he certainly would have been if they'd been at home on Sphinx—reminded Anders that while it was autumn on this part of Sphinx, temperatures were much warmer on Manticore.

"Do you want me to see what anyone at the Adair Foundation knows about this DeWitt?" Stephanie was saying. "They didn't select the team members, but they did vet their credentials. They may know something your dad and Dr. Nez don't, and Gwen Adair seemed really nice. If there's something going on that she doesn't know about, I'm sure she'd be more than happy to help us get to the bottom of it. Let me know, okay?"

The rest of Stephanie's message was mostly about classes. She was so busy she hadn't even made it off campus except for the foundation dinner.

"...Mom and Dad are coming out in about two weeks so they can have a holiday before they attend my graduation. They're talking about extending their visit for another week or two so I can do some touring, but I don't know... I really want to get home and see you and help with the x-a's. We'll see. I may not have a lot of choice in the matter."

Anders considered Stephanie's offer, then set up his reply. Knowing Stephanie would be eager to hear what he thought about her plan, he started in on that first thing.

"Let's hold back on using the Adair Foundation until we see how DeWitt behaves. It's been almost a week now, and he's been a perfect angel. Jess and I asked Chris and Chet to keep an eye on him—or, I guess you could say, to keep an eye on whether or not he was staying with the rest of the x-a's or off doing his own thing. They say he's definitely staying with the herd. Maybe Dr. Radzinsky chewed him out after Mr. Pheriss got done talking to her. I hope so! It takes a special kind of slime-sucker to use kids that way.

"Hard to imagine you still have at least an entire month away—maybe more if your folks decide to take you touristing. Don't miss the chance just for me, though. I was feeling too lonely and sorry for myself to really enjoy it when I was stuck on Manticore and you were stuck on Sphinx, but there are some really spectacular spots on that planet. If you get a chance to take one of the cruises on Jason Bay—not the air cruises, the *water* cruises—do it. You won't be sorry, and there's time. Dad said again the other night that we'll definitely be here through autumn. For once, I'm so glad the seasons on Sphinx are fifteen T-months long."

He chewed his lip for a moment. It was hard to be supportive when what he wanted most of all was to urge her to come back to Sphinx, but he resisted the impulse as unworthy.

"You look really cute in those shorts...I guess that's one good thing about you taking that trip, Sphinx is so cool that even in summer I never would have had the pleasure if you'd stayed. Take care of yourself. Don't study too hard. Give the fluffball a piece of celery for me. Hi to Karl...Miss you...Bye..."

Keen Eyes feared that the time of toleration had ended on the day Red Cliff disappeared.

Red Cliff had not been born to the Swaying Fronds Clan, but to a distant clan which lived where the rocks were a lovely sunset color. He had come to Swaying Fronds' range many turnings before, drawn—or so he always said, and no one who had shared his thoughts had any reason to doubt the accuracy of this statement—by the most beautiful mind-glow he had ever sensed.

That mind-glow belonged to a young female of the Swaying Fronds Clan. In those days, she had not earned a name but was simply called "Speckles" for the pretty flecks of white that showed against her brown coat. Today, Speckles was called "Beautiful Mind," in recognition both of the quality that had brought her a mate and for her undeniably warm and pleasant way with others. Together, Red Cliff and Beautiful Mind had raised several litters. The last had been born the previous spring and were showing themselves as fine a lot of scamperers as had ever delighted their parents and enriched their clan.

But those very scamperers were the reason Beautiful Mind was probably dying and Red Cliff was going slowly insane. When the fires had come, Swaying Fronds had done its best to get the weaker members to safety. The kittens had behaved with admirable composure, guided by the promise that if they passed through smaller flames they would escape the worst of the raging conflagration that was destroying their homes.

Then one little male had been hit by a flaming branch, breaking the hips of both his hand-feet and true-feet on that side. Beautiful Mind had sent her other kittens ahead, then raced back for the injured one. Lacking the dense oils that gave the older People some protection, the kitten's fur had caught fire and his injuries had made it impossible for him to roll free of the flaming branch, much less smother the flames.

Beautiful Mind had thrown the branch clear, beat out

the flames, and then attempted to carry the injured kitten clear, breathing in lung-scorching smoke all the while. The kitten had died in her arms. When Red Cliff raced back to pull her to safety, she was already far gone after her little one. Yet, despite her injuries, Beautiful Mind continued to draw ragged breath after ragged breath. Her mind was untouchable except in fragments, and those fragments mostly dreams of better days, but Keen Eyes wondered if she held onto life because she knew that without her Red Cliff would likely fade away. So many bonded pairs could not live without their partners. Sometimes a parent would survive if their kittens needed them, but Red Cliff's bond to Beautiful Mind had always come first. He loved the kittens truly, but always because they were part of her.

When Keen Eyes returned to where the Landless Clan was currently camped near a stream that offered good water, he found Sour Belly fuming that Red Cliff was gone.

<Gone! And gone beyond the range of my mind-voice.>

This was not good. A Person's mind-voice carried a long distance, especially when seeking someone well-known. Clearly, Red Cliff had ventured farther than was prudent or he was refusing to answer. Neither of those were promising.

<Which way did he go?> Keen Eyes asked.

<How should I know?> Sour Belly's thoughts were as unpleasant as his breath. *<You are the scout. I am just a retired hunter turned caretaker of kittens.>*

A cough came from where Beautiful Mind lay. She was hardly more than a matted heap of brown and white fur, yet one true-hand rose and pointed, holding the position until Keen Eyes said *<I see, sister. I will go after him. I will bring him back. I promise.>*

But his heart moved uneasily within him, for Beautiful Mind had indicated the very heart of the territory held by Trees Enfolding Clan.

❖   ❖   ❖

Anders had just finishing messaging Stephanie when his uni-link chimed. He glanced at the ID and took the call with real relief. Stephanie's last message had been full of impending finals and her parents' upcoming visit. Somehow, all her excitement had made her seem farther away than ever.

"Hey, Jess."

"Hey, Anders. Listen. Mom's asked me if I could do a favor for her. Tiddles isn't feeling too well—"

Tiddles was Jessica's youngest sister, a sturdy, determined three-year-old. Her given name was Tabitha, but Anders had never figured out where the nickname came from.

"—and Mom needs to take her to the doctor. Problem is, today is Mom's day for recording plant growth in some of the burn areas, then collecting soil and plant samples. Timing's really important with this. She asked if I thought I could handle it. I said I thought I could."

Jessica sounded unusually nervous, and Anders thought he knew why. Naomi Pheriss was collaborating with Dr. Marjorie on a study of succession growth. The project was important for a lot of reasons—not all of them scientific. Dr. Marjorie had promised coauthorship to Mrs. Pheriss, which could mean a lot for future projects. The gang had gone along on a couple of Mrs. Pheriss' collecting outings already, but they'd definitely been assistants, not in charge.

"Need company?"

"Seriously," Jessica agreed. "I'm going to call the others, but I wanted to get you... Well, I mean, before you promised your dad you'd distract the x-a's for him or carry buckets at the site or something."

Anders laughed. "Honestly, I think Dad has me in mind for bucket duty. I was looking for an out. I'll call you back if there are any problems, but otherwise you can count me in. Where should I meet you?"

"I can pick you up," Jessica said. "Would you mind our leaving relatively early? We're going to where the big fires were, up in the northeast Copperwalls."

"No problem. See you then."

When Jessica picked Anders up the next morning, he was surprised to see that—other than Valiant—she was alone. He'd figured she'd have at least grabbed Toby, since he didn't live far from her in Twin Forks.

She saw him glance at the empty interior of her battered air car before he got into the front seat on the passenger side and, almost as if she was reading his mind, began to speak.

"Toby can't make it. Today's some special holy day for his family's religion. Christine and Chet are on guard duty. I hope you don't mind."

Suddenly, Anders felt a touch shy. It wasn't as if this was the first time he'd been alone with Jessica. And not only Jessica, but with her empathic treecat...He wondered why that should bother him.

He realized Jessica was staring at him, an expression of dismay spreading across her pretty features. He shook his head and hurried to answer her question.

"Mind? I don't mind. Sorry. When I realized Chet and Toby weren't going to be here, I tried to remember if I'd packed my handgun. We shouldn't be out there, just the two of us, with no protection."

"Do you need to go back for it?"

Anders made a pretense of checking his pack, even though he was absolutely certain he had the gun with him. He'd inspected it before coming down and made sure to put in a spare box of ammunition.

"I've got it," he said.

"Great." Jessica set the air car to rise. "I've never learned to shoot. I have a stun gun and a CS sprayer, but my dad is sort of into nonviolence. He doesn't mind if I learn to defend myself. He even signed me up for an aikido class back on our last planet, but he says we should learn to defend ourselves without turning into our own enemy."

"Tell that to the hexapumas," Anders said. "Somehow I doubt they'd see it that way—or that CS would stop them. A stun gun, maybe, on full power, if you hit exactly the right spot."

"Yeah," Jessica said. "Stephanie says the same thing. Since I usually went hiking with her and Karl—and they're always carrying some sort of shooting thing, sometimes more than one—I figured I was safe enough. Anyhow, we'd probably just use our counter-grav to get out of the way."

"Well," Anders said. "I'm still glad I've learned to shoot. I'm not as accurate as Karl or Stephanie, but I think I could at least slow down something the size of a hexapuma."

They were speeding over the green canopy. Twin Forks and its outliers had vanished, but the northeastern Copperwall Mountains didn't look a whole lot closer. Jessica set the autopilot and leaned back.

"Funny," she said. "It was learning Stephanie was so good with a gun that made me pretty certain all the stories Trudy told me about Steph being nova violent must be right."

"Stories?" Like any young man in love, Anders was eager to hear stories about his beloved's life before he'd met her, even—or maybe even especially—those she wouldn't be likely to tell herself. "Stephanie uncontrollably violent? You've got to be kidding."

"Apparently," Jessica said, "it's true. I heard about it first from Trudy. When Stephanie first met the local kids, there was a fad on for catching critters for pets. Chipmunks were popular. They're ground burrowers, about the size of a small dog, and though they can climb, they're nowhere near as good at it as, say, a wood rat, so they're not that hard to catch. Almost everyone in Trudy's gang had at least one chipmunk for a pet, and Trudy had a near-otter and a couple of range bunnies, too.

"Anyhow, one day Stephanie came into Twin Forks with her folks, and they made the usual attempt to get Stephanie to play with some kids her own age. When she found out that the game was dressing chipmunks up in bandannas and hats, she went ballistic. She punched out a couple of kids, gave Trudy a bloody nose, and basically made herself *really* unpopular."

Anders found himself laughing uncontrollably. He'd seen images of young Stephanie Harrington from long before he'd met her. Marjorie and Richard Harrington were very proud of their only child and numerous holos of her were displayed around their house. He had no trouble imagining the cute little urchin in those images walloping a bunch of kids because they'd dressed up their pets.

"Oh, boy. Great way to make friends and influence people!"

"For sure." Jessica shared his laughter. "When I got to know Stephanie, I asked her if that had really happened. She admitted it had—and admitted that it had happened more than once before her folks gave up on making her socialize in anything but an organized group like the hang-gliding club."

"I guess Trudy wouldn't have wanted to admit that her gang got repeatedly assaulted," Anders guessed. "Once makes Stephanie sound mean and out of control, but more than once—Well, it doesn't exactly make Stephanie sound much better, but it makes Trudy and her friends sound like the limpest sort of lettuce leaves."

"That's what I think, too," Jessica agreed. "I think Lionheart brings out the best in Stephanie—and there's a lot of good there. She's admitted that she finds it easier to hang on to her temper these days."

"Does Valiant help you?" he asked, and Jessica considered.

"Not with my temper. I don't really have one, like Stephanie does, I mean. I get cold mad, not hot mad. But Valiant does help me, I think. My family's moved so many times that I'm good at making friends, but inside I'm really shy. Valiant is so confident I'm worth knowing that, these days, I find it easier to talk to people about big things, not just make small talk."

"You mean you wouldn't have talked like this about Stephanie before?"

"I might have," Jessica said. "I mean, I know you care a lot about her and so do I. It's not like I'm trashing her. I figure she's probably told you some of this already."

"She did tell me she has a temper," Anders admitted. "But she didn't tell me about giving Trudy a bloody nose."

"Oops!" Jessica giggled. "Still, I don't think she'd mind your knowing. It's not as if Trudy ever fooled you about the sort of manipulative bitch she really is. Trudy thinks there's not a guy on the planet—maybe even in the whole system—who can resist her."

"But she dates a doper like Stan Chang." Anders shook his head. "I just don't get it."

"Figuring out other people's relationships," Jessica declared, "is impossible. I'm not sure anyone will ever construct a formula that will precisely explain why certain people fall for each other."

Valiant reached over and patted her, so Anders knew she must be thinking about something specific, but before he could ask, she shifted the conversation, talking about how her parents had met—an unlikely courtship if ever there'd been one.

From there it was natural that they talked about her little brothers and sisters, about how much the whole family liked Sphinx. Anders wondered if Jessica thought talking about Stephanie might make him feel bad, if she was trying to save him pain. Even so, Stephanie's name kept coming up. It was impossible not to talk about her since she'd become so deeply entwined in both of their lives since they'd each come to Sphinx.

Eventually, Jessica glanced at the navigation readout on the HUD.

"We're getting close. I'm going to slow us down so I can be sure we don't miss the right areas. Mom's trying to collect data on precisely the same plants, along with doing a more general study."

"Right," Anders said. "Bring us down, Captain. It's time we went a'hunting the infant forms of Sphinxian super-gigantic plants."

Jessica's giggle wasn't Stephanie's but it sounded pretty good. It cut through the loneliness, reminding Anders that—no matter how far away his girl might be—he still had friends.

Keen Eyes raced through the net-wood trees. Knowing how acutely aware of each other bonded pairs were, he'd set his course in the direction indicated by Beautiful Mind's pointing finger. However, he kept his attention sharp for any other signs the Person he sought had come this way. He found precious few: fresh claw marks in the bark where Red Cliff had apparently leapt too far and had to grip in, a bit of shredded leaf, a patch of matted feathers. This last looked as if the hunter had sprung after a potential bit of prey and missed.

All of these worried Keen Eyes. They indicated haste and carelessness, neither of which boded well for the

Person he pursued. Then, too, though he called repeatedly after his friend, there was no reply, not even the faintest flicker of a mind-glow. True, Red Cliff could be out of range. Since the fires, there were fewer People to relay messages than there would have been in the past. Nonetheless, Keen Eyes' heart hammered hard in apprehension.

Keen Eyes knew when he crossed into the heart of the Trees Enfolding Clan's range. He'd known he had been in what a stiff-tail like Swimmer's Scourge would call that clan's territory practically from the start. Now, however, there could be no claiming ignorance. He'd passed—and avoided—snares set for bark-chewers along the limbs of the net-wood. He'd seen pads made from leaves and branches set in convenient areas where a hunter might wait in stillness for prey animals to become convinced the forest was quiet and safe. He'd seen a spring, its tiny natural basin sculpted into a perfect pool. These, and a dozen other reworkings of the landscape, told him that People lived here.

Still his calls, kept as tight and directed as possible in the hope that he could avoid the attention of the Trees Enfolding Clan, met with no answer. Only a passionate desire to find Red Cliff and convince him to go home to his mate and kittens kept Keen Eyes searching. He was about to give up when he smelled blood—not prey blood, but Person blood—and mingled with that horrid reek was the odor of fear.

Without considering the consequences, Keen Eyes bounded towards the scent. Even if it wasn't Red Cliff, to bleed so heavily a Person must be in danger. Any Person, no matter the clan, would come to offer aid. But when he burst into the clearing at the heart of a cluster of net-wood trees, Keen Eyes found no Person, only a patch of earth soaked with blood and ornamented with tufts of fur. This close to the source, Keen Eyes could have no doubt whose blood it was: Red Cliff's.

Red Cliff was sorely wounded or—more likely—dead. Intent on keeping hope alive, Keen Eyes sought for any trace of Red Cliff's mind-glow, but found nothing. He reminded himself that this did not necessarily mean the other Person was dead. The range over which People could sense each other's mind-glows was much smaller than that over which they could speak. However, this did mean one of two things. Either Red Cliff was dead or so close to dead that his mind-glow had all but vanished. Or Red Cliff had managed to escape, despite his wounds.

Keen Eyes sniffed the air, examining his surroundings carefully with the acute vision and sense for detail that had won him his adult name. Mingled in with Red Cliff's own scent he found that of another Person. It was not a familiar scent in the sense that Keen Eyes had met the Person to whom it belonged face-to-face, but it was familiar in that he had encountered traces of it before. It belonged to someone who regularly hunted in this area, so probably a Person belonging to Trees Enfolding Clan.

Keen Eyes sought additional information, but it was curiously lacking. A skilled hunter learned how to conceal his scent trail. Keen Eyes wondered just who had been here with Red Cliff—and had he proved a friend who bore the injured Red Cliff away or the enemy who had wounded him?

<Looking for your friend?>

The mocking mind-voice was familiar: Swimmer's Scourge! It did not wait for Keen Eyes to reply but went on in the same taunting fashion.

<I took him back where he belongs. If you want to find him, don't look in our lands. Look in your own.>

<Was he alive? Did you get him help? How badly was he injured?>

But there was no answer. Nor, no matter how determinedly Keen Eyes cast about, could he find the faintest trace of another's mind-glow. Swimmer's Scourge must have moved out of range as soon as he had issued his challenge.

Briefly, Keen Eyes considered going after him, but his concern for Red Cliff won out. Gathering all six limbs under him, he raced along the interconnected limbs of the net-wood trees, his tail flowing behind like a banner.

The first place Keen Eyes checked was where the Landless Clan currently had gathered. It was easy to tell Red Cliff had not returned, even without drawing attention to himself. If he had, the news would have shone in the mind-glows of those present.

Wanting to keep his fears to himself, Keen Eyes stayed in the vicinity of the camp for as little time as possible. The mocking words of Swimmer's Scourge had repeated themselves over and over in Keen Eyes thoughts as he ran.

<I took him back where he belonged. If you want to find him, don't look in our lands. Look in your own.>

Keen Eyes thought he knew what that meant. He even thought he knew where within the wider range to look. If Red Cliff had been taken "home," it would be to where the burned lands touched the lands of Trees Enfolding Clan. He knew, too, that this almost certainly meant that Red Cliff was dead. However, he would not rest until he knew for certain.

Although enough time had passed since the fires for the foliage to begin to shift color in reaction to the cooler temperatures, the air nearest to the fire ravaged areas still stank of burned matter. For once, Keen Eyes hardly noticed the smell. He was seeking an odor even less welcome. Before too long, he found it.

Red Cliff lay reduced to a crumpled heap of bloodied and torn flesh and fur. His mind-glow had long gone silent and his heart ceased to beat. Bereft of the fierce intensity that had filled him since his mate had been injured, Red Cliff looked small and pathetic.

Reaching out a hesitant true-hand, Keen Eyes patted the still form, wishing there was some way he could forget this broken creature and remember his friend only as he had been. He wondered if Beautiful Mind knew her mate was dead. He suspected she did. Would he return to the camp to find she had given up her fragile hold on life? He had sensed no such thing when he had checked in, but often the process took longer, the remaining partner simply wasting away in a terrible misery.

So the Landless Clan—already small—had now been reduced by not one but two. Anger replaced sorrow in Keen Eyes heart. Swimmer's Scourge—for even with the smell of death and ashes he could catch traces of the same scent he had found in the bloodied glade—must have guessed that Red Cliff had a mate. Perhaps he'd even seen her image in Red Cliff's thoughts. Had Red Cliff begged? Begged for mercy? Begged for passage? Begged for food for his starving kits?

But Swimmer's Scourge had shown no mercy. Worse, he had not only killed, he had made a cruel joke of his killing by moving Red Cliff's body so that there would be no doubt that in life or in death the members of Landless Clan were not welcome in the lands of *his* clan.

Very well. No mercy. No passage. Not even a handful of roots or a couple of tough old bark-chewers to ease the slow starvation Landless Clan faced with the coming of winter. Swimmer's Scourge had made his point clear. The search for a new home for the Landless Clan had become something far grimmer. This was a declaration of war.

12

"ALL RIGHT," JESSICA SAID, STRAIGHTENING FROM inspecting a hearty seedling. "That finishes this area. Mom's going to go nova over what we're finding. There's always been a lot of interest in the way crown oak puts out broad leaves for spring and summer, then generates filament leaves for the winter months. From what we've seen today, I'm guessing they're also very adaptable in fire recovery. No wonder they're becoming the dominant tree in this region."

"Definitely," Anders agreed. "Where next? Another crown oak grove?"

Jessica shook her head, which caused her thick, wildly curly hair to toss very attractively around her face. She was apparently unaware of the appeal. With an annoyed sniff, she dug a band from one pocket and corralled the curly mass into an abundant ponytail.

"Nope. Both Mom and Dr. Marjorie are really curious about how picketwood handles fire. Dr. Marjorie was already studying picketwood, because it has some interesting disease control mechanisms. It'd have to since what looks to us like a whole grove is actually one tree with lots of trunks."

"Weird," Anders said. "But from what I've seen, really useful if you're a treecat."

"Exactly!" Jessica said, miming applause before she gathered up her collecting gear and started walking toward the air car. "The treecats are super-dependent on the picketwood. Aerial imaging's shown that the groves cross mountains, go all over continents."

"That means," Anders said excitedly, loading various buckets and bags into the back of Jessica's air car, "the treecats can travel just about anywhere."

Valiant leapt gracefully into the front seat, then moved so he could sit on the back of the seat behind Jessica's head. He made a bleeking sound and tugged at her ponytail, clearly protesting that the abundant massive hair was crowding him.

Jessica sighed and undid the ponytail, sweeping her curls into untidy order with the tips of her fingers. "I wish Valiant wanted to stick his head out the car window the way Lionheart does. Instead, he likes to snuggle. Sometimes I think I'm going to have to cut my hair all off—wear it really short, like Christine does."

"Oh, don't!" Anders protested impulsively, then felt himself color.

"What?" Jessica looked surprised at his vehemence, then laughed. "My hair's just so inconvenient. It always was, but now that Valiant likes to sit on it..."

Anders swallowed his embarrassment and tried to sound casual. "Oh, I just...I mean, it looks really pretty. I like the curls. It wouldn't look the same all short."

Jessica laughed. "I know. It was short when I was small. Mom said I looked like an angel, but I think I looked more like a frizzly-leone."

"Frizzly-leone?"

"It's a sort of plant they have on Sankar. Seedpods as big as my head that stick out in little parasols. They come in pink and pale blue. I think they'd be really popular, but the seeds get everywhere so they're considered a weed."

Relieved—though he wasn't sure why he was suddenly so flustered—Anders hurried to ask, "What makes something a weed, anyhow?"

Jessica' explanation—that basically the difference had more to do with humans than with plants—effectively got them off the subject of her hair. Jessica went on to tell a story about the time her family had been so low that they were making a living by pulling weeds in some rich man's garden.

"Dad's client didn't want the sound of machinery to intrude," she said. "What he didn't ever guess was that we were taking about half of what we pulled home and cooking it. He was pretty greedy, I bet he'd have tried to dock—"

She stopped and peered down, then glanced at the HUD.

"What's wrong, Jess?"

"I thought I saw something moving down there, but I'm not sure. The zoom on this junker is busted. Did you see anything?"

"No. I've got to admit, all this burned forest gives me the creeps, so I wasn't really looking. Was what you saw large?"

"Like a hexapuma or something? No. Probably just a near-otter or like that. Steph would know."

"Yeah." Anders felt the familiar pang. "She probably would, and—if she didn't—she'd want to go after it and get some images."

"Well, we'll leave the poor critter be," Jessica decided. "This is our last stop. Then I want to get home. Mom commed that she has medicine for Tiddles but, if I know her, she's going to have worn herself out. She'll need help."

And your dad's pretty useless for that, Anders thought. *A nice guy, but useless or your family wouldn't end up eating weeds.*

He wondered why the thought should make him so angry. Jessica had clearly thought the idea of "stealing" the rich man's weeds had been pretty funny. He was still trying to come to terms with the strength of his reactions when Jessica touched the air car down. Valiant, who'd been drowsing, woke up. All at once, he stiffened, gave a demanding bleek, and tapped the window.

Puzzled, Jessica opened the door. Valiant was out in a flash, loping over the burned ground in the direction of something that lay in a heap on the dirt. Jessica ran after him, then called back.

"Anders! It's a treecat. I think it's dead!"

Dirt Grubber awoke feeling distinctly unsettled. He had been dreaming of his gardens, inspecting the three different plantings side-by-side, as he never could do in reality. The plantings that grew within the protected confines of Plant Minder's transparent plant place were larger and healthier than those that grew either near Windswept's clan's home or those that grew near Damp Ground's central nesting place. Waking and sleeping, Dirt Grubber considered how to help those plants that must grow strong outside the shelter of the transparent plant place.

In his dream, he was sorting through the difficulties. The plantings near the bog were troubled by insects. He was considering the best way to protect them when, to his utter astonishment, the strong plants in the transparent plant place lifted off the roof, reached over, and began to rip the other plants out of the ground. The other plants fought back. Faced with two opponents, even the stronger plants could not escape injury. The destruction was horrible.

When Windswept touched the flying thing down, Dirt Grubber awoke. He felt very happy when he realized his plants were safe, that their destruction had been only a terrible dream.

He barely had a moment to enjoy his relief before his mind—reflexively searching the area as he always did when they arrived at a new place—touched that of another Person. The mind-glow Dirt Grubber encountered was dark and violent. If mind-glows had come in colors, this one would have been the purple-black of thunderheads.

<Who? What is wrong? How can I help you?> Dirt Grubber reached for the other Person and felt himself repelled by the force of the other's anger.

He tapped the flying thing's transparent side panel and Windswept let him free of the confined space. When he landed on the bare earth, he felt the brittleness of cinders beneath his feet. Without pause, he ran in the direction from which he tasted the other's mind-glow. Before he reached it, he came upon the body of another Person.

Dirt Grubber stood aghast, sending forth his query once more, this time not relying upon words, but instead projecting a heartfelt desire to give whatever help this stranger required of him.

<I am beyond help.> Pain and desperation now tinted the purple anger with lightning streaks of dark green and deep indigo. *<My clanmate is dead. Our clan is doomed. There is nothing left for us but death. Keep away lest I number you among my enemies, Bright Water Person.>*

<I am not of Bright Water,> Dirt Grubber protested, but the other was gone, his mind closed against hearing. Nor could Dirt Grubber tell in what direction the other had fled. People could easily trade information—entire life histories could be shared in moments. However, such a sharing took willingness on both sides. This angry stranger desired a privacy so complete that it made a mockery of sharing.

Dirt Grubber heard Windswept's feet pounding on the ashy ground. Bleached Fur followed her a few paces behind. In a moment, they would see the dead Person. Would they realize the cause of that one's death? Would they realize that, in defiance of custom, tradition, and common sense, one Person had killed another?

If they did not, could he keep them from realizing? Could he somehow hide this horrible crime from the knowledge of the two-legs?

Anders raced to where Jessica crouched next to the cream and gray figure that lay so unnaturally still upon the ground.

"I wonder how long he's been dead?" He asked. "Not long, I think. I mean there aren't any—well, there aren't any bugs crawling on him."

Jessica started to touch the still form, then drew her hand back. "No. We'd better handle it as little as possible. We don't know what killed it, but if it was disease, we might spread whatever it was to Valiant."

Certainly the treecat had retreated a good distance from the body and seemed eager to stay away from it.

"Good point." Anders, however, was his father's son, and he couldn't resist trying to figure out a little more. Picking up a stick, he gently lifted the corpse's head. "I'm not sure this guy died from disease, Jess. Look. There and there. Those look like bite or claw marks to me. I hate to say it, but it seems to me that something ripped this poor guy's throat out."

"There's not a lot of blood," Jessica protested. "Sure, there's some on his fur, but not much anywhere else. Maybe he caught a disease that caused itching or hives or something and those marks are from him trying to get at it. My little sister Melanie-Anne had to wear gloves all the time when she had reesels while we were living on Tasmania or she might've left scars. Or maybe something shot him with a poison spine. The problem with Sphinx is that we know too little about what lives here. Most of what's been recorded is because those creatures interact in some way—usually a negative one—with humans. There are zillions of small animals, plants, birds, and insects we don't know anything about."

"You've got a point," Anders agreed, lowering the corpse's head and gently manipulating the torso with his stick. "It's hard to tell with all that fur, but the poor guy does look skinny. Maybe you're right. Maybe he'd been sick for a while and couldn't eat. Maybe he left his clan or was chased out to avoid contagion. I guess the question is what we do with him?"

"We could bury him," Jessica said. "That way if he was sick, the sickness won't spread."

"We could take him to Dr. Richard," Anders countered. "He could probably find out the cause of death."

"I'm not sure," Jessica said. "Mom mentioned he's crazy busy. The Harringtons are getting ready to go away to Manticore so they can have a holiday before Stephanie's graduation. Anyhow, I hate the idea of the poor 'cat's body being poked it. I mean, it's okay for humans to do that to humans, but we don't really know how the treecats feel about their dead. I'd hate to do something that would make Valiant uncomfortable. I can't tell what he's thinking, but I can feel he's pretty miserable."

"I wonder if Valiant knew this guy?" Anders mused. "He seems really upset. How far can treecats communicate?"

"No idea. And this isn't the time to start trying to figure that out. Whether or not Valiant knew this treecat isn't important. What we need to figure out is what we should do that won't make him more unhappy."

"Can you ask Valiant what we should do?"

Jessica shook her head. "Nothing that complex. The best I can do is see how he reacts if we try something like burying the body. Valiant knows how to let me know not to do something, just like he knows how to encourage me if I'm doing something he likes."

Anders sighed. "Still, I feel funny not knowing how this treecat died. What if there's a plague? Shouldn't someone know?"

Jessica shook her head again, this time so violently her curls bounced and covered her face. "Not necessarily. Anders, as much as people like your dad and the other xenoanthropologists like to forget it, the treecats were dealing with issues like death and dying for a long time before humans came to this planet. Just because this is the first dead treecat either of us has seen doesn't mean there haven't been others."

"I understand." Anders frowned. "Okay. How about this? We see how Valiant reacts if we try to bury this guy. If he doesn't mind, we do it. But before this fellow goes in the ground, I take some images. I won't give them to my dad or anything like that. I'll just have them on file. We'll mark the coordinates here, too. That way if something happens—like disease breaking out—we can at least add information."

Jessica considered for a long while, staring at Valiant as she did so. Anders wondered if she was trying to guess her companion's reaction. Eventually, she nodded.

"Okay. But the images don't go to your dad. Promise?"

"Not without your permission. Not to my dad, not to anyone else on the team, not to anyone at all without your permission."

Jessica smiled at him. "Thanks. You know, I wonder if we should ask Stephanie?"

"I don't think so. Steph's pretty busy getting ready

for finals. Besides, what could even Stephanie tell from a bunch of images?"

Jessica turned toward the air car. "Well, one good thing about being out collecting plants. We have shovels. I'll get them."

"I'll start taking images."

"Stop if Valiant seems unhappy."

"Right."

But Valiant didn't seem to care in the least when Anders started recording images.

When Jessica returned with the shovel and started digging a hole over where the grave would neither be obvious nor interfere with her mother's test area, Valiant loped over and started digging with her.

"I guess he agrees," Anders said. "Unless he just thinks you're getting ready to plant another garden bed and he's eager to help."

"No, it's not that," Jessica replied. "I think he knows why I'm doing this. I can't explain how, since it's just a feeling, but I think I'm right. He's helping and he's eager we get this taken care of. I wonder if he was so worried because he thought we were just going to leave the body to rot out in the open."

Anders finished with his images and came over to help with the digging. They didn't need as large a hole as they would have for a human body, but the ground had been baked hard enough that even with the modified vibro blade cutting edge on the shovel, it was hard work.

Valiant wandered off once both humans were at work and returned as they were finishing up. He'd filled one of his larger carrying nets with the reddish autumn leaves from the picketwood trees. When the humans stepped back, he dropped most of these in to line the grave.

"Well, I guess he approves," Jessica said. "If we lift the body on one of the shovels, we can disinfect the blade afterwards. Better than using our hands. We didn't see any bugs, but there might be some."

"I'll do it," Anders said. "You stay in tune with Valiant and make sure I'm not doing anything wrong."

But the stout treecat didn't do anything in the way of protest. Instead, he sprinkled the last of his picketwood leaves over the corpse, then began digging the dirt back into the grave. The two humans helped him. Before long, only a small mound of broken dirt remained to mark where a fellow creature had ended his life's journey.

"I wonder if treecats pray?" Jessica said. "My family's lived on so many planets, I don't really have any set religion. Still, I don't suppose it would hurt to be quiet for a moment."

"Not at all," Anders agreed.

They bent their heads but kept their thoughts to themselves. Anders wondered what Valiant made of this, but he figured that the treecat was enough in touch with Jessica's emotions to sense that respect was intended.

When Jessica raised her head her hazel-green eyes were bright with tears, but she only shook back her curls and raised her chin as if defying Anders to comment.

"Come on," she said. "We need to record those images for my mom and take samples. I want to be back in time to help cook dinner."

"And what do you have to say about Ms. Harrington and Mr. Zivonik now, Harvey?" Mordecai Flouret inquired genially.

Smoke drifted from the barbecue grill between him and Harvey Gleason and the shouts of children splashing in the waves rolling in from Jason Bay competed with the curious, warbling cries of the wave-cresters circling overhead. The wave-cresters were the planet Manticore's equivalent of Old Earth's seagulls, and the silver and brown bird analogs were just as determined when it came to scavenging any tasty bit of garbage that came their way. Which was probably why they were keeping such an avid eye on Flouret's grill at that very moment. He rather doubted they'd have any objection to snatching one of the sauce-coated chicken breasts if the chance came.

At the moment, though, he was more interested in Gleason's response. They might be colleagues on the Landing University faculty, and their wives and children might like one another (which was the reason for this afternoon's picnic), but there were times he wasn't very fond of Gleason.

The other man was very good in his field, and LUM was fortunate to have him, especially this early in the process of developing its curriculum, but he was also full of a sense of his own importance, and he sometimes seemed to resent the fact that Flouret was the chairman of a fully established department. He'd tried to downplay his irritation at being required to make room for "runny nosed kids" (as he had rather injudiciously expressed himself on one occasion) into *his* forestry studies courses, but he hadn't fooled anyone who knew him. And he had a well-developed capacity to cherish grudges for a long, long time, as well, but this time he surprised Flouret.

"Actually," he said, "I've been very impressed with them. Both of them, to be honest, although given how young she is, I suppose its inevitable people are going to be even more impressed with her."

He met Flouret's gaze levelly as he made the admission, and the criminology professor found himself forced to reconsider a few prejudices of his own. Maybe Gleason had something rather closer to an open mind than he'd thought.

"Really?" he asked.

"She's mastered every bit of the course material without breaking a sweat," Gleason said. "And to be honest, she already knows more about Sphinx's flora than ninety percent of my students know *after* they graduate. More holes on the Manticoran side of her knowledge, but that was only to be expected, and she's worked hard to fill them. Despite—" he acknowledged dryly "—a certain suspicion on her part that she's never going to need that particular body of knowledge and that a certain professor's only insisting she learn it to be a pain. And Zivonik's just as sharp as she is, in his own way. Not as quick, perhaps, but...steadier, I think. The two of them are a team, of course. You only have to glance at them to see that. But I think his job is to be the balance wheel while hers is to go rushing off to find the next challenge. They're surprisingly formidable for such youngsters, when you come down to it."

"That was my impression, too," Flouret agreed. "I have to admit I'm a little surprised to hear you share it, though, Harvey."

"I know." Gleason's eyes glinted with an unusual flicker of amusement. "Didn't expect me to admit I did, either, did you?"

"Well, no," Flouret admitted, using his tongs to turn the chicken breasts sizzling on the grill.

"Thought not." Gleason took a sip from his bottle of beer, then shook his head. "I suppose I had it coming, too. But do me a favor and don't rub it in *too* hard, all right?"

"I'll try," Flouret promised with a grin. "It'll be hard, you understand, but I *will* try."

13

KEEN EYES DID NOT TRY TO SPEAK TO ANY MEMBER of his clan before he reached their current nesting place. Instead, he sat while the darkness passed, striving to gain mastery over his thoughts and emotions so that he would not give himself away when he was once again close to People. There was a remote chance Beautiful Mind had not felt her mate's death. If so, he was not going to be the one to let her know that Red Cliff had gone further than merely out of range of their mind-voices. If she did know and somehow still kept her grasp on life, he did not wish her to know that Red Cliff's death had been horribly unnatural, that his life had been ripped from him by the claws of another Person, that even his dead body had been rejected as anathema.

He managed this nearly impossible task before he reached the grove near the river where the Landless Clan now squatted. He was relieved to learn Beautiful Mind was still alive. The females who were attending her reported that she had been very agitated at one point, so Keen Eyes suspected she already knew of her loss.

Sour Belly and some of the other elders had been lucky in their fishing that day. When Keen Eyes arrived, most of the clan were shredding their way into the tender flesh. It was an indication of their reduced circumstances that fishheads, tails, and even bones were being set aside for a later meal. Nothing even remotely edible would be wasted in these hard times.

Although Keen Eyes had returned with nothing to add to the feast, Wonder Touch, Sour Belly's mate—a Person as sweet and nice as her mate was sour and unyielding— called out to him.

<*Welcome back, Keen Eyes. We have saved you enough dinner to put some fat back on your bones. Tiny Choir and her littermates found a lake builder's cache from last season, so we have some fruit as well.*>

Keen Eyes thanked her enthusiastically, then invited Tiny Choir and her siblings to tell him all about how they had found the dry fruit. They had really been quite clever, guessing that the pool near which the clan now camped had probably been the result of some lake builders' beginning work.

<*Probably a death fang got them,*> Tiny Choir said, her mind-voice wildly excited. <*Lake builders usually store food, so we went looking and we found it.*>

Even as he praised the kittens, Keen Eyes could not but think how far the clan had fallen. To be glad to have these shriveled and bitter fruit when before their home had been destroyed these would have been tossed away as inedible. However, he *was* grateful. The nights were already too cold for lace leaf to thrive. The green-needle nuts had turned to ash along with the trees that bore them. Any supplement to the thin hunting was welcome.

When he had eaten, Keen Eyes considered who he

could tell about Red Cliff's death. As much as he would have liked to keep the matter secret, there was too much risk to the clan. Already, he suspected they were in lands Trees Enfolding Clan viewed as their own. Any roving hunter might meet the same fate as Red Cliff.

Keen Eyes would have preferred to take the matter up first with the clan's memory singers, to learn what precedents were in place for such a situation, but Wide Ears and her juniors were gone. For a moment, he considered consulting Tiny Choir, but he knew this impulse for the cowardice was. Even if Wide Ears had begun teaching the kitten, she would not have shared information about past wars between clans. Memory songs were vivid, perfectly re-creating all of the thoughts and emotions—bad, as well as good; ugly and vile as well as courageous and selfless—that the events at their heart had evoked. Songs recounting the anger and hatred, the wrenching loss of mates and kittens, the extinguishing a beloved mind-glows, were hard enough for adults to accept. They would almost certainly warp the sensibility of a growing kitten who believed that all possible problems could be resolved because shared mind-glows made misunderstandings impossible, and so they were passed only into the keeping of those made strong enough by age and experience to bear them.

In the end, he did what he had known he must all along and reported what he had learned to all the adult members of the clan. The reaction was as bad as he had dreaded it would be.

Only respect for the young and injured kept mind-voices within their lower registers. Red Cliff's death would have been upsetting enough, but the contempt for the entire clan shown by how his body had been dumped was enough to enrage even the most moderately tempered Person.

<I notice something very interesting in your report,>

commented Bowl Shaper, a senior female highly respected for her work in clay. *<Twice you have spoken with this Swimmer's Scourge. Once his nephew Nimble Fingers was also present. However, they have taken great care to stay outside of the range at which you might have tasted their mind-glows.>*

<You are correct,> Keen Eyes agreed. *<I think it was deliberate. My ability to taste another's mind-glow is not as strong as it would be if I were bonded with a mate. I guess that one or both of these is stronger than I am and would be able to detect me before I detected him. It would then be a simple matter for him to speak to me. He would know that once I heard his voice, even if I could not see him, I could reply and the advantage would remain his.>*

<This speaks of a cunning individual,> Bowl Shaper replied.

<Or sneaky,> cut in Sour Belly.

<Or both,> a younger female, Knot Binder, said pacifically. *<Trees Enfolding Clan has chosen its border guards carefully. We should respect this and take it into consideration when we plan what to do next.>*

<And we will *do something,>* Sour Belly asserted. *<Red Cliff may have come from elsewhere, but he had become a valued member of this clan. His children will not grow up to learn that we did not care that their father was murdered.>*

<I have wondered,> Keen Eyes said, trying to share a half-formed idea that had come to him as he made his way back to the clan with news of Red Cliff's death, *<if perhaps the Trees Enfolding Clan does not understand how dire our need is. Perhaps the one who spoke to me—Swimmer's Scourge—was so worried about the fate of his own clan this coming winter that he could not find sympathy for strangers. The fact that he was able to stay at the very fringes of my mind-glow would have made it easier for him to think*

*only about the needs of his own clan, to see me only as an
invader, a threat.>*

<*So?*> scoffed Sour Belly. <*Would you have us go to
them, force our mind-glows upon them?*>

<*Not quite,*> Keen Eyes replied, striving to project
patience rather than the irritation he felt. <*What if we
brought one of them close enough so that he could not
ignore what our mind-glows would show him? Let them
taste the fear of the kittens who have lost parents, the
hunger that gnaws the bellies of all our people. Once even
one Person of their clan knows how terrible things are for
us, surely they would at least let us pass through their
territories and seek refuge elsewhere. They might even pity
us and take us in.*>

Keen Eyes was pleased to feel that many members of
the clan were interested in his idea. Others still projected
doubt. He turned to Knot Binder.

<*Something about my idea troubles you? Perhaps if
you would explain, we could use your ideas to make a
stronger plan.*>

<*I am afraid of what might happen if we brought some-
one here. You have said that you think Trees Enfolding is
tolerating our living on this poor fringe of their territory.
What happens if we force the clan as a whole to take
notice? What if they decide to drive us out?*>

Keen Eyes was about to reply when Bowl Shaper surprised him by speaking with great force.

<*I share your fear, clan sister, but either Trees Enfold-
ing will chase us out or the coming of winter will do so.
This is a decent nesting place now, but what will happen
when the stream freezes and even our best fishers can no
longer find prey? We have already been forced to eat the
leavings of lake builders. We have scraped the stones bare
of rockfur. I am no memory singer, but I recall the tales
Wide Ears told of when winter stretched unreasonably*

long. Then hunger-maddened clans fought each other to the death over a handful of green-needle nuts. Our Landless Clan cannot avoid conflict. We can only choose whether we will make our move while we still have some strength or wait until desperation pushes us.>

<I understand, Bowl Shaper.> Knot Binder shivered as if she felt the icy winds that Bowl Shaper had evoked in memory. *<I withdraw my objection.>*

<How then,> asked Sour Belly, *<shall we go about issuing an invitation to visit us? Somehow, I fancy that if anyone in the Trees Enfolding Clan actually cared to know us, they would have come by now.>*

Keen Eyes stroked his whiskers with one true-hand. He had thought this part out with care but had deliberately withheld the details of his plan until he knew the clan would at least consider it.

<I have an idea,> he said. *<Let me show you.>*

"So what did your mom have to say?"

"Um?"

Stephanie looked up from her reader. She sat crosslegged on the bench under the shading branches of the Manticoran blue-tip tree, the reader in her lap. Lionheart stretched companionably beside her with his chin propped on her thigh, and she blinked.

"I asked what your mom had to say," Karl repeated with a smile. Stephanie in "I'm studying hard" mode had about as much situational awareness as a rock, he reflected.

"Oh." Stephanie blinked again, then grinned crookedly, recognizing his amusement. "Sorry. I was really locked in. She said she and Dad are having a wonderful time seeing all the sights. And they darn well should, too! This is the first vacation they've had since we got to Sphinx."

"I know." Karl nodded. "They've worked their butts off

ever since you guys got here. I'm glad they're having a good time. Wish you could be showing them around?"

"Show them *what?*" Stephanie snorted a laugh. "Aside from the meetings with the Adair Foundation, we haven't been off campus more than twice! They're making out better with the standard guide package and their uni-links than anything *I* could tell them."

"You're probably right," Karl agreed, and looked back down at his own reader. Despite Stephanie's laugh, there'd been at least a little bite in her response, and from the corner of his eye he watched Lionheart's ears twitch. He'd learned to read the 'cat's body language almost as well as he could read another human's, and he could tell a lot about Stephanie's mood by reading Lionheart's. And just that moment, she obviously wished she *could* be touring Manticore with her parents. Unfortunately, it was exam week, and even Stephanie was finding herself pushed by the pressure. Both of them carried averages which would see them successfully complete their courses even if they blew the finals pretty badly, but neither of them was interested in just scraping by. Doing the best they could would have been a point of pride with them under any circumstances, but given Ranger Shelton's decision to expend precious slots on a couple of kids, they had a special responsibility to do him proud.

Not that there'd ever been much chance *Stephanie* wouldn't do just that, he reflected wryly.

"You want to go back over Dr. Flouret's discussion questions again?" Stephanie asked, as if she'd been able to read his mind, and he chuckled.

"Couldn't hurt," he acknowledged. "But, truth to tell, I'm more concerned about Dr. Tibbetts." He shook his head. "I know it's going to be open-link to the library, but I'm not as good at searching precedents as you are, Steph!"

"You're better than you think you are," she scolded,

and Lionheart bleeked emphatically, arching his spine and stretching luxuriantly.

Karl was always putting himself down where the purely academic side of their courses were concerned, she thought. He *did* do better when it came to fieldwork, true, but he was better than three quarters or more of their classmates when it came to the more sedentary portions of the curriculum, as well.

"Doing better than I think I am wouldn't be all that hard," he pointed out with a chuckle. "Don't bite my head off, Steph! I don't think I'm going to tank the exam, you know. But the truth is, you're a lot more comfortable with jurisprudence than I am. And I'm not all that clear on why a ranger needs Jurisprudence 101, anyway. We're not going to be judges or magistrates!"

"No," she agreed. "But it does make sense for us to have at least a basic understanding of how it works. Right now, ranger field assignments are basically common sense and seat-of-the-pants, but it's not going to be that way forever. That's why Ranger Shelton's trying to build up the supply of trained, *professional* rangers, and having at least some notion of what the courts are likely to do with anybody we end up dealing with in a...professional capacity, let's say, isn't going to hurt a thing."

"Probably not," he agreed. "But the truth is I'd rather take Dr. Gleason's exam twice than take Dr. Tibbetts' once! She always makes me think she's going to throw me into jail somewhere if I screw up."

"That's a terrible thing to say!" Stephanie's tone was severe, but her lips twitched. Dr. Emily Tibbetts—also known as Justice Tibbetts—was a senior member of the King's Bench who taught introductory jurisprudence courses at LUM. She had a severe way about her, but Stephanie had caught something suspiciously like a twinkle in her brown eyes on more than one occasion.

Besides, she'd not only decided Lionheart could accompany Stephanie to class, she obviously liked the treecat. More to the point, perhaps, Lionheart liked *her*. "Dr. Tibbetts is perfectly nice," she continued. "And even if she weren't, I promise I'd file a writ of *habeas corpus* as soon as her minions dragged you away."

"Gee, thanks."

"You're welcome. But, you know," Stephanie went on more thoughtfully, "we could always pick Jeff's brain. He took the same course last semester, and he's taking Jurisprudence 102 *this* semester. If anyone we know knows the kinds of questions Dr. Tibbetts is likely to ask, it's him."

Karl raised an eyebrow at the suggestion. Jeff Harrison was one of their classmates in Dr. Flouret's criminology course. A native of Manticore, not Sphinx, he obviously intended to pursue a law-enforcement career on the capital planet, and he was several years older than Karl, much less Stephanie. He was also ridiculously citified in Karl's opinion, but he was fascinated by Lionheart and he'd become one of their Manticore-born friends.

Besides, Karl reminded himself, *he might be hopeless in the bush*, but *you're not that much better in a* city, *now are you?*

"That might be a very good idea," he said after a moment. "No way she'd use the same questions over again, but I really would feel better if I could talk it over with someone who's already survived her course once!"

With Knot Binder providing direction, the Landless Clan set about building a net in which they could catch and hold another Person. This was not an easy task, for a Person's claws were very sharp and could slash through just about anything, if given time. Nor was it a fast one. However, because they were small compared to enemies such as death fangs and snow hunters, People were also very patient, and Knot Binder's assistants knew careful preparation could mean the difference between living and dying.

Knot Binder supplied an exceptionally tough cord that combined the fibers of several different plants with the shed fur of People. This type of cord required so much time to make that, even with fire raging closer and closer, Knot Binder had insisted on bearing a coil of it away with her. Now she showed the others how to work it into a net with a noose closure, so that it could be pulled into a sort of bag.

As a final refinement, Wonder Touch—who was one of the clan's healers and wise about plants and their properties—supplied a bitter-tasting paste with which the strands of the net could be coated.

<*It burns a little*,> she cautioned, <*so apply it with a brush. However, it should keep our captive from either biting through the net or tearing it apart as quickly.*>

Keen Eyes thanked her. <*We do not wish to keep him imprisoned very long, but anything that will gain us a little time is very welcome.*>

The next stage of Keen Eyes' plan was more complicated. After conferring with the Landless Clan's scouts and hunters, he had confirmed his own impressions. He was the scout who had gone most deeply into the territory held by Trees Enfolding Clan and the *only* member of the clan who had actually encountered a member of Trees Enfolding.

Well, other than poor Red Cliff, and he cannot help us now.

This likely meant the Trees Enfolding Clan was actively avoiding the area. It was not as if there was much incentive to go into the sun-rising parts of their range, given the poor pickings. In any case, with winter coming on, every spare adult would be involved in preparing whatever food the hunters and plant gatherers brought in.

<I have encountered only Swimmer's Scourge and Nimble Fingers,> Keen Eyes explained. <My guess is that Swimmer's Scourge is in charge of watching our edge of their territory and that he has taken a few family members as assistants. We all know that it is easier to speak to a Person once he is known to you. Since I am at least somewhat known to these two, they will hear me before anyone else will. I will go into the general area where I found Red Cliff's body and set the net. Then I will think angry thoughts. My hope is that one or both will come to confront me.>

<Why would they do that?> asked Sour Belly, who was not in the least happy with the prominence young Keen Eyes had recently acquired. <Why would they not just ignore you?>

<I am counting on basic curiosity,> Keen Eyes replied. <But if that is not enough, I have other tactics in mind.>

Sour Belly sniffed as if he did not believe this was the case, but he did not ask for details. Keen Eyes did not volunteer them, either. He was committed to this course of action and though he thought he had some good ideas, he did not want Sour Belly's nasty comments to undermine his confidence.

<What help do you need from the clan?> Bowl Shaper asked. In the absence of a fully-trained memory singer, she seemed to be taking on some of the leadership role that would have belonged to Wide Ears.

<I could use a couple of strong hunters to come with me to help carry my captive if he will not come willingly,> Keen Eyes responded promptly. <I had thought about asking Hard Claw and Firm Biter if they can be spared from the hunt.>

<There is nothing to hunt,> Hard Claw replied promptly.

<Red Cliff was life-partner to my own littermate. I would be happy to capture the one who killed him.>

Anger flooded Hard Claw's mind-glow, showing how dangerous his "happy" cooperation could be. Keen Eyes had suggested Hard Claw and Firm Biter because, like him, they were among the Landless Clan's unbonded males. Now he wondered if he had been unwise.

<We are not seeking revenge,> Bowl Shaper cautioned. *<We are seeking a place where we have a hope of surviving the winter. All hope will be lost if you use your much-storied claws out of turn. You do realize that?>*

<I do,> Hard Claw replied. His mind-glow brightened, although not all the anger left it. *<Perhaps making this killer see what he has done will be a better revenge than death's quiet. You can count on me. I will follow Keen Eyes' commands and do my best to make sure his plan succeeds.>*

<Thank you,> Keen Eyes said, flooding his mind-glow with the tremendous gratitude he felt. He was relieved to feel honest pleasure balancing Hard Claw's anger. *<I will ask you and Firm Biter to stay to sun-rising of me, out of the range where your mind-glows could be easily detected. I will also ask you to concentrate on muting your mind-glows as much as possible.*

<Our plan will work best if the one we seek to trap believes me alone. I will bait the trap. When I call to you that we have our captive, you will race forward and help me bear him away as quickly as possible.>

<But this captive is sure to call for help,> Sour Belly sneered.

This time Keen Eyes was not even tempted to offer any further explanation. *<I think I have a way to keep him from calling.>*

Knot Binder fluffed her tail in a nervous fashion. *<Keen Eyes, you keep speaking of "he," as if you are certain you will face a single opponent. How can you be so sure?>*

<I am not sure,> Keen Eyes admitted, *<but I plan to do what I can to make matters go the way I wish. First, I will direct my mind-voice to one and one alone. I had thought to try to call Nimble Fingers, because he seemed more sympathetic than his uncle. Nimble Fingers also seemed quite junior to me. I will go out at a time when it is likely his senior will be taking his ease...I was thinking of the hours when night is giving way to dawn and neither the day-prey or night-prey are active. That is when a senior hunter would rest.>*

<And if your cleverness does not work?> Needless to say, this came from Sour Belly.

<Then I must rely upon courage,> Keen Eyes returned levelly. *<As Bowl Shaper said, winter will remove all our choices. We must act while choice remains.>*

"We're running out of time, Gwen," Oswald Morrow pointed out a bit diffidently across the table. The two of them were dining in an expensive restaurant whose clientele were prepared to pay inflated prices in return for guaranteed privacy as they dined. "They've only got another week or so before they head back to Sphinx."

"Really?" Gwendolyn Adair's response dripped irony. "Do you know, Ozzie, I do believe I read something about that somewhere already!"

"I'm not the one joggling your elbow," Morrow pointed out. "It's Frampton. She's getting impatient."

Gwendolyn started to snap at him, then stopped. Angelique Frampton, Countess Frampton, was the grand-daughter of a first shareholder whose son had improved upon his father's originally fairly modest position through a lifetime of aggressive (some would have said unscrupulous) financial maneuvers. Over the course of his and Angelique's lifetimes, the Framptons had moved into the uppermost ranks of the Star Kingdom's wealthy, and as part of that climb, they'd acquired a huge portfolio of Sphinxian land options and leveraged it for all it was worth. At the moment, those land options were valued at "only" four or five hundred million dollars. Over the course of the next thirty to forty T-years, that value would at least triple, and the bankable value they already represented had been used as security for loans totaling just over a billion dollars. Those loans were critical to the Earldom of Frampton's solvency, and their terms required full payment or refinancing within the next ten T-years. Repayment would be difficult or even impossible; refinancing would be a routine transaction…as long as the options' value was maintained.

That would have been cause enough for Angelique to seek proactive means of protecting their worth, yet that was hardly her only motivation. Nor was the sizable stash of options in Gwendolyn's portfolio *her* only motivation. True, both she and the countess stood to lose heavily in purely financial terms if they were invalidated or even simply declined in market value, although Frampton stood to lose far more. But the countess also possessed a vindictive streak at least a kilometer wide. Those were *her* land options. No stinking clutch of misbegotten, ratlike little aliens was going to take what was hers! She would probably survive financially if she lost the options, but her fortune would be brutally reduced…and she was just the sort of person to use what was left of it taking vengeance on whoever had allowed—or caused—that to happen.

On someone like Gwendolyn Adair, for example.

"I imagine she's not the only one who's feeling impatient," Gwendolyn said after a moment, instead of biting Morrow's head off, and he snorted.

"*All* of them are getting antsy, if that's what you mean."

He shook his head. "For someone who's only gotten off campus twice—aside from her visits to the Adair Foundation, anyway—Harrington and that little monster have attracted an awful lot of favorable press. Every time I think about that puff piece the *Landing Observer* did on her I want to throw up. Even *Harvey's* in her corner now! He says she's one of the best students he's ever had, and the last time I talked to him, he went on *forever* about how smart her treecat is, too."

"I know." It was Gwendolyn's turn to shake her head. "She's more personable than I'd hoped, and she's got those idiot friends of George's eating out of her hand at the foundation."

Stephanie and Karl had visited the Adair Foundation five times now—three times to meet with the foundation's directors, who also happened to be its most generous donors. There wasn't much doubt what sort of impression she'd made on *them*, unfortunately. Not that it had come as much of a surprise to Gwendolyn.

"It was your idea to invite her," Morrow pointed out.

"Yes, it was. And if *I* hadn't thought of it, someone else would have—probably George himself."

Gwendolyn's tone was acid. Her cousin George Lebedyenko took his position as Earl of Adair Hollow—and CEO of the Adair Foundation—seriously. Usually, she found that more useful than not, but there were times (and this looked like one of them) when his personal interest could become more of a hindrance than a help.

"The treecats are exactly what the foundation was set up to protect," she continued. "That's one reason Angelique sent you to me in the first place on this one, Ozzie. At least by issuing the invitation I was in a position to control how much contact young Stephanie actually had with them."

"Granted." Morrow shrugged. "But Frampton would be

a lot happier if we could've at least managed to give the 'oh-aren't-treecats-cute' lobby a bit of a black eye while we had them here on Manticore."

"Oh, I haven't given up on that," Gwendolyn assured him. "In fact, I have good news for Stephanie and Karl. The management at the Charleston Arms has finally agreed to allow Lionheart not just on the premises, but into the private dining room."

"*What?*" Morrow stared at her across the table. "I thought we'd agreed that the last thing we wanted—"

"—was the foundation's membership getting a chance to meet the little monster personally and fall under his spell," Gwendolyn finished for him, and waved one hand impatiently. "Of course we did. But I was in two minds about that from the beginning. And since George has decided *he* wants Lionheart admitted to the next foundation meeting, I decided it would probably be less than desirable for him to find out *I've* been the one discreetly dragging my heels on that from the beginning. Especially when he's actually going to be able to be present for the next meeting instead of delegating to his faithful proxy cousin."

"Well, that's the game," Morrow said gloomily. Unlike Gwendolyn, he hadn't personally met Lionheart, but he'd watched quite a bit of covertly obtained long-range imagery of the treecat, and he *had* met Stephanie. "Once they see the two of them together, they're going to jump right on the treecat bandwagon."

"Oh, grow up, Ozzie!" Gwendolyn looked at him irritably. "*That* was going to happen no matter what we did! What? You expected the *foundation* to come down in favor of exterminating all treecats? And that doesn't even count George! It's been a given that they'd feel compelled to come to the little beasties' rescue."

"So you decided to get behind and push them in that direction? Is that it?"

"Exactly." Gwendolyn smiled at Morrow's expression. "The best we're going to be able to do with them is get them to sign on for the reservation option, Ozzie. George will be inclined in the direction of 'protecting them from human contact' no matter what—it's going to be an automatic reflex on his part—and the foundation's board almost always follows his lead. You know that as well as I do. What we need to do is to steer George in the direction he'd take anyway...and do it in a way which will push the board even more strongly into supporting him."

"And giving them an opportunity to actually meet Lionheart is going to do that?" Morrow looked skeptical. "You've read Dr. Radzinsky's reports, and we've both watched the vids of Lionheart scampering around the campus with Harrington. They're sentient, Gwen, and you know it. In fact, they're probably even smarter than we were afraid they were! If the board gets a chance to spend any time in Lionheart and Harrington's presence, a lot of them—I'm thinking of Turner and Fitzpatrick, especially—are going to see this as some kind of healthy symbiotic relationship between two highly intelligent species. And it'll be the first time humans have ever managed anything of the sort, too. If they decide that's what's going on on Sphinx, they're almost certain to vote in favor of some act granting the treecats the legal status of full sentients!"

"First, Turner and Fitzpatrick are going to do that anyway. Second, anybody with half a brain who's actually listened to how Harrington and Lionheart met ought to realize treecats can be dangerous. Third, *dangerous* aborigines need to be isolated, both to protect them from corruption—not to mention the sorts of reactions that interaction with the threats and challenges of a high-tech society are likely to provoke—and to protect innocent bystanders from injury if something triggers their fight-or-flight mechanism. And fourth, Ozzie, who ever said Harrington and her little friend were actually going to *get* to the next meeting?"

Morrow had opened his mouth to reply. Now he shut it very slowly, eyes narrowed in speculation at her across the table, and her knife-sharp smile was cold.

14

HARD CLAW AND FIRM BITER HELPED KEEN EYES POSI-
tion the net trap where any Person trying to reach Keen
Eyes must trigger it. Then they retired to the agreed-
upon distance. Keen Eyes concentrated on Nimble Fingers, focusing on the sense of the other Person he had
gained during their brief encounters. Then he shaped his
mind-voice into notes of anger and pain. He let himself remember Red Cliff as he had been when they had
last met, half-mad with grief over his beloved Beautiful Mind, weak in body because he kept insisting that
his share of the food be given to either his mate or
their kittens.

Keen Eyes shaped the images into mockery. <*I suspect
whoever slew Red Cliff thinks himself a hero, protecting
the home territory. What sort of hero gives death when
comfort is needed?*>

Making his memories into a coherent mind-voice image
was painful in and of itself. Keen Eyes let that pain

intensify the message. He showed the listener where he was, how he sat within Trees Enfolding's own territory.

At first, Keen Eyes thought his plan to lure Nimble Fingers to him had failed. He let his despair come forth to color his mind-voice. Perhaps this last was what made Nimble Fingers finally hear.

Nimble Fingers spoke to Keen Eyes, mind to mind.

<What do you mean by this insult?> Nimble Fingers said indignantly. *<If your clan brother is dead, we did not have anything to do with it. If this Red Cliff was as weak as you say, perhaps he fell victim to a young death fang or a flock of death-wings.>*

In reply, Keen Eyes sent a detailed image of Red Cliff's body as he had found it, claw-slashed and bloodied but with no indication that any part of it had been eaten, as surely would have been the case if the killer had been either of the fearsome predators suggested. He focused on showing how those wounds were very like those made by a Person's claws.

Nimble Fingers' reply was not so much a statement as a sense of uncertainty, a hint that perhaps Keen Eyes was not providing the full tale.

As he shaped his own reply, Keen Eyes also sensed the first hints of the other's mind-glow. In it he tasted no indication that Nimble Fingers had yet called for help from others in his clan. Whether this was because Nimble Fingers was young and impulsive or because what Keen Eyes had accused Trees Enfolding of having done made him uncertain, Keen Eyes could not be sure.

Keen Eyes kept projecting his own anger and grief, his certainty that his clan mate had been slain by another Person and that the killer belonged to Nimble Fingers' own clan. He kept his mind-voice narrowly focused, so that what he said would be heard only by Nimble Fingers. He sought to disorient Nimble Fingers, so the younger 'cat would hurtle forward, leaping from point to point without thinking very hard about what he might meet at the end.

Keen Eyes knew his own mind-glow would reflect his current state of mind. To the approaching Nimble Fingers, Keen Eyes would be a vibrant emotional storm in which his current intense anger and grief would dominate less immediate emotions. Keen Eyes knew his own excitement that his plan seemed to be working would blend into the storm. In such a situation, excitement and tension were only natural. Indeed, he had to fight not to attack when Nimble Fingers at last burst from the cover of the sheltering trees. Instead, Keen Eyes shifted his position so that when Nimble Fingers took his next leap he would land squarely in the trap prepared for him.

Nimble Fingers leapt. The spread net snapped shut into a ball with Nimble Fingers caught on the inside.

Before Nimble Fingers could call for assistance from his clan, Keen Eyes bombarded him with a shout of command.

<Hold and listen!>

With the swiftness of thought, Keen Eyes hammered into Nimble Fingers the one part of his discovery of Red Cliff that he had withheld to this moment—how when he had found his murdered friend's body he had been taunted from afar by Swimmer's Scourge. Keen Eyes had considered sharing this memory from the start, but he had chosen not to because he had worried that rather than racing forward in indignant defense of his uncle, Nimble Fingers might have chosen to confront Swimmer's Scourge.

Now the memory, perfect in every detail, hit Nimble Fingers like a blow. He stopped struggling against the tightly knotted mesh and hung limp.

<Swimmer's Scourge said that to you?> The statement

held no doubt as to the accuracy of Keen Eyes' reporting of the event, only shock and pain that a Person Nimble Fingers thought he knew so well could be capable of such cruelty. *<I knew Swimmer's Scourge was ferocious beyond measure in his desire to protect our clan's territory. He has said that the fire's invasion was enough for us to bear. He would not tolerate another invasion. Yet...that he could kill your Red Cliff and then brag of it to you—return to the clan and reveal nothing...>*

<He said nothing to the members of Trees Enfolding?>

<Nothing. Of course we could all tell he was overwrought and excited, but so have we all been. There has been much argument in the clan of late. There are two factions regarding where we should locate our winter central nesting place. There are those who believe we should let your clan pass through our lands, and others who believe with equal certainty that we should chase you from where you currently den. There are many other, smaller, arguments, as well, so that our memory singers and mind healers are worn out trying to mediate them.>

Nimble Fingers could easily have shared all the details of these clan quarrels fully with Keen Eyes. However, he clearly felt he had no reason to trust the other. Nonetheless, although Nimble Fingers could conceal details, he could not conceal the confusion and pain that now dominated his mind-glow.

Keen Eyes carefully tasted that mind-glow, but he saw no indication that Nimble Fingers was about to call for help. Soon, however, Nimble Fingers would get over his initial shock and call for someone—perhaps the senior memory singer. Therefore, Keen Eyes could not delay his next move, no matter how much sympathy he felt for the younger Person's confusion.

<If Swimmer's Scourge did not tell your clan what he did,> Keen Eyes said, abating some of his anger and replacing it

with a thoughtfulness that came easily because it was more natural to him, *<then perhaps I should tell them. Perhaps Swimmer's Scourge doubts that the rest of the Trees Enfolding clan would agree that he took the right course in killing Red Cliff. Perhaps he feels ashamed at how he added to my pain at the death of my clan mate through the cruelty of his taunts. Perhaps Trees Enfolding clan needs to hear this.>*

<No! Don't... It would... I told you, we are already...>

The younger Person's thoughts muddled into frantic incoherence. Keen Eyes hurried to offer a compromise.

<Perhaps I will wait... But if I agree, then you must promise not to call out for help. I want you to come with me to see my clan. I want you to be able to testify how severe our need is. Thus far, you of Trees Enfolding have kept your distance. You have been able to consider our plight as if it was merely a question of your convenience. I want an end to such denial.>

Keen Eyes opened himself to the younger Person, letting him see without reserve that Keen Eyes meant him no harm, that he could be set free this moment—but that Keen Eyes was equally sincere about carrying out his threat.

Nimble Fingers did not offer an answering openness, but remained thoughtfully silent for a long moment. When his reply came, it was lit with sincerity.

<I will come with you, Keen Eyes of the Landless. I promise that I will take back to my clan what I learn about your own. In return, will you spare my uncle?>

<For now. I do not see how the truth can be withheld forever, but I also do not see how causing more conflict within your clan will help my own.>

<Fair enough. You may take this net off of me. I will run with you of my own free will.>

Keen Eyes accepted his promise. Mind-voices might be able to withhold some aspect of an event. In such a manner, Swimmer's Scourge might have disguised his own emotional state as merely a reaction to the strain of current events. However, it was impossible for a Person to be dishonest to another Person when they stood close enough to read one another's mind-glows. He saw no indication that Nimble Fingers was anything less than vibrantly interested in doing what he could to preserve his clan's internal peace—and if that would also help the Landless Clan, then that was good, as well.

Keen Eyes spoke to Hard Claw and Firm Biter, sharing with them what had passed. Then he said, *<I will take Nimble Fingers back to our clan's current nesting place. You two should patrol this border and send warning if anyone misses Nimble Fingers and comes seeking him. Do not cause a confrontation. That might undo all we have managed to this point.>*

The two hunters agreed. Reassured that their backs were being watched, Keen Eyes led Nimble Fingers toward a meeting that they both hoped would change the fates of their clans.

Keen Eyes called ahead to the members of his clan that he was bringing Nimble Fingers in with him.

<He is a young Person, still very much in shock over the news of what Swimmer's Scourge has done. If you have it in you, be gentle with him. Even if you do not have much patience left, remember that our clan's fate may rest on how this Person sees us.>

He wondered what Nimble Fingers would see. Even in its prime, Swaying Fronds had been only a moderate-sized clan, for the mountains were not hospitable to the largest sized clans. Yet they had also been prosperous and well-fed. The mountains gave them good stone for their tools. They had strong stands of green-needle and gray-bark from which they harvested the seeds. The females with small kittens tended stands of golden-ear and other such bark-growing plants. Both seeds and bark-growing plants were kept against the thin days of winter, when hunting and fishing became more difficult.

Now they were poor beyond measure. Even thickening coats could not hide that most of them were growing gaunt. Moreover, many members of the clan had perished in the fires, others soon after it, for it took great need and support from the clan for the survivor of a bonded pair to carry on once one of the pair had died.

To make matters worse, many of the survivors were the very old, the very young, and the infirm. Swaying Fronds Clan had started its evacuation with these. Younger, stronger members of the clan had remained behind to salvage what they could of the stored food and tools—a task that had been viewed as especially important because even then the clan's elders could tell that the fires would destroy much of their territory and they would need every advantage if they were to make it through the winter.

It was a decision which had cost them dearly when the winds swirled suddenly, driving the flames before them like a tempest.

He was desperate to know how Nimble Fingers saw them. Would he see their need, or would he see a group of refugees—too many young, too many injured, too many elderly to be anything but a burden to Trees Enfolding clan? Keen Eyes was certain this was how Swimmer's Scourge had viewed them. Was it too much to hope his nephew would be any different?

Silently, Nimble Fingers passed among the members of the Landless Clan. Very few spoke to him, but their mind-glows were eloquent of their hope and need. Only the kittens—who had only heard tales of winter—were less eloquent of their desperation, but even they were scarred with grief and loss.

Keen ears paced behind Nimble Fingers, ready to protect him if any of the Landless Clan forgot that he was there as a guest, not an enemy. He tasted Nimble Fingers' mind-glow carefully, hoping for a clue as to how he would judge them. Surely there were the echoes of sympathy, of shared pain. Surely, Nimble Fingers was seeing them as they saw themselves—wounded but not beyond healing and growing strong again.

Hope was budding in Keen Eyes' heart when a sudden loud cry reached his mind. It came from Long Voice, a scout who had stationed himself where he could relay messages from Hard Claw and Firm Biter.

<*They come! They come! Trees Enfolding has tracked Nimble Fingers. They come to his rescue and intend our doom!*>

Any Person old enough to be accepted as an adult by the clan had heard the memory songs that recalled those rare and horrible times when People fought each other. Such times *were* rare, and the memory songs preserved from them were old, faded, yet still dreadful in their intensity. But Keen Eyes soon discovered that even their savage intensity fell short of reality.

Fangs and claws were the least of the weapons brought to bear. For clan to fight clan, the empathy that connected even People of different clans must be washed away in a tide of emotion so strong and fierce that it eliminated the awareness of the others as People, transforming them into Enemies.

So it was among the members of Trees Enfolding who descended upon the temporary nesting place of the Landless Clan. Their mind-glows were one loop of fury, of rage that their kindness had been met with cruelty, of fear for Nimble Fingers, of visions that horrible torments had been visited upon him. The attacking mass of People were beyond reason, for if they had been capable of reason, they could have reached for Nimble Fingers' mind, discovered that he lived, learn from him what had actually happened.

But reason was gone. All that remained were fangs and claws.

Already ravaged by their own many losses, by starvation, by dread of the coming winter, the Landless Clan rapidly mirrored Trees Enfolding in senseless rage. Elders swept panicked kittens into hiding, mated couples swept forth in terrible battle pairs, their linked mind-glows intensifying their shared fears into a berserker rage.

Caught as he was between these two emotional storms, Keen Eyes struggled to maintain some slim thread of reason. He felt Nimble Fingers striving to do the same. He heard as Nimble Fingers shouted at the top of his mind-voice that he was well, that there had been a mistake... that there was no need to fight.

But Trees Enfolding was deaf to reason. The tide of fear had risen beyond the triggering cause for this attack. As their grouped minds now perceived matters, the Landless Clan must be wiped out, eliminated before they could threaten Trees Enfolding further. Glimpses of the vision within their mind-glows showed Keen Eyes the Landless Clan not as it was, but as a combination of the cold, white power of winter and the cramping constriction of lands suddenly seen as too small to support them.

And in this image, Keen Eyes thought he smelled one mind more mad than all the rest—the stress-corrupted mind of Swimmer's Scourge.

Struggling to retain his own identity, Keen Eyes stretched his mind-voice to touch that of Nimble Fingers. *<Hide yourself, for if you die there is no hope! Hide!>*

Then he bunched his muscles for a great leap, seeking with all his power to separate the voice of Swimmer's

Scourge from the mind-glow storm that swirled in many-colored emotions around him.

He found the mind-glow he sought. Swimmer's Scourge was wild with glee as he tore into Tiny Choir's mother, battering her not only with fangs and claws, but with a determination that she understand that neither she nor her kittens deserved to live, anathema as they were in a land strained beyond the ability to support them.

<You should have died! Died! *Flesh and bones turned to ash. Fertilizer to feed the damaged forest. Die now! Let blood heal the wounded earth!>*

The images were nearly more than Keen Eyes could bear. He leapt forth, stretching his limbs to their utmost, six sets of claws extending to rend and tear. He hit his mark, felt blood flow, drowned in insanity beyond his comprehension.

Yet Keen Eyes struggled to retain a thread of sanity, fought for his clan but also for Trees Enfolding Clan, fought for the hope of the reconciliation that had seemed possible a bare moment before.

His mouth wet with a Person's blood, matted with fur, Keen Eyes felt Swimmer's Scourge's voice fade down the dark trails towards unconsciousness. Yet the reverberations of his insanity could not be so easily quieted. The battle storm raged around where they were entangled.

Keen Eyes did not know who hit him, whether one or many. His pain was a wind howl within a storm of fear and suffering.

The blackness that took him would have been welcome, but for the regret that he had failed.

"I think Mom's gotten to depend on us to make this run," Jessica laughed as she picked Anders up. "I hope you don't mind."

"I really don't," Anders said, sliding into the air car

next to her and presenting a piece of celery to Valiant by way of greeting. "Ever since the x-a's arrived, Dad's whole team's been incredibly focused. It's not that I don't like anthropology, but there are times I seriously need a break."

Valiant bleeked thanks to Anders and hopped into the back seat where he could eat his celery without dripping all over Jessica. Jessica set the car on course and leaned back in her seat.

"Mom asked if I'd expand my collecting zone. She wants samples of plants from the surrounding area to compare with those in the regrowth regions."

"That makes lots of sense," Anders replied. "Want to start today? The weather's really nice."

"You wouldn't mind? I don't want to bore you."

"Hey, Jess, take it easy. You never bore me."

"I..." Jessica leaned forward and made an unnecessary adjustment to the air car's controls. "I guess I've wondered...Worried. I mean, you're used to Stephanie. She's so much more interesting. I mean, look at this class she's taking, the people she's meeting...I'm just not in that league."

Impulsively, Anders reached out and laid a hand lightly on Jessica's shoulder. "Jess...Stephanie is great, really great. I have a lot of fun with her, but she's pretty intense, too. You're interesting, but you're not as intense."

"I get it," Jessica replied, and there was no ignoring the bitterness in her voice. "Stephanie's like a strong, sparkly jazzberry soda. I'm sort of like warm milk."

Anders was all too aware that his hand was still on her shoulder, but he felt that if he pulled it away, she'd take it as a rejection. He left it there, trying not to think about how nice it would be to slide over little closer, to put his arm around her. Jessica was taller than Stephanie and usually seemed so balanced and mature. Right now, she seemed small and delicate, very much in need of reassurance.

He drew in a deep breath. "Jessica, you're not like warm milk. I don't like warm milk, and I do like you. So, just stop it."

Jessica gave an unsteady laugh. "Sorry, I guess. I shouldn't be fishing for compliments from you of all people. It's just been a hard time with Tiddles sick. Did I tell you Dad almost got himself laid off again? He stayed home to take care of Tiddles and sort of forgot to call in. There are times I don't know why Mom puts up with him."

She sighed. Valiant bleeked from the backseat, then leapt gracefully up to pat his human comfortingly on the cheek before sliding down into her lap. Anders decided that the treecat had given him a good excuse to remove his own hand and did so, but he was amazed at how reluctant he was.

It can't be because Stephanie's been away. I mean, it's not like I'm that desperate. It's just that Jessica is ... She's really so sweet. She's always doing stuff for other people. I'd like ... I'd like to do something for her, *something to show her she's appreciated. Her dad doesn't appreciate her, and her mom relies on her too much to really appreciate ...*

His thoughts spiraled off into an uncomfortable muddle, not helped in the least by the fact that he thought Valiant was eyeing him in an amused fashion. Anders knew he was reading human expressions into that furred face, but still, there was something in the angle of the whiskers and cant of the ears ...

He realized the silence had been going on uncomfortably long and grabbed for the first thing he could think of.

"I guess your mom puts up with your dad because she loves him. Love makes people do some really incredible things. I mean, I sometimes wonder why *my* mom stays with my dad. He so obsessed, and it's not as if being married to a college professor does anything for her career. But when he got into trouble, she was right by his side, fierce as a neo-tiger. I'm pretty sure he'd have gotten into a lot more trouble with the university without her connections."

"Love..." Jessica said musingly. "It makes as much sense as anything. I can't figure out why people love each other. Sometimes it seems like a pretty lousy way for a species to perpetuate itself. People in love make the dumbest mistakes. Mom should have married a nice man who could have given her stability. People who like plants need to put down roots."

"But maybe," Anders countered, thinking of how Buddy Pheriss had confronted Duff DeWitt, "maybe what your mom wanted was someone who'd keep her from getting— well, like pot-bound. You know how they say 'opposites attract.'"

Jessica laughed without any tension this time. "Well, my folks could be the illustration for that one. I don't think I'm like my mom, though. I don't want someone I'd always have to worry about. I want someone who's steady in a crisis, someone who isn't well, a charming mercurial flake like Dad."

She said the words so firmly that Anders almost asked if she had anyone specific in mind. He swallowed the question before it could come out, realizing he wasn't sure if he wanted to know the answer.

And why not? Shouldn't you help her out? Maybe you could act as a go-between. Or is it that you don't want to know because you're afraid of the answer for some other reason?

Now Anders was sure Valiant was studying him quizzically and realized he was blushing. Bad enough that he could barely shape a coherent thought without some alien running private commentary.

"Well," he said a bit lamely, "at least you think your dad is charming. That's better than hating him for what he's put your family through."

"Good point," Jessica said. "Tell me about your mom. You've got the advantage on me. You met both my parents. I've only met your dad."

Anders was grateful for the change of subject, even if he suspected that once again Jessica was displaying her talent for thinking of others, this time to his advantage. He launched in, determined to be amusing at least.

His stories of his mother's rise in politics and how she'd made an effort to be an attentive mother despite the demands of her career kept them occupied for the rest of the trip. He was finishing up his story when the autopilot shifted to landing mode.

"So there's Mom at this function for the foreign ambassador, but with her mind on my birthday. When they struck up the national anthem, she started singing the Birthday Song, instead. She lucked out, though. Turns out it was the ambassador's wife's birthday and everyone thought Mom had been really up on her research. She told us the truth later though...."

Jessica brought the car around to a landing in their usual spot at the edge of the burned-out forest. "She sounds great. You must miss her a lot."

"I do, but... Well..." Anders got out of the car and headed to help Jessica unload equipment. "It's not like my family's ever been like yours or Stephanie's. If we eat a meal together, it's maybe once a week, and that's scheduled. I'm used to scattered contact."

Jessica nodded understanding. "Want to take the images? Coordinates are preloaded if you have any doubts as to which plant we want. I'll do the soil samples and moisture readings."

"Right."

They did the first set of readings, then moved to a new area, closer to the tree line.

"We'll go into that stretch of forest when we're done," Jessica said. "I spotted a clearing from the air where we can land. That should be a good place to get the samples Mom asked for."

"Good with me."

They hadn't even set down in the new location when Valiant showed every evidence of great agitation.

"I wonder if he smells a predator or something?" Anders asked, reaching nervously to make sure his handgun was where it should be. "We're high enough we could be in the lower parts of peak bear territory. Hexapumas are all over this area."

Jessica shook her head. "It doesn't feel like that. Valiant's eager but apprehensive. That's not how he reacts when he smells something dangerous."

She settled the air car on the ground and Valiant sprang out as soon as she opened the door. He bleeked urgently at Jessica, then sprinted off.

Jessica tore off after him, not even pausing to shut the door. Anders did so, thinking of all the nasty Sphinxian wildlife that otherwise might come in to investigate. Then he rushed after.

They were in a picketwood area, so the understory was mostly open, without a great deal of scrub growth. Anders followed the flashes of blue and yellow that were Jessica's shirt. About a hundred meters into the forest, she cried out.

"Anders! Get my med kit from the car. We found another treecat. This one's badly hurt, but still alive!"

15

ANDERS FOUND JESSICA AND VALIANT CROUCHED ON the ground next to a bloodsoaked treecat. Valiant was making loud, rough purrs, but Anders thought the 'cat was anxious, not happy.

"This 'cat's hurt, badly hurt," Jessica said, accepting the med kit without looking up from her patient. "But he's not dead."

"What can I do?" Anders asked.

"Not much, right now," Jessica said, her hands already busy pulling out a spray anesthetic. "Cover us. Whatever did this might still be around."

Anders obeyed. He found himself wishing that Stephanie or Karl were there. Not only would they have a better idea what type of creature might have done this, but Lionheart might have something to offer. Valiant certainly wasn't much help. He remained crouching by the wounded treecat as if his thrumming purr might help the other hold on to life.

And it might, Anders admitted to himself. *I have no idea how treecats work.*

A flick of motion ahead and to the left caught his attention. For a moment, he thought it might have been caused by another 'cat. Then he realized it was nothing so large. Some sort of bugs were darting over a huddled shape on the ground. He pulled out his binoculars. What he saw made him gasp.

"Jessica! There's another treecat about ten meters to the east. I think this one's dead for sure."

Jessica continued her frantic labors. "Take a look? Or do you want to wait until I can go with you?"

"I'll go," Anders said. He unholstered his gun, slung the binoculars around his neck, and marched toward the still figure. The bugs scattered when he got close, but he saw that they'd been clustered on a gaping hole in the treecat's thick throat fur.

"Definitely dead," he called back. "And definitely not disease. Something tore his throat out."

Her response was calm and resigned. "This one's been attacked, too. Do you suppose they went after a hexapuma—like Lionheart's clan did to rescue Stephanie—only this time they weren't so lucky?"

"Maybe," Anders agreed. "I'm going to scout around a bit, see if I can find a body or something."

He did, but the body he found was not that of a hexapuma. Instead, it was another treecat, this one a brown and white female, very slender and incredibly pathetic in death. A few steps further, he found another body—this time a male.

Anders might not be an expert tracker like Stephanie or Karl, but his time with his father's anthropological crew had made him sensitive to detail.

"Jess, I think you might be right about the treecats going after a hexapuma or something. There's a lot of damage here, both on the ground and up in the trees as well. The area gets more torn up the farther I go."

"Did you find what they were fighting?"

"No sign. Maybe it got away. Maybe these 'cats weren't as good at fighting as Lionheart's clan. How's your patient?"

"I think I have him stabilized, but he needs more help than I can give him. Normally, I'd take him to Dr. Richard, but—"

She shrugged and Anders bit his lip. What a time for Stephanie's parents to be off Sphinx!

"I don't know if we should take him to the clinic," he said. "Dr. Saleem is good, but I'm not sure how much he knows about treecats. He'd have the files, but I don't think he's done much hands-on work. Dr. Richard always handled the treecats himself. What about Scott MacDallan? Stephanie told me Dr. Richard's been sharing all of his notes with Scott, and he treated Fisher himself after the two of them first met. Is your car up to a flight to Thunder River?"

Jessica nodded. "It'll take a bit longer than it does in Karl's car. My junker just can't go as fast. I'll have to com Mom, though. What should I tell her?"

Anders noticed that without having discussed it, both of them were already agreed that the injured treecat—and three dead ones—were not matters for general discussion. The x-a's would probably insist on seeing the injured treecat and poking it, no matter how hurt it—no, he—was. Heck, Anders couldn't even be sure *Dad* would keep off!

"Stephanie's a big fan of telling the truth," he said, "just leaving out the awkward parts. Let's do that. Tell your mom we found an injured treecat and that we think Scott would be the best person to treat it. Ask her to keep it to herself."

"I think she'd do that," Jessica agreed, "especially given how those x-a's were looking for dirt on Valiant. She'd understand the need to protect this one."

Naomi Pheriss did indeed understand. "Take your time, Jessica. Call if you decide to stay the night in Thunder River, all right?"

Anders called his dad, too, but Dr. Whitaker was—as usual—too distracted by his work to worry about why his seventeen-year-old son might not be home until late or the next day. "Have fun with your friends," he said.

"I suppose," Anders said after he'd disconnected "we should call Scott and warn him we're coming. We should probably have called him before we called our folks."

"Yeah, and given Scott a chance to tell us to take this poor fellow to the clinic in Twin Forks, instead," Jessica added.

But MacDallan made no such suggestion. Instead, the redhaired doctor asked Anders and Jessica for any details they could give and viewed images of his future patient over the uni-link.

"I'll have a treatment room ready," he promised. "Call again when you're about fifteen minutes out."

"We will," Anders promised. "And thanks for helping out on such short notice."

When Anders disconnected, he helped Jessica clear a spot in the rear seat of the air car and settle in the wounded treecat.

Then he said, "I think we should bring those bodies along. I noticed you had some tarps in the trunk."

"Mom and I always carry some in case we need to wrap a root ball or something," Jessica said. "I've got boxes, too. Do you think the other treecats will mind?"

"I don't see anyone making funeral arrangements," Anders said brutally. "Let's do this like last time, let Valiant see what we're doing. If he protests or the other treecat wakes up and gets upset, then we stop and settle for images. Otherwise, we bring the bodies, too. We'll take the same precautions as last time, handle the bodies as little as possible, and disinfect afterwards."

Jessica nodded and, when Valiant showed no signs of being upset, they carried out their grisly task as quickly as possible.

"I suppose we could have buried these like we did the other one," Anderson said, "but I'm edgy about all of this."

"You, too?" Jessica said. "I thought Valiant's worry over the other 'cat was making me nervy."

"It's not just you," Anders assured her. "It can't be a coincidence that we've found four dead and one injured treecat all in the same region. What if something's hunting them—some predator displaced by the fire, maybe? I'd like to see if Scott can make a guess at what got them. Then maybe the SFS can do something."

"Good idea," Jessica agreed, tucking a tarp to secure the load packed in the air car's trunk. "We'll call Scott on the way and tell him what to expect. Now we'd better fly."

Keen Eyes realized the pain had gone away. He still felt very weak, but it was a delicious sort of weakness. He felt cared for, protected, relaxed in a manner he hadn't felt for a long time—certainly not since the fires destroyed his clan's home range, perhaps not since he'd been a kitten.

His lids were so heavy that he could not open his eyes, but he did twitch his nose. The odors around him were very strange. He was certain he had never smelled them before, yet they were not completely alien. . . . He let his mind drift. That, at least, was easy. And in the depths of memory, Keen Eyes found the connection he sought. He had never smelled these things, not with his own nose, but he had experienced them in one of the memory songs Wide Ears had given to the scouts.

The song had been at several removes, but Wide Ears had been a strong singer. Moreover, she had been showing them these particular memories to help them in their scouting. For that reason, she had been even pickier than usual about making sure the various sensory details were as refined as possible.

The song was from the memory of two young People from the Damp Ground Clan. They had been trapped by one of the earlier fires in the past fire season—one in the lowlands, near the large central nesting place of the two-legs. These two—Right-Striped and Left-Striped—would certainly have been burned alive had their cries for help not been heard by Climbs Quickly of the Bright Water Clan, companion of the young two-leg called Death Fang's Bane.

Without help, Climbs Quickly could not have saved them, but he had managed to make his two-leg companions understand that they were needed. After they were rescued, Right-Striped and Left-Striped had been taken to Death Fang's Bane's nesting place. Her sire, Healer, had treated their burns.

Some of the smells from that memory were what Keen Eyes was smelling now. Medications. The odor of the interior of one of the two-legs' flying things. And, not at all in the least, that of several two-legs. He was very tired, but as a scout he was good at sorting through scents. Many of the two-leg scents were older. Those who had left them were not present. However, there were two sharper scents, strong enough to indicate that those who had made them were close by. Keen Eyes registered another scent, as well; that of a male Person of some years. Now that he had this focus, Keen Eyes realized he had been aware of this Person's mind-glow since he had awakened. Its calm, comforting presence had a great deal to do with the feeling of being protected and relaxed that had been wrapped around him.

Tentatively, Keen Eyes spoke, <*I thank you...I am Keen Eyes of the Landless Clan. You are?*>

The comforting mind-glow replied, <*I am Dirt Grubber of the Damp Ground Clan, although now I live with the two-leg called Windswept and her clan. The ones you smell are Windswept and Bleached Fur. We are in their flying thing, up in the sky.*>

The mind-voice was accompanied by images. Keen Eyes recognized both Windswept and Bleached Fur from the background of Right-Striped and Left-Striped's memories. However, he had had no idea that yet another Person had chosen to bond with a two-leg. He felt lost and confused. Dirt Grubber immediately moved to reassure him.

<*There is no reason you should have known. My clan lives in the lowlands. Perhaps your memory singers have been too busy to share songs with another clan.*>

<*We have no memory singers.*> Keen Eyes did not try to hide his pain and bitterness. His mind was muddied, perhaps from whatever had taken away the pain, but he managed to share something of the Landless Clan's history since the fires. He deliberately held back its problems with Trees Enfolding Clan, for he had no idea whether or not Dirt Grubber or his clan was friendly with Trees Enfolding. They might even be related clans.

<*You have had a bad time,*> Dirt Grubber replied. <*I would ask more, but you are very weak. Windswept has given you something to help with the pain. She is taking you to Darkness Foe, who will help you, but it is a long journey. I think you should try to rest.*>

Keen Eyes wanted to protest, but he really was very tired. Dirt Grubber started purring, his mind-glow filling with slow, easy images—of plants unfolding their leaves, of sunlight warming fur, of eyes heavy with sleep after a good meal.

Keen Eyes did not resist, but gave himself over to sleep.

Scott MacDallan's red hair shone like a landing beacon as Jessica brought her air car down behind the house he shared with his wife, Irina Kisaevna.

Fisher had been on his customary perch on Scott's shoulder, but as soon as the car landed, he came racing across, waiting with obvious impatience until Anders opened the door. Flirting his tail in a gesture of thanks, Fisher leapt inside, where he joined Valiant.

Valiant had sat cuddled up next to the wounded tree-cat for the entire flight and now he made room so that Fisher could join him.

It takes absolutely no imagination at all, Anders thought, *to figure out that something more than a group hug is going on here.*

In the background, he could hear Jessica speaking to Scott: "Anders and I just lifted the hurt 'cat in, but do you think we should use a stretcher or something getting him back out?"

"I'll give him a first exam here," Scott said, shoving head and shoulders into the back of the air car. "Then we'll decide. Move over, guys. I realize you're helping him, but I need to take a look and I can't do with you in the way."

Valiant and Fisher moved aside as one, leaping to frame the doctor from new perches on the back of the seat.

"Stars above," the doctor said softly a few moments later. "He's really been slashed· up. Some of those claws went deep. Internal organs might've been perforated. I don't think there's any bone damage, but..."

He activated his uni-link and spoke without pausing. "Irina? I'm going to need a small stretcher."

"Coming."

Feeling as if he was going to jump out of his skin if he didn't do something, Anders turned and ran back toward the house, meeting Irina as she emerged. He took the compact stretcher and sprinted back to the car.

Scott was pulling himself out of the enclosed space. His worried expression momentarily brightened when he saw Anders and Jessica holding the stretcher ready.

"Okay. Slide it over here. Now I'll lift a little...Good..."

Within a few minutes, they had the injured treecat in the room already prepared as a surgery. Scott frowned.

"I hate to do this," he said, "but I'm going to insist you two stay out unless you have some surgical experience. Irina, scrub up."

"What about the 'cats?" Irina said, for Valiant and Fisher had resumed their posts next to the patient.

"I'm going to let them stay," Scott said. "Jessica? Do you think Valiant would wear a surgical mask? And put up with a sterile spray-down?"

"Sure," she said promptly, "if he sees Fisher doing it. He's used a respirator, and he's seen Dr. Richard—and me—spraying wounds to disinfect them. He may not understand *why* we do it, but he knows it's part of making them better."

"Good." The doctor paused. "We've emptied a cooling unit. Put the bodies in there. I'll look at them after I've done what I can for this guy."

"Right."

As Jessica and Anders left the surgery, Irina called after them, "Make yourselves free of the house and grounds. Patients don't normally call here at the house. If anyone shows up, tell them the doctor's unavailable because of an emergency."

"Right."

When the door closed firmly after Irina, Anders was

aware of a tremendous sense of relief. He'd been terri-
fied that the treecat would die during the long flight to
Thunder River. If he had, he knew he and Jessica would
never have forgiven themselves for not taking the shorter
route to Dr. Saleem, even if Scott did have far more
experience with treecat injuries.

"I think," Jessica said, sinking down on a cushioned
bench in the entryway that was the closest available seat,
"I'm going to start either blubbering or screaming."

"Delayed shock," Anders reassured her. "This has been
a blackhole of a day. You really kept it together. I won't
think the worse of you if you start crying." He gave a
crooked grin. "I might even join in."

With a funny little choked noise, Jessica bent forward
slightly, her long hair curtaining her face. For a moment,
Anders thought she was laughing. Then he realized that
Jessica's shoulders were shaking with an effort to contain
her sobs. It seemed the most natural thing in the world to
reach over and hold her, to let her press her face against
his chest while he stroked her back.

"There, there," he said inanely. "You did great, really
great. It's going to be all right."

After a while, she pulled away. "I'm sorry. I just...I
just...I've always been really good at keeping my head
when something's wrong, but afterwards...Mom says I
always pay twice what I would if I just admitted how I
felt, but I can't help it."

Anders nodded. "What's wrong with crying? You know,
it would've been okay even if you'd broken down when
we found that hurt 'cat. I mean, it was scary."

Jessica grinned ruefully. "I bet Stephanie never cracks
up. I love her like a sister, but she's always so, so...
intellectual. Weighing the odds, figuring out the angles."

"I think," Anders said, feeling a bit awkward, "that
Stephanie does crack up. She just does it differently. She

loses her temper instead of crying. Anyhow, she told me she cried her eyes out when Lionheart got hurt saving her. I bet she'd understand. I really do."

"You're right." Jessica scrubbed at her eyes with the back of her hand. "Stephanie's one of the best friends I've ever had. I don't know why, but I'm always measuring myself against her and feeling like I come up short."

"You're several centimeters taller," Anders said, trying to make a joke out of it, then stopping when he saw that Jessica looked hurt. "No, seriously. I know what you mean. Stephanie's pretty extraordinary, but what makes her that way is that she has lots of heart to go with the brains and the talent."

"Yeah..." Jessica's expression turned wistful. "Anyhow, thanks for letting me sob all over your shirt. I'd offer to return the favor, but maybe we should raid the fridge instead. I think I read somewhere that food is a good antidote to shock, and we're not done today. Not by a long shot."

While Darkness Foe worked on the unconscious Keen Eyes, Swift Striker and Dirt Grubber did what they could to help the other Person remain comforted.

<What do you think happened to him?> Swift Striker asked.

<I am afraid he was injured by another Person,> Valiant replied. Somewhat reluctantly, he shared with Swift Striker what else they had found that day.

<Three other People dead? And one of them a female? This is not good....>

<And the odor of blood on the ground for many others,> Dirt Grubber added. *<And fur. Bleached Fur is not the tracker that Death Fang's Bane or Shadowed Sunlight have shown themselves to be, but he may have guessed*

that many more People than those four were present—and that many more died or were injured. Yet Windswept and Bleached Fur might have suspected how Keen Eyes came to be injured in any case, even if there had been no other bodies.>

<What reason would they have for that?>

<This is not the first dead Person they have found near that place.> Dirt Grubber showed Swift Striker his memories of that other day. *<I am certain the mind I touched that day was Keen Eyes, although he fled quickly, before I could do more than get the faintest glimpse of his mind-glow. Still, I tasted enough to tell he was upset . . . and to feel he was not personally responsible for that death.>*

<Now though . . . > Swift Striker's sorrow was acute. *<Now I think Keen Eyes is personally involved in the fighting. His confusion and pain are bright in his mind-glow, complicating his ability to let his body heal. Some part of him believes he should die because he was doing harm.>*

<Yes. I think you are right. I have been doing what I can to bring comfort, but it is difficult. He slides away as soon as he remembers how he got his wounds.> Dirt Grubber shifted uncomfortably, as if he could move away from these unpleasant thoughts. *<Do you think Darkness Foe will guess? The younglings carried the bodies of the dead ones with them here. I did not stop them because I did not like the idea that other two-legs might find them. There have been too many in that area since the fires.>*

<Yes, I think he will,> Swift Striker replied with certainty. *<He was quick to realize the truth of what had happened to True Stalker's two-leg and his clan. I do not believe he will be slower in this case.>*

<What do you think he will do?>

<I am not sure. I wish I knew, but I really am not sure.>

<What should we do?>

<I do not know that, either,> Swift Striker admitted.

<It is never good for People to kill other People. However, at this time and that place, it is even worse. As you say, the two-legs are all over that area, and the tree cover is thin. If the killing goes on, then the two-legs are likely to learn about it. That thought makes me very uncomfortable. Not all of them are our friends, as we both know too well, and some—like the new ones who have come to study us with Garbage Collector's two-legs—do not wish us well, however hard they may seek to convince the other two-legs that they do. If those who are not our friends discover that People are killing other People, how will they use that knowledge when they speak to the two-legs' elders about us?>

<I agree that this could go ill for the People,> Dirt Grubber said soberly. *<If Keen Eyes lives, we must ask him more about what has caused this clash.>*

<Yes. That is where we must start,> Swift Striker agreed, *<but where the trail will end, that is far less clear.>*

It was very late when Scott and Irina emerged from the surgery.

"We think we've saved him," the doctor said immediately in response to the unspoken question Anders knew must be visible in both his and Jessica's eyes. "One can never be completely sure, but his vital signs are good. I'm grateful that Richard Harrington updates my treecat biology files every time he learns something new. It was the next best thing to having him available to consult."

"Valiant's staying with him, right?" Jessica said.

"Valiant and Fisher, both." Scott sank wearily into a deep, soft chair. "I'm absolutely certain they were doing everything they could during the surgery to keep our patient calm and relaxed. Richard says fear is one of the greatest enemies a veterinarian has to face, since a panicked animal may harm itself. At least we can be confident that won't be a factor here—and that means I don't need to risk added tranquilizers."

"What was..." Anders began, then realized how tired both Irina and Scott looked. Sure, they were both used to medical emergencies, but Scott was accustomed to human patients, and Irina wasn't even a doctor.

He began again. "Why don't you two get comfortable? I can play butler or whatever. We had a pretty good chance to scout out your kitchen, and I think I can manage to find whatever you'd like."

Irina, who'd resisted sitting to this point, now heaved a great, relieved sigh.

"Anders, that would be wonderful. The blue-green container on the middle shelf has a nice ice potato and cream soup. There's some roasted prong-buck in the meat drawer and a loaf of dark bread. We could have soup and sandwiches."

"And a salad," Jessica added impishly. "Don't forget your vegetables."

"And a salad," Irina agreed. "If you two can handle that, Scott and I will collapse in front of the fire in the living room. The chairs in there are more comfortable."

"Can I take Valiant and Fisher some celery?" Jessica asked. "I won't bother the patient. Promise."

Scott heaved himself to his feet with some effort. "I'll take your promise. Tell the guys not to drip all over the patient."

"I'll do my best," Jessica pledged.

In the kitchen, Anders set the soup to warm, then started slicing prong-buck. With both of his parents out as often as they were, he'd become a pretty good cook early on. These last months on Sphinx had provided ample opportunity to add to his skills, since Dr. Whitaker was likely to forget to eat unless his son reminded him.

He cut the bread into thick slices, then layered meat, cheese, greens, thinly sliced onions, and a nice spicy sauce. At another counter, Jessica put together a huge salad, using a beautiful handmade pottery bowl that Irina had assured them had been created for the purpose.

"I don't make pottery just to put it on a shelf," she'd explained. "You'll find soup bowls and plates that go with the salad bowl. Anything that's in the kitchen is meant to be used."

Anders couldn't help but think how pleasant it was working with Jessica this way. Maybe because of her higher metabolism, Stephanie was a picker. He'd often teased her that by the time she'd finished making a meal, she'd eaten one already. Jessica, by contrast, occasionally sampled something, but only to check whether it would go well with the items she'd already put into the salad bowl.

I like Jessica, Anders thought, wondering why the thought should come as a revelation. Hadn't he always known he liked Jessica? If he didn't like her, why would he have spent so much time with her since Stephanie left for Manticore?

I like Jessica . . . a lot. Too much. I—

"Did you say something Anders?"

Anders looked up and found Jessica staring at him. *Had* he said something? He swallowed hard. He hoped he hadn't.

"No, I don't think so. I was muttering at the sandwiches. I think I got carried away and made them too thick. They keep falling over."

Jessica laughed. "They look good to me."

Relief washed over Anders. He hadn't given himself away.

"I'll take them out and come back for the soup."

"Great."

When the first edges of hunger had been taken off— although they'd been given permission to raid the kitchen, both Jessica and Anders had been too shy to do more than nibble—Anders decided to ask the question that had been nagging at him ever since they'd found the injured treecat.

"Scott, do you have any idea what did that to the treecat?"

"I have some ideas," Scott said, "but I'd prefer to keep them to myself until I've had a chance to look at the bodies you brought with you."

"Tomorrow," Irina told him with a firmness that brooked no argument. "It's already past midnight. You had a full schedule this morning, and this is not the time to start doing autopsies."

Scott started to argue, but when a huge yawn interrupted him mid-phrase, he had to admit his wife was right.

"Fine, tomorrow morning. First thing. I don't think I have anything early at the clinic."

Irina glanced at her uni-link. "Not until noon, when Mr. Alvarez comes in so you can check that compound fracture."

Jessica cut in. "I'd like to stay and hear what you find out. I already have permission, and so does Anders. Would it be okay?"

"More than okay. I wasn't going to let you fly back this late." Irina set aside her tray and got to her feet. "I always keep a couple of guest rooms ready."

Jessica rose and started carrying her tray to the kitchen. "I'll just go say good night to Valiant. I'm sure he's staying with the patient."

"Fisher, too," Scott said. "I must admit, I'll sleep better knowing Fisher will wake me the instant he senses anything going wrong. You folks sleep in as late as you want. I promise I'll make sure we talk before I go in to the clinic."

After the dinner things had been cleared away, Irina

showed Anders and Jessica to their rooms. "Each of your rooms has its own bath. I put towels and robes in your rooms, along with spare toiletries. When you've washed up, bring me down your dirty stuff and I'll toss it into the wash so you'll have clean in the morning."

Anders realized that he hadn't even thought about any of that.

"Thanks, Irina. I appreciate that."

"Are you sure it won't be too much trouble?" Jessica added. "I'm betting you'll be up early with Scott. I could stay up and do the wash, so you can get some sleep."

"It's all automatic," Irina assured her. "Between my pottery and Scott's medical practice, we create a lot of laundry."

An expression that wasn't quite envy flickered across Jessica's face. Once again, Anders was reminded that her family probably did without a lot of the laborsaving devices he took for granted—and with all those kids, laundry was probably a constant chore.

"Okay, then. If you're sure."

"I'm sure." Irina gave Jessica a quick hug. "Stop worrying. If we're not out in the morning, go into the kitchen. I'll leave some breakfast stuff where you can find it."

After he'd gotten cleaned up, Anders sat on the edge of his bed, trying to sort through the confusion of feelings raised by the day's events. He started a new message to Stephanie, but when he found he couldn't get beyond the first few sentences he erased the whole thing.

What's wrong with me? Am I just tired? Is it that I want to be able to give her a full report? Right now I'd just be speculating. Tomorrow, after Scott looks at the bodies, we'll have a better idea what killed those 'cats. Sure. That's it. It must be…

But after he'd snuggled himself under the covers and turned out the light, images of Jessica flooded his mind. Jessica working over the injured treecat. Jessica sometimes talking, sometimes thoughtfully silent, during the long flight to Thunder River. Jessica in the kitchen, making a salad. Jessica, kneeling to gently dig a sample from the soil, her expression intent. Jessica...

His lips shaped her name in the softly whispered plea, though he had no idea what he was asking.

"Jessica?"

16

ANDERS THOUGHT HE'D WOKEN UP PRETTY EARLY, BUT when he washed up and came downstairs, he found he was the late riser. His cleaned clothing had been set inside the door to his room, so he'd guessed Irina was already up, but he was a bit surprised to find Jessica in the kitchen, already halfway through her breakfast.

"Hey," he said, trying hard to sound like his usual self. "I thought you'd take advantage of no kids jumping up and down on you and sleep in."

Jessica grinned. "I did sleep in—for me. Anyhow, even though I knew from Valiant that the injured 'cat was doing fine, I wanted to check."

"And he is? Fine, I mean?"

"Well, for someone who was hurt that badly, he's doing great. He's been moved to a room around the back where he can see out the window."

"Is he nervous?" Anders moved to where Irina had left an assortment of cereals and poured himself a bowl.

"Not really. I think Valiant and Fisher have reassured him he's among friends."

"'He,'" Anders said, bringing his bowl to the table. "Anyone give him a name? It's sort of awkward calling him 'he,' or 'the injured treecat.'"

Jessica shrugged. "Scott's calling him 'Survivor,' since it looks like he's going to. That works for me."

"Me, too. Optimistic. Can I go see Survivor, or would it be better if I stayed clear?"

"Scott didn't say for you to stay out. If you want to see him, we could go in after breakfast. Valiant will let us know if we should stay clear."

When they went into visit Survivor, Anders knew immediately why Scott and Irina had chosen this room. A large curving bay window looked out into a tangle of late autumn shrubbery, providing not only privacy but an illusion of being up among the branches. Survivor was sitting on the padded seat beneath the window, flanked by Fisher and Valiant.

All three treecats turned to look as the two humans entered, and the contrast between them made Anders gasp.

"Oh, poor guy!"

Jessica nodded. "Yeah. Scott had to shave a lot of fur to get at the injuries and make sure they were clean."

"Oh . . . poor guy . . ." Anders repeated. Knowing that treecats sensed emotion, he tried to project that he felt sympathy, not pity or revulsion or anything like that. Still, there was something pitiful about Survivor. His thick fur had been shaved in a wide band around his neck. Other areas along his back had been shaved, as well, as had one side of his face.

"Whatever went for him went for the vitals," Anders said thoughtfully. "Throat, spine, maybe an eye."

"You can't see it from here," Jessica added, "but there's a big strip down his belly, too. Still, since Scott didn't have to guess what medications to use, the wounds are already healing."

"I wonder how long until Survivor grows his fur back?" Anders asked, thinking about their discussion with Dr. Hidalgo. "I mean, we've still got months of autumn, but the nights are pretty cold already."

"Good question," Jessica said. "I bet Stephanie and Dr. Richard have a good idea from when Lionheart was hurt. Dr. Richard might even have put it in his notes. I wonder, though...maybe we can get Survivor to wear a sweater?"

Her lopsided smile made it clear that she, too, remembered Dr. Hidalgo's disdain for the contamination of pristine cultures.

A voice behind them spoke. "That's an interesting idea," Irina said from the end of the hall near the kitchen. "Scott's cleaning up. Then he wants to talk. You two ate breakfast?"

"We did," Jessica answered for them both. "I put the bowls in the washer."

"Come on then," Irina said. "I've put on water for tea and a pot of coffee. We'll have our conference in the kitchen."

Scott was waiting for them. He looked tired and drawn. Even the red of his hair seemed duller. Irina sat close to him, her hand on his shoulder. Something about her posture reminded Anders of how he'd seen treecats offer support in emotionally stressful situations.

"So, Scott," Anders asked. "Do you have any idea what sort of creature did that to Survivor and the others?"

The doctor bit into his upper lip, as if he wished he could keep back the answer, then spoke three words. "Treecats did it."

"Treecats?" Jessica's hazel eyes opened wide in astonishment. "That's not possible. Maybe there's something the size of treecats...a natural enemy of some sort that we haven't seen so far. Something that competes for the same resources."

Scott shook his head slowly. "No. Treecats. I'm not a forensic pathologist, but out here in the boonies, there's a lot of overlap. I know the basics."

He activated the portable holo-projector. "Some of these images are going to be a bit upsetting, but I've kept the focus tight so you can concentrate on just the injuries."

An image of something marbled pinky-gray and over-laid with red streaks appeared. Remembering Survivor, Anders realized that this was the shaved skin of a treecat. The pinkish areas were where light gray fur would have been, the darker gray the tabby barring. The red streaks were the wounds, cleaned of clotted blood, so that only the lines showed.

"Look at this first series," Scott said. "Here's a neck wound. Now, here I've superimposed an image of a tree-cat's true-hand. Look at how tightly it matches. This next image is a longer shot of the same body. See here and here...that's where the attacker's hand-feet and true-feet dug in. Unless you really want to see it, I'll spare you the headshot. The attacker landed on his opponent's back, dug in, and then went for the face with his fangs. The attack to the head probably provided the kill, though at least some of the back shots must've paralyzed the victim first."

Jessica shuddered. "I think we can skip the head view, but if Anders wants to look, I'll close my eyes."

Anders shook his head. "I'll take the doctor's word for it. But, Scott, this isn't absolute proof. I mean, most creatures on Sphinx are hexapedal. Couldn't something *like* a treecat have done this? Near-otters are about the same size. They're carnivores. Maybe they're more adaptable than we realized."

"I want to believe treecats didn't do this as much as you do, Anders." The weariness was back in the doctor's eyes. Now Anders recognized it as something like shock. "Remember, Fisher saved my life—saved it of his own accord, without any reason other than that he saw another person in trouble. We suspect that Lionheart and Stephanie were already bonded when he saved her from the hexapuma. Jessica and Valiant sort of saved each other, but Fisher was a stranger, and still he risked his life to save me. I've got more reason than anyone to think of treecats as the 'good guys.'"

"Sorry, Doc," Anders apologized. "I just...I can't believe this."

"Here's more evidence," Scott said. "Like I said, I'm not a forensic expert, but I know enough to check under fingernails—or claws, in this case. These images are magnified. I'll show them to you unenhanced, then enhanced. See what I mean?"

"That's blood, isn't it?" Jessica said quietly. "Blood and—" She made a little gagging noise, but went on, "Blood and flesh—I guess doctors call it 'tissue.' That's easier. Blood and tissue."

"Right. Needless to say, I analyzed it. Treecat blood. Treecat tissue. Some treecat fur. All three of the dead ones show indications that they were fighting other treecats. I haven't tried to type for specific individuals, and I'm not sure we need to."

"And Survivor?" Anders asked. "Was he fighting, too?"

"Oh, yes. I'm afraid he doesn't get a free pass. Survivor was fighting, and Survivor lost. My guess is that he was left for dead. He was close enough."

"Valiant must've heard him," Jessica said. "That's why he went tearing off. Survivor must've regained consciousness, been lying there calling for help, but no one came. No one at all."

Her voice choked up, and Anders had to bend his head to hide the tears that came hot and unbidden to his eyes.

"Look," he said. "I know the jury's still out on the range of a treecat's mental abilities. But I think all of us here agree that not only are they powerful empaths, among themselves, they're probably telepaths. We've seen Valiant and Fisher—who aren't related to each other or to Survivor—giving Survivor a huge amount of support, practically willing him to live. How could creatures capable of such compassion fight each other? Wouldn't it be impossible?"

"I would've thought so," Scott said. "I thought that among treecats we'd finally found a sentient species that had no need for war. Why should they fight when they're capable of perfect understanding?"

"Yeah," Jessica agreed. "So something has to have gone very wrong. We found the bodies near where the fires had been pretty bad. I wonder if the two things are related?"

Scott nodded. "I wondered the same thing. Survivor and two others were very thin, as if they'd been on short rations. The other male wasn't exactly robust, but he was in somewhat better shape."

"Oh!" Jessica said. "I hadn't exactly forgotten, but I'd been waiting to bring this up until a better time. These three treecats weren't the first dead ones we've seen. There was another one. He was pretty skinny, too."

"Another?" Irina looked startled. "Where? What did you do?"

"We recorded images," Anders said. "Then we buried it."

Quickly, bouncing the story back and forth between them, Anders and Jessica told about finding that first dead treecat.

"We didn't mention it," Anders said, "because there wasn't anything we could do. Also, because we didn't want anyone—up to and including my dad—"

"But especially those blackhole x-a's," Jessica added.

"—taking the body back to some lab," Anders finished. "I mean, the anthropologists might be arguing about their status, but as we saw it, the treecat was a person and deserved some respect."

"Can we see the images?" Scott asked. After he'd reviewed them, he went on, "It's hard to tell from an image, but that 'cat does look on the skinny side. I'd like copies."

"Sure."

Jessica was clearly excited. "What if the fires have physically stressed the treecats to the point that they're susceptible to some disease? A disease might affect their empathic abilities."

"Or just make them crazy," Anders added. "One of Dad's hobbies is looking at old legends in a medical context. There was a disease on Old Terra called rabies that made the victims become very violent and afraid of water. Animals could get it, too. There's some evidence that hallucinogens and parasites on domestic crops contributed to outbreaks of belief in witchcraft. Stuff like that."

"So maybe the treecats are eating things they shouldn't be," Jessica said eagerly. "Maybe stuff they wouldn't usually eat, but are eating now because they are extending their foraging range. We know they eat various fungi. Valiant even cultivates it on trees near our house. Maybe they ate some bad mushrooms."

"Or maybe," Irina said quietly, "they're just competing for territory or food. Let's not rush too fast to assure ourselves that treecats have escaped our human failings. No matter how hard it is to accept, we need to keep that on our list of possibilities."

"So what do we do next?" Anders asked. "I mean, do we tell anyone? Do we try a food drop?"

Scott considered. "How much right to we have to interfere? Fighting like this might be part of their natural life cycle."

Jessica snorted. "Valiant and Fisher didn't seem to think

Survivor should be left for dead. Remember, Valiant's the one who showed us where to find him."

"But we've got to be careful, whatever we do," Anders said. "I don't think those x-a's are up to any good. I'm sure they'd put this into the worst possible light."

He paused, then shrugged. "I'd like to ask Stephanie's opinion."

Jessica frowned. "Me, too, but isn't she in the middle of exams?"

"Yeah, but I think she'd be furious if she knew something about treecat culture that might help us and we hadn't asked her."

"I agree," Scott said. "All of us are seriously committed to treecats, but I think Stephanie—well—thinks of herself as part of Lionheart's family." He bit his lower lip, clearly searching for a better way of expressing himself. "I'm certainly deeply attached to Fisher's clan, but when Fisher and I met, I was an adult. I wasn't a lonely only child."

Jessica nodded. "I like Valiant's people, but I have the impression he's a bit of an oddball among them. I mean, he's a gardener among 'cats who are mostly hunters. And I have lots of brothers and sisters. So, yeah, I'm with you, Anders. Let's tell Stephanie and hope we don't mess up her exams."

Irina smiled. "I think she'll be fine. Maybe an A or two instead of an A++, but at her age, she can afford to lose a few percentage points."

Usually, Jessica and Anders messaged Stephanie separately, but this time they sat side-by-side, so they wouldn't forget anything. After giving the background, they moved to speculation.

"There's a lot we're worried about," Anders said. "Especially what caused this. Scott doesn't leave any room for hoping that anything other than treecats did these killings."

Jessica took over. "Here our our theories: disease, insanity, eating something like bad mushrooms, competition over territory."

"That last has to include the possibility of war," Anders said, "no matter how disgusting the idea is."

Jessica nodded. "Yeah. We'd love to hear if you have anything more to add."

"We're attaching a bunch of images," Anders went on. "Some are kind of grim, but you and Karl have been studying forensics, so we figure you're up to them. One thing that's bugging all of us is the dead female. From what you've implied and Scott has seen—"

"And, me, too, with Valiant's clan," Jessica cut in.

"—females don't seem to hunt much. I know you were in bad shape when Lionheart's clan came to help you, but were there any females? We're trying to get any information we can that might help us find patterns, but for obvious reasons—"

"Like those stupid x-a's," Jessica inserted.

"—and my dad's group," Anders agreed with a rueful grin, "we don't want to take this public. Too much of a chance the wrong person might get curious. We're not even talking to Frank and Ainsley. Scott felt that wouldn't be fair to them—put them in the middle."

"We'll keep you posted," Jessica said, "but try and concentrate on those exams, okay? We're counting on you not to disappoint us."

Anders nodded. "Yeah, Wonder Girl, do us proud."

They waved, signed off, and hit send.

"I hope we did the right thing," Jessica said.

"Well, right or not," Anders replied, "it's done."

✧　　✧　　✧

"We've got to go home!" Stephanie said urgently.

She and Karl sat on their favorite bench under the blue-tip, but there was no hot sun overhead. Instead, the light of Thorson, Manticore's single moon, trickled down through a break in the overcast. The well-lit quadrangle didn't need moonlight, and as always, it was well populated as the student body enjoyed the relative coolness before turning in for a good night's pre-exam sleep. Not that Stephanie was enjoying it all that much at the moment.

"We *can't*, Steph." Karl's expression was grim.

"We've *got* to!" Stephanie looked at him, as if unable to believe her own ears, and hugged Lionheart tightly. "If Scott's right—if treecats are *killing* each other!—we need to get home and help Jessica and Anders figure out what to do about it!"

"Steph, we're here as *rangers*. We don't have the option of just turning around and going home whenever we feel like it." Anger sparkled in Stephanie's eyes, but Karl looked at her levelly. "I'm not saying you want to go home on a *whim*, Steph! But we've got responsibilities right here, and Ranger Shelton stuck his neck out a kilometer or two to get us here in the first place. We owe him more than to cut and run before we've even taken our finals." She opened her mouth, but he went on ruthlessly before she could speak. "Besides, how are you planning to *justify* it? A health emergency? Some kind of family crisis—with both your parents right here on Manticore? Or do you want to go ahead and send the chief ranger—or Frank or Ainsley—a copy of Jessica's message?"

Stephanie shut her mouth with an almost audible click and stared at him. He looked back for several seconds, then reached out and laid one big hand on her shoulder.

"I understand what you're saying, and I wish we could just hop the first flight home, too. But we can't, for a lot of reasons. Not unless we want to drag all of this out into the open before we even know for sure what's going on, and God only knows how people like the Franchittis are likely to react if they realize 'cats are capable of... of fighting some kind of *war!*"

Stephanie felt her eyes brimming with unaccustomed tears, but he was right. She hated it, but he was right.

"I don't know if I can do this," she admitted in a tiny voice, hugging Lionheart still tighter. "I don't know if I can just pretend nothing's going on at home."

"You've got to, at least as far as anyone else is concerned." Karl squeezed her shoulder. "And it won't be easy for me, either. But we can't start just chucking our schedule out the window without raising all kinds of questions."

Climbs Quickly suppressed an urge to squirm as Death Fang's Bane's arms tightened about him. It was uncomfortable, but not as uncomfortable as the stress and worry flooding from her mind-glow. He had no idea what was causing her distress, but he knew it had begun while she was watching the moving images from Windswept and Bleached Fur. And whatever it was, it was as frightening to her as anything he'd tasted from her since the day they'd faced the death fang together. It was greater even than her fear for Windswept when the burning tree fell on her!

He crooned gently, patting her forearm with his remaining true-hand, trying to radiate calm, but whatever had her so frightened resisted stubbornly. And somehow, he knew, it focused on *him*, as well. The frustration of his inability to communicate clearly with her burned hotter than ever, but all he could do was snuggle more closely against her, purring loudly, offering her the physical comfort of his presence and wishing with all his heart he could make her hear his mind-voice as clearly as he could taste her emotions.

Stephanie looked down as Lionheart patted her arm encouragingly. He was purring so hard she half expected his bones to vibrate right out of his body, and he stared up at her intensely, green eyes gleaming in the light washing under the blue-tip's branches from the quadrangle.

She realized she'd been crushing him and eased her embrace, lifting him to drape him over her shoulder and run her hand down his spine. If only she could explain it to him! Even better, ask him if Scott and the others had it right. If only *he* could explain it to *her*!

But he couldn't. And in the absence of any ability to talk it over with him, she had to make the decision for both of them.

Only there's nothing to decide, really, is there? Because Karl's right.

"You're right," she told him bleakly, still stroking Lionheart, as if somehow she could comfort whatever was driving those other treecats back home on Sphinx to attack each other. "You're right. But I wish you weren't, and I don't think I'm going to enjoy finals week very much after all."

"You're weird, Steph," Karl said, trying to lighten the mood. "Finals are to be endured, not enjoyed."

Anders and Jessica were babysitting Tiddles and Nathan, Jessica's two youngest siblings, when Scott MacDallan commed.

"I've got a more detailed autopsy report on the three dead 'cats," he said. "I went through their stomach contents very carefully and analyzed everything. Short answer is I think we can rule out hallucinogens as the reason behind the treecats fighting each other."

"Nothing so easy," Jessica sighed. "There's something more, though, isn't there?"

Scott flashed a quick grin. "Nothing so easily quantified, but I'll offer it without any theory. Two of the dead 'cats—one of the males and the female—were very undernourished, as was Survivor. They weren't starvation-thin, but they were already burning stored fat. I doubt they'd have made it through winter, and their stomach contents were eclectic, to say the least. Most of the treecat diet is meat of some sort. They eat other things, but more or less as a garnish. These two had been eating a diet that was at least half roots, tubers, leaves, dried berries, things like that. Their primary meat element appears to have been fish.

"The third 'cat was better fed. He wasn't plump and sassy, but he wasn't to the point of burning stored fat, either. He'd have made it through the winter. Again, the proportion of nonmeat in his diet was a bit higher, but only by about twenty percent. He showed evidence of having eaten a good sized rodent—I'm guessing a chipmunk—not long before.

"What do you two make of that?"

Anders jumped right in. "I'd guess they were from different groups. Wait! Hear me out...'Cat Three might have been just a better hunter, but from what we've observed of treecats, there's no way one member of a clan would let two others get that starved down. If we're right about their empathy, he couldn't—he'd feel their hunger as his own."

"Then," Jessica said, nodding agreement, "there's the difference in proportions. If there was ever a 'vegetarian' treecat, I'm living with him. Valiant actually likes trying different plant foods. But he's still mostly a meat-eater.

Those other two 'cats wouldn't have been eating that many tubers and seeds and things if they'd had a choice."

"And that means?" Scott said. "Go on."

"That means," Jessica said, "that 'Cats One and Two came from a clan that's having a hard time finding enough food. We found the bodies near one of the burned-out areas. I'm guessing they lost a lot of their range."

Anders took over. "'Cat Three, by contrast, shows more typical 'cat eating habits. I'm guessing he came from a clan that lost some of its range to fire but is still doing all right." He grinned and poked Jessica in the ribs. "Or he's just weird, like Valiant."

"I agree with you," Scott said. "About two different clans—not about Valiant being weird. I'll add that the proportion of fish in those two 'cats' diet is also off. My friend Fisher, is a fanatic. Most 'cats, given the choice, eat a more balanced selection, but a river or stream would replenish more quickly than a burned forest, so that's more evidence for that male and female coming from a territory hard-hit by the fires."

"And that brings us to the ugly conclusion that the treecats really are fighting over territory and resources." Anders sighed. "Why don't they share?"

"Why wouldn't human share in a similar situation?" Jessica retorted, her voice holding all her eloquent awareness of how often humans did not.

"I know, I know..." Anders replied. "It's just, I guess, I hoped they were better than we are."

"I think in some ways they are, most of the time," Scott spoke up. "But these two clans have been badly stressed by the fires. Remember, they were extraordinarily bad last year. We shouldn't be surprised that the side effects are just as bad."

"You're right," Anders conceded. "And all we know right now is that one group's range seems to be in better shape than the other's. We don't know how much better, or how large each group is, or *anything* about their situations, really. Maybe they aren't sharing resources because they don't have enough for both groups." He shook his head, his expression sad. "If they don't, this may be the only way they can settle who gets to survive the winter."

There was silence for a moment, until Jessica broke it.

"So, what next? Any ideas?"

"I have a couple," Anders said. "Why don't you and I try to locate the Skinny 'Cat Clan? We've got some good clues. They're probably near a river. They're probably not too far—as the treecat runs—from where we found the bodies."

"And they're probably using picketwood," Jessica added. "I'm for it. We can fly to the general area, then hike. Valiant might be able to help us."

"I'm not sure how I feel about you two running loose in what might be a war zone," Scott cut in.

"We should be all right," Anders said. "There aren't any registered cases of treecats attacking humans without being provoked. Heck, even when they *have* been provoked—"

"Like by that slime-sucker Tennessee Bolgeo," Jessica inserted.

"—they've shown a lot of restraint. And we'll have Valiant."

"Okay. But you go armed," Scott said, then paused. "You do know how to handle a gun?" he asked.

"Anders does," Jessica said, "and I have my stun gun and my sprayer. They might not faze a hexapuma, but treecats are a lot smaller than that."

"It's not as if I could stop you," Scott said, "so go with my blessing. That way I'll know when you set out and you'll have someone to check in with."

"We could look for the other clan, too," Anders added. "But if their territory wasn't so badly hit, finding them is going to be harder."

"Start with the Skinny 'Cat Clan," Scott advised. "One step at a time."

"We'll go tomorrow," Anders said.

"Weather permitting," Jessica added practically, looking up at the clouds gathering overhead.

"Bleek!" Valiant added, but whether the 'cat's comment indicated enthusiasm or resignation—or simply a desire for lunch—Anders could not tell.

"MAN, AM I EVER GLAD THAT'S OVER!" JEFF HARRISON
said emphatically, dropping into a chair across the table
from Karl, Stephanie, and Lionheart in the LUM student
union. "Hi, Lionheart!" he continued, handing over the
stalk of celery with which he'd thoughtfully provided
himself on his way past the salad bar.

"Gee, thanks, Jeff," Stephanie said, watching the 'cat
pounce on the treat as if no one had offered him celery
in the last decade or two. She knew she shouldn't really
indulge him the way she'd been doing for the past week,
but her heart wasn't in it. "That's his ninth piece today,"
she continued, doing her best to sound completely normal.
"But, hey! Who's counting?"

"Sorry, Steph." Harrison smiled in what looked like
genuine apology. "It's just that I'm not going to get
many more chances to spoil the little guy before you
and Karl—and Lionheart—head back off to the boonies."

"Let's watch just exactly whose planet we're going to

call 'the boonies,'" Karl suggested. His voice sounded a little unnatural to Stephanie, but Harrison's smile turned into a grin.

"If the shoe fits, buddy," he said, then looked back at Stephanie. "I've got to admit I was sweating that final. But I suppose you aced it?"

There was no malice or resentment in his teasing tone, and Stephanie managed to smile back at him.

"Nope," she said. "I did pretty well, and I figure I'll get out of the course with a 4.0, but only because Dr. Flouret gave us that extra credit question. I checked my notes after I saved the final and mailed it in, and I blew the question about the Draper Precedent."

"*You* blew a question?" Harrison pressed a hand to his chest and goggled his eyes at her.

"It happens . . . from time to time," she told him, not mentioning that she'd performed at less than her best on at least three of her four finals. She wasn't used to having something like that happen. Then again, she wasn't used to being worried sick over what was happening back on Sphinx.

"I suppose you got it right when you took the course?" she challenged after a moment.

"Darn right I did." Harrison elevated his nose. "It just happens that the Draper Precedent was critical to a case I had to analyze as part of my midterm research paper last semester. I had to practically commit the majority Bench opinion to memory word-for-word. Which," he acknowledged just a bit complacently, "came in very handy for the final."

"Figures," Karl said just a bit sourly.

"Got you, too, did it?" Harrison asked more sympathetically. "I admit it's tricky. But that reconstructive nanotech's been critical to at least a dozen high-profile cases since 1487. Anyone who expects to be a career cop needs to understand when it's admissible and when it isn't. I'd, ah, been a little sloppy about that early in the semester; that's why Justice Tibbetts assigned it for my research paper. I didn't much enjoy it, but she did have a point about that."

"You're probably right," Karl acknowledged. "On the other hand, it's not something we're going to need all that often out in 'the boonies,' now is it?"

"Probably not," Harrison agreed. "Of course, I probably won't need to know a hexapuma's vital areas anytime real soon, either. And even if I did—"

A server moved past their table, slapping Harrison's beer down in front of him, and he took a deep, appreciative sip. Then he looked back across at Stephanie.

"So, you guys are done now, right?"

"Yes, we are." She leaned back in her chair, gathering Lionheart in her arms as he swarmed into her lap. "Of course, the grades haven't been posted yet." She grimaced. "Dr. Flouret says they won't be up until day after tomorrow, and Dr. Gleason's probably won't be up any sooner."

"What's the rush?" Harrison's eyebrows arched. "You're that eager to run away from Manticore? I thought you guys were going to spend a week or so with your parents on the Bay before you went home!"

"Well, yeah. Sure!" Stephanie produced another smile, hoping it looked more natural than it felt. "But Ms. Pheriss—she works with my mom, sometimes, you know—says there's a problem that needs looking into. So we'll probably be heading back a little ahead of schedule, and I hope you won't take this the wrong way, but much as I know you love Manticore, I'm really missing Sphinx right now."

And that's not really stretching the truth all that much, she told herself. *After all, Jessica is "Ms. Pheriss," and she does work with Mom sometimes.*

"I'm sorry to hear that," Harrison said sincerely. "I'm going to miss you guys—and Lionheart. Let's at least try to stay in touch, okay?"

"Sure thing," Karl agreed.

"Hey!" Harrison cocked his head. "Does that mean you're going to have to head home without addressing the Adair Foundation again?"

"No." Stephanie shook her head. "That's scheduled for tomorrow night, and we can't leave—that is, we don't *want* to leave—" she amended, not entirely truthfully, "until grades are officially posted. So we've got plenty of time for it, and Earl Adair Hollow's invited my parents, as well." This time her grin came more naturally. "I'm looking forward to it, especially since they finally managed to get Lionheart invited, too!"

Dirt Grubber was aware of Windswept's excitement the next morning as she tossed a variety of bags and bundles into her flying thing and motioned for him to jump in. He knew part of the reason for her happy mood was that they were going to get Bleached Fur. Even when Death Fang's Bane had still been close, Windswept had clearly found Bleached Fur an attractive male, but Dirt Grubber had gradually come to realize that she had held back expressing her feelings because she felt that Death Fang's Bane had a claim on him.

That sort of confusion would not have arisen among the People, given their ability to taste one another's mind-glows, but he admitted that there were still many things he did not truly understand about two-legs. For example, he was far from certain how they chose their mates. There were pairs he had met who behaved outwardly like bonded pairs. Inwardly, however, each was indifferent to the other. Sometimes parts of an apparent pair even despised each other. That was troubling enough, but this question of conflicting claims on one person—this uncertainty and pain when there was no indifference in any of them—would not happen among the People.

Not for the first time, Dirt Grubber wished he and Windswept could talk Person to Person. Since they could not, he settled for watching the landscape passing in a blur which was still mostly green beneath the flying thing. Even with the clear partitions closed, Dirt Grubber could tell that once again they were over one of the areas where the fires had been very bad, for the green shifted to blacks and browns. He thought it might even be near the area where they had found Keen Eyes. That reminded him of their last meeting.

When he had awakened after Darkness Foe's treatment, Keen Eyes had shared very little with Dirt Grubber and Swift Striker. Part of that was clearly because the medicines Darkness Foe had used to make him comfortable muddled his thinking, as both Dirt Grubber and Swift Striker knew from first-hand experience. But part was certainly because he was deeply miserable and did not care to share his innermost thoughts.

Dirt Grubber had to depart when Windswept did, but Swift Striker had promised to stay with the stranger and offer him comfort. That Swift Striker would also try to learn what had so disturbed Keen Eyes, Dirt Grubber did not doubt. However, Swift Striker would not be able to share that information over the enormous distances that separated them, so revelation would need to wait until their two-legs brought them together again. Judging from the number of times the feelings Windswept associated with Darkness Foe flowed through her mind-glow after she had gathered up Bleached Fur and they were making their mouth noises at each other, Dirt Grubber did not think that meeting would be too long in coming.

Death Fang's Bane was also much on the young two-legs' minds. Dirt Grubber was interested to see that Bleached Fur's mind-glow became a rich complex of conflicting emotions at these times. Dirt Grubber could not taste the young male as easily as he could Windswept, but he thought that the strong affection Bleached Fur had always felt for Windswept was growing into something more complex.

These poor two-legs! How hard it must be not to be able to easily taste emotions and thoughts. Mind blindness must lead to so many misunderstandings among them.

But, then again, he thought, remembering Keen Eyes and the three dead People, even mind-voices and mind-glows could not solve all conflicts.

"How about putting down over there?" Jessica said, indicating a pocket meadow at the edge of a picketwood grove.

"Good choice," Anders said. "River and picketwood enough for shelter, but near enough to the fire zone that it's likely the hunting isn't great. Looks like a logical place to find a bunch of 'cats who're eating a lot of fish."

Jessica landed her air car, got out, and shrugged into her pack. Anders—he was doing the same thing—thought he'd need to be both blind and neuter not to admire how her torso moved when she did this.

He forced himself to look away and saw Valiant flowing up into the branches of one of the closer picketwood trees. Anders himself moved over by the river so he could splash some cold water over his suddenly hot face.

"I see some little fish," he said, "so the river at least is 'live.'"

Jessica hunkered down next to him. "Over there," she pointed. "See that matted plant with little heart-shaped leaves floating in the shallows?"

Anders nodded.

"I've seen Valiant sample it. Usually, the mats are larger, so I'm wondering if this one's been foraged lately. There's a lot of evidence that treecats—like human hunter-gatherers—have the sense not to take all of the plant. They cut it back but leave enough so the plant will regrow."

"We saw some evidence of that when we were trapped by the swamp," Anders agreed. "Valiant's people—you know, I never thought about it until now, but it was probably Valiant himself—had left some near-lettuce that we harvested ourselves."

He turned to grin up at the 'cat. "Thanks, fellow!"

Valiant replied with a polite "bleek," but his attention was firmly fixed upstream, in the general direction of the mountains.

"I have a feeling we should go that way," Jessica said. "And we shouldn't rush."

"Did Valiant tell you that?"

"Not so much told, but, yeah. Ready?"

They fell into step side by side. The picketwood canopy was shading toward the deep red foliage of autumn. It contrasted nicely with the dark gray and black of the trees' rough bark.

Really a nice place to go for a stroll with a pretty girl, Anders thought. *I just wish I didn't feel so—*

His thoughts were interrupted by a sharp, commanding bleek from Valiant. The treecat had been guiding them, scampering from branch to branch or leaping gracefully when he needed to alter direction. Now he'd halted and was holding up one true hand to indicate "stop."

The humans did. Anders tried not to move even his head, but his gaze scanned both the branches and the surrounding area. He let his hand drift to the butt of his holstered handgun.

"He's spotted someone," Jessica said very softly. "A treecat someone, I mean. More than one treecat someones."

Anders felt the thrill of discovery. He knew his dad would give anything to be where he was at that moment.

Valiant bleeked and motioned for them to follow him. Jessica stepped forth without hesitation, Anders a pace behind. He caught up with her quickly, and—shoulders almost touching—they walked to where the treecats waited.

When he sensed the People ahead of them in the netwood trees, Valiant made no effort to dim his mind-glow or slow his advance.

<I am Dirt Grubber of the Damp Ground Clan,> he said, sharing images of his home clan. *<Although these days I live with the two-leg called Windswept, who is my bond mate. That is her, along with the two-leg called Bleached Fur. Perhaps you have heard the songs?>*

But these People did not seem to know about him and Windswept—evidence that they were of Keen Eyes' clan.

<I am Firm Biter, hunter of the Landless Clan,> said the larger of the two males who confronted him.

<I am Long Voice, scout for that same clan. Once we called ourselves Swaying Fronds, for our range high in the mountains was filled with them. We lined our nests with them and used them to pad shelters against the snow. They smelled sweet even when dry.>

This came to Dirt Grubber as a rush of shared images from Long Voice. Scent, color, shape, the beauty of the forests high in the mountains. Memories of climbing high into the trees to feel the caress of the wind fingers and admire the sharp whiteness of distant mountain peaks. Truly, Long Voice had a scout's heart, for he delighted in the smallest detail and yet had room for beauty, as well.

Firm Biter was made of sterner stuff. He was the one who explained how these mountain People had come to live in the relative lowlands.

<Fire season was our doom. The burning began to moss-growing, but the winds drove the flames to rush across valleys and rises alike. We thought we would be safe, for there are many deep gorges cradling rivers. We had reckoned without the dryness of the land. Tall golden-leaf trees that should have shrugged off the flames instead fell prey to licking fires that ran like bark-chewers up their sides. Gray-bark and green-needles burst into torches. Even the net-wood betrayed us, providing bridges although we had faithfully kept the proper gaps.>

Dirt Grubber knew shared pain made bridges as firm as any net-wood branch, and so he opened his own memories in return. <Even in the lower lands where my clan has its nesting place, we were not safe. A green-needle bursting into flame went from tree to death trap in a single breath. Had it not been for Windswept, I would have been burned alive. When we crawled back into life, we found ourselves as tightly bonded as ever two hearts have been.>

He shared the incredible wash of emotion that was still as fresh to him now as on that day. Then he waited patiently, for though memories could be shared in a moment, the thoughtful tasting that led to deeper understanding took time. It was Firm Biter who shook himself from nose tip to tail tip and made a gusty sound that combined astonishment and distinct pleasure.

<And is the light-furred creature next to Windswept her mate?>

Dirt Grubber sighed. <He should be, if either of them had the sense of rocks, but two-legs are mind-blind and must learn such things in their own way and time. Still, mate or not of my Windswept, Bleached Fur is brave and very determined.>

He shared images of when the Damp Ground Clan had joined in rescuing the stranded two-legs from a whistling sucker. Bleached Fur stood defiantly between the monster and the weaker members of his group—this though he was a youngling still only on the threshold of being adult and many of those he protected were adults themselves.

<*You choose your friends well,*> Long Voice said. <*What brings you in search of us? I can see that this is no accidental meeting.*>

<*I bring you news of Keen Eyes, scout of your clan,*> Dirt Grubber said. <*I see you believed him dead, victim in the recent fighting, but he lives.*>

He shared with them the finding of Keen Eyes and how he had been tended by Darkness Foe and his mate. In doing this, he also showed images of Swift Striker.

<*Our memory singers had shared with us Swift Striker's song before the fires,*> Long Voice said. <*So where is Keen Eyes now?*>

<*He remains with Swift Striker and Darkness Foe,*> Dirt Grubber replied. <*Darkness Foe is a marvelous healer, but even with the medicines of the two-legs, such wounds will not heal in a day.*>

Firm Biter's mind-voice was gruff with relief, flickering memories of his association with Keen Eyes—whom he had obviously liked—shading all he said. <*It is a wonder beyond belief that such wounds would heal in even six hands of days. We owe you welcome. Will you come to us so that our clan may hear your tale from your own mind, not through our memories?*>

<*Gladly,*> Dirt Grubber said. <*My two-legs as well?*>

Firm Biter's mind-glow flickered with hesitation, as if he might protest, but Long Voice rebuked him.

<*Remember, Firm Biter. These two saved Keen Eyes as much as Darkness Foe did. They have shown they are worthy of trust.*>

The hesitation vanished from Firm Biter's mind-glow, replaced with shame. <*I apologize. These days, trust is hard to remember. There has been so much death and unkindness. That should not make me forget how People should believe. My mother, had the flames not eaten her, would rebuke me for my behavior. Follow us. We will call ahead your coming.>*

Although both Firm Biter and Long Voice had been friendly enough, they had not chosen to share histories with Dirt Grubber when they met. For this reason, many surprises awaited him when they came to where the Landless Clan had set up a central nesting place of sorts.

One was the size and composition of the clan. While it still had members enough to manage, this was a tree with many limbs lopped off. Worse, many of the remaining limbs were very old, very young, or suffering from injuries—old and new. Dirt Grubber sensed that the most severely injured had already died. These were the ones hanging on because of their clan mates' careful nursing.

Based on his contact with Keen Eyes, Dirt Grubber had been prepared to find a clan both underfed and emotionally overwhelmed, but the sheer poverty of their situation touched him at once. They lacked all but the most basic necessities...and he saw no evidence of stored food.

Do they realize that if something does not change they cannot survive the winter? he thought, hoping this horrible revelation would blend into the other shocks swirling through his mind-glow. No wonder the Landless Clan had reached the point of fighting another clan! They must find a better place than this.

Horrible as that discovery was, the second shock was worse. Keen Eyes had told him that his clan had no memory singers. Still, when the elders came forth to meet him, he found himself looking for the clear brilliance of the memory singers among them. Not finding it was like not finding his own teeth within his mouth. In a very real sense, a clan *was* its memory singers, for they held all its shared history. The loss of Wide Ears and her assistants had robbed the Landless Clan not only of an important part of its leadership, but of its sense of self.

In the second rank, Dirt Grubber tasted a bright spark of a mind that watched him very carefully. This youngling had potential, great potential, but who would teach her what she needed to know? Some of her clan's history would have been shared with neighboring clans, but still...

The understanding of just how much the fires had taken from this Landless Clan struck Dirt Grubber like a blow.

He was still reeling when a wizened elder called Sour Belly offered his version of events since the fires had made Swaying Fronds into the Landless Clan. Whatever flaws Sour Belly had—and Dirt Grubber tasted both pettishness and ill-temper among them—his account caused none in his clan to protest as to its fullness of detail. It all came forth: flight, struggle, constant moves, death after death, eventual settlement, hope changing to despair as scout after scout (Keen Eyes prominent among them) reported that all ways from this place seemed blocked.

Then came the disappearance and murder of Red Cliff. In the image, Dirt Grubber knew the body he and his two-leg friends had buried. He sought for and found Beautiful Mind among the invalids, still holding to life because she would not make her mate's sacrifices mean nothing.

Finally, the events that had led to battle... Keen Eyes' plan. The plan working. Nimble Fingers. Hope rising, chased by despair and loss as a kitten chases its own tail. The horror of the battle. Bringing home the dead and wounded. Waiting... waiting...

For Sour Belly, that wait was one for death, for now all knew Trees Enfolding blocked the only way out and Trees Enfolding had no mercy in its heart.

<*But what of this Nimble Fingers?*> Dirt Grubber asked

in desperation. *<He did not seem like a bad fellow. Surely he would help you.>*

Sour Belly's reply hit as hard as the claws of a death wing in the night.

<Nimble Fingers wishes to help us, but he was badly injured when he tried to stop the fighting. His own clan mates were too caught up in battle rage to know when they rent the very one they had come to rescue. His life is safe, but he is too weak to go to his clan, and surely we cannot aid him.>

Anders contacted Scott MacDallan as soon as they were aloft.

"It's a bad situation. Neither of us is a treecat expert—"

"Who is?" Scott asked dryly. "Even Stephanie would be the first to say we've barely touched on their complexities. Go on."

"Okay, then. It's a small clan. They didn't stand still for us to count or anything, but we're guessing there were no more than seventy-five individuals—and that includes a lot of kittens and some adults who were obviously invalids. Not only from the fighting, either. There were what I guess you'd call chronic cases, too."

"Probably smoke damage to lungs," Jessica cut in. "We saw a lot of healing burns, too. Scars by now, but ugly."

"And a lot of the healthier adults were seniors."

"How could you tell that?"

"Valiant just gave me that impression," Jessica replied for Anders. "Then there's that theory that males get more rings on their tails the older they get. If that guess is right, well, we saw a lot of tails with a lot of rings."

"Oh!" Anders added. "Again, we're guessing because we didn't trying get too close, but under all that fur they seemed pretty skinny."

"So you think this is Survivor's clan."

"Well, I hope it is," Jessica snapped, "because the thought of another group of treecats that miserable makes me want to cry!" She paused. "Sorry. It's just that I think Valiant's as upset as I am. We're not doing each other any good at all right now."

Scott's tone was soothing. "I understand. What else?"

"They're poor," Anders said. "My dad's been studying treecat garbage, remember? I know what they should have, and they don't. I didn't see *any* gourds, and they don't have many baskets, either. And the handful of those I did see were clumsily woven, like just getting them done was enough. I saw some nets, but...I've visited Lionheart's clan with Stephanie, and how they live is different. They have nice baskets. They have perches in the trees with pads on them—some are practically pillowed! They weave weatherproof nests thick and insulated enough to stand off even a Sphinxian weather. They keep furs. They store food. This clan had none of that."

Jessica agreed. "I've gone home with Valiant. His clan's on the small side, too, but the difference is obvious. It's not just stuff this clan doesn't have. It's how they move around. These guys were sluggish, like they were tired right down to their bones."

"Are you sure they weren't just on guard because there was a strange treecat and two humans in their settlement?" Scott asked.

"Absolutely," Jessica said. "Even the kittens looked beat. You can't tell me that even the best-behaved kids in the universe would just sit and watch. They're not only starving physically; I think they're emotionally beaten. I think they know they're not going to make it through the winter with what they have and they're giving up."

"That's a lot to say based on one visit," Scott said, "but I'm not saying I don't believe you. You say Valiant is down?"

"Very. Utterly despondent. When we first got in with the clan, he was really pleased, especially when he and this other male treecat were nose to nose. I'm guessing they were talking up a storm, but somewhere in there he got sad. He's in my lap now, and he's never there when I'm flying."

"I took a bunch of images on my uni-link," Anders said. "None of them are going to be art pieces, but I'll copy them over to you, if you want. Take a look. You're not going to get the emotions, I know, but you'll have more than our word for it."

"Do it," Scott said. "I'm going to have to go back to my patients for a few hours, but I'll view the images as soon as I can. Are you two heading back to Twin Forks?"

"Yeah. Jessica promised her mother she'd be back to make dinner. Ms. Pheriss is doing her best to get everything at the Harringtons' spiffy before they get home next week."

"Closer to four days now," Scott reminded him. "Richard e-mailed me their ship schedule. We're all going to meet at the Harrington steading for a conference as soon as they're home."

"Good!" Anders said. "I'm glad."

But somewhere deep inside, he wondered why he didn't feel gladder.

Dirt Grubber was haunted by memories of the Landless Clan. He was all too well aware that without the intervention of Death Fang's Bane, Windswept, and their friends, his clan could be in much the same position—if not worse. Like the Landless Clan, they would have found it difficult to move to a new location without trespassing on territories already claimed by other clans or, worse, settled by the two-legs.

There but for the kindness of some impulsive younglings go we, he thought. *Surely I can do something. But what?*

He brooded during the flight to Windswept's home. Even after the evening routine was over and she had fallen into troubled sleep, he tried idea after idea, much as he would have tested plants in various types of soil and light. Somewhere in the darkest hours, he came up with the plan.

The Landless Clan needed to be transplanted. That was certain. However, their route to new lands was blocked by the Trees Enfolding Clan. Nimble Fingers was willing to act as ambassador, sharing his experiences with the Landless Clan with his own, but he was too wounded to travel.

If Windswept could treat Nimble Fingers, perhaps even help bring him close to where Trees Enfolding nested... Surely the Landless Clan would have had enough time by now to realize that the outsiders could help them. He was sure he could convince them of what must be done.

The only problem was, how could he explain to Windswept what he wanted?

18

"WHAT IS BOTHERING YOU, STEPHANIE?" MARJORIE Harrington inquired. "You're squirming inside your skin like a demented stutter bug!"

Despite herself, Stephanie giggled at the image. Stutter bugs were one of Meyerdahl's more colorful insect analogues. They were also about the size of her hand, and they communicated by drawing air over vibrating spicules that covered their garishly decorated sides. A stutter bug in full mating chorus looked like a bright orange, hairy beanbag someone had stuffed with a vibrator.

"Sorry, Mom!" She shook her head contritely. "I guess I'm just more nervous tonight."

"Well, sure," Karl put in, supporting her excuse loyally. "It's the first time they've let you take Lionheart anywhere off-campus, Steph!"

"I'm sure that explains it," Richard Harrington said in a tone which—to his daughter's knowledgeable ear— suggested he was rather less certain of it than his words implied. Fortunately, he let Karl's explanation stand, although the look he gave Stephanie suggested she might well find herself revisiting the topic with him later.

Well, of course I will! We really should've told them already, but if we had, they'd have climbed onto the next Manticore-Sphinx shuttle come hell or high water. And the same people who would've wondered why Karl and I were running for home would wonder why they were scooting back to Twin Forks while he and I were still stuck on Manticore. Especially when they hadn't even seen us in the last three months!

"It was nice of the foundation to lean on the restaurant's management," Richard said instead of following up on the reasons for his daughter's obvious anxiety.

"It sure was," Stephanie agreed sincerely as the taxi grounded at the entrance to the park around the Charleston Arms. The same footman who'd opened the door for her and Karl on their first visit opened it again, but this time he smiled at them.

"Welcome back," he said. "I understand you two are heading home to Sphinx in a day or two?"

"Yes, we are," Stephanie acknowledged, and gave him a sincere smile. He'd turned out to be a much more worthwhile person than she'd assumed that first evening. "Steve, this is my mom and my dad. Mom, Dad—this is Steve Cirillo."

"Pleased to meet you," Cirillo said, shaking hands with Marjorie and Richard in turn. "You're probably tired of hearing it, but you've got quite a daughter here."

"That's not really the kind of thing a smart parent admits she's tired of hearing," Marjorie replied, and he chuckled.

"And this—" Stephanie reached up to touch Lionheart's ears "—is Lionheart."

"So those old...fogies in the front office finally said you

could bring him, did they?" Cirillo glanced at Stephanie's parents from the corner of one eye as he changed nouns in mid flight. "Good for you!"

"I think Ms. Adair had a lot to do with it. She and her cousin," Stephanie said.

"The earl usually does get what he wants," Cirillo agreed, and waved them through the ornamental gate. The days when he'd assigned a minder to make sure they didn't get lost—or steal any doorknobs—were long past, and Stephanie smiled at him again before her parents followed her and Karl past the gate and along the gravel walk across the restaurant's manicured park.

There was less traffic about than usual, although the paths were seldom very crowded. It had taken Stephanie a couple of visits to realize that the Charleston Arms wasn't actually a public restaurant at all. In fact, the entire facility was a private club which belonged to the Earl of Adair Hollow. The restaurant was open to the public three days a week, but not on Fridays, which was when the foundation regularly met here. She'd wondered, since she'd discovered the way things were actually organized, why it had taken so long to clear her to bring Lionheart along. She knew Landing had stricter regulations than Twin Forks about permitting "animals" into eating establishments, but they made plenty of exceptions for service dogs and Beowulfan fox bears. Probably just bureaucratic inertia, she'd decided, and the fact that the earl himself had returned to the Star Kingdom this week from his extended business trip probably explained why they'd suddenly managed to overcome that inertia.

Of course—

Lionheart's sudden, rippling snarl cut her off in mid-thought.

❖　　❖　　❖

Climbs Quickly tensed, muscles coiling tightly. His ears went flat to his head and his bared fangs showed bone-white in the illumination spilling from the tall pillar of light behind him and his two-legs.

I should have tasted them sooner! he told himself fiercely. *Am I a scout of the People or a just-weaned kitten who cannot be trusted out of the nest on his own?!*

Even as he thought it, he knew he was being unfair to himself. Death Fang's Bane's mind-glow had been clearer and brighter since her parents had arrived at the learning place, but it remained more shadowed than it ought to be, and he was no closer to understanding the reasons for those shadows. Except for the increasing certainty that they had much to do with the People, that was. And the echo of her fretfulness had seeped into his own mind-glow. It had not dimmed his perceptions, but it had focused his own thoughts on his effort to understand what concerned her so, worrying at it like a death gleaner at a two-day-dead horn blade.

Two-leg mind-glows were always strong, but that was part of the problem. He had grown accustomed to being forced to barricade himself against their intensity, like someone shielding his eyes against too-bright sunlight. And he had been allowing himself to luxuriate in the mind-glows of Death Fang's Bane's parents—and in the way her own mind-glow had taken comfort from their presence, even if she had not managed to release whatever was causing so much anxiety. But even so, he knew his own preoccupation with her worry was the only reason he had missed the oncoming mind-glows until it was almost too late.

Stephanie's head snapped up, turning automatically to the left. It wasn't until much later that she grasped the real reason she'd looked in that direction and realized she'd *felt* it from Lionheart. At the moment, all she saw was a blur of movement coming out of the shadows and the undergrowth...and headed straight at *her.*

"What the—" her father began.

"*Richard!*"

That was her mother's voice, and adrenaline rocketed as she realized her parents were in danger, as well.

"*Steph—!*"

Karl called her name in a hard, harsh-edged voice, but she scarcely heard him through the high, snarling crescendo of Lionheart's warcry, and she felt herself dropping into a half-crouch.

Five of them, a ridiculously calm corner of her brain reflected. *At least five. How—?*

But there was no time to worry about how they'd gotten onto the Charleston Arms' grounds, and she felt Lionheart catapult from her shoulder.

Climbs Quickly launched himself into the overhead branches, snarling his challenge. It wasn't the first time his two-leg, his *person*, had been in danger, and the red fury of rage roared through him. The People knew how to deal with threats to those they loved, and his scimitar claws slid from their sheaths.

Yet even as he snarled, even as he tasted Death Fang's Bane's fear—for her parents, not for herself—he tasted a sudden spike of fresh and different apprehension flooding out of her. Apprehension with a familiar tang, even if he had never tasted it so strongly before. She was frightened for *him*, and not just that he might once more be injured as he had been when they faced the death fang together. In its own way, this fear was even sharper than the fear she had felt then, because it was more focused, something which had been with her longer, and he hissed again, more fiercely, as he realized what it was.

I do not want *to realize!* The thought flashed through his mind. *They mean us evil—they mean* her *evil—and evildoers deserve whatever comes to them!*

Yet even as he rebelled, he knew she was right. This was no death fang, devoid of reason. These were two-legs, and he could not slay such as they as he would have slain a death fang or a snow hunter. Not unless there was clearly no other choice.

Perhaps not, he thought grimly. *But if they do not* leave *me another choice...*

Later, it was all a blur in Stephanie's memory.

She felt Lionheart flash from her shoulder into the branches of an overhead tree. She sensed her father grabbing her mother, pushing her behind him and reaching for Stephanie herself. But she ducked under his hand, because one of the vague shapes coming out of the shrubbery carried a weapon of some kind in his right hand, and Stephanie dived for it.

He was a third again her height and undoubtedly outweighed her two-to-one, but she didn't think about that at the moment. She got her hands on his wrist, shoved it upward with all her strength, and kicked him in the right knee as hard as she could.

Stephanie Harrington would never be a tall woman, but she was a genie, genetically engineered to live in a gravity well thirty percent higher than that of humanity's birth world, and she was scared to death. The combination of her enhanced muscles and that blast of pure adrenaline had unfortunate consequences for the lead mugger, and he screamed in anguish as his kneecap shattered.

Something hissed past Stephanie's ear, and the trank dart buried itself in the tree's bark. She twisted from the hips, getting her shoulders and back into it, and the

injured mugger released the tranquilizer pistol. It thud-
ded to the ground, and she heard a high, falsetto squeal
from the second assailant in line.

Climbs Quickly recognized the sound. He had heard
it before when Speaks Falsely had faced the young death
fang at Bright Water Clan's nesting place. It was one of
the two-legs' weapons, but not one of the ones that killed
instantly, and he saw another one of it in one hand of
the second attacking two-leg.

He launched himself from his tree-branch perch as the
two-leg Death Fang's Bane had kicked collapsed, wailing
and clutching at his injured limb. He arced over Death
Fang's Bane's head and struck the second two-leg's weapon
hand with both hand-feet and his remaining true-hand,
and his claws sank deep.

His victim howled, waving his right arm frantically as
the knife-clawed demon ripped at him. The thug had no
idea how fortunate he was, how easily Climbs Quickly
could have shredded his entire forearm. In fact, he thought
that was *exactly* what the treecat was doing, and he flung
away the tranquilizer pistol, beating at the hissing cream
and gray monster with his left hand.

Climbs Quickly's true-feet raked the two-leg's other hand,
and he hissed again—this time in fierce satisfaction—as the
evildoer cried out in fresh pain. He would have preferred
to spend a little more time dealing suitably with anyone
who threatened *his* two-leg, but there were more of them
behind the first two, and he abandoned his initial victim
to hit a second assailant in the chest.

Stephanie released the first mugger's wrist to go bound-
ing after Lionheart. It was a mistake.

Despite the anguish of his broken kneecap, the thug managed to get one hand up and grabbed her ankle as she went by. She fell, sprawling forward, just managing to catch herself on her hands before she landed flat on her face.

"*Stephanie!*"

She'd never heard Karl sound quite like that, but she had no time to dwell on it at the moment. Instead, she twisted to one side and her free foot slammed into her attacker's chin. It wasn't as clean and powerful as the kick which had broken his kneecap, but it was more than sufficient to encourage him to let go of her ankle.

She rolled away from him, flinging herself back to her feet, but before she could come back upright, Karl went past her. She couldn't see exactly what happened next, but whatever it was, it didn't take very long. She heard a sharp, meaty thud, then a grunt of exertion, a gasp of what was probably pain, and over all of that a strange voice screaming "Get it off! *Get it off!*"

And then, suddenly, it was all over.

The man she'd kicked was curled in a knot, cradling his broken kneecap with one hand and trying to comfort his equally broken jaw with the other. The first man Lionheart had hit was on his knees, clutching his freely bleeding hands and forearms against his chest. The one who'd been screaming to "Get it off!" was backed against a tree trunk, his tunic and shirt shredded, his chest oozing blood from at least a dozen shallow cuts, while Lionheart crouched in front of him, lashing his tail and hissing. It was obvious from the thug's expression that he had absolutely no interest in challenging the treecat's obvious rage a second time.

And then there was Karl, and Stephanie's eyes widened as she saw one man lying unconscious and another down on one knee, bent sharply forward and obviously trying not to whimper in pain while Karl twisted his arm up behind him, high enough to press his wrist against the back of his neck.

"Are you all right, Steph?" Karl demanded, and she nodded.

"Y-Yes," she said, and flushed furiously as she heard the catch in her voice. Then she whirled. "Mom! Dad!"

"We're fine, Steph!" There was a shaky edge in Richard's voice, too, but he managed to smile as he stood hugging her mother. "We're fine. Thanks to you and Lionheart—and Karl." He cocked his head, looking at the younger man. "That was very, ah, *efficient* of you, Karl," he said.

"My dad always said it was important to know how to take care of yourself, Dr. Richard," Karl replied with a brief smile. "He was pretty serious about teaching us how to do it, too." He shrugged. "I earned my black belt three T-years ago. Never really expected to need it, though."

He gave Richard another smile, but his attention seemed to be focused on Stephanie.

"You're bleeding, Steph," he said a bit sharply, and Stephanie looked down as she realized she'd bloodied one knee through her shredded trousers when the first thug tripped her.

"Only a scraped knee, Karl," she said quickly.

"Good. In that case—"

"Security!" a voice snapped, and the beam of a powerful hand lamp speared the battered group. "Everybody just stay where you are till we get this straightened out!"

"Stephanie, I am *so* sorry this happened!" Gwendolyn Adair shook her head, her expression more distraught than Stephanie had ever dreamed she could look. "I can't imagine how they managed to get onto the grounds in the first place!"

"Whoever hired them must've hacked our security protocols, ma'am," the senior uniformed guard said unhappily. "The LPD says they were loaded to their uni-links, anyway."

"But why?" Marjorie Harrington asked. "I mean, I'm sure the members of your cousin's club have to be rich enough to be worth mugging, Ms. Adair. But why go to all the trouble of hacking your security and then jump on *us*, instead?"

"'Fraid I can answer that one, too, Dr. Harrington," the security man said heavily. "The police found an animal carrier in the shrubbery. I'm guessing they meant to trank the lot of you, including Lionheart, then shove him into the carrier."

"They wanted to *kidnap* Lionheart?!" Stephanie demanded.

"We don't know that yet, Stephanie," Gwendolyn replied. "It does sound as if it could make sense, but I wouldn't jump to any conclusions yet."

Stephanie looked at her, feeling the residue of too much adrenaline still burning through her. It wouldn't be much longer before she started to shake, she reflected, but something about Gwendolyn bothered her. There was a flicker of uneasiness, as if something wasn't quite right. It was almost like . . .

Of course something isn't "right," you dummy! she told herself. *Someone just tried to mug you all and kidnap Lionheart!*

She snorted mentally at the thought. She was pretty sure she was still feeling the echoes of Lionheart's emotions along with her own, which probably helped to account for at least some of the tension jangling down her nerves. And whatever else might be true, Gwendolyn Adair was nothing like Tennessee Bolgeo, no matter how frazzled her nerves might be at the moment! Besides—

"I'm quite sure they would have thought of it as *stealing* him, not a kidnapping, Ms. Harrington," another voice said, and she turned to find herself facing a man who looked so much like an older version of Gwendolyn that she knew instantly he must be the Earl of Adair Hollow. Now he shook his head, his expression regretful in the bright lights his security personnel and the police were stringing up around the crime scene.

"Like Gwen, I'm terribly sorry that this could have happened to you here at the Charleston Arms," he said sincerely, holding out his hand to her. She shook it almost dazedly, and he extended it to her parents, in turn. "I assure you that we usually take much better care of our guests," he told them.

"These guests seem to have turned out to be able to take care of themselves, George," Gwendolyn pointed out, and he smiled slightly.

"Indeed they do," he agreed and shook hands with Karl. "Nicely done, Mr. Zivonik! In fact, all of you did remarkably well...including you, Lionheart."

The earl went down on one elegantly tailored knee, showing rather more aplomb—and nerve—than most of the security and police personnel had as he extended his open palm to the bloodstained treecat. Lionheart cocked his head, looking at him for a moment, then laid his own three-fingered true-hand on the exposed palm. The earl stayed that way for several seconds, then nodded courteously to the treecat and stood.

"I realize this wasn't exactly the beginning of the evening you had in mind when we invited you," he told his guests. "Nonetheless, I do hope you'll honor us with your company after all. I deeply regret having been out of the Star Kingdom until tonight, and I would consider it a personal favor to have the opportunity to speak with all of you—and especially you and Lionheart, Ms. Harrington."

He smiled winningly at Stephanie. "Speaking on behalf of the foundation, I believe this may be the beginning of a long and close relationship."

Climbs Quickly rode on his two-leg's shoulder as she, Shadowed Sunlight, and her parents moved towards the enormous living place. The echoes of combat still reverberated deep inside him, and he forced himself to draw a deep mental breath as he fought to damp them out.

It was hard, and not least because yet again he had discovered evildoers among the two-legs. He had no idea exactly what *these* evildoers had had in mind, but did it matter? How was he to convince the rest of the People that they could truly trust the two-legs when things like *this* kept happening? And did even the two-legs around him truly know what had just happened and why? The mind-glows were so brilliant, and so roiled by the two-legs' reactions, that he could taste very little of their deeper emotions, and he reminded himself not to read too much into that stormy sea of feelings. There was a great deal of shock in most of them—and almost as much anger as shock, in some—and the intensity of it all made his head ache.

And, oddly enough, the two who seemed angriest of all were the ones who were clearly in charge of all the other two-legs in this living place. Perhaps, as its elders, they felt a special responsibility for what had almost happened? That much, at least, would make sense.

"Well, *that* didn't work out very well, did it?" Oswald Morrow muttered as he and Gwendolyn followed Adair Hollow and the Harringtons across the park.

"No, it didn't," she conceded with an icy smile which contained very little humor.

At least she didn't have to be concerned about anything leading back to her. She'd hired the thugs through an anonymous electronic intermediary. All they'd known was that someone was prepared to pay them upwards of a quarter million Manticoran dollars if they could deliver the treecat to him. They'd been informed that they would receive the location for the delivery once they had proof the treecat was in their possession. Nothing had been said one way or the other about the humans in the treecat's vicinity, although given the caliber of her disposable henchmen she'd anticipated a certain amount of serious injury.

Of course, she'd also anticipated that they would never get off the Charleston Arms' grounds with their prize. The access code she'd provided them with had gotten them *in* through the facility's security, but their mysterious employer had obviously missed the fact that getting *out* again required a different code entirely. Besides, if things had gone properly, they would have been in no condition to think about going anywhere.

Anything that could hold a hexapuma at bay even briefly should have made short work out of shredding faces and throats with gory abandon, and that was exactly what she'd expected. What she'd *planned* on. Who would ever have imagined the treecat would show such restraint? Especially when Gwendolyn had gone to the trouble of making sure Stephanie's parents would be present for the event. If anything could have been calculated to send her into a panic and goad Lionheart into an . . . extreme reaction, that should have done it. But had he cooperated? No, of course he hadn't!

"Countess Frampton's not going to be very happy about this," Morrow whispered as they approached the restaurant's front steps. She shot him a venomous glance, and he shrugged. "At least I'll be able to tell her it wasn't *my* fault," he said.

"Well, she's just going to have to be unhappy then, isn't she?" Gwendolyn replied sharply. "It didn't work out as planned, but the fact that the little monster *didn't* kill anyone isn't going to get anywhere near as much coverage as we'd have gotten if he *had* killed someone." She showed her teeth in another humorless smile. "Like I said before, it's not like we would've changed the foundation's mind whatever happened, and I should be able to spin the 'exotic animal poacher' threat in a way to help encourage the protective reservation mindset. It'll be a harder sell, of course, but I've had lots of practice managing Cousin George and his little band of philanthropists. And sweet little Stephanie and Karl are going to go home thinking of me as their friend. That offers all kinds of possibilities, don't you think?"

Morrow started to reply, but they'd reached the stairs, and he contented himself with a short nod before the two of them started up.

◆ 19 ◆

ANDERS COMMED JESSICA THE MORNING AFTER THEY'D found Survivor's clan and caught her finishing up her morning chores.

"I've been looking at maps, Jess," he began excitedly. "I didn't realize how much of the unburned land east of the mountains is already in use by humans, and I'm guessing that population pressure's definitely part of the picture with those treecats."

"Interesting. Link me to your map." When she'd had a chance to look at it, she said, "I see what you mean, but there's still a lot of unclaimed land."

"Unclaimed *as far as we know*," Anders said. "Remember that third treecat body. We all agreed that from Scott's autopsy evidence that it really looked like another clan was involved, like this wasn't infighting in one clan. If we find that other clan, then we can add their location to the map and color in the zone with their probable holdings. No one knows exactly how much land a treecat clan needs, but from hanging around with anthropologists I've learned that hunter-gatherers—like treecats—need a lot of it. I think we should go find out how much the other clan—if there is one—is using, where it is relative to our Skinny 'Cat Clan, and how badly it's being pinched by the human-occupied areas."

Jessica nodded. "It sounds like a good idea to me. And I was going to call you anyway. I've got some babysitting money saved. I called the discount warehouse and they have a crate of freezer-burned poultry they'll sell me cheap. I was going to drop it off for the Skinny 'Cats."

Pleased that she hadn't rejected his theory out of hand, Anders risked teasing. "But what would Dr. Hidalgo say? Aren't we interfering with a pristine indigenous culture?"

"I am, and with pleasure—and so are you, Mr. Population Pressure. Somehow, I don't think you plan to stop with coloring in a map."

Anders grew serious. "I don't, but I think we're going to need some help. I almost messaged Stephanie with this, but I remembered that she's giving her big talk today. I'm sure she won't have any trouble at all, but I didn't want to distract her. Still, if anyone can help us talk the SFS around to relocating Survivor's people, it's going to be Steph. Let's get her all the ammunition we can."

"I'm with you," Jessica said. "I'll pick you up, then we'll get the stuff from the warehouse, and go. Mom's already given me the day off. She's taken all the kids over to the Harringtons' steading. Some sort of berry is coming ripe. The bigger kids are going to help pick and we're going to have berry ice cream. I was told you could come, too."

"I'd love that," Anders said. "Okay. Listen, since you're giving me dinner, let me chip in for the treecat chow, okay?"

Jessica paused, but she was too practical to be proud. "Okay."

✧   ✧   ✧

Dirt Grubber was pleased by the taste of Windswept's mind-glow. As soon as she awoke that morning, she turned to the image showing thing and studied the images she and Bleached Fur had captured of the Landless Clan. Her sorrow for the terrible straits to which Keen Eyes' clan had been reduced flowed to him through their link, and with it the determination to do something about it.

That determination stayed with her, burning in the depths of her mind-glow as she bustled about, clearly preparing for another lengthy trip. Relieved that she seemed to want to go where he did, Dirt Grubber concentrated on convincing her to pack extra healing things.

He knew the boxes in which they were kept, both within the large stone place where the family lived and in the flying thing. The problem was telling her she should bring them, and he resolved it by taking the smaller box from the flying thing and going and sitting on the larger box. When Windswept called for him, he bleeked until she found him.

He tasted the interest and delight that flashed through her mind as she figured out what he wanted. The surging cadence of mouth noises she made meant nothing, but the efficiency with which she gathered a large selection of items from the bigger box and moved them not only into the small box he held but into another box showed she was willing to help many more than Nimble Fingers.

When they got into the flying thing, he snuggled up close to her, patting her and purring. She chuckled warmly and patted him back. Wrapped in the warmth of mutual love and approval, they sped off to collect Bleached Fur.

Valiant was first out of the air car when they set down a short distance from where they'd found the Skinny 'Cats the day before. He bleeked at them, holding up his hand in the stop/wait gesture, then flowed off through the branches.

"I hope he'll be okay," Jessica said nervously. "Things *seemed* to go pretty well yesterday, but we know these 'cats aren't exactly friendly to everybody."

But Valiant was back before Anders could frame a reassuring reply. With him were two other male treecats. Anders thought they might even be the same ones from the day before. Valiant leapt down to join the humans, bouncing up on the lid to the air car's storage compartment, just in case they'd missed that they could unload.

"I'll take the 'cat chow," Anders said. "Even with countergrav, it's a big enough crate that steering it through the trees could get tricky."

Jessica tilted her head and thought. "Let's stack all three boxes, and then I'll go in front and steer. You can be manly and push."

"Aye aye, Captain," Anders said. When the boxes were stacked, he found he could just see over the top. Following Valiant's guidance, they quickly came upon the treecat clan's settlement.

Jessica looked at Valiant. "Food first?" She asked, tapping the crate. "Or medicine?"

"Bleek!" Valiant said, pointing to the crate of poultry. "Bleek! Bleek!"

Freezer-burned or not, the poultry proved to be a huge success. Soon the surrounding trees were filled with treecats shredding their way into what might have been their first big meal in weeks. Anders found himself particularly delighted by a cluster of kittens who had claimed an entire bird for themselves. One even climbed right inside the body cavity, like a particularly furry bit of stuffing.

"Look," Jessica said softly. "Those 'cats are carrying food to some of the others, even though they haven't had any themselves. I bet they're feeding the injured ones."

Her guess proved correct. A moment later, Valiant
returned. He picked up the smaller first aid kit and
motioned for them to follow him with the larger box, into
which Jessica had dropped quick heal, bandages, sponges,
and a huge thermos of hot water. She'd had only a little
of the other medications Dr. Richard had approved for
treecat use, but Anders had insisted on buying more at
a local pharmacy before they set out.

"I'm not a doctor," Jessica was muttering. "I'm certainly
not a vet. Survivor was unconscious. Most of these are
awake."

"I'm not a doctor, either," Anders said. "But Valiant
believes you can do what he thinks needs doing. We've
got the guidelines Dr. Richard wrote down for you so
you could care for Valiant in an emergency. If we come
across something we can't deal with, we'll com Scott.
We're in this together, remember? If you take the risk
of getting bitten or clawed, then so will I."

She smiled bravely. "Thanks, Anders. That means a lot."

Valiant seemed particularly eager that they treat one of
the younger males first, even though his injuries were not
the worst. He'd been badly slashed and seemed to have
trouble moving. One eye was swollen nearly shut, as well,
and the tip of an ear was missing. Giving him a dose of
pain medication first, they concentrated on cleaning and
disinfecting the ugly, open wounds, spraying them with
quick heal, and gently washing out his injured eye with the
same sterile solution Richard Harrington used for similar
injuries. They followed that with a Richard Harrington-
approved broadband antibiotic and, although neither of
them would ever confuse their skills with those of a trained
xenovet, they were pleased to see him sitting up so that he
could chew on a chicken leg when they'd finished.

They didn't stay to watch, but moved on to others,
starting with those with more recent battle wounds.

"Frankly," Anders said, spraying on more quick heal, "it's easier to figure out what to do with a cut or a gouge than the older injuries."

"I agree," Jessica said, "but I want to look at those, too. We have a couple of the same inhalers Dr. Richard used for Valiant and the twins. Maybe it's not too late for some respiratory therapy."

Valiant hovered near as they worked, making the same thrumming purr he had when they'd been treating the injured Survivor. Several other treecats, mostly females, joined him. Anders quickly noticed that these females watched what he and Jessica did very carefully—not as if they were suspicious but as if...

"Jess, I think we have the local doctors here," he said, as one of the females moved his current patient's limb so he could see a nasty cut he might otherwise have missed. "If treecats have healers, it would make sense that many of them would be female, since they'd be staying 'home' with the kittens and the injured. I bet they have field medics, too..."

"You're beginning to sound like an anthropologist," Jessica warned teasingly. "But I bet you're right. A lot of the wounds I've been looking at have been kept clean, the fur around them trimmed back so it won't grow into the scabs, stuff like that."

Eventually, they finished. Valiant had been a great deal of help, especially demonstrating how the inhalers worked and convincing the treecats to use them. Then, when Jessica and Anders were packing away their gear, he stiffened, turned, and went loping off in the direction of the young male who'd been their first patient.

"Wonder what that was about?" Anders said.

Jessica grinned. Although she was tired, she was also radiant with pleasure that they'd been able to do so much. "No idea. The other one called him. That's all I know, but I can assure you, if Valiant thinks we need to know, he'll figure out a way to tell us."

<Dirt Grubber, can you take me to my clan?> Nimble Fingers' mind-glow was brilliant with urgency. <Whatever your two-leg did to my wounds has me feeling almost myself. I am shaky on my legs, true. But if Windswept would carry me, I am certain I could manage.>

Dirt Grubber considered the other Person with concern.

<Are you certain? The medicines they have for pain may have given you a false sense of what you can do.>

<I think this is more than mere deadening of pain. I truly feel as if flesh that was torn has been pulled together and is healing. No matter the reason, I do not feel there is time to waste. I have heard my uncle calling to me. He is careful to keep out of mind-glow range, but even though I have told him otherwise, he is certain I am a prisoner. The traces of pain he tastes in my mind-voice only affirm his certainty. For the safety of these poor People who have already suffered so much, I must get away from here before his sanity becomes completely unbalanced. Too many would be hurt as he fought to get to me. If you doubt how fero-cious he can be, I tell you this, it was Swimmer's Scourge who nearly killed Keen Eyes.>

<Then he must be terribly wounded himself.>

<Not as severely as you might imagine. Keen Eyes bit down on his throat so that Swimmer's Scourge passed out, but furious as he was, Keen Eyes is not a killer at heart. He did not rip and tear as he would some bark-chewer or ground runner, and Swimmer's Scourge's other injuries were minor enough.>

Dirt Grubber flipped his tail in comprehension. <And if you leave here, Swimmer's Scourge will have no reason to come. I understand. It is unlikely he would be any threat

to us, even though we will need to travel on foot since you would not be able to guide us to your clan's central nesting place from the flying thing.>

<I fear I could not. I do not think I would recognize the landmarks if I were flying through the air like a death wing. Would you be willing to try this? When we leave here, I will call to my uncle that I am going back to our clan. He may track us, but I doubt even he is mad enough to attack.>

Dirt Grubber agreed. No Person, not even one driven by stress, would attack a Person of another clan and—especially—a pair of two-legs. The prohibitions against becoming involved with the two-legs had lasted for many turnings before Climbs Quickly had accidentally broken them. Although they had been gently bent these last few seasons, still they were firmly in place in most clans.

<Very well. Windswept and Bleached Fur are done with treating the sick and injured. I will try to make them understand.>

As with his last attempt, Dirt Grubber found his task made easier because his two-legs already had a similar idea. When he came up to them, they were sitting on the front of the flying thing, eating some food they had brought along and watching the now replete Landless Clan with definite satisfaction.

He could taste their pleasure that the big box held as much again of the dead birds as the clan had already eaten, so that hunger would be a while returning.

And if we are fortunate, by the time they are hungering again, we will have found a means of transplanting them from this place.

That thought gave him great satisfaction as he paused before Windswept, cradled his arms the way that she did when she scooped him up to hug and cuddle, and then pointed at Nimble Fingers.

❖   ❖   ❖

Anders and Jessica were a bit surprised when Valiant gestured that Jessica was to pick up and carry one of the treecats.

"Do it," Anders urged. "I'll carry a pack with all the basics. We're probably not going too far."

Jessica nodded and went to inspect her passenger.

"It's the same one Valiant had us treat first," she said, examining the 'cat's injuries before she helped it get into position with true-feet on the pad set into the back of her jacket and true hands on her shoulders. "He seems steady enough, but keep an eye on him."

"I'd love to tie a sling around him," Anders said, "but he probably wouldn't understand. Don't worry, I'll make sure he doesn't fall off—or if he does, that I catch him."

Jessica nodded. "I noticed when we were treating him, and it's more obvious now that he's on my shoulder. This guy's heavier than Survivor was. His ribs don't stick out nearly as much. Do you think he might be from that other clan?"

Anders shrugged. "Maybe. Was he a prisoner of war, then? A hostage? Someone they took in when he got hurt?"

"I'm not sure we'll ever know," Jessica said. "But maybe he's the guide we've been hoping for."

As they hiked deeper into the spreading trees, they felt the forest coming back to life around them. Where the Skinny 'Cats had been, there were few avians, certainly no small creatures. Even the plants were thinner. Now their passage disturbed numerous living things, only partially glimpsed as they retreated. The leaves overhead lost much of the singed look.

"But there's still fire damage," Anders said, "and with everything around burned out, whoever lives here isn't going to be able to count on natural migration. Those burned areas will act as a sort of moat, at least for ground creatures."

"Flying ones, too," Jessica said. "Only hunters like open

areas, though large herds will risk them, because the chance of being attacked is spread among so many. But there's nothing out in those blackened areas for a flock to forage on."

They didn't talk much. Once Jessica said, "Valiant's taking point, but I think the guy on my back is actually giving directions."

"Guide," Anders said. "Let's call him 'Guide.' 'The guy on my back' sounds kind of kinky."

Jessica laughed. "Okay. 'Guide' it is. There's something else, though. They're both edgy. I'm not sure why, but they are."

Anders patted his handgun. "I'm ready. Want me to carry the gun in my hand like a holo drama hero?"

Jessica's reply turned into a scream as something came tearing at terrific speed from behind them and landed directly on her head.

Later, Dirt Grubber would realize that the taste of menace that was Swimmer's Scourge's muted mind-glow had been with them for some time before the attack. At the time, his own dread of what might happen when they reached Trees Enfolding Clan, combined with the need to follow directions from Nimble Fingers, serve as a scout for their little group, and filter the strong emotions flowing to him from both Windswept and Bleached Fur, were enough to make him not as aware of the approaching enemy as he might have been.

Then, too, like Nimble Fingers, Dirt Grubber did not really believe that Swimmer's Scourge would attack when the two-legs were present. In the end, both he and Nimble Fingers were wrong—and they were right.

When Swimmer's Scourge attacked, he was aiming not for Windswept, but for Nimble Fingers who rode with his true hands on her shoulder and his head level with her own. What this meant was that both of them suffered the violence of the insane Person's assault.

Nimble Fingers had thick fur and was a fighter, besides. Windswept, however thick the long hair that grew atop her head, was a poor naked-faced creature. Swimmer's Scourge's leap carried him so that his fangs, true-hands, and hand-feet could rend at Nimble Fingers, but this left his true-feet—and their wicked claws—scrabbling at Windswept's head.

Dirt Grubber felt his two-leg's shock and pain as immediately as if they were his own, but since they were *not* his own, he was free to leap to her rescue. He was not alone in this. Feeble as he was, Nimble Fingers was fighting as much in the two-leg's defense as in his own. His wrath lashed out at his uncle, even as his wounds made his return attacks weak.

But it was Bleached Fur who resolved matters—although at terrible risk to himself. Taller than Windswept, he was in a good position to grab Swimmer's Scourge in both hands and pull him away. Shocked by the feeling of large, alien hands grasping him firmly and a strong voice shouting right in his ears, Swimmer's Scourge actually released his hold. It was only for a moment, but a moment was enough.

Dirt Grubber knew Swimmer's Scourge would not be quelled for long. Leaving his two-leg bleeding and uncomforted was its own pain, but he must stop Swimmer's Scourge. The Person was a menace to himself and to all around him. If he fled into the forest, what new harm might he cause?

Flinging himself on the other, Dirt Grubber struggled to hold Swimmer's Scourge without hurting him—for killing another Person out of hand was not the action of a sane Person and although angered and frightened, Dirt Grubber was not insane. Yet he was built for hunting, and six sets of razor-sharp claws longed to treat Swimmer's Scourge as he would a particularly difficult lake builder.

The roiling currents of Swimmer's Scourge's mind-glow—for he seemed beyond speech—were enough to remind Dirt Grubber that this was no lake builder. This was a Person, a Person as wounded in mind as Keen Eyes had been in body.

Yet could he hold him without doing him harm—or being injured himself? Dirt Grubber was beginning to doubt his abilities when someone else took a hand.

Anders knew how quickly a pleasant day could turn into a nightmare, but he'd been so enjoying being out for a walk with both Jessica and two treecats—one of them "wild"—that even with Jessica's apprehensions he was completely unprepared for the sudden attack.

Jessica's screams first froze him, then brought him into furious action. The gun he'd been about to draw would be useless in such close quarters. Instead, hoping with all his heart that he wouldn't make matters worse, he grabbed the attacking treecat firmly by its midsection and lifted it up and away from Jessica and Guide. He wanted to keep a hold on it, but the treecat swiveled its midsection with the clear intent of turning those murderous claws on him next.

Faced by that threat, Anders threw the treecat to the ground as hard as he could. He hoped he'd stun it or something—after all, Sphinx's gravity was very high—but treecats were made to live in that environment. This one would have sprung up almost immediately, but Valiant leapt on it.

Anders expected to see blood gush forth, but he quickly realized that while Valiant was trying to stop the other 'cat, he was also trying to wrestle it to inaction without inflicting more than minor injuries. Although he had no idea why Valiant would be so merciful toward an attacker, Anders knew he must follow the 'cat's lead.

We're trying to stop a war, he thought, *not make it worse. Maybe that's what Valiant is trying to do.*

As he thought that, he had an idea. Dashing forward, he unbuckled the counter-grav unit from where he always wore it at his waist and adjusted the dial.

If I can just get this on top of the other 'cat . . .

As he struggled beneath the suddenly greater pull of gravity upon his own body, Anders sought to get the counter-grav unit on top of the pitching bundle of fur. Like many great ideas, it wasn't nearly as easy to implement as he'd thought it would be, but in the end he managed to set the unit on top of the attacking treecat and switched the setting over so that the 'cat would suddenly feel much, much heavier. At the same time, he used his free hand to push Valiant away.

His idea worked wonderfully. The attacker 'cat gave a strangled wail and struggled to move, but Anders knew firsthand what an incredible burden even a third more gravity could be, and he'd given this fellow quite a bit more—although he hoped not enough to cause him injury.

Anders then stripped off his jacket and bundled it around the attacker's front end, doubtless ending the jacket's usefulness but assuring that those deadly fangs and claws were tearing into nothing more important than fabric.

Valiant joined him. Together, using various items (including the spare socks Anders always carried), they bound the kicking true-feet, then the hand-feet, and lastly the true-hands. Certain that the treecat could not escape, Anders reclaimed his counter-grav unit. Leaving the treecat's head shrouded, he raced to Jessica's side.

Both she and Guide were bloody messes. Her lovely face was marred with long claw marks, one of which narrowly missed her left eye. She'd been knocked to the ground by the force of the sudden attack and she was shivering with pain, but even so she had the presence of mind to pull out the first aid kit.

"Anders!" she said, looking at him in shock. "You're bleeding!"

"So are you," he said, kneeling next to her and taking the kit from her shaking hands. "And I can honestly say 'just a flesh wound' about mine—really just a few scratches. Let's look at you."

"Guide!" she said.

"You," he insisted, speaking sternly to cover his own fear that he was going to find horrible injuries. "Even Valiant agrees. Now be good. Can you lie back? There, rest your head on my pack."

In preparation for the trip to Sphinx, Anders had brushed up on his first aid. He'd even had a chance or two to use it, but he was relieved to see that despite the amount of blood, Jessica's attacker had missed any vital areas. Most of the claw marks were on her forehead, scalp, and upper face. Her eyes had been missed, so had her nose, except for a thin scratch.

First, he gave her something to dull the pain, then set about cleaning the wounds. Once he was pretty sure he'd gotten rid of any chance of infection, he pressed loose flaps of skin into place, then sprayed on quick heal.

To one side, Anders glimpsed Valiant at work on Guide, licking various wounded areas clear of blood. At one point, Valiant came over and took a thick gauze pad from the kit, but Anders didn't pause to see what he wanted it for. However, when he finished doing what he could for Jessica, he squeezed her hand.

"Rest quietly for a moment. I'm going to see if Guide needs any help."

Valiant was sitting next to Guide, holding the gauze pad—now bloodsoaked—to the other 'cat's right ear. He bleeked at Anders, pointed to Guide's now cleaned wounds, and made a gesture very like using a quick heal sprayer.

"Got you," Anders said, and followed directions, adding on his own initiative a spray or two of antiseptic. He figured treecat spit was probably good enough, but why take a risk? "Now, let me see that ear."

He motioned and Valiant understood. Very carefully, Valiant pulled away the pad to reveal the complete ruin of what had only moments before been a perky treecat ear. The wreckage was still seeping blood, and Valiant clamped the pad back down.

Anders fought an urge to gag, swallowed hard, then reached back into the first aid kit.

"First stop the bleeding. If you can't, figure out if something major has been cut and seal the wound . . ." he muttered to himself.

He managed the first two steps. Since none of the treecats they'd tended back at the camp had been freshly wounded, the kit still held all its trauma supplies. With Valiant's help—he'd started that thrumming purr again—Anders got the wound cleaned and treated. He didn't think anything could be done to replace the ear, but at least Guide wouldn't be in so much pain.

Anders was finishing up when he heard an urgent "bleek" from Valiant. The 'cat had risen all the way onto his true-feet and was pointing in the direction in which they'd been heading. Anders turned to look.

The attacking treecat lay where they'd left him, still bound, although he'd managed to toss his head free from the enclosing folds of Anders' jacket and lay glowering.

But that wasn't what had Valiant's attention. He was looking beyond their captive, up into the forest canopy. Anders looked into the trees and gasped.

The branches were full of treecats and, if he was any judge of that species, they were not at all happy.

20

DIRT GRUBBER'S MIND WAS ALMOST OVERWHELMED by the flood of unfamiliar mind-glows. Normally, he would not have found meeting even an entire clan all that difficult, but these People were unhappy and the force of their emotions was directed fully at him.

Complicating matters was the swirl of dark and incoherent emotions coming from where Swimmer's Scourge lay bound. The elder Person's mind voice was silent, but the anger and tension that flowed from him was so powerful that it made Dirt Grubber anxious and tense. He found it difficult to shape a coherent thought, and he wished he could simply beat away this newest complication.

Fortunately, Nimble Fingers was a tough sort—or maybe he was more accustomed to the madness that was Swimmer's Scourge. He broadcast as loudly and firmly as he could, <*This is my friend Dirt Grubber of the Damp Ground and Windswept Clans. Without the help of him and his two-leg friends, I would not be speaking with you.*>

He went on, swiftly sharing images of how Swimmer's Scourge had attacked them, how Bleached Fur had broken the assault, then tended the injured. Without leaving room for comment or debate, he segued immediately into images of what he had learned from Keen Eyes regarding the death of Red Cliff. In the manner of the People, this vast wash of information was shared even more quickly than the original events had unfolded.

As Nimble Fingers concluded, a brown figure with white spots separated herself from the general throng. Politely, she introduced herself to Dirt Grubber, <*I am Pleasant Singer, senior memory singer of the Trees Enfolding Clan.*>

She did not need to say how shocked and appalled those assembled were by what they had just learned, nor that the news would be relayed to those of the clan who had remained behind at their central nesting place. Dirt Grubber could taste that in the framing of her thoughts.

Pleasant Singer continued, <*Can you believe that we knew nothing of this? Nimble Fingers' report is like the breeze that sweeps away the fog. I see now that our minds have been fogged since the days when the fires threatened us and gnawed at our territory. Our losses were not as great as those of this Landless Clan, but they were enough to leave us in turmoil.*>

Dirt Grubber understood. Pleasant Singer's words were accompanied by images that made him shiver. Most of the time a clan benefited from shared mind-glows. If one mind was out of balance—due to illness or injury—then there were mind healers to rebalance it, as a more usual healer would clean and treat physical wounds.

But the mind healers of Trees Enfolding Clan had been overwhelmed by the need of their clan mates. Then, too, Swimmer's Scourge had possessed the cunning of his insanity. He had hidden his deeper unbalanced state within the cloak of the general unsettled situation of the clan. As a scout, he had also had ample excuse to stay away from the central nesting place. Lastly, the mind healers, so over-stressed by the many demands upon them, had simply not looked deeply beneath the surface of the thoughts of such a respected senior. However, the inner turmoil of Swimmer's Scourge had not been unfelt. It had seeped into the general mood of the clan, eventually tipping the balance so that the members who felt most threatened by Landless Clan's presence when their own range was so reduced had overreacted when Nimble Fingers had been taken.

After that, there had been yet more injured bodies and minds to be treated, for the Landless Clan had fought back with a ferocity born of sheer desperation. The end result was that Swimmer's Scourge had been lost—and only this moment was he found out for the poor, danger-ous, tormented Person that he was.

<*If you will give Swimmer's Scourge to us,*> Pleasant Singer went on, <*we will take him home and see what our mind healers can do for him. We would like to take Nimble Fingers home, too. I promise you, the Landless Clan will not be harmed. I will send one of my junior memory singers to them with our promises. We will bring them what food we can spare.*>

Dirt Grubber listened thoughtfully. Then he said, <*I see, though, that you believe that your territory will not support the Landless Clan, even if the members of both clans combine their efforts.*>

Pleasant Singer twitched back her ears in unhappiness. <*I fear not. Perhaps if this was the middle of the growing season and there was time to gather more food. Perhaps if the fires had not driven away so many of the larger prey animals, perhaps then. But the days of deep snows are coming. Already many of the prey animals that remain are drifting to even lower reaches than these.*>

Dirt Grubber had to agree. If they pooled their efforts,

the two clans might manage to survive, but they would be taking a tremendous risk. From the sense of her territory that Pleasant Singer shared with him, he could also see why she did not think that simply permitting the Landless Clan to move through to seek a new home would solve the problem. Time and again, there were reasons against new settlement in a particular area beyond Trees Enfolding's borders. Some were natural, but all too many were caused by the two-legs claiming the same lands.

<*Then you and your clan will help for now,*> he replied, <*and I will see what can be done to find these landless People a new nesting place, one rich enough to carry them through winter.*>

Pleasant Singer did not ask how this could be done for he had shared with her his hope the two-legs could somehow be enlisted. Dirt Grubber felt that Windswept and Bleached Fur were as devoted as he was to making sure the Landless Clan could live through the cold months. He felt they were wise enough to realize that doing this would take more than a few boxes of dead birds.

When the conference was ended, several of the strongest males came forward with a litter made from net strung between branches. They lifted Nimble Fingers with great gentleness.

<*We will meet again, Dirt Grubber,*> Nimble Fingers assured him. <*A friendship like ours will not fade with distance or time.*>

Next the members of Trees Enfolding came for Swimmer's Scourge. Swimmer's Scourge was left bound, for Pleasant Singer had decreed that he was dangerous to himself and others until he was calmer. Then he, too, was lifted onto a litter and born away. As soon as Swimmer's Scourge was outside of immediate mind-glow range, Dirt Grubber felt a tension he had not known had crept into himself fading away.

He shivered. Who would have thought that Swimmer's Scourge had a weapon more dangerous than sharp fangs or six sets of claws? Dirt Grubber, himself, had always pitied the two-legs for their mind-blindness. Now he understood more fully that sharing minds could be dangerous, as well.

When the last of Trees Enfolding had left, Dirt Grubber came and tapped the two-legs' shoulders, then pointed back to where they had left the flying thing.

"Bleek!" he said, wishing he could share with them all these complications. "Bleek! Bleek!"

"They're talking," Jessica said. "I can't tell what about, but they're talking, not arguing." She shivered violently. "Stars! I'm freezing."

"Shock," Anders said, moving over to her. "Here. Let me put my arms around you."

Jessica gave a wan smile. "Share body heat? Okay. I mean, you've got to be pretty cold without your jacket. Even if you could get it back, it's seriously ruined."

Anders settled so that Jessica could nestle against him, then wrapped his arms tightly around her. She fitted very well, there. He put his chin on top of her head, careful to avoid any of the places the treecat had gored her. After a few minutes, he thought she'd stopped shivering, but his own heart was beating so fast he couldn't be sure.

"Feeling better?"

"Uh-huh." Jessica's voice was distant and dreamy. "I've decided I'm going to be a doctor."

"What?"

"A doctor. Lately, I seem to be spending all my time patching people up. If I'm going to keep doing that, I'd better know more. I want to be a human doctor, though, not a vet. Maybe I'll have a side specialization in treecats. They're people, too, right?"

She giggled, and Anders heard the shrill note that said better than any words that Jessica was still on the edge of hysteria. No wonder. She'd been under a lot of pressure lately. He'd been shocked by the dead treecats, but it would be different for her. She would have felt Valiant's reaction, as well as her own. Her mother covering for Marjorie Harrington had put more responsibility on Jessica, too.

And then...

Anders realized all at once what the other factor just might be. At least it was a factor in his own wildly beating heart. His voice suddenly thick and rough, he managed to get the words out.

"I don't know what I want to be," he said. "But I know what I want to *do*. Jessica...I...I want to protect you."

"Protect me?"

Anders felt her tense and quickly explained. "Not because you're weak, Jessica Pheriss, but because you're one of the strongest people I've ever met. You're always there for everyone else. I want you to know always there's someone there for you."

Her tension didn't ease. "Valiant! I have Valiant."

"Hush, girl. Of course you do. But he's also someone else you need to look out for, protect him from blackholes like the x-a's, deal with spite and envy. Besides, just because you have Valiant, are you saying you don't need anyone else?"

Jessica said nothing, but her silence was a listening one, so he went on, words tumbling over each other.

"Jess, darling, I've been falling in love with you for weeks now, but I didn't want to admit it. When I saw that treecat tearing into you, I felt something I've never felt before. I had to protect you. Your safety meant more to me than my own. That's what gave me the courage to get in there and grab that thing, even with blood all over the place and knowing he could shred me, too. I had to because you mean more to me than anybody I've ever met."

One word, hardly more than a whisper. "Stephanie?"

Anders tightened his hold. "I know. I—Stephanie is great, but 'us,' that was her idea, and I...I was swept up. I mean, after treecats, the thing on Sphinx I wanted to see most of all was the person who'd discovered them."

"Thing?" Another tense giggle.

"Yeah...I mean, I knew Stephanie Harrington was a person, but she was a thing, too. The discoverer. First contact with aliens. Brilliant, creative, pretty in a cute way. Then she liked me. Really liked me." He let out a gusty sigh and Jessica's curls danced. "Steph told me she thought I was something special from the first moment she saw me."

"Yeah...She told me that, too. She was floored. In love at a breath."

"Aw, Jess, don't you get it? Love at first sight is wonderful and romantic, but it also means you're in love with an impression, an idea, an appearance."

"Fate?"

"You mean, do I believe in fate?"

"Uh-huh."

"I don't know...I mean, I could say that it was fated I meet you, too. Fated we'd be put through stuff like this that would mean I'd get to know you as someone who otherwise wouldn't step out of Stephanie's shadow. Stephanie, well she sort of claimed me. I'm not saying I didn't like being claimed or her. I did. I do. I think I always will...but Steph isn't...she isn't *you*, Jessica."

They sat quietly. The treecats were moving now. Some had vanished back into the thick green canopy. A couple of hefty males were bringing the stretcher and loading Guide onto it.

Jessica spoke very quietly. "I didn't exactly envy Stephanie, but I thought she was really lucky. I thought she was luckier than she knew... When she went off to Manticore, oh! I had such thoughts. I tried not to show them, though."

"You mean...you liked me, too?"

"Idiot! Of course I did. But I'm not the sort of person to poach my best friend's boyfriend. And I'm going to be a doctor."

Anders blinked, but he thought he understood. Jessica had mentioned how her mother had settled down with her father—though "unsettled down" might be a better way to put it—fairly young. He hoped she wasn't so much rejecting him as offering terms.

"Okay. You be a doctor," he said. "I'll figure out something that will let me be the doctor's boyfriend. I'm good with people. Maybe I can be a receptionist."

She giggled. Anders relaxed a little, but he didn't loosen his hold on her.

"You're going to need to stay in the Star Kingdom because of Valiant, right?"

Jessica shrugged. "No one's made rules yet. Remember, Lionheart's the first treecat ever to leave the planet even temporarily."

"Still..." Anders' thoughts twisted through all sorts of complications. One loomed in front of the others. "I'm going to have to tell Stephanie. And I'm not going to be a coward and do it in a message. I've got to do it face to face."

The treecats had carried both Guide and the Attack 'Cat away. Valiant had stayed, nose to nose with a female who radiated authority. Now she turned away and Valiant loped over to them.

"Bleek!" he said, patting them both on the shoulder and pointing back toward the air car. "Bleek! Bleek!"

✧　　✧　　✧

When they were back at Jessica's air car, she made no fuss about letting Anders pilot.

Instead, she leaned back in the passenger seat with Valiant thrumming in her lap.

"The question is," Anders said, "where do we take you?"

"It's got to be Scott again," Jessica said. "If I go to the clinic in Twin Forks, I'm going to have to come up with some explanation. Or I could skip seeing a doctor. I think I'm pretty well patched up."

"No!" Anders said. "That's out of the question. What will we tell your parents?"

"Mom gave me the day off," Jessica said. "I'll com and let her know we decided to go to Thunder River and see how that 'cat we rescued is doing. Even with everything that's happened, it's not all that late. We might make it back by evening."

"Okay," Anders said, lifting the air car above the canopy and setting the coordinates. "My dad won't miss me, but I'll message him I'm going to be late. I'd already told him I'd be out for dinner."

"I'll com Scott first this time," Jessica said. "Just in case he's off with a patient."

But Dr. Scott said he'd be available when they arrived. He didn't ask many questions, only asked Jessica to show him her wounds via her uni-link.

"Looks like they've been treated fine," he said. "But I'm with Anders. Better you have me look at them. Survivor's doing well enough, but he's edgy. I'm sure having a chance to talk with Valiant will help. See if you can stay the night so they can confab."

"I'll check," Jessica said.

Naomi Pheriss gave permission cheerfully. "I'll save you some berry ice cream."

"Thanks, Mama."

As Jessica shut off her uni-link, Anders glanced over

at her. "No offense, Jess, but you look tired. I won't crash the car. Why don't you cuddle up with Valiant and nap?"

She gave him a grateful smile. "I think I will. I think I will."

Dirt Grubber was pleased when he realized they were going to Darkness Foe and Swift Striker. He had a great deal to tell Keen Eyes. He spent much of the journey organizing his thoughts and soothing Windswept so that her sleep would be a healing one. Every so often, he went over to pat Bleached Fur. The young man was very thoughtful but, despite a certain tension, his mind-glow held the serenity of a decision made and accepted.

Dirt Grubber stayed with Windswept while Darkness Foe checked her injuries. When he was sure she was not injured more severely than she had seemed to be, he patted her on the arm and pointed in the direction of the room where Keen Eyes and Swift Striker waited.

Windswept gave him a gentle shove, accompanied by a few mouth noises and a glow of agreement Dirt Grubber took to mean she understood. From the relaxed under notes of her mind-glow, he gathered that they were planning to stay the night. He was pleased. Today had been very full and he needed time to let new ideas take root and grow.

When he joined his friends, he shared with them the events of the day. Keen Eyes' mind-glow brightened, taking strength from his pleasure in learning so many of his clan had survived the battle. There were dark notes, for some had died, and the injured were many, but the damage was clearly not as extreme as he had dreaded.

<I am pleased, too, that Nimble Fingers lived and is devoted to making sure the truth about my clan's situation is spread. He is a very strong Person. I have no doubt he will be a treasured elder of his clan someday.

What Pleasant Singer said fills in many things that had puzzled me.>

Swift Striker curled his whiskers forward. *<Now what will we do? From Pleasant Singer's words, it is clear Trees Enfolding Clan's range will not bear both clans. Landless Clan must be moved to a healthy range of its own, yet how can we do this? Windswept and Bleached Fur are clever enough to have understood this for themselves, I am sure—if they did not, why did they take the box of birds? Clearly they realize Landless Clan is in dire straits. And Darkness Foe is a healer, who has seen the marks of hunger on Keen Eyes and the bodies of his dead clan mates. So I believe it is possible the two-legs would be prepared to aid us, but People are not rocks or twigs to be moved at will. Keen Eyes, do you think your clan would cooperate?>*

Keen Eyes rubbed his fingers along his throat, where a fine downy fur was growing back... and causing a degree of itching.

<I believe they will want to, but the condition of our clan is much like that of Trees Enfolding. Our mind healers are already extended to their limits. Worse, we have no memory singer to tell us how such events fit into the greater pattern of events in the history of our clan. We lost many adults. Our elders are not bad People, but they are not adept at change.>

All three of the People gazed at one another, thinking, tasting and sharing their mind-glows, for what Keen Eyes had said was clearly true. People did not seek change the way ground runners sought out lace leaf. It did not come easily to them at the best of times, and these were scarcely the best of times for the Landless Clan. But then, after several moments, Dirt Grubber chortled deep in his throat.

<I have an idea. My clan was recently saved from fire. To escape, many of our young and elderly rode in one of the flying things. Most found it very exciting. I could share

my experiences but, because of my bond with Windswept, your elders might consider me suspect. Perhaps one of our memory singers could come speak to your clan. She could share not only our adventure but also the history of clan migrations.>

Keen Eyes bleeked in astonishment. *<Memory singers are very valuable People. Would your clan agree to risk one?>*

Dirt Grubber nodded. *<When you have none and we have several? I believe so.>*

Swift Striker added, *<I would go to my clan, but the distance between my clan and yours is quite far, even in a flying thing. Perhaps when Climbs Quickly returns, he could find someone from Bright Water to help. His sister, Sings Truly, is their senior memory singer and, as we have all heard, a very adventurous female. Now that I consider matters, I suspect we would have more trouble keeping her away than getting her to help.>*

Dirt Grubber cocked his ears as if listening for a distant sound. *<I cannot be sure, but I believe Pleasant Singer might help. She did not say so directly, but when we spoke I had the feeling that she was considering asking one of her own juniors if they would consider joining the Landless Clan and teaching Tiny Choir. The clan lore will not be exactly the same, but their borders touched, and some events will be known to both.>*

<If this is the case,> Swift Striker said, bouncing happily, *<then we will have several memory singers to help convince your elders!>*

Keen Eyes agreed. *<Can you tell how long Darkness Foe will wish to keep me here? I know it has been only a short time, but I am eager to be there to help my clan.>*

<I cannot say,> Swift Striker replied. *<But I think he will understand if we show him your desire. Mind-blind he may be, but he has understanding that bridges the silence.>*

❖   ❖   ❖

The humans spent much of the evening discussing the possible relocation of the Skinny 'Cat Clan.

"We're going to need to bring the SFS in on this at some point," Scott concluded. "Stephanie and Karl's return home may be the perfect excuse for a private meeting—one that won't alert the x-a's that something's up."

"I don't expect to hear from Steph today," Anders said. "It's already evening in Landing, and tonight's when she's giving her big talk to the Adair Foundation. I'll message her and time delivery so there's no chance she'll get it until that's over. Knowing Steph, she'll be eager to help."

He hoped so, especially given what he'd be telling her as soon as he could. What if she got in a snit and refused to have anything to do with them? No. He wouldn't believe that. Stephanie had always been an advocate for treecats. If she got upset, she'd probably just channel it into finding a solution.

He hoped.

The next morning, he found a message from Stephanie waiting. He opened it, expecting tales of triumph, and met with a shock. As soon as he had the details, he went tearing downstairs where Irina and Jessica were chatting over tea. Scott emerged from where he'd been checking over Survivor's wounds just as he arrived.

"Someone tried to kidnap Lionheart!" Anders said, and quickly gave them the details.

"Wow!" Jessica said. "If I believed in astrology, I'd say the stars must've been out of alignment. We tangle with the Attack 'Cat. Stephanie and the rest face 'catnappers."

"But everyone's all right?" Scott pressed. "No serious injuries?"

"None," Anders assured him. "Stephanie even went in and gave her talk, just like planned. She says the earl seems like a good sort, even nicer than his cousin, and she seems to like this Gwendolyn a lot, too."

"I bet Richard and Marjorie are relieved they'd already made plans to come home early," Irina said. "When do they get back?"

"Three days," Anders said.

Scott nodded. "Right. I'm going to talk with Frank, if I can catch him alone. I think our presentation to Chief Ranger Shelton would go better if we can suggest a couple of possible locations. I think I could talk Frank into giving us a few suggestions without letting his boss know."

"Wait!" Anders said. "My dad and his team have been working out a program that models the sorts of areas that would best suit treecats. They've gone beyond the simple things like the need for picketwood, into plants and other materials the 'cats seem to use. They've even included things like preferred prey animals. That would help identify possible relocation sites, wouldn't it?"

"Would he give you a copy?"

"Sure. I have one already. When I've had time, I've been helping with data entry. I get automatic updates."

Jessica grinned. "We can overlay that onto the Crown lands, add in where we already know treecats are, and plug in human holdings."

"I like it," Scott agreed. "Ever since that bit with Tennessee Bolgeo, the SFS has been really guarded about confirming anything to do with where treecats are currently living. This way Steph and Karl can go in, make suggestions, and Shelton can tell them whether or not those locations will work."

"And if he refuses to let them be moved?" Irina asked.

Jessica's grin faded. "He won't. But if he did, well, I've got some images cached that would go straight to where they'd do us the most good." Her expression brightened again. "But he won't. He's not the sort of man to let even a bunch of chipmunks starve to death if he could help. He'll find a way to make it work. He'd better."

STEPHANIE'S HEART BEAT RAPIDLY AS THE SHUTTLE
touched down. So much had happened in the last three
months—and so much was about to happen. Already the
demands of her coursework seemed unreal, especially in
the face of the challenges to come.

When debarking began, Stephanie was immediately
aware of the change in gravity. For a moment, she thought
about switching on her counter-grav unit, but she resisted.
From his carrier, Lionheart gave a heartfelt "bleek" and
waved his true-hand to show that he, too, felt the changes.

Stephanie's parents and Karl were chattering, bags were
being gathered, general motion began towards the exit.
On some level, Stephanie took part in all of it, but most
of her was focused on what would happen in just a few
moments. Anders had promised he'd be there to meet her,
yet she felt suddenly nervous. What if he wasn't there?

But Anders was there, tall and lean, his wheat-colored

hair pulled back in its usual ponytail, his dark-blue eyes intent. His smile flashed when he spotted her in the queue. He loped forward.

"Steph! Welcome home!"

Anders hugged her, then turned and greeted the senior Harringtons. Karl was being hugged by his parents and various siblings, so the young men settled for clasping hands over the assorted dark heads.

"Your dad and I can wait for the luggage, Stephanie," Marjorie Harrington said playfully. "If Anders wants to give you and Lionheart a ride home, you can leave now."

Without waiting for Stephanie to answer, Anders grabbed her carry-on from her father, leaving Lionheart's carrier to her. "Thanks!"

Stephanie considered letting Lionheart out right away, but the treecat would certainly attract attention. Better wait until they were outside. She waved to Karl.

"Later!"

Karl was now wearing some sort of homemade paper crown. He gave her a sheepish smile. "Later..."

Outside, the air was crisp, sharp with autumn in a way it hadn't been when Stephanie left for Manticore. Or was the change she felt just the contrast between the planets? Lionheart certainly felt it. When she let him out of his carrier, he wrapped his tail around himself, then jumped into the air car.

"He did lose a lot of fur," she said thoughtfully, talking to cover her sudden nervousness. It was one thing to message a guy just about every day. It was another to finally be alone with him. "I wonder if I should get him a sweater?"

Anders laughed. "If you do, don't let Dr. Hidalgo see him in it."

"Right!" Stephanie joined the laughter; both he and Jessica had messaged her about Dr. Hidalgo's devotion to pristine cultures. "I'm all for letting the treecats live treecat lives, but not to the point where Lionheart gets sick." She slid into the passenger seat. "How did Survivor do when you took him home? He'd lost a lot of fur, too, hadn't he?"

"Scott and Irina felt pretty much the way you do," Anders said. "They sent him home with a couple of jackets they'd cobbled together. All the fastenings can be undone by a treecat, so Survivor can wear them or not as he pleases."

"That's good. Maybe I should com for the pattern and make a couple of jackets for Lionheart."

Anders nodded agreement, but Stephanie felt a throb of apprehension. There was something tight about his features. She couldn't help but notice that his hand didn't reach for hers as it would have before. Her sense that something wasn't quite right wasn't helped when Lionheart jumped onto the back of the seat and wrapped his tail around her neck instead of bleeking for the window to be opened the way he usually did.

"Steph," Anders said, biting down on his lower lip. "There's no easy way to say this, so I'm going to just be honest. I'm ... I'm in love with someone else."

"Jessica." The answer was so obvious that Stephanie didn't even need to guess. A sick feeling flooded the pit of her stomach, followed by a flash of anger. How could they betray her? She'd loved them both, though in different ways. She'd *trusted* them ... Then, as soon as her back was turned, they'd gone against her!

"I don't know," Anders went on stiffly, "if Jessica loves me. I know she likes me but ... She's been keeping her distance ever since I told her how I felt. That was after the Attack 'Cat went for her."

The air car was on autopilot, but Anders had been staring at the HUD as if he were piloting through a storm. Now he hung his head. "I feel like an utter blackhole, telling you this when you haven't even gotten your planet legs back, but I thought holding out, acting like nothing had changed, would be worse."

To Stephanie's surprise, Lionheart stretched to pat Anders on one arm. For a moment, she felt a flare of jealousy. Then she understood. Lionheart could feel Anders' emotions—and that meant the pain she saw on his face was genuine. He wasn't acting. He really did feel terrible.

"I don't..." she managed. "I don't know what to say."

"Yeah," he said, shrugging in mute understanding. "Listen, don't blame Jessica. She didn't encourage me or anything. We haven't been dating or anything...I'd been keeping my feelings to myself... Then, there she was, all covered in blood, her eye nearly slashed out... You've talked about how you felt when Lionheart was being attacked...I...I couldn't lie to myself anymore. And I'd never lie to you."

Stephanie reached into herself, wondering if this extraordinary calm she felt was Lionheart's doing, but she didn't think so. She could feel him there, watchful, attentive, ready to intervene if she needed him, but the treecat seemed to have learned that there were things she had to deal with without the comfort he so easily offered.

"I... Talk to me... I'm confused."

"Me, too. What do you want me to talk about?"

"Is there something wrong with me? Are you still my friend? Is Jessica? I...I feel like the universe's gone through a blender and everything is all different shapes. I guess I'm glad you were honest. I know I am, but I can't..." She felt hot, fat tears running down her cheeks. "Just talk to me."

He did. Slowly at first, then with greater detail. Eventually, she started talking, too. Back and forth, back and forth. He still thought she was great. So did Jessica. Both of them were torn up....

Was there a point when Lionheart intervened, letting

Stephanie feel just how lost and confused Anders felt? She didn't know, but throughout it all the 'cat stayed close, wrapping her within the fluffy length of his tail.

Climbs Quickly did not need to understand mouth noises to figure out the reason for the emotional storms he was caught between. The next day, when he and Death Fang's Bane went to the two-legs' gathering place and met with Windswept and Dirt Grubber, his friend filled him in on the details he could not gather from Death Fang's Bane's mind-glow.

After showing him how Swimmer's Scourge had assaulted Windswept and Nimble Fingers, Dirt Grubber said, <*I had been aware that both Windswept and Bleached Fur had feelings for each other beyond what they were admitting. I had no idea how matters would be resolved. I know that none of those involved are completely happy right now, and the two-legs are certainly very different from the People when it comes to knowing their own feelings, far less anyone else's. But I cannot help feeling this will all be for the best in the end.*>

Climbs Quickly chewed thoughtfully on the cluster stalk he had been served. Maybe it was just being home, but it tasted so much better than it had in the Hot Lands.

<*At least Windswept and Death Fang's Bane have not parted in anger. If they can weather this, I think their friendship will be stronger than before. Now, tell me more about what has happened between Trees Enfolding Clan and the Landless Clan. I knew even in the Hot Lands that Death Fang's Bane was worried and the moving images she showed me told me that it was because of events among the People, but that was all I knew.*>

As methodically as he would have set one of his gardens in place, Dirt Grubber began with the finding of the body he now knew to have been Red Cliff's and his first sensing of Keen Eyes. He interwove what he had later learned from Keen Eyes and Nimble Fingers, so that by the time Climbs Quickly had taken it all in, he actually had a better understanding of events than had any of those who had been more immediately involved.

<*I will certainly speak with Sings Truly about all of this,*> Climbs Quickly said. <*And she will just as certainly insist on helping. And Death Fang's Bane took me to examine her flying thing last night, which is how she tells me when she intends to take me to visit Bright Water. I believe she wanted me to understand that we will fly there tomorrow.*>

<*I have already spoken with Brilliant Images,*> Dirt Grubber said. <*Windswept has wanted to avoid Bleached Fur—I think she wishes to understand her own feelings better before seeing him again—so we made a long visit to my clan, and I used the opportunity to arrange matters. Now we need to see if the two-legs will take action as we expect.*>

<*If they do not,*> Climbs Quickly said with confidence, <*then we will find a way to make them take action. But I do not think we will need to go that far. I cannot speak with Death Fang's Bane as I can with a Person, but I can taste when she is planning and plotting. Even in her grief, those sensations are present.*>

He reached for another piece of cluster stalk, expecting Death Fang's Bane to take it from him because he had already eaten over a hand of them, but she remained intent on her conversation with Windswept. He could only hope that some of it was about starving People and not all about one young two-leg with bright hair.

"Jessica commed me," Karl said when he picked Stephanie up for their meeting with Chief Ranger Shelton. "So you don't have to tell me anything. She said she talked to you, too."

"She did," Stephanie agreed. "We had shakes at the Red Letter Café a couple of days ago. We decided not to let a guy get in the way of our friendship. I mean, she's not to blame for Anders' feelings changing."

Karl sighed. "Steph, I've never really told you about Sumiko, have I?"

Stephanie blinked, startled by the change of subject. "Well, I know a few things. She lived with your family, right? Some things Irina's said...I think she was your girlfriend. And she...she died in an accident."

Karl nodded. "Those are the basics. But I'm going to tell you something no one else knows—no one, not my mom or my dad or anybody."

From the thin trickle of emotion flowing into her through Lionheart, Stephanie could tell this was very important to Karl, so she didn't say any of the usual things, "If you really want to" or "I don't want to pry"—all those "kind" things people say when what they're really saying is, "Don't take me into your pain."

"Go on. I'm listening."

"Sumiko came to live with us after all her family died in the Plague. My folks legally adopted her. Sumi and I were pretty close in age. I was just a few months older. Since our families' freeholds shared a border, we'd known each other all our lives. For a while, it was just like having another sister, but as we got older..."

He paused and made an unnecessary adjustment on the air car's panel. Stephanie held her breath, not wanting to break the moment.

"I'm not sure who started thinking we'd get married when we got older. I think it started with adults joking around the way they do when they think kids are too young to really take them seriously. The thing is, we did take them seriously. We'd talk about it when we were alone. Whether we'd live in the house her family had built or build one of our own, stuff like that..."

Karl swallowed hard. "When I turned fifteen, Sumi started getting really serious. Maybe it's because girls mature faster than guys or something. I don't know. She wanted us to get engaged or at least betrothed. I wasn't against it. I mean, marrying Sumiko was as much a part of my future life as going to Landing for college. But I did want to go to college, and I didn't want to get married and start a family before I was done."

"Oh..."

Karl rushed on. "On the day Sumi and I took the kids sledding, we'd been fighting. She'd been hinting that she thought I'd be giving her a betrothal ring for her fifteenth birthday. I just told her flat out I wasn't, that I thought eighteen would be better—we'd both be legal adults then. It wouldn't be kids' games.

"Sumiko was furious with me, said what *she* felt wasn't kids' games, that she loved me, and if I didn't love her enough to give her a stupid promise ring, then..."

Karl's fists were clenched tight, but the words came rushing out. "Normally, we'd probably have figured out a way to go off on our own, cool off. Then we would've made up. But we'd promised the kids, and so, still really mad, we went out. Looking back, we probably shouldn't have. The tree branches were heavy with snow and we weren't too young to know conditions were dangerous. But, well, if we'd backed off, it would have been like one of us was giving ground.

"It's probably because I was so pissed that I didn't see that one of the branches of the crown oak my sister Larissa was sledding under was weak. Sumi did, though. She screamed a warning and ran all out, knocking Larissa out of danger... Sumiko didn't get clear, though. The branch hit her from over a hundred meters up."

Stephanie could see it all in her imagination, the crown oak limb tearing free, the fragile black-haired girl smashed. She knew all too well how hard things could fall in heavy gravity.

Karl went on, his voice stiff. "I hollered for someone to call for help. I ran and hauled that tree limb off, but there was nothing I could do. Sumiko's chest had been crushed, her lungs punctured. There was blood on her lips. She said something about our having at least six kids, that she loved me, and then...she died."

Karl was crying now, his calm, stiff tone a frightening contrast to the tears that rolled down his cheeks. "She was dead and I'd killed her. Killed her because I wouldn't give her a stupid ring that would have made her happy."

"Karl...you didn't! It wasn't your fault..."

Karl gave her a twisted grin. "Yeah. Except it felt like it. It still feels like it. There's not a day I don't think about it, don't wonder how things might have worked out. When I turned eighteen, I realized this would've been the year I gave Sumiko her ring...And I also realized that maybe I wouldn't have. I mean, people change a lot. Three years? Would kids' dreams have lasted that long? I don't know."

Stephanie fought back tears. "Kids' dreams? That's why you're telling me this? Because of Anders?"

"Some." Karl looked directly at her. "Maybe other reasons. Maybe because I'm beginning to be ready to let go of the ghost. Look, I don't think what you felt—feel—for Anders isn't real, but the fact is that most people don't end up settling down with the first person they fall in love with. Even if they do, not all those relationships work out. I'm finally accepting that even if Sumi and I had gotten married, maybe it wouldn't have been as perfect as we dreamed."

"And maybe," Stephanie said slowly, "if Anders hadn't

fallen for Jessica, something else would've come along to break us up. Still, there have got to be easier ways to get dumped than having your guy fall for your best friend."

Karl poked her with one long finger. "*Yours?* They don't really belong just to you, you know. And you don't belong just to them. No matter what words you use, Jess and Anders have lives beyond how they relate to you... And you wouldn't have gotten involved with them if you hadn't thought both of them were pretty great people, right? Imagine how you'd feel if Anders had dumped you for Trudy!"

Stephanie actually found herself giggling. "I see what you mean. Okay." She grew suddenly somber. "And, hey, Karl... Thanks. I won't tell anyone."

Karl nodded his appreciation. "Actually, I'm thinking it's time I told my family. Maybe I'll start with Irina. She's pretty understanding. It's time I stopped carrying this shadow on my heart. Sumiko deserves more than to be remembered for her last few hours."

Stephanie nodded. "I think so. I think, you know, she'd probably like that a lot."

"So, essentially," Chief Ranger Shelton said, "you want to move an entire clan of treecats. You're just giving the SFS a chance to pick where."

Stephanie felt as if this was another test—and one where a lot more than the final mark rested on her answer.

"Well, sir, it's sort of complicated. First of all, there *is* precedent—SFS relocated the remnants of the clan the Stray came from."

"Ah, but in that case," Shelton said, "the treecats were endangered by human actions. In this case, the fires were completely natural."

Karl pointed to the holo map they'd brought with

them. "Sir, humans are involved here, too. Not by causing the fires, but indirectly. Look at how many possible areas are blocked by human settlement."

"Point taken," Shelton said. "Still, why should the SFS get involved?"

Stephanie drew in a deep breath. "Well, sir, like I said, it's complicated. If the treecats are animals, then this particular clan is living on Crown Lands, which makes them Crown property. If we just move them, say to a space on the Harrington freehold or on Karl's family's lands, then we'd be stealing. We don't want to do that."

"I am vastly relieved. Continue."

"If, however, as a lot of people—"

"Including some members of the Adair Foundation," Karl inserted helpfully, with an innocence that didn't fool anyone.

Stephanie glared at him. "*If*, as some people seem to think, the treecats are sentient, then they should have the right to move wherever they want as long as where they go doesn't get in the way of other people's claims. I mean, if the 'cats are people, not property, then they can't be stolen. If, say, Chet parked his truck and a bunch of 'cats got on, and then he gave them a lift, that wouldn't be theft, right?"

"Perhaps letting you take those law courses wasn't a good idea after all, Ms. Harrington. You have the makings of a bedroll lawyer." Chief Ranger Shelton steepled his fingers and peered thoughtfully at his two probationary rangers. "Still, that's an interesting point. I've been reading the interim reports from both Dr. Whitaker's expedition and Dr. Radzinsky's team. Certainly the balance seems to be tipping in favor of ruling the treecats as at least marginally sentient."

Karl nodded. "We've been looking at those, too. I must say, sir, with all due respect, that I think the question of sentience is settled. The level, now—that's quite different. Dr. Whitaker's in favor of a higher ranking. Dr. Radzinsky's arguing for a *lower* one, especially since there's no evidence the treecats have any form of writing or even a complex spoken language."

"I expect," Shelton said, "the debates will continue for a long while to come. And even when the scientists have submitted their papers, the question of the treecats' legal status will take even longer to settle."

He sat in thoughtful silence for long enough that only Lionheart's calming presence stopped Stephanie from fidgeting.

"Still, I think it would be all for the best if in this instance we erred on the side of protectiveness," he said finally. "We don't want future generations to judge us for knowingly letting an entire group of 'people'—no matter how unsophisticated—freeze and starve through our inaction."

He sighed. "I mean, we drop hay for near-deer and prong bucks. The only thing that makes this different is that problem of interference—"

"—with a pristine indigenous population," Stephanie and Karl chorused, made a bit giddy by relief.

"Yes. For that reason, I think that, other than suggesting a location, it would be better if the SFS didn't take an official role. From the images Anders and Jessica sent, this Skinny 'Cat Clan is fairly small. Could you arrange for, say, Chet's truck and a few other vehicles to be in the area on a day to be named later? I'll make certain neither of you are on the duty roster that particular day. In fact, it might be a good time to arrange a field trip for all our anthropologists to some distant location...."

"Yes, sir!"

"Anders won't mention any of this to his father?"

"He hasn't so far, sir," Stephanie said, "and he and

Jessica have known about this the longest of anyone. By the way, in case you didn't know, they took Survivor back to his clan yesterday."

"I'd heard. Very well, start making arrangements. These maps narrow possible relocation areas, but we'll need to make sure prospective locations are indeed uninhabited. Recruit Jessica Pheriss and Scott MacDallan to help with that—we'll need Fisher and Valiant to help scout, since treecats are so good at hiding from humans. I'll be in touch. For now, you're dismissed."

Stephanie shot to her feet. She was halfway to the door when she turned and blurted out impulsively. "Thank you, sir. I hope I can be half as good a ranger as you."

Chief Ranger Shelton smiled. "Go. We've got a job to do."

Keen Eyes had expected the strange sense of dislocation he had felt since he had been wounded by Swimmer's Scourge to fade once he was home again with his clan, but he found that it persisted. Even when he learned that he had not been abandoned, that his hopelessly calling mind-voice had been heard and a group had been on their way to get him when the flying thing had landed, he still felt isolated. He had spent time with the mind healers and that always helped, but when he was alone, he found himself remembering the twisted violence that had been Swimmer's Scourge. And the violence it had evoked within him, as well.

He reassured himself that all would be well when they moved to their new territory. That the two-legs planned to help the clan was certain now. For the last few days, the clan had been visited by those People who had bonded with two-legs and their partners. Each of the People had carried with him a scout's report of places the two-legs hoped would serve the clan's need. Even Sour Belly's attitude had softened when he realized how hard the two-legs were working to assure the Landless Clan would be landless no more.

The two-legs had also shown the clan images of all those places—images that moved and made sounds. Marvelous though they were, they told less than the mind pictures of the People who had also seen them, but Keen Eyes and his clan mates had realized the reason the two-legs had shown the images to them. They had tasted the question and the desire in the two-leg mind-glows and known the two-legs wanted them to choose from among all the possible ranges and indicate which they preferred.

In the end, the clan had chosen a place where swaying fronds grew tall in the shade of the net-wood trees, for this reminded them of their former home. The area was well watered, and possessed both flint for tools and some hard red clay that shaped well. The new land was less high in the mountains than their former range had been, and untouched by the ravages of the past fire season. Storing supplies away for winter would not be impossible.

Keen Eyes was sitting high in a golden-leaf when he heard Nimble Fingers calling out to him. *<I would like to come and say farewell. Also, my clan has a gift for yours. May I bring it to your central nesting place?>*

<Come and welcome.>

When Nimble Fingers arrived, Keen Eyes saw the other had recovered well from his wounds. Except for some patchiness to his fur and the tattered state of his damaged ear, he looked much as he had when Keen Eyes had first met him. Nimble Fingers had with them a female Person of considerable presence. For a moment, Keen Eyes thought Nimble Fingers had brought his mate, but the female's mind-glow was so powerful that he immediately knew her for what she was.

<*This is Perfect Recollection,*> Nimble Fingers said. <*She is the first junior to our senior memory singer, Pleasant Singer.*>

Perfect Recollection spoke to all the clan. <*I would very much like to come with you to your new home. Since our clans shared a border, I know some of your lore. I could also teach your promising young so that your clan would not be without future memory singers.*>

Her mind-glow was so vibrant and her passion to provide help was so strong that there was no need for discussion. Tiny Choir scampered forward and embraced Perfect Recollection, twining her tail around the other's in spontaneous joy.

Keen Eyes found himself purring. A clan needed a memory singer to be truly a clan. He groomed his whiskers and reached to pat Nimble Fingers in thanks.

The sound of one of the two-legs' flying things broke into the celebration. Perfect Recollection announced, <*I taste Climbs Quickly. He is chuckling over something.*>

<*That one is a prankster,*> Sour Belly said indulgently. <*But there is no harm in him. It will be good to learn what has him so pleased.*>

When the flying thing touched down a few moments later, they discovered that Climbs Quickly was not the only Person it had carried to them.

<*This is my sister, Sings Truly, senior memory singer of the Bright Water Clan. With her is Song Spinner, who was her teacher.*>

Song Spinner, a dignified female of some years, spoke for herself. <*Since Sings Truly proved herself the best senior memory singer for our clan, I have been hoping to make myself useful. May I join your clan in its journeys? I know a great deal about the two-legs. Also, the songs of our clan may not be too strange to yours, since we are all mountain Peoples. I would be very happy to teach them to you.*>

Perfect Recollection spoke for the clan. <*Accepting not just one new memory singer but two is an enormous change. When we take your songs and make them our own, we will become a new clan. Yet, with all we have been through, perhaps this is the best choice. There is a time to hold onto the past, but there is also a time to move forward.*>

A ripple of understanding flowed among the clan members, but there could be no doubt that all the Swaying Fronds Clan were thrilled by this second promising omen for their future.

<*We are happy to have you,*> Perfect Recollection said to Song Spinner. <*Let neither of us be senior or junior, for what we have to share differs in substance but not in value.*>

Song Spinner flirted her tail in happy acceptance. <*Yes. Let us be sisters, bonded by our desire to make our new clan strong.*>

Joy washed over the gathered People. Tiny Choir bounced, her mind-glow alight with pleasure mingled with brilliant streaks of relief. Keen Eyes knew the kitten would have tried her best to serve as memory singer, but that role was a huge responsibility even for an adult, which was why most clans had more than one. Now she could grow and learn as a kitten should. Keen Eyes had no doubt that someday Tiny Choir would be a legend among the People.

Looking over his rejoicing clan, Keen Eyes noticed that Death Fang's Bane stood near the flying thing. The darkness of tension that had shadowed her mind-glow was fading away as it became very obvious that the people of Swaying Fronds were welcoming their new members. Behind her stood Shadowed Sunlight. The tall, dark young male always seemed to vanish behind the brilliance of Death Fang's Bane's powerful mind-glow, but today—

Keen Eyes shook his head so hard his ears flapped. Nimble Fingers said something to him, but though they stood close enough to touch, Keen Eyes felt as if a sudden, unexpected brilliance was making him blind to the other's contact.

He raced forward, leaping from limb to limb until he stood in the net-wood closest to Shadowed Sunlight. But this was a Shadowed Sunlight he had never seen, never tasted before. His mind-glow held subtle hues that reached and touched Keen Eyes, fitting into place as to pieces of a broken pot fit together.

Shadowed Sunlight was turning, turning, his mind-glow brightening as he realized the source of the feelings flooding into him. Again Keen Eyes was impressed by the strength of this young two-leg. Death Fang's Bane was the flash of light on water, of sunlight blazing against the sky, unmistakably brilliant, but Shadowed Sunlight was the force that held the trees tall, the rock that carried the weight of all the land.

Keen Eyes dropped from the net-wood branch and landed, carefully keeping his claws sheathed, trusting the other to catch him. He laid a true-hand on his new partner's cheek.

"Bleek!" he said.

And he felt Shadowed Sunlight laugh, the shadows vanishing from his heart forever.

22

ON THE DAY OF THE BIG MOVE, ANDERS DROVE THE air van. His dad's entire crew, plus Dr. Radzinsky's x-a's, were all on a special field trip hosted by none other than Chief Ranger Shelton himself, with Senior Rangers Ainsley Jedrusinski and Frank Lethbridge as support. The SFS had even supplied vehicles, officially because they would be going into some rough terrain.

The real reason, of course, was that this way there was no chance any nosy x-a—Duff DeWitt immediately sprang to mind—would slip away and show up where he wasn't wanted.

A lot had happened over the last few days. Anders' breaking up with Stephanie had been superseded by the amazing news that Karl had bonded with Survivor. When Anders commed to congratulate him, Karl had shaken his head in obvious wonder.

"I get the feeling Survivor had been through too much. I know what that's like, really. So I guess we're both survivors, but we're survivors looking into the future, not back at the past."

The Skinny 'Cat Clan took the invasion of air vehicles with composure. Chet was there with his truck. Christine, for once, didn't ride with him, but came in her family's flatbed. Karl had arrived in one of his family's heavier farm vehicles. Toby had borrowed a van used by his church. Stephanie had the bulky vehicle her mom used for moving plants. And Jessica was flying her family's battered sedan.

Mostly the humans stood around waiting and keeping out of the way. Loading was arranged by the treecats themselves.

"Now I know what it's like to be a chauffeur," Stephanie laughed. "Remember everybody, when we leave we're staying below the tree line."

Chet's laughter shook the air. "We've filed the flight plan, ma'am. We'll follow orders." In a softer voice, he said to Anders, "That girl is wasted as a forest ranger. She should be commanding battle fleets."

"You going to tell her that?" Anders grinned.

"Oh, no. I like Stephanie a lot, but I'd never try to *tell* her anything." Chet looked appreciatively over to where Christine was tying down a net over a heap of treecat luggage. "Actually, I wouldn't try to tell Christine anything, either. That's the secret to a happy relationship. No one is boss...."

He clapped Anders on the shoulder, sympathy guy-fashion, and hurried off to pull away an inquisitive group of kittens who apparently thought they could fly his truck.

Given all the advanced planning, it should have been no surprise that the relocation went smoothly. At last, Anders unloaded a heap of handmade cord that his father would have loved to have for his collection, wondering vaguely if treecats had something like ropewalks. Then he stepped back.

"I guess we're done," he said.

Karl nodded. "I'm still learning how to read Survivor, but I think what I'm getting is 'Thanks so much, folks, but we're fine,' from his family. They need to settle in without us around."

Jessica came up, Valiant riding on her shoulder. "I'm getting the same feeling. Should we clear out?"

Stephanie nodded. "Let's. My folks said everyone was welcome back at our place for a picnic and some hang-gliding."

"We'll be there," Christine said, "after we drop off my parents' truck and grab our rigs."

"Me, too," Toby agreed. "I don't want to keep the church's van, though. Can someone give me a ride?"

"Sure," Chet said. "No problem."

"I can come straight out to your place, Steph," Jessica said quickly. "I've got my gear in the trunk."

Anders hesitated. These days, he wasn't sure how welcome he was. Jessica was still keeping her distance, and Stephanie... He wasn't sure how much the general invitation had been good manners. Neither of the girls' expressions helped much, but Karl gave him a lopsided grin.

"Come on. You know what good cooks Dr. Marjorie and Dr. Richard are. And there are always spare gliders."

"All right..."

The picnic would only have been called a picnic by the Harringtons. Anyone else would have called it a banquet. Anders had slipped over to the buffet for another slice of tanapple pie when he felt a tap on his shoulder.

It was Stephanie.

"Hey, Anders..."

She motioned for him to follow her onto the back porch, where she sat down on a swing. He sat down next to her, realizing with a shock that this was the first time he'd been alone with her since that fateful drive back from the shuttleport.

"I just want you to know," she said, "that I think I'm

okay now. I needed time to think, but flying around, checking stuff out for the treecats—that gave me the time."

Anders nodded. "Okay? Maybe you don't hate me?"

"I don't hate you." She managed a grin. "I think I still even like you. I'm not saying I'm ready to dance at your wedding...."

He shrugged. "*I'm* not ready to dance at my wedding. And I'm beginning to think that the girl...I mean, I don't know what I think anymore."

"I think," Stephanie said deliberately, "that Jessica likes you a lot. But, you know, she's had a lot dropped on her at once. She knows she was one of my first 'real' friends, so she doesn't want to hurt me. She's also got a lot of defenses up...No offense, Anders Whitaker, but you seem to be the sort who falls in and out of love pretty fast."

"I'm really not that way," he protested.

Stephanie put a light hand on his arm. "Actually, I know that. That's one of the problems of my bond with Lionheart. He's pretty polite about not sharing what other people are feeling, but if he thinks I need to know, he's also pretty ruthless. I wanted to be angry at you. I wanted to be completely furious—cast you as the handsome heartbreaker from a distant world..."

"But Lionheart?"

"Wouldn't let me sit around buried in self-pity. He made sure I knew you were really hurting. That sort of ruins the fantasy."

"I guess..." He laughed. "What's wrong with me that I keep falling for girls who bond with treecats? I'm not really into having my heart paraded for public display."

"It's not like that," she assured him. "I mean, the 'cats may know, but the human side of the partnership's only in on what the 'cat shares."

She leaned forward. "Valiant likes you. He's not going

to *make* Jessica like you, but it does mean you have, well, an advocate."

Anders' heart had wings.

"Stephanie Harrington, you really are the best."

"Friends?" she suggested.

"You bet!"

Up against the crisp blue sky, the young two-legs soared like birds. For once, Climbs Quickly had chosen not to go with Death Fang's Bane. He had stayed on the ground so he could talk with his friends.

He liked Keen Eyes—and this was a very good thing. Given the close friendship and shared interests of Death Fang's Bane and the newly named Shining Sunlight, they were certain to spend a great deal of time together.

Dirt Grubber was thinking about plants with blue leaves. <*I wonder if they would grow here? Maybe in one of the plant places. I would like to see some for myself. You do not look at plants as carefully as I do.*>

<*From what you have been telling us about the changing shape of Windswept's mind-glow,*> Climbs Quickly said <*I think it very likely you will see such trees yourself. Windswept seems hungry for learning, and as best I could gather, the reason we went to the Hot Land was because that is the central nesting place for those among the two-legs who have a great deal of learning. They are not memory singers, precisely, but I think they serve much the same purpose for the two-legs.*>

Keen Eyes bleeked with laughter. He had cheered up a great deal in the last few days. Clearly, his new bond gave him what he needed to clear from his spirit the guilt he felt for having been part of violence between People.

<*I would like to see those places, too, and I taste that*

hunger for learning in Shining Sunlight, as well. I think he will return to the Hot Lands, and I will go with him.>

Climbs Quickly agreed. More and more, the People's lives were becoming intertwined with the lives of the two-legs. That meant scouts such as he and Keen Eyes would need to take careful note of all they saw, so that the memory singers could teach the People about their changing world.

He twitched his whiskers, amused at the image that came to him that moment. *<Yes, Keen Eyes. Who would have thought the lights in our night skies were other worlds, each as vast and wonder-filled as our own? But they are, and they have many surprises, the two-legs who move between them. I think it will be a long, long time before we even begin to truly understand them all. But we will understand, and it will be scouts like you and me who leap from light to light all across the two-legs' net-wood who will bring that understanding back to the People.>*

NOTES

Ante Diaspora — the notation Ante Diaspora (or AD) indicates the T-year counting backwards from 2103 CE, Year One of the Diaspora. That is, the year 2102 CE would be the T-year 01 AD.

bark-chewer — treecat term for wood rat.

burrow runner — treecat name for a Sphinxian chipmunk.

cluster stalk — treecat name for terrestrial celery.

condor owl — a nocturnal flying predator of the planet Sphinx. An average adult condor owl's body is 1.4 meters (4.5 feet) long, with a wingspan of 2.9 meters (9.5 feet) and a body weight of 5.4 to 6.35 kilos (12 to 14 pounds). Despite the name assigned to it by the Sphinxian colonists, it is actually mammalian and is covered with fine down, not feathers. It has very acute vision and is fully capable of taking even an adult treecat if it can surprise it. Indeed, it has been known to take considerably larger game and is considered a dangerous threat even to humans. Unlike Sphinxian "birds," it has only a single set of wings but four sturdy legs, each ending in a set of powerful talons.

crown oak — a deciduous, hardwood tree that looks much like a *really* big white oak but has large, arrowhead-shaped leaves. It also sheds its leaves *twice* in the course of a planetary year, once shortly after the end of spring and again at the end of autumn. The summer-autumn foliage turns a bright, deep gold, rather like terrestrial maples, before falling, hence the treecat name for it. The spring-summer foliage does *not* change colors before it falls. Average height of a mature crown oak is 80 meters (263 feet), although some as tall as 102 meters (335 feet) have been reported.

death fang — treecat name for hexapuma.

death gleaner — treecat name for peak vulture.

death-wing — treecat term for condor owl.

Diaspora — humanity's expansion to the stars, dated from September 30, 2103 C.E. and the departure of the first manned interstellar vessel from the Sol System. 2103 thus became officially Year One of the Diaspora.

fox bear — a species native to the Beowulf System. Fox bears are collie-sized, ground-going marsupials whose vaguely bearlike bodyform and tall, mobile ears gave rise to their name. They have powerful, otterlike hands and are considerably more intelligent than dogs, though still short of full sapience, and have been trained as service animals for centuries.

golden ear — treecat name for range barley.

golden-leaf — treecat name for crown oak.

grass runner — treecat name for a Sphinxian range bunny.

gray-bark — treecat name for red spruce.

green-needle — treecat name for near-pine.

ground runner — a generic treecat term for small, non-arboreal prey animals.

Gryphon — Manticore B-V, the fifth planet of Manticore B, a G2-class star which is the secondary component of the Manticore Binary System. The planet of Gryphon is the sole habitable planet of Manticore B and has an orbital radius of 11.37 LM and a gravity of 1.19 Old Earth standard gravities.

hexapuma — a six-limbed Sphinxian predator. Hexapumas are very quick for something their size and extremely territorial. There are several subspecies of hexapuma, which vary in coloration depending on the season and the climatic zone in which they are found. The largest species are located in Sphinx's temperate zones, and adults of those species can be as much as five meters (16.4 feet) long with tails 250 centimeters (8.2 feet) long and weigh as much as 800 kilograms (1,763 pounds), more than most terrestrial horses.

horn blade — treecat term for prong buck.

ice potatoes — a Sphinxian tuber, about twice the size of a terrestrial Irish potato, edible by humans. It is a winter-growing root with a rather nuttier taste than potatoes.

lace leaf — treecat name for near-lettuce.

lace willow — a willowlike tree found mainly along water-ways or in marshy territory. It is relatively low growing and bushy, with very long, streamerlike leaves. The leaves have a pierced look, because they form insect-trapping openings (thus the name "lace willow").

lake builders — treecat name for near-beavers.

lowland vulture — a winged Sphinxian scavenger. Lowland
vultures average approximately 90 centimeters (3 feet) in
length with an average wingspan of 2 meters (6.5 feet)
have been verified, with two pairs of wings and powerful
talons. Lowland vultures are found primarily in coastal
and lowland areas (as the name implies) but are closely
related to the much larger peak vulture.

Manticore — Manticore A-III, the third planet of Manticore A, a G0-class star which is the primary component of the Manticore Binary System. The planet of
Manticore is the inner habitable planet of Manticore A
(orbital radius of 11.4 LM) and the capital world of the
Star Kingdom of Manticore. Manticore has a gravity
of 1.01 Old Earth standard gravities.

Manticore Binary System — the home star system of the
Star Kingdom of Manticore, consisting of Manticore A,
the GO primary component of the system, and Manticore B, its G2-class companion star.

moss-drying — treecat name for south.

moss-growing — treecat name for north.

mountain eagle — a bird analogue of the planet Sphinx.
It was two sets of wings and a single pair of powerful,
talon-tipped legs. An average adult mountain eagle's
body is 1.0 meters (3.2 feet) in length, with a wingspan
of 2.4 meters (7.9 feet) and a body weight of 4.1 to 5
kilos (9 to 11 pounds). The mountain eagle is a very
efficient hunter, but prefers small prey and seldom
attacks treecats.

near-beavers — a Sphinxian mammal approximately 51
centimeters (20 inches) long. Although the colonists have
named it the near-*beaver*, it is actually closer to a six-
legged otter in basic body form. Unlike terrestrial otters,

however, the near-beaver is an industrious dam-builder. Various species of near-beaver are found in virtually every Sphinxian climate zone except the high arctic.

near-lettuce — a native Sphinxian plant very similar in size and shape to terrestrial head lettuce, although its leaves are perforated in a lacy pattern. It is edible by humans and is quite popular in salads, with a flavor which combines that of terrestrial lettuce and onions.

near-otter — a Sphinxian mammal approximately the same size as a treecat. Although they look very similar to the Sphinxian near-beaver, they have clearly carnivore teeth without the tree-gnawing incisors which gave the near-beaver its name. They do not build dams, but they are very fast, strong swimmers and skilled hunters and fishers.

near-pine — an evergreen tree with tough "hairy" seed-pods and a rough, deeply furrowed bark. The seeds are about the size of peanuts and have a strong, nutty flavor. They can also be crushed for oil. Average height of a fully mature near-pine is 62 meters (203 feet) although at least one specimen 76 meters (249 feet) has been recorded. After the crown oak, near-pine is the tallest Sphinxian tree. Mature trees are branchless for the lowermost third of their height.

net-wood — treecat name for picketwood.

peak bear — a six-limbed omnivore found primarily in mountainous territory. It stands about a meter (3.3 feet) tall at the shoulder and can be up to 2.5 meters (8.2 feet) in length and weighs up to 550 kilograms (1,212 pounds). Although not as territorial as the hexapuma and not a pure carnivore, the peak bear is a ferocious hunter and is considered the second most dangerous land animal of Sphinx.

peak vulture — a large, winged Sphinxian scavenger. Peak vultures may be as much as 1.5 meters (4.9 feet) in length and wingspans of up to 3.5 meters (11.5 feet) have been verified. They have two pairs of wings and very powerful talons, and it is not uncommon for them to kill small game rather than relying solely on carrion. Peak vultures are found primarily among mountains (as the name implies) but are closely related to the much smaller lowland vulture.

peak-wing — treecat term for Sphinxian mountain eagle.

picketwood — a deciduous tree which spreads by sending down runners from its lower branches. Each runner eventually becomes its own nodal trunk, sending out branches of its own to form huge, extensive networks of branches and trunks which are all technically the same tree. Picketwood has very straight, very rough-barked trunks which are a deep gray and black. Leaves are long and splayed, with four distinct lobes. They turn a deep, rich red before falling at the end of the year. The average height of a mature tree is 35 to 45 meters (114 to 148 feet).

Post Diaspora — the notation Post Diaspora (or PD) indicates the T-year counting from 2103 CE, Year One of the Diaspora. That is, Year 2103 CE is considered Year 01 PD.

prong-buck — a vaguely deerlike Sphinxian herbivore with a powerful, elongated neck and a single, branching horn growing from the center of its forehead. They range between 2.5 and 3.4 meters (8 to 11.2 feet) in length and stand between 90 and 124 centimeters (2.9 to 4.1 feet) at the shoulder. They are found in virtually all Sphinxian climate zones, although the mountain-dwelling species tend to be larger than their lowland cousins, and prefer to browse on the foliage of trees rather than grass. The prong buck's horn is sharp edged and quite capable of dealing with any predator much smaller than a hexapuma or peak bear.

purple thorn — the treecat name for a low, densely growing, thorned plant which is nearly impenetrable and almost impossible to eradicate. It has small, very bitter-tasting berries, but it is a necessary component of treecat diets, since the berries provide critical trace elements required for full development of their empathic abilities.

quick heal — a family of therapies which accelerate healing and recovery times. It reduces tissue healing times by a factor of four but is only about half that efficient at speeding the knitting of broken bones.

range barley — a native Sphinxian grain. Range barley is an alpine grass with a bearded head. While edible by humans, it has a rather astringent taste which is not widely popular. It can be ground into flour and baked or be more coarsely ground and made into a porridge.

range bunny — human name for a small, ground dwelling Sphinxian animal, approximately two thirds the size of a treecat. It runs with a distinctive "two-stage" leaping motion, hence the name, despite the fact that it doesn't really look very much like a terrestrial rabbit.

red spruce — another evergreen, this one with scaled, very dark blue-green leaves and a pyramidal form. Its seedpods are smoother than the near-pine's, but the seeds themselves are bitter tasting (to humans, at least; Sphinxian critters like them just fine). It is called "red spruce" more because of the almost russet color of its wood, which is prized for decorative woodwork. Average height of a mature red spruce is about 17 meters (56 feet).

ribbon-leaf — treecat name for lace willow.

rock raven — a cliff-nesting Sphinxian bird analog.

rock tree — a Sphinxian hardwood, so called because of the extreme hardness and density of its wood. A mature rock tree stands about 13 meters (42 feet) in height. It has long, slender, sword-shaped leaves of a particularly rich, bright green which turn dark purple in the fall. It is noted for its very straight trunk. The brown rock tree is the most common species, named for its light-brown, rather rough bark. The next most common species is the yellow rock tree, named for the deep, golden yellow natural color of its timber. Various species of rock tree can be found in almost every Sphinxian climate zone, although it does not like mountains.

rockfur — treecat term for moss growing on rocks.

snow hunter — treecat name for peak bear.

Sphinx — Manticore A-IV, the fourth planet of Manticore A, a G0-class star which is the primary component of the Manticore Binary System. The planet of Sphinx is the outer habitable planet of Manticore A (orbital radius of 21.15 LM) and has a gravity of 1.35 Old Earth standard gravities.

Sphinx Forestry Service — The Sphinx Forestry Service (SFS) is a Sphinxian planetary agency charged with the combined functions of wildlife and natural resources protection, exploration, environmental conservancy, and law enforcement. It is an arm of the planetary government, not the Crown, and consists of a very small cadre of fulltime professional rangers assisted by a larger force of part-time sworn volunteers.

spike thorn — a native Sphinxian flowering shrub which fills much the same niche as azaleas or laurels, attaining a maximum height of about 3.6 meters (12 feet). Its leaves are dark green and spade shaped, and it produces very sharp thorns up to 10 centimeters (4 inches) in length. Its blossoms, which come in many different colors, are vaguely tulip shaped and are prized for the flavor their pollen gives to honey produced by imported terrestrial honey bees.

stag horn fern — a Sphinxian fernlike plant which actually greatly resembles the Old Earth plants of the same name but is found almost exclusively in highland locations. Sphinxian stag horn fern grows a bit taller, reaching heights of up to 2 meters (6.5 feet). It is a seasonal plant, dying back in late fall and winter, but is far more cold-hardy than its Old Earth namesake. It prefers shady growing conditions and is often found in association with picketwood.

Star Kingdom of Manticore — a star nation consisting of the three habitable planets of the Manticore Binary System. Those planets are Manticore (the capital world) and Sphinx, which both orbit the primary stellar component of the Manticore System; and Gryphon, the sole habitable planet orbiting the secondary component of the star system.

sun-rising — treecat term for east.

sun-setting — treecat term for west.

swaying frond — treecat term for Sphinxian stag horn fern.

tanapple — a native Sphinxian fruit, so named because it looks very much like a bright green, somewhat outsized terrestrial apple with a thick, easily peeled skin rather like a terrestrial tangerine. It is sweet tasting but tart.

T-Day — Terrestrial-Day; the standard day used to keep track of all dates for interstellar purposes.

T-Month — Terrestrial-Month; the standard month used to keep track of all dates for interstellar purposes.

tongue-leaf — treecat name for rock tree.

T-Week — Terrestrial-Week; the standard week used to keep track of all dates for interstellar purposes.

T-Year — Terrestrial-Year; the standard year used to keep track of all dates for interstellar purposes. It is one Old Earth year in length. Because the Star Kingdom of Manticore has three separate planets, each with its own local year, Manticorans tend to use T-years in all of their dating conventions. The planet Manticore's year is the "official" year of the Star Kingdom but is seldom used (except by a handful of diehard purists) outside purely official documents.

uni-link — an all-purpose, multifunction device. It combines the functions of timepiece, communicator, GPS navigator, data net interface, data storage device, and emergency locator beacon. Although it is commonly worn as a wrist bracelet, it also comes in pocket versions, which tend to be larger and even more capable.

wave-crester — Silver and brown bird analogs on the planet Manticore. The equivalent of Old Earth's seagulls.

white root — treecat name for ice potatoes.

Wildlife Management Service (WMS) — Meyerdahl equivalent of the Sphinx Forestry Service.

wood rat — a Sphinxian rodentlike, marsupial arboreal, about a third the size of a treecat. They are small and fast-moving creatures which live primarily on the bark and leaves of the crown oak, although they also infest other types of trees when no crown oak is available. They are also very fond of finished timber products, such as lawn furniture or wooden paneling. Enough of them can do significant damage to or even kill any tree, but such concentrated infestations are rare.

The following is an excerpt from:

A CALL TO DUTY

★ BOOK I OF ★
Manticore Ascendant

DAVID WEBER &
TIMOTHY ZAHN

A Novel of the Honorverse

Available from Baen Books
October 2014
hardcover

CHAPTER ONE

"Mom?" Travis Uriah Long called toward the rear of the big, quiet house. "I'm going out now."

There was no answer. With a sigh, Travis finished putting on his coat, wondering whether it was even worth tracking his mother down.

Probably not. But that didn't mean he shouldn't try. Miracles did happen. Or so he'd been told.

He headed down the silent hallway, his footsteps unnaturally loud against the hardwood tiles. Even the dogs in the pen behind the house were strangely quiet.

Melisande Vellacott Long was back with the dogs, of course, where she always was. The reason the animals were quiet, Travis saw as he stepped out the back door, was that she'd just fed them. Heads down, tails wagging or bobbing or just hanging still, they were digging into their bowls.

"Mom, I'm going out now," he said, taking a step toward her.

"I know," his mother said, not turning around even for a moment from her precious dogs. "I heard you."

Then why didn't you say something? The frustrated words boiled against the back of Travis's throat. But he left them unsaid. Her dog-breeding business had had first claim on his mother's attention for as long as he could remember, certainly for the eleven years since her second husband, Travis's father, had died. Just because her youngest was about to graduate from high school was apparently no reason for those priorities to change.

In fact, it was probably just the opposite. With Travis poised to no longer be underfoot, she could dispense with even the pretense that she was providing any structure for his life.

"I'm not sure when I'll be home," he continued, some obscure need to press the emotional bruise driving him to try one final time.

"That's fine," she said. Stirring, she walked over to one of the more slobbery floppy-eared hounds and crouched down beside him. "Whenever."

"I was going to take the Flinx," he added. *Say something!* he pleaded silently. *Tell me to be in by midnight. Tell me I should take the ground car instead of the air car. Ask who I'm going out with. Anything!*

But she didn't ask. Anything.

"That's fine," she merely said, probing at a section of fur on the dog's neck.

Travis retraced his steps through the house and headed for the garage with a hollow ache in his stomach. Children, he remembered reading once, not only needed boundaries, but actually craved them. Boundaries were a comforting fence against the lurking dangers of absolute freedom. They were also proof that someone cared what happened to you.

Travis had never had such boundaries, at least not since his father died. But he'd always craved them.

His schoolmates and acquaintances hadn't seen it that way, of course. To them, chafing under what they universally saw as random and unfair parental rules and regulations, Travis's absolute freedom had looked like heaven on Manticore. Travis had played along, pretending he enjoyed the quiet chaos of his life even while his heart was torn from him a millimeter at a time.

Now, seventeen T-years old and supposedly ready to head out on his own, he still could feel a permanent emptiness inside him, a hunger for structure and order in a dark and unstructured universe. Maybe he'd never truly grown up.

Maybe he never would.

It was fifteen kilometers from Travis's house to the edge of Landing, and another five from the city limits to the neighborhood where Bassit Corcoran had said to meet him. As usual, most of the air car pilots out tonight flew their vehicles with breathtaking sloppiness, straying from their proper lanes and ignoring the speed limits and other safety regulations, at least until they reached the city limits. Travis, clenching his teeth and muttering uselessly at the worst of the offenders, obeyed the laws to the letter.

Bassit and two of his group were waiting at the designated corner as Travis brought the Flinx to a smooth landing beside the walkway. By the time he had everything shut down the three teens had crossed the street and gathered around him.

"Nice landing," Bassit said approvingly as Travis popped the door. "Your mom give you any static about bringing the air car?"

"Not a word," Travis said, reflexively pitching his voice to pretend that was a good thing.

One of the others shook his head. "Lucky dog," he muttered. "Guys like you might as well be—"

"Close it, Pinker," Bassit said.

He hadn't raised his voice, or otherwise leaned on the words in any way. But Pinker instantly shut up.

Travis felt a welcome warmth, compounded of admiration and a sense of acceptance, dissolving away the lump in his throat. Bassit was considered a bad influence by most of their teachers, and he got into trouble with one probably twice a week. Travis suspected most of the conflict came from the fact that Bassit knew what he wanted and wasn't shy about setting the goals and parameters necessary to get it.

Bassit would go far, Travis knew, out there in a murky and uncertain world. He counted himself fortunate that the other had even noticed him, let alone been willing to reach out and include him in his inner circle.

"So what are we doing tonight?" Travis asked, climbing out and closing the door behind him.

"Aampersand's is having a sale," Bassit said. "We wanted to check it out."

"A sale?" Travis looked around, frowning. Most of the shops in the neighborhood were still open, but there didn't seem to be a lot of cars or pedestrians in sight. Sales usually drew more people than this, especially sales at high-end jewelry places like Aampersand's.

"Yes, a sale," Bassit said, his tone making it

clear that what they *weren't* doing was having an extended discussion about it. That was one of his rules: once he'd made up his mind about what the group was doing on a given evening, you either joined in or you went home.

And there wasn't anything for Travis to go home to.

"Okay, sure," he said. "What are you shopping for?"

"Everything," Bassit said. Pinker started to snicker, stopped at a quick glare from Bassit. "Jammy's girlfriend's got a birthday coming up, and we're going to help him pick out something nice for her." He laid his hand on Travis's shoulder. "Here's the thing. We've also got a reservation at Choy Renk, and we don't want to be late. So what I need you to do is stay here and be ready to take off just as soon as we get back."

"Sure," Travis said, a flicker of relief running through him. He wasn't all that crazy about looking at jewelry, and the reminder that other guys had girlfriends while he didn't would just sink his mood a little deeper. Better to let them stare at the diamonds and emeralds without him.

"Just make sure you're ready to go the second we're back," Bassit said, giving him a quick slap on the shoulder before withdrawing his hand and glancing at the others. "Gentlemen? Let's do this."

The three of them headed down the street. Travis watched them go, belatedly realizing he didn't know what time the restaurant reservation was for.

That could be a problem. A couple of months ago, when Pinker had been looking for something for *his* girlfriend, they'd all spent nearly an hour poring over the merchandise before he finally bought something. If Jammy showed the same thoroughness and indecision, it could be like pulling teeth to get him back outside again.

Travis smiled wryly. Maybe it would be like pulling teeth for *him* to get Jammy out. For Bassit, it would be a stroll down the walkway. When it was time to go, they would go, and whenever the reservation was for they would make it on time.

Assuming, of course, that Bassit remembered how Travis insisted on sticking to the speed limit. But Bassit wouldn't forget something like that.

Putting all of it out of his mind, Travis looked around. Businesswise, he'd once heard, this was one of the more volatile neighborhoods in the city, with old shops closing and new ones opening up on a regular basis. Certainly that had been the case lately. In the two months since he'd last been here one of the cafés had become a bakery, a flower shop had morphed into a collectables store, and a small upscale housewares shop—

He felt his breath catch in his throat. In the housewares shop's place was a recruiting station for the Royal Manticoran Navy. Behind the big plate-glass window a young woman in an RMN uniform was sitting behind a desk, reading her tablet.

A series of old and almost-forgotten memories ghosted across Travis's vision: his father, telling his five-year-old son stories of the years he'd spent in the Eris Navy. The stories had seemed exotic to Travis's young and impressionable ears, the stuff of adventure and derring-do.

Now, as he looked back with age and perspective, he realized there had probably been a lot more routine and boredom in the service than his father had let on. Still, there had surely been *some* adventure along with it.

More to the point, everything he'd read about militaries agreed that they were steeped in tradition, discipline, and order.

Order.

They probably wouldn't want him, he knew. He was hardly at the top of his class academically, his athletic skills were on a par with those of the mollusk family, and with Winterfall, the family barony, long since passed to his half-brother Gavin he had none of the political clout that was probably necessary to even get his foot in the door.

But Bassit and the others would be shopping for at least half an hour, probably longer. The recruiter was all alone, which meant no witnesses if she laughed in his face.

And really, there was no harm in asking.

The woman looked up as Travis pulled open the door.

"Good evening," she greeted him, smiling as she set aside her tablet and stood up. "I'm Lieutenant Blackstone of the Royal Manticoran Navy. How can I help you?"

"I just wanted some information," Travis said, his heart sinking as he walked hesitantly toward her. *Blackstone* was a noble name if he'd ever heard one, her eyes and voice were bright with intelligence, and even through her uniform he could see that she was very fit. All three of the probable strikes against him were there, and he hadn't even made it to the desk yet.

Still, he was here. He might as well see it through.

"Certainly," she said, gesturing him toward the guest chair in front of the desk. "You're looking for career opportunities, I assume?"

"I really don't know," Travis admitted. "This was kind of a spur-of-the-moment thing."

"Understood," Blackstone said. "Let me just say that whatever you're looking for, the RMN is the perfect place to start." Her voice, Travis noted, had changed subtly, as if she was now reading from an invisible script. "Career-wise, we have some of the best opportunities in the entire kingdom. Alternatively, if you decide the Navy isn't for you, you'll be out in five T-years, with the kind of training and technical skills that will shoot you right past the competition for any job or career you want. There's going to be plenty of opportunity in the civilian economy for decades still, rebuilding from the Plague, and someone with the skills and discipline of a Navy vet can expect to command top dollar. It's as close to a no-lose situation as you could ever imagine."

"Sounds pretty good," Travis said. Though now that he thought about it, wasn't there a faction in Parliament that was determined to shut down the Navy? If that happened, there wasn't going to be much left of careers *or* exotic training.

"Are you interested in the Academy?" Blackstone

continued. "That's where the men and women in our officer track start their training."

"I don't know," Travis said, starting to relax a little. If she thought this was a joke, it didn't show in her face or voice. And that officer's uniform she was wearing definitely looked sharp. "I might be. What kind of requirements do you need to get in?"

"Nothing too horrendous," Blackstone assured him. "There's a vetting process, of course. Certain academic standards have to be met, and there are a few other credentials. Nothing too hard."

"Oh," Travis said, his brief hope fading away. There it was: academics. "I probably won't—"

And then, from somewhere down the street came the boom of a gunshot.

Travis spun around in his chair, a sudden horrible suspicion hammering into his gut and morphing into an even more horrifying certainty. Bassit—Jammy and his girlfriend's supposed birthday—that bulge he now belatedly remembered seeing beneath Pinker's floppy coat—

There was another boom, a double tap this time and somewhat deeper in pitch. Travis started to stand up—

"Stay there," Blackstone ordered, shoving down on his shoulder as she ran past him, a small but nasty-looking pistol gripped in her hand. She reached the door, slammed to a halt with her left shoulder against the jamb, and eased the door open.

There was another pair of deep booms, then another of the slightly higher-pitched ones as the first weapon answered. Travis jumped up, unable to sit still any longer, and raced over to join Blackstone.

"What's going on?" he breathed as he shoulder-landed against the wall at the other side of the door.

"Sounds like we've got a robbery going down," she said. Her eyes bored into Travis's face. "Friends of yours?"

Travis's tongue froze against the roof of his mouth. What was he supposed to say?

"I thought they were."

"Uh-huh." She turned back to the door as two more shots echoed. "Well, I hope you're not going to miss them, because one way or another they're going down. The cops will be here any minute, and if they're not gone by now, they're not going. What was your part of the job?"

Briefly, Travis thought about lying. But Blackstone had probably already figured it out.

"They told me we had early reservations at a restaurant," he said. "They said they were going to do some shopping and that I needed to be ready to head out as soon as they got back."

"Where was this supposed shopping? Aampersand's?"

"Yes."

Blackstone grunted. "Big mistake. Aampersand's apprentice goldsmith is a retired cop. Why you?"

"My mom has an air car," Travis said. "I guess they thought they could make a faster getaway in that than in a ground car."

"Were they right?"

Travis blinked. "What?"

"Would an air car have made for a better getaway?"

Travis stared at her profile, confusion coloring the fear swirling through his gut. What in the world kind of question was that? Was she trying to get him to incriminate himself? Hadn't he already more or less done that?

"I don't understand."

"Show me you can think," she said. "Show me you can reason. Tell me why they were wrong."

Some of Travis's confusion condensed into cautious and only half-believed hope. Was she saying she wasn't going to turn him in?

Apparently, she was.

He took a deep breath, forcing his mind away from what was happening to Bassit and the others and focusing on the logical problem Blackstone had presented.

"Because air cars are faster, but there aren't as many of them in the city," he said. "That makes them more easily identifiable."

"Good," Blackstone said approvingly. "And?"

Travis's throat tightened as he abruptly noticed that the gunfire had stopped. Whatever had happened was apparently over.

"And as soon as you get above rooftop level, you're visible for five kilometers in any direction," he went on. "The cops would have you in sight the whole time they were chasing you."

"What if you wove in and out between the buildings?"

That's illegal, was Travis's reflexive thought. But of course someone who'd just robbed a jewelry store would hardly be worried about traffic regulations.

"Well, if you didn't crash into something and kill yourself," he said slowly, trying to work it through, "you'd pop up as a red tag on every other air car's collision-avoidance system. Oh— right. The police could just follow the trail on their readouts and have their pick of where to force you down." He dared a wan smile. "They could also slap a dozen traffic violations on top of the armed robbery charge."

To his surprise, Blackstone actually smiled back.

"Very good. What else?"

In the distance, the sound of approaching police sirens could be heard. Again, Travis had to force his mind away from Bassit as he tried to come up with the answer Blackstone was looking for.

But this time, he came up dry.

"I don't know," he admitted.

"The most basic flaw there is," Blackstone said, turning a thoughtful gaze on him. "They picked the wrong person for the job."

Travis grimaced. "I guess they did."

"I'm not talking about your piloting skills," Blackstone assured him. "Or even your loyalty to people who don't deserve it. I'm talking about the fact that someone who's not in on the plan isn't exactly going to burn air when the gang comes charging up with guns smoking and pockets bulging with rings and bracelets."

She tilted her head to the side.

"Especially when that person comes equipped

with an ethical core. You *do* have an ethical core, don't you, Mr.—?"

Travis braced himself.

"Long," he said. "Travis Uriah Long. I guess so." He tried another half-smile. "Is an ethical core one of the requirements you mentioned for naval officers?"

"If it was, the officer corps would be a lot smaller," Blackstone said dryly. "But if it's not a requirement, it's certainly a plus. Shall we go back inside and get started on the datawork?"

Outside, two police air cars appeared, their flashing lights strobing as they settled onto the street.

"I don't know," Travis said, feeling a fresh tightness in his chest as cops began streaming out of the vehicles, guns at the ready. Blackstone was right—if Bassit and the others weren't out of the neighborhood by now, they were done for.

And if they were still alive after all that shooting, they were going to talk.

"It can't hurt to try," Blackstone pressed. "The vetting process will take two to four weeks, and you can change your mind at any time."

And if part of their confession included such facts as the name of their intended getaway driver...

"How about regular Navy?" he asked. "Not officer, but regular crew. How long does that take?"

Blackstone's forehead wrinkled.

"Assuming there are no red flags in your record, we could ship you out to the Casey-Rosewood boot camp by the end of the week."

"You mean no flags other than armed robbery?"

"Pretty hard for anyone to link you up with that one," Blackstone said. "Especially given that you were in here with me when it went down. Are you sure you wouldn't rather go the academy route?"

"Positive," Travis said, wondering briefly what his mother would think of this sudden right-angle turn in his life. Or whether she would even notice. "You said there was datawork we had to do?"

"Yes." Blackstone took a final look outside and closed the door on the flashing police lights. "One other thing," she added as she holstered her gun. "Back when I told you to stay put, and you didn't? Bear in mind that once you're in the Navy you're going to have to learn how to obey orders."

Travis smiled, his first real smile of the day. For the first time in years, he could see some cautious hope beckoning from his future.

"I understand," he said. "I think I can manage."

—end excerpt—

from *A Call to Duty*
available in hardcover,
October 2014, from Baen Books